TRUTH
OR
DEAD

A gripping crime thriller full of twists

T.J. BREARTON

JOFFE
BOOKS

Published 2017 by Joffe Books, London.

www.joffebooks.com

ISBN-13: 978-1-912106-46-2

For Lee and Smitty.

CHAPTER ONE

WEDNESDAY

Livingston Road was a speedway of morning commuters, three lanes going east, three west, the sun bright and glaring off the rushing vehicles, everything one false move away from destruction. The ringing phone was just out of reach, in her bag in front of the passenger seat.

Heather stretched for it, had to take her eyes off the road a second, and a nearby vehicle blared its horn. She jerked the car back into her lane as the motorist passed, yelling and pointing a finger.

The phone kept ringing and vibrating. She decided to risk it again, stretched farther, fished around in the green bag, grabbed it without causing an accident. The phone stopped ringing. "Oh for God's sake . . ." She tossed it on the seat beside her and checked her mirrors. There was an open lane to her right, a gas station at the next intersection. She flipped on her blinker and started over.

But, the gas station was on the northeast corner. Once she pulled in she'd have to wait for a break in traffic before getting back onto the road, and she was already running late. The traffic light coming up was green.

The phone numbers for Abby's day care and Olivia's school were programmed into her cell, and the incoming number had been neither. Heather didn't know anyone with a 945 area code, come to think of it. She didn't even know where the code indicated.

She hit the gas and ripped through the traffic light as it changed to yellow and kept to the middle lane. Her next turn was in two intersections, a left onto Golden Gate Parkway. From there it was a straight shot to the clinic.

Florida driving was nuts.

Most days she was exactly on schedule. She had it timed down to the minute, from getting up with the two girls, taking her shower, feeding them breakfast. By 7:10 each morning she was clicking their seatbelts and pulling out of the driveway.

She always stopped first at Olivia's school, where she'd wait as Livy ran inside, her oversized backpack jouncing along with her bright curls. Then to Abby's day care, where she'd say a quick few words to Gillian, kiss Abby goodbye. The drive to work ate up the rest of the time.

But this morning she hadn't been able to find the damned shoes that went with her outfit, and Olivia had sat on the toilet for an eternity, feet dangling, like she had all the time in the world, while her baby sister played hide and seek with the car keys.

The phone rang again. It had landed upside down on the seat.

Heather flicked a look in the mirrors — the traffic crowded around her like stock cars at a NASCAR race.

"Shit."

She got hold of the phone, checked the screen: 945-212-1974. Who the hell was it? Telemarketers didn't usually call back, did they? Maybe it had something to do with work. But all the work-related numbers from her supervisor on down to the jail were on her phone …

"Hello?"

There was a pause. "Mrs. Heather Moss…"

The voice sounded artificial, like a machine.

"Who is this?"

"I need you to listen very carefully, Mrs. Moss."

A finger of fear traced up her spine.

"I'm driving to work. Who is this? What—"

"I know you are driving to work, Mrs. Moss. That is what I want to talk to you about."

The fear bloomed into anger.

"Excuse me? If this is the approach of whatever company you represent — if you're even human — I gotta tell you, it sucks."

"Your work, Mrs. Moss. You are a clinical therapist for Everglades County."

Heather tried to keep focused on the driving — her left turn was coming up at the next intersection and she still hadn't pulled into the proper lane. A white pick-up truck flanked her, a crew of landscaping workers piled in the back, grimacing in the hot morning sun.

She flipped on her turn indicator.

"Tell me who you are or I'm hanging up."

"As a clinical therapist, you make regular visits to the county jail for counseling and evaluations."

"Listen, whoever you are, goodbye."

"Stay on the line. Olivia is doing just fine, and Abigail is happy and healthy. And you're going to want to keep them that way. Aren't you, Mrs. Moss." The inhuman voice dropped on the last word instead of rising with the question.

Heather's hands went numb at the mention of her daughters; her heart clutched by an invisible hand. The part of her running on automatic pilot — she'd made this trip to work five days a week for eighteen months now — checked the mirror again and saw that the white pick-up had slowed. The driver was attempting to let her into the lane. She could see his face behind the glass, his hand waving her in.

Heather spun the wheel. Her heart was pounding too hard; it felt like she was short of breath. Some rational part of her mind attempted to override the racing emotions and make the right choices.

Say you don't know who those people are.

"Listen to me, I'm gonna call the police. I'm gonna pull over right now and call them."

"You are not going to call the police either. Olivia is sitting in her classroom; she has that nice little blue jumper on. And Abby is playing with the big doll house at Gillian's. They are very nice girls."

She started to make the turn, someone beeped their horn, and the white pick-up loomed in the rear-view mirror.

The caller could see them. Could somehow see the girls.

Heather was going too slowly through the intersection, her mind not coordinating with her body. When she hit the gas it was with too much force and she shot forward.

Pull over. Pull over, hang up, and call the police.

The clinic was just a mile down Golden Gate. By the time she maneuvered off, called the police, or even 911, and explained the situation, she could be at work, where she could summon help.

"Good. Mrs. Moss, just keep going like that. Don't let the other cars bother you. That white pick-up looks like it is full of illegals anyway."

The panic mixed with confusion. The caller could see her, too? She checked all her mirrors again. The pick-up was still behind her — she'd widened the gap — but was that a black SUV after the pick-up?

Heather concentrated on the road. The speed limit was 45 miles per hour and she got going up to fifty. The faces of her daughters teased at her, bits of the morning replayed themselves.

No. Relax. Keep talking until you get to work.

"Okay," she said. "Where are you? You can see me?"

"Yes, Mrs. Moss. I can see you."

She couldn't help but search the mirrors again. But it was hard to tell where the caller might be. As Golden Gate Parkway curved and passed a large plaza with a Publix grocery store, she could see the white pick-up with several others following, but no black SUV. Still, if the caller was in one of them, she could lead him right to her job. End this thing before it really began, whatever the hell it was.

"Howard Declan," the voice said.

"What? Who? I don't understand."

"You're scheduled to visit him this morning at the jail. To evaluate him."

"Don't hurt my girls." It just tumbled out. Heather's lower lip trembled and tears sheeted her vision. She couldn't help it. "Don't hurt them."

"I don't want to hurt them. I like them. I like you, Mrs. Moss."

"Tell . . . tell me . . ." Her tongue wasn't cooperating. She passed another familiar landmark. Almost there. The clinic was just half a mile. Another glance in the rear-view mirror. She thought she saw the dark SUV again, about a hundred yards behind her. The white pick-up had its blinker on, about to turn off into one of the business plazas rolling past.

"Florida is nice, isn't it?" The mechanical-sounding caller was making no sense now. "Just look at those palm trees everywhere. As if, no matter what is happening in the world, it is still okay here."

"Tell me what you want. Why don't you— We're almost to my job. Pull in and let's talk."

"You have everything you need with you."

Heather looked around the car, suddenly alarmed in a whole new way. What did he mean? Need for what?

Less than a quarter mile to her office at the clinic. She was pushing sixty miles an hour.

"I am sure you like Florida. Almost two years with the clinic. People are starting to know you, trust you. You go to the jail so regularly; they have come to trust you, too."

Something sank in her stomach with the weight of a stone.

"It takes time to settle into a place," the voice said. "But you are personable, attractive. That gives you an advantage, don't you think."

The wide, flat building where she worked slipped into view. She automatically flipped on her blinker for the turn and started to slow down, checking behind her for the black car. She saw it, and she slowed, turned into parking lot, and watched as it continued cruising past on Golden Gate. The big dark vehicle drove out of sight.

The voice was still right in her ear.

"It's small enough to slip in your pocket. A small manila envelope with a red string. You will find it in your bag on the seat beside you."

Heather scanned for a parking spot as she listened. It was eleven minutes past eight and all the other clinicians had already arrived. She spied an open spot far away from the entrance and headed that way, putting a picture together of what this might mean just as the caller spelled it out for her in that unearthly voice.

"You are going to take that small package into the jail this morning at nine a.m., and you are going to give it to the inmate named Howard Declan."

Heather pulled into her spot and hit the brakes, threw the transmission into park. "I can't do that. I have to go through security."

"Listen to me, Mrs. Moss. We have been watching you. Security lets you pass right in, they don't even take you through the metal detector anymore."

We.

We've been watching.

6

How did they know this? Were they right now watching her girls? Heather started to feel angry, invaded. So many emotions mixing together. She banged the neighboring car with her door as she threw it open.

"You're wrong. Security is very tight. There's no way I can—"

"Stop lying. You have not gone through the metal detector in months. They check your ID badge, off you go. Sometimes they take your pen, true. It is sharp. But this little package, no one is even going to notice."

Holding the phone to her ear, standing beside the car, Heather bent and peered in. Her green bag just sat there on the passenger seat, looking just like it always did. The car was giving off a chime — her keys dangled from the ignition. She stared around the parking lot, hoping to see someone.

No one. Everyone was already inside, at their desks, preparing for the day's work.

The caller knew she was scheduled to provide the jail a psych evaluation for Howard Declan. She hadn't learned the details yet, but she had an app on her phone that let her see County arrests. Declan had been taken to jail the previous day for a non-violent crime.

And the caller was right about the guards, they greeted her by name, smiled at her, made small talk, and it had been at least a month since anyone had run her through the security portal. She used a face-scan for identification when she first came in, then an ID badge got her the rest of the way.

Worse than any of that, the caller knew her daughters' names. What they were wearing. Where they were. Why would he need to know that?

"You can't hurt my girls." She was trembling, shivers running up and down her legs. Despite the early morning heat, she felt cold. Her brain kept urging her to run inside and tell her supervisor what was happening. Police could be at the school and day care within minutes. Surely whoever this was couldn't just—

"They will not be hurt if you do exactly as you are told. We are sitting right outside the school. And right outside Gillian's. You are probably thinking we cannot really do anything. But that is because you are a rational, normal person. Rational people would not shoot Gillian Hough in the face, then take your Abby. They would not then pose as your late husband, and take Olivia out of her spelling class with everyone smiling."

Heather couldn't move. The little Honda was still chiming, the keys swinging from the steering column.

"But we are not normal, rational people, Mrs. Moss."

She found it hard to swallow, harder to speak. If this was a prank, it was utterly convincing and cruel. If it was amateurs pretending to be more capable than they were, it was still motivation to cooperate — even if the caller was just part of some group of idiots, they still might try to accomplish what they were setting out to do.

Howard Declan. He wasn't part of any mafia or organized crime group she'd heard anything about. From what little she knew, he'd been arrested for walking around outside his house naked, ranting and raving. Police had shown up and Declan had tried to take one of their guns. Not to use on them, but, according to the report, on himself. A sad, lonely man with possible mental health problems. What relationship could he have to the caller? What was the package in her bag?

"Mrs. Moss. Are you still with me."

"Yes." She barely recognized her own voice.

"You need to check in with your supervisor now, get ready to head to the jail. No one can know anything, or your daughters will die. Stop standing there, pick up your bag, and go inside. You are already late."

Heather spun around, suddenly sure she'd spot the caller somewhere, or at least one of "them" — the clinic parking lot was adjacent to a Walmart shopping center, maybe someone watching her had turned in over there — but saw nothing. Nothing but people coming and going from the Walmart, their tiny shapes in the distance. A hot breeze swept through, the royal palms surrounding the clinic bobbed and rustled. She thought she smelled the sharp, chemical stink of brakes from the roadway.

"Okay." Heather ducked into the Honda, plucked the keys from the ignition, grabbed her bag and dropped them in. Then closed the door behind her. She headed toward the entrance to the clinic — therapists had their own back door to come and go.

"Good. Remember, Mrs. Moss, we will be watching."

"When will my girls be safe? How will you know I've delivered this . . . envelope?"

"We will know. We will see everything. Your appointment with Declan is for nine o'clock. Do all the normal things you would do. It is important that you are smiling. Do not look upset, Mrs. Moss. Do not give any signals, do not pass any notes. We will know."

She was almost to the door. Once she opened it she'd be in the vestibule with the clinic's facial recognition scanner. Then through a final door and she'd be surrounded by her co-workers. The seconds drained away.

"When will my girls be *safe?*" She fought to keep her voice under control.

"Your evaluation of the inmate takes about forty-five minutes. About ten minutes after that, it will all be over. We will be long gone, your girls will know nothing about it."

"And what will happen to me? Whatever I'm doing — it makes me some kind of accessory . . ."

She reached the door and paused. She checked the windows on the other side of the entrance — sometimes Mandy, the clinician who specialized in PTSD, complained the air conditioning was too cold and kept her window open. But it was sealed. So was Jake's on the other side.

"Nothing will happen to you. If you do exactly as you have been instructed, you will return to your rational, normal life. Just make sure you do."

The line went dead.

CHAPTER TWO

Tom lay in bed, staring up at the ceiling. There were still some mornings he expected to awake at the condo in Naples, but he was gradually getting used to the new place.

A phone vibrated. He grabbed his from the side table and puzzled at the blank screen. Katie sat up in bed beside him, rubbed her eyes, leaned over and fished her phone out of her pants, which lay in a heap on the floor.

Tom watched her. He could see the curve of her spine, the tan line across her backside as the sheet fell away. She answered, "Mills," and swung her legs out of the bed.

She listened. "Okay. Alright, I'm on my way." She dropped the phone on the bed and pointed her toes out, slipped on her underpants, drew them up. Grabbed her pants and flapped them in the air before stepping in. Her bra was buried in the mess of clothing.

Tom propped up on an elbow, staring at her perfect shape. "I thought you were off today?"

"I'm on call."

"No time for a shower, huh?"

She kept her back to him as she buttoned her white shirt. "CSB just got called to county jail. An inmate is dead. Apparently, it's a real mess. I'm going to stop at the office to suit up and grab gear; I'll shower there."

She turned and bent to pick up her phone from the bed, a lock of thick brown hair tumbling free. She pulled an elastic tie from her pocket and drew all the hair back into a ponytail, accentuating her smooth skin, small nose, a slender cleft in her chin.

Their eyes connected. She had dark brown irises, similar in color to his.

"So, I'll see you later?" he asked.

She slipped her holster around her waist. Her Everglades County badge was clipped beside her Glock. "I don't know."

Their gaze lingered, then Katie turned away, found her shoes, her bag, and headed toward the bedroom door. She stopped before leaving and turned her head.

"Good luck today, okay? This is your last session, right?"

Tom sat up and put his bare feet down on the carpeted floor. "Yeah. Then I'm officially head-shrunk and released back into the wild. Katie, what do you mean you don't know? Listen—"

"I gotta go, Tom."

"I know, I just . . ."

She turned a little bit more but kept her eyes averted. She was smart, she was pretty, she was an excellent crime scene technician. And it felt like she was leaving for the final time.

"Hang on a minute, okay?" He rose to his feet, naked and suddenly self-conscious despite their many nights together. He ripped the sheet from the bed and wrapped it around his waist, crossing the room.

"What's going on?" he asked.

"We can talk later."

"Katie . . ."

He reached her, touched her arm, and she withdrew. "I can't do this now, Tom. I've really got to go."

"Do what now? That's it? We're done?"

She made eye contact. "Don't. You've got your last session — you're doing good, Tom. Almost to the end. Okay?"

"That doesn't make any sense. I've jumped through their hoops, maybe they're going to let me start catching again, and you're leaving? What are you . . . The work is done, time to cut me loose? Like them?" He regretted the line instantly.

Katie's face bloomed with color. "Hey — I can't imagine what you've been through, okay? You lost someone very important to you. And maybe I took pity on you — I can own that."

"Katie that's not — you know that you—"

She put up a hand. Her expression said: *you asked for this, so here it is.* "No, that's not all this has been. Not all I wanted it to be either. But it seems like it's all you have room for."

"What's that mean?"

Her eyebrows went up: he knew what it meant.

She'd showed him compassion after Nick had died, and while they'd wound up spending a lot of time together over the past six months, he'd probably kept her at a certain distance. She deserved more.

She shook her head. "Bye Tom."

"We can talk about it later, right?"

She let him kiss her, but it was brief, perfunctory.

"Be safe out there," he said. "Okay?"

Katie seemed to force a smile. "Always."

Tom leaned against the wall, listening as she went down the stairs. A moment later the door to his place opened and she was gone.

He let out a held breath, tossed the sheet aside and stayed leaned against the wall for another few seconds.

When he heard a phone vibrate this time, he knew it was his. He moved to the bed and grabbed it off the table.

"Blythe? Hey . . . What's up?"

"Tom, good morning. Been a while."

He'd worked with Lauren Blythe on the case leading up to his brother's death, and she'd left an indelible impression. Even though her phone call was unexpected and he had the day off, he suddenly felt guilty for lying in.

"How are you?" she asked.

"I'm good."

"Governor Protection been keeping you busy?"

"Yeah."

"How would you like to jump back into IFS?"

Tom started gathering his strewn about clothes. "Yeah, I mean, I'd love to start catching cases again. As soon as the state psychiatrist gives me the green light, and Turnbull is ready to—"

"Turnbull has already put in your paperwork. You're good to go."

He jumped into his jeans. "You talking about this thing at the county jail?"

A pause. "How did you know about that?"

His eyes fell on a couple of long, coppery hairs on the pillow where Katie had slept. "I have my sources."

"Well, yeah, that is what I'm referring to. How soon can you meet me over there?"

He checked his watch again, thinking. The recent move to Bonita Springs put him a little bit farther than he would have been. "Half an hour?"

"I'll see you there."

"Alright." He jammed the phone in his pocket and stuck his head through his undershirt. After fastening his shoulder holster and checking his Glock Gen4, he hurried out of the bedroom.

Katie had commented that he needed some furniture, but he liked the emptiness of his new townhouse. There was a clarity to it. With its arched doorways and high ceilings, it reminded him of Nick's house.

One of the few things he'd brought from his old condo was the coffee maker, which had been set to brew an hour earlier. Tom slopped some of the hot liquid into a to-go mug, grabbed his car keys and left.

* * *

Everglades County Jail was massive, the perimeter fence topped with razor-sharp cyclone wire. It was the first stop for all suspected criminals whether they were being charged with local, state or federal crimes. Some, depending on their convictions, spent the entirety of their sentence there.

Tom pulled up to the security gate. One guard scrutinized his badge while another circled his department-issued Crown Victoria with a dog and a mirror on the end of a long pole, checking underneath the chassis. A third guard was on the phone inside the booth. He looked out at Tom, his lips moving, then nodded and hung up. He approached the car and handed Tom a generic visitor's pass to clip to his suit jacket.

They waved him through.

An ambulance was parked near the main entrance, its lights twirling but the siren off. Two unmarked cars sat behind it — Tom recognized Blythe's Crown Vic. He parked and entered the building, greeted in the main receiving area by a female deputy who showed him to a locker room. Florida was like most states in the US in that each county had a Sheriff's Department. Since each county had a jail, it was the department's responsibility to run it. Corrections officers were hired to do the grunt work, but deputies served some functions. The ones that walked you in and out were called floaters.

"We're going to take you to the east wing," the deputy said. "That's where the inmates are kept who are on watch."

Tom climbed into the forensic suit laid out for him and zipped it up. "On watch? You mean — what? Suicide risk?"

"Correct."

"So what happened? Did someone complete a suicide?"

She returned his gaze. Tom thought she looked anxious.

"I don't know, sir. You can put your service weapon and phone in that locker there. Pick them back up when you're on your way out. Can stick your watch and wallet in there, too. It'll all be safe."

Tom stowed the items, then grabbed the bag of protective gear, which included booties, gloves, and a facemask.

She showed him out of the room and to the security entrance. He placed his bag in a plastic tub and shoved it into a tunnel where it was X-rayed, then he stepped through the metal detector.

On the other side, he was asked to raise his arms by a guard who then feathered a wand over his body.

"All set."

The deputy rejoined him and led him along a corridor to a door she keyed for entry. They stepped into an air-locked chamber. After a hiss, the lock cracked open and they moved through the next door, down a final corridor. A group of crime scene techs were coming from the other direction, Katie Mills among them. Their eyes connected just before she passed him, and Tom thought she looked uneasy, too.

The deputy stopped at a room with a transparent door. There were two more rooms like this one, each with someone posted outside.

"We watch the inmates here around the clock," she said.

Tom peered through the reinforced, bulletproof glass and sucked in a breath.

A man was lying on his stomach, wearing inmate fatigues, some kind of gunk splattered around him. Blythe stood near the body. At least, Tom thought it was her — she was dressed in a white jumpsuit, her face partly covered by a mask, alone in the room.

Tom opened the bag, pulled the booties on over his hard-soled shoes, wriggling into the latex gloves after he'd affixed a mask to his own face.

The deputy keyed the door and Tom stepped through.

The smell hit him right away — an acrid, bilious odor — unmistakably vomit. That and the metallic smell of blood.

There was a path laid out, marked with thin strips of yellow tape. It led to the body, then the strips widened out and encircled the area around the dead man and Blythe.

She stared down at the corpse, then looked at Tom as he approached.

"I cleared the room. Wanted a minute with you."

"That's romantic."

"You know me." Her eyes glistened in the bright overhead lights. "I'm glad to see you."

"You too."

"Been a couple months?"

Tom nodded. "Since October. Alan Ward's sentencing."

Both of them turned to the body, Tom asked, "Who's our friend?"

"A retired auto mechanic from North Naples. Sixty-six years old."

Tom looked around the room. There was an undressed cot, decorated with only a plain, wafer-thin pillow without even a pillow case. A stainless steel toilet and sink in one corner. In the other, an apparatus resembling a massage chair crossed with Puritanical stocks for hands and feet. Inmate restraints.

Tom focused on the body again. The man was prone, one hand sprawled above his head, which was thick with hair that was, surprisingly for his age, still mostly black. The other arm was tucked beneath him, out of sight. There were no bullet holes or slashes Tom could see. The only blood was spread around his head, mixing with the other bodily fluids. Tough to say where it was coming from since he was face-down.

The smell of vomit in the room was so powerful Tom felt his stomach binding. And he was coming to detect another, even worse, odor. Blythe said, "He defecated before dying."

"Before?"

She flicked a look at him. "Yes."

"So how did he do it? There's blood there, but not enough that he bled out . . ."

"He bit his tongue almost completely off," Blythe said flatly.

"What happened?"

"You'll see it on the video. He had a pretty violent seizure."

Tom saw the camera in a high corner. Then he lowered his voice, despite that the room was probably sound proof, or close to it. "You got something to tell me, Agent Blythe?"

She lowered into a squat. Tom joined her, and they locked eyes over the dead man.

"First, tell me what you think," she said. "You've come in fresh: What does this look like to you?"

Tom took a beat. "Was he on anything? If he was on suicide watch, been here a day already, maybe they medicated him? Benzos or something? And he had a bad reaction?"

She shook her head. "No. They had him sign a release of information, heard back from his primary care physician, and he wasn't on benzodiazepine or antidepressants, no antipsychotics, nothing."

"Well, it looks to me like he took something or ate something, had this reaction. I think maybe a man on suicide watch found a way to get his wish? Poisoned? I also think you haven't told me his name."

The skin around her eyes wrinkled like Blythe was smiling behind her mask. But when she spoke there was no humor in her voice. "His name is Howard Michael Declan."

It clicked right away. Their last case had involved a man named Mario Palumbo, a known drug trafficker being investigated by the County vice and narcotics bureau. Tom wasn't supposed to be involved in it any longer, but he'd kept certain tabs.

"I know the name," he said. "County VNB questioned Declan a few months ago as a witness in their Palumbo investigation. I'm probably not even supposed to know that much, and I honestly don't know more." A silence developed, Blythe seemed to be waiting. "Were they trying to get him to flip on Palumbo?" he asked. "Is that why we're here?"

"Well, we're here for the death investigation, but also for a security breach."

Tom felt exhilarated but managed to lower his voice to a whisper. "Someone here is working with Palumbo?" He instantly imagined guards and organized criminals in collusion, making hand-offs, having back alley meetings. Someone at the jail murdering a potential state witness. After months of being sidelined Tom felt like he was right back in the middle of things.

At the same time, a man had lost his life. Never a good thing.

Blythe stared back, clearly excited, but warned, "We're not there yet. Just a security breach in general."

"Okay, we're not there yet. What did the ME say?"

"Well, before I kicked him out, he said it looked like Declan had some kind of brain embolism. The preliminary theory is that, yeah, someone gave him a pill."

"Okay, so . . . Who has access to these rooms?"

She rose, grunting a little, and Tom stood along with her. "That's the interesting part. On-watch is run by the sheriff's deputies," she said. "Sometimes there's a C.O. in here, the captain who supervises the jail, the sergeants. Otherwise, no one but the mental health clinicians."

Tom waited.

"The clinician who came in this morning is named Heather Moss."

Blythe started to the door, sticking inside the path of yellow tape, and Tom followed. "She saw him at nine o'clock, was out of here by nine forty-six. And she left a little envelope behind. County CSB took it, but they're passing the chain of evidence to us." Blythe waited at the door for the guard to open up. She gave him a direct look. "Less than ten minutes after Heather Moss walked out the door, Declan was soiling himself, vomiting and convulsing."

"So, she passed him this envelope? Some sort of suicide pill inside?"

"It's possible."

"And the guard on duty saw her?"

"Everglades County spoke to the captain. The deputy on shift, Rizzo, says he was distracted, looked away for a minute. So he didn't see Heather Moss passing anything to the inmate. But the camera did."

The door opened and they stepped into the corridor. It smelled like roses compared to inside the room. Tom tore off his facemask, wondering about the likelihood of a therapist assassin working for Mario Palumbo. "Where is Heather Moss now?"

"Well, while she comes here twice a week, her office is at the mental health clinic, a few minutes away. County is on their way to pick her up."

Tom was already moving down the corridor, headed for the exit.

CHAPTER THREE

Heather Moss was not at the clinic.

Her supervisor, a painfully thin man with a ponytail and goatee, named Finn Shaver, gestured a lot with his hands while he spoke to Tom. "Yeah, she was in there this morning — got here late — and I thought something was wrong. She told me it had been a tough morning with her girls and she thought they all might be coming down with something. But then she was on her way to the jail, and I didn't think any more about it. What's going on? What happened over there?"

"Can I have a look at her office?"

"Right this way."

Each therapist had a small room with a door for privacy and a window. Heather's window viewed the back parking area for a Walmart Supercenter. The room was scented with some kind of pleasant incense, like sage. A small couch by the window, a Monet painting on the wall, a couple of Taoist and Buddhist books on the shelf by the couch. As therapy meeting places went, Heather Moss's wasn't bad; she'd made it comfortable. Tom browsed the pictures on her desk. "Are these her daughters?"

"That's Olivia, she's six. And that's Abigail, who recently turned two."

"Where are they?"

"Olivia goes to Bonita Springs Elementary. Abigail goes to a day care not far from the school. The woman's name is Gillian Hough."

Tom glanced at the other therapists who were looming outside Heather's office. He gave the framed photos on her desk another look. Heather Moss, blonde-haired, with sky blue eyes, smiling as she hugged her two girls.

He envisioned her coming into the jail that morning, carrying a tiny lethal package she'd managed to get past security.

While he'd been required to store his phone, gun, and personal effects, then been frisked and passed through a metal detector, Moss had somehow gotten through with a murder weapon. It was either oversight on part of the jail staff, or, one of them, perhaps also working with Palumbo, could have let her slip through on purpose.

But the idea that she was working with Palumbo had immediate holes. Organized criminals worked in the shadows. They covered their tracks. This woman was a clinical therapist who had eighteen months working with County Mental Health and no criminal record. She'd given an inmate a lethal pill right in front of the camera.

What if she'd been coerced? If so, what would she do now?

Blythe called. "County just swung by her home, and she's not there either. They're issuing the BOLO now."

"I'm going to the school where the older daughter goes."

"Alright."

Tom thanked Shaver and quickly left the clinic. He got up to speed on the highway, listening as the BOLO came over the radio: Female, thirty-five years old, driving a white Honda Civic, last seen at Everglades County Jail.

* * *

Tom made a quick turn and the tires gave a shrill squawk. A national flag rippled in the warm breeze out in front of the two-story school. A curved access road led up to the main entrance where he stopped and got out. He found the front doors locked, pressed the Call button on the intercom mounted to the wall.

"Hi, how can I help you?"

"Agent Tom Lange, FDLE." It had been a while, and it felt good to say.

He held his badge up for the camera. The door buzzed and he hooked a right turn into the main office. An older woman with a pile of gray hair looked up from behind her desk. The others in the room tried to hide their gawking.

"Hi. I'm looking for a student, Olivia Moss. Her mother is Heather Moss. Is she here?"

A look of concern spread over her face. "Her mother picked her up about a half an hour ago." The woman consulted a piece of paper on her desk that looked like a sign-out sheet. "She wrote here that the girl had a doctor's appointment. Is she alright?"

"Okay, thank you." Tom glanced at the paperwork, noting the neat, legibility of Heather Moss's signature. Then he gave the main office a quick look, seeing a computer near the back, its screen split into nine images. Each showed a different camera view of the school, some inside, some out. He headed for the doors.

As he got back to the car, a County police car pulled in. Tom presented his badge again as the deputy got out.

"The girl is gone," Tom said. "Moss picked her up."

The deputy ducked into the cruiser and poked at his mobile data terminal. "Well, we've got someone on the house at 1415 Tangerine Drive." He pulled his head back out into the open air. "Still no one there."

Does she know, or not? Tom wondered. *Does she know what she's done? Is she running?*

23

"Alright. Need you to follow me to that address, okay?"

"I can do that."

Tom trotted back to his vehicle. The Crown Vic came equipped with its own mobile data terminal and he tapped the screen. Information on Heather Moss was filtering in, including her official clinic photo. She smiled in the picture but there was a touch of distance in her eyes.

He scrolled down to her birth date, known kin. A husband predeceased her; Glenn Moss. He had worked as a store manager for Home Depot in New York State. Dead for almost two years, but it didn't say how.

She had a brother, Paul, from Nevada. Her parents were in upstate New York, both still alive, a handsome retired couple. Maybe they had a winter home in Florida? It was just past Christmas and New Year's, the time when many "snow birds" flew down to escape the cold. But there was no Florida address for Theresa and Henry Hutchins.

He flipped back to the main screen just in time to see the BOLO updated.

Suspect located 1415 Tangerine Drive.

His phone rang a second later. He answered the call.

"Lange."

"Agent Lange, this is Sergeant Sanchez. Heather Moss just pulled into her driveway. I was told to contact you as soon as we had visual confirmation."

Tom put the Crown Vic in drive and tore away from the school. "What's she doing?"

"She's, ah, looks like she's — well she's loading up the car with bags, or something."

"Anyone with her? Little girls?" He turned onto the main road and got up to speed.

"Yeah, but they're in the car, strapped in their car seats. Okay, now — Moss is looking over. She's approaching."

"Take it easy," he said to Sanchez, "take it easy . . ."

"She's got her hands up. Looks like she's turning herself in."

"Copy that. I'm there in five."

* * *

A deputy cruiser had pulled in behind the Honda, blocking any exit. Another cruiser was parked nearby on the street. Tom jumped out of the Crown Vic and hurried over.

The back hatch of the Honda was open, a couple of tote bags in the cargo space, each overflowing with kiddie things; books and stuffed animals. A box of diapers was tucked between the bags.

Heather Moss wore an ash gray pantsuit, her hair tied back, standing beside one of the rear doors. Tom heard a child crying as he got closer. Heather made a move for the back seat and the deputy beside her grabbed her arm. She jerked away. "I have to take her to the bathroom. I need to go back inside."

"Ma'am," Sanchez said, "please, we just need to stay put until—" He cut off when he saw Tom.

Tom displayed his badge for the two deputies and Heather Moss to see, then put it away.

"Mrs. Moss, I'm here to help, alright?"

Heather Moss gave him a look — she was terrified but determined. She turned back to the crying girl. "Then let me take her into the bathroom, for God's sake, before she wets her pants."

Tom swept the packed bags with his gaze. "Are you going somewhere?"

She brushed sweaty strands of hair from her forehead and fixed him with a look. "Yes. To the police. To explain what happened . . ." She trailed off, glancing past Tom and Sergeant Sanchez. Behind them, another officer pulled up to the curb.

That fierce determination was draining from Heather Moss, and she seemed to sag as she put a hand to her mouth, realization dawning: "Oh my God," she said. "What happened? What happened to that man?"

Tom kept his voice low so the girls couldn't hear. The little one's crying nearly overwhelmed his words anyway. "Howard Declan is dead. We need you to come with us."

Her eyes welled with tears, but she uncovered her mouth and nodded. "That's why, I guess — that's why I wanted them to have their things. In case — oh God."

Tom moved a little closer, suddenly afraid she was going to collapse. But Heather straightened her back as her eyes dried up. "Just let me take Abby to the bathroom, okay? She's made a mess, and it's just a pull-up, okay? Please? I'm not going to go anywhere, just bringing her inside. Alright?"

"Okay. We can do that."

"Thank you." Heather leaned in and unbuckled the child from the seat. Abigail's face was wet with tears, but she settled down the moment Heather gathered her in her arms. Heather moved off toward the house with the girl on her hip.

Tom said to Sanchez, "Can you follow her in for me?"

"You got it."

Sanchez headed up the short walk after Heather. The house was modest, single-story with a red clay-tiled roof, beige stucco siding. There were trimmed shrubs flanking the door. A string hung in the window with a child's drawings attached by clothespins.

Tom ducked down to look in at the other girl, Olivia, who had a coloring book in her lap.

"Hi."

She kept her eyes on her work shading some cartoon character's face with a green Crayola.

"My name is Tom."

Olivia finally looked at him. "Are you a police?"

"I am."

She seemed to think about it, then she held up the coloring book for him to see. She'd colored the Disney princess in bright, unusual shades. Green skin, blue hair, a striped dress. "See? I gave her mojo."

"Mojo?"

"Yeah. I gave her mojo. You know what mojo is?"

"I think so. Or maybe moxie?"

"No." Olivia set the coloring book down on the seat beside her. "Abby had to pee. She sometimes pees her pants."

"Does she?"

"Yeah, poops too. She's potty-training. My mom does everything by herself. Sometimes she lets me help."

"I bet you're a big help. Could you show me inside your house? Let me see some of your drawings?"

"Sure."

Tom waved over the second officer. Pierce agreed to hang outside, keep an eye on things while they went in. Tom stooped to the back seat again. "Now how do I—?"

Olivia had already unbuckled herself and opened the car door. She climbed out, tossed her hair back, and headed toward the house. He followed her up the two steps and in through the open front door.

The place was cozy, toys everywhere. A simple couch and a couple of cushioned chairs, lots of bookshelves and books. A small TV sat in a far corner, looking neglected.

Straight back was a hallway where Sanchez stood with his arms folded outside a closed door. Tom could hear Heather talking in a soft voice to Abigail.

Olivia plucked a drawing from the line hanging in the window. "This one is for you," she said.

"For me, huh?" He took the dried watercolor, an abstract jungle, it looked like, people in the foreground. "Thank you."

Olivia explained about the picture as Tom had a look around: the next room was just a small open space with a modest dining table, three chairs around it, one higher than the others. The kitchen was bigger, a bit of a mess, dishes piled in the sink. A window above the sink overlooked the small backyard.

"I'm going to get a drink." Olivia went to the fridge and got out a juice box. As she carefully worked the straw out of the packaging and punctured the juice box with it, Tom looked over the photographs held to the refrigerator by magnets.

Most of them were of the girls: the girls at the beach with pails and shovels; the girls out in the street on little manual scooters; the girls with cake and ice cream smeared on their faces at what looked like a birthday party. There was one with them dressed in winter clothes in a snowy setting. The older people smiling along beside them were probably Theresa and Henry Hutchins, Heather's parents.

In the center of it all was a family photo showing Heather and Glenn Moss with a much younger Olivia, but no Abigail. Glenn was handsome with a boxy chin and thick eyebrows. They looked happy.

Tom's phone rang — the incoming number was Blythe's.

"How's it going?" Blythe asked.

He set the drawing down on the kitchen table and tracked behind Olivia, now moving back into the living room.

"I'm at Moss's house. She's cooperating, says she was about to turn herself in. She seemed to not know what happened after she left the jail." Tom was aware of Olivia's proximity, but the six year-old didn't seem to be paying attention. She'd taken a book from a shelf and had sat on the couch with it, still slurping from the juice box.

"You make the arrest yet?"

Tom glanced at the bathroom door. "No. She's got the little one in the bathroom. I don't think she's a flight risk at this point. I've got two deputies here; the house is secure."

"Okay. Declan is being moved to the District Medical Examiner's Office. I'm meeting with Turnbull and Sheriff Jacobsen in about five minutes. We're going to start interviewing the C.O.s and deputies."

Tom walked to the front door and looked through the window at the Honda in the driveway.

"Who is he?"

"We're going to find out."

"Alright." Even though the child appeared engrossed by the book, Tom lowered his voice further. "I'll call family services, have them come take the girls. Better here than at the jail. Then we'll bring Moss in."

Deputy Pierce was between the Honda in the driveway and the front of the house. Out on the street, a dark SUV was driving along, its windows smoked. The vehicle slowed.

Blythe was saying something.

Tom leaned toward the glass for a closer look. "Hang on, Lauren . . ."

The SUV came to a complete stop and the driver's side window rolled down. Something dark protruded from the window. Tom took a breath and held it.

A window exploded in the living room. The front of the house was pummeled by gunfire. Tom leaped away from the front door and dove for the couch where he grabbed Olivia and yanked her to the ground.

The barrage of gunfire thundered as Tom shielded Olivia with his body. It sounded like a jackhammer was working on the front wall of the house. More glass shattered, but outside, like the vehicles were being shot up, too.

Tom heard a shriek of fear behind him.

He yelled toward the back of the house. "Stay in the bathroom!"

The volley of gunfire went on, everything seemed to tremble like an earthquake. Tom covered Olivia with his body, able to sense her rapid breathing and fluttering pulse. He squeezed his eyes shut for a second, opened them, took a deep breath.

The shooting ended.

An engine revved, tires squealed, and then the sound of the motor faded as the gunman's vehicle sped away. Tom didn't move. He waited, still covering Olivia. Gradually, he eased off her and checked her for wounds. She didn't seem hurt, just frightened, staring up at him in shock.

He got to his knees but didn't dare stand fully upright. "You okay?"

Olivia blinked, her eyes wide and glassy. "Was that fireworks?"

"No." He took her hand, helped her to her knees. "Stay low like this, okay, crawl towards the hallway there, okay? I'm right behind you."

She did as she was told. As they rounded the couch Tom stretched to see around her. Sanchez was in the hallway, sitting against the wall, stunned. He was looking away from them, towards the back of the house. His gun was out and in his lap.

"Sergeant . . ."

Sanchez didn't respond.

"Sergeant *Sanchez*!"

At last, he turned his head. His face was pale as a cloud, his eyes unfocused with shock. But he gave his head a little shake and his eyes cleared. "Yeah, okay. I'm alright, I think."

Heather shouted from inside the bathroom. "What happened? What *happened out there*?! Is Olivia okay? Livy?!"

"I'm okay, Mommy." Despite her recent composure, Olivia's face crumpled and she started to cry.

Tom urged her forward until they were just outside the bathroom door. He reached up and turned the knob. The door swung out and Heather was there, sitting on the closed toilet, Abigail in her lap. The little girl was sucking on her thumb and twirling her hair. Her little chest jumped, the way children spasmed after a hard cry.

Olivia crawled into the bathroom, sobbing now.

Tom spoke gently but firmly. "Get in the tub, honey, okay?"

"The tub?"

Heather reached out, took her daughter and drew her into a quick, tight embrace. "Yes, get in there, Livy, like he says, go ahead . . ."

"But it's still *wet* . . ." Olivia wailed and shook, but finally straddled her leg over and slipped into the tub.

Tom locked eyes with Heather. Heather climbed in after with the other girl. Then he got his gun out and shut the door.

Sergeant Sanchez was still sitting there in a daze. Tom checked the man over, but he appeared unharmed. Sanchez raised his arm and Tom looked where he was pointing.

There was a single bullet hole punched in the back wall of the hallway. One of the framed pictures hanging there had been knocked askew.

Sanchez was showing Tom where the round that missed him had wound up. A bullet that had come from the vehicle on the street, through the window of the front door, narrowly missed Sanchez and embedded in the wall. "Almost got nailed," Sanchez said, a bit breathless. "Ah, God."

"Stay here. Keep them safe. I'm going to have a look out front."

Tom crawled back into the living room and toward the front door. A piece of glass bit into his palm. He winced and got to his feet, staying as low as possible. He shouted up toward the shattered window. "Deputy Pierce? Can you hear me?"

"I can hear you!"

"You hit? You alright?"

"I'm alright! I'm behind the Honda!"

"Where is the vehicle?"

"Gone!"

Tom slowly unfurled, now gripping the gun with both hands, blood from his cut palm oozing out and threading down his wrist. He looked through the broken window.

A bad scene out there. His Crown Vic had been all shot up. The glass was cracked on one of the Sheriff's Department cruisers. Tom saw Pierce on the ground in front of the Honda's engine, his gun held at his chest, pointed at the sky. He rolled his head and looked at Tom, his eyes wide.

Sirens rose in the distance.

CHAPTER FOUR

A blur of lights and faces. Tom stood on the front lawn and relayed events to a County investigator, but he was distracted by Heather Moss and her two daughters.

Heather was in the back of a police cruiser, the door ajar. Abigail sat in her lap as Olivia sat beside her, clutching her coloring book. The medical team had already looked them over. Not a scratch on the girls beyond a rug burn on Olivia's knee.

Nearby, the deputy who'd been sprawled out in the driveway, Pierce, was back on his feet, talking to another investigator. Tom knew her.

Detective Felicia Machado watched him closely as he approached. "Tom. What a morning. Are you alright? Did they check you over yet?"

"I'm fine. How you been, Machado?"

"Good."

Machado was friends with Katie Mills, the woman who'd walked out on him that morning. Tom could see something in the investigator's eyes that betrayed knowledge of his personal life, but it disappeared in a blink. "Deputy Pierce was able to make the vehicle."

"Yeah? Good."

"Chevy Tahoe." Pierce said.

"You're sure?"

He nodded. "I'm sure. I wasn't able to get the tags, though." The deputy's face fell with disappointment. "Car was coming toward me."

Tom knew it wasn't Pierce's fault. Cops were trained to read license plates — getting the first numbers was particularly helpful since they were assigned by county. But Florida was one of nineteen states not requiring front plates.

"By the time I could have gotten a chance to read it, he'd opened fire," Pierce lamented. "Should be pretty easy to locate, though, right? Had blacked-out windows."

Tom stepped beside Pierce and put a hand on the smaller man's shoulder. "I'm just glad you're okay."

Police tape had been stretched out around the house and front lawn, forming a perimeter. Orange cones blocked street traffic, no one was allowed to drive through. Techs in white jumpsuits labeled "IFS" worked the scene, examined the rubber burns, placed yellow markers where spent shell casings lay glinting in the sun. A tech set down a marker numbered twenty-eight while Tom watched.

An estimated thirty bullets fired at Heather Moss's home. A spray of ammunition that chewed up the house, damaged multiple vehicles, caused Sergeant Sanchez to see God. Heather Moss and her two daughters were shaken up, but safe. It was amazing no one was hurt.

Machado shook her head, incredulous. "Broad daylight, the guy just rolls right up, gangland-style drive-by — and you're sure it was driver's side? I mean I guess it had to be if he was coming from that way."

"That's right," Tom answered. "I saw the gun come out."

"Yeah," Pierce echoed. "Driver's side."

"Sounds like a single shooter," Machado said, "which is odd."

"Odd, but not unheard of I guess."

"Well, I'll work with DMV on it, but we're going to see thousands of registered Tahoes; we'll see if we can narrow it down with the window tint. But even if we can, and we look at registrants with a record — felons — it'll take days to chase down all those leads. I wish it could have been a friggin' Packard Panther or an Aston Martin."

Tom smiled but Pierce continued to look forlorn.

Machado nodded toward Heather. "And I already talked to her. She was in the bathroom, didn't see anything, has no idea who this could be. No one has threatened her before today, nothing like that. What have we got going on, Lange? This woman doesn't strike me as a murderer, or some contract killer."

He looked at Heather Moss again. Her blonde hair was tousled, her eyes wide. She kept darting looks at the two people at the lawn's edge, social workers with the Department of Family Services. The girls were going to be separated from their mother here at the house after all.

Moss had fled the scene at the jail before even knowing what had happened. She'd gone for them in a blind panic like she wanted them safe. Hadn't packed a suitcase, just two tote bags for the girls, saying she'd been planning to go to the police.

But then whoever it was came after her anyway. Boldly, recklessly. Sheriff's Deputies had been present, but it didn't matter. An agent with the state bureau had been present, but that didn't matter either. Like whoever it was sought to tie up loose ends, execute the person whom they'd either hired or suborned into murdering a potential witness.

It had to be Palumbo and his crew.

Palumbo's crew was drug-runners. Heroin, meth, a little grass, but the big product was cocaine. Palumbo also made millions on gambling, using the dog track in Bonita Springs to run his poker racket. They were underground enterprises that had pulled Nick, a guy who struggled to stay straight, into the thrall.

Tom had known Palumbo was a piece of shit, dangerous, but executions and drive-bys took it up to a whole new level.

Blythe pulled up outside the crime scene tape in the street, got out, looked around. She spied Tom through the chaos and started over, showing her badge to a deputy who lifted the tape and let her through. Then she was standing with them, surveying the scene.

"You alright?"

He held up his bandaged hand.

She gave it a sidelong look and said. "Lucky."

"I should have gotten them out of here as soon as I showed up."

"Nah. Nobody expected this."

"*We* should have. If someone was willing to go to such lengths to get rid of Declan, we should have expected Heather Moss could be in danger, and that someone might come after her."

"Tom, this whole thing happened in less than two hours. We don't know anything."

* * *

They rode together in Blythe's car. Tom's own department-issued vehicle, riddled with bullet holes, was being processed for evidence.

"And I just got that thing . . ." he muttered.

The cruiser carrying Heather was two cars ahead. Behind them was the DFS car, with the daughters strapped into their car seats in the back. It had been a difficult, emotional separation. There were promises made by Heather that she would see the girls tonight, tuck them into bed, but Tom doubted it.

"Okay," Blythe said, driving. "What do we know about her?"

"We know she recently relocated to Florida. We know that her husband died and she moved here a little while after that."

"Can she do that? As a social worker? Just pick up in a new state?"

"She's a licensed clinical mental health counselor," Tom said.

"That's not a social worker?"

"Sort of; not really. Nick and I used to have a case manager — *that's* a social worker. Mental health counselors like Heather have their master's. So, she's a clinician. I think there's about thirty states she can work in and Florida is one of them."

"So she saw a job opening and moved here from New York?"

"Maybe."

Blythe followed the vehicles along the three-lane highway. The sky was clouding over, an afternoon storm impending. The palm trees along the median strip were lashed by the wind.

Tom glanced at his bandaged hand. He could smell the antiseptic the paramedic had swabbed over his glass cut. There was a bloom of blood in the white gauze, the size and color of a rosebud. "Lucky" barely touched it. It seemed miraculous.

"You're still beating yourself up," Blythe said. "You don't have to do this right now, Tom. You can take the rest of the day. Take whatever time you need. You'll need to speak to IAB tomorrow."

With her dirty blonde hair drawn back in a tight braid, her tanned skin, light wrinkles around her eyes, Blythe was a perennial Floridian, born and raised. They'd had their ups and downs together. Mistakes had been made on their first case, and they'd been costly. Their second case was now off and running at full speed. He wondered how they would do.

"I'm fine, Lauren. Good to go."

"Listen, if you and County hadn't been there, the shooter might have walked right up to her front door. So you can pat yourself on the back for a fast response time."

Tom looked at the deputies cruising along the lane beside them, a veritable motorcade. Still, he kept scanning the highway, his heart speeding up with every intersection. When they stopped at a red light, he broke out in a sweat despite the Crown Vic's cool, air-conditioned interior. He put his hand on the grip of his gun, ready to pull, imagining that blacked-out Tahoe barreling through the traffic, window rolled down, tip of an automatic rifle poking out . . .

The light turned green and they continued on. Tom watched the traffic going by in the other direction. All these people, living out their lives.

CHAPTER FIVE

They stowed their phones and weapons in the locker room, passed through security and were led to a control room. The captain greeted them, a broad-shouldered man named Aaronson who was the direct supervisor of the jail, and a corporal named Cordova. The control room featured a bank of monitors displaying various areas of the jail, and one main monitor with a frozen image. On the screen, Heather Moss was seated in a chair later removed from the room. She had her legs crossed and balanced a notepad on her knee. Howard Declan, still alive, sat on his bare cot.

"Go ahead and play it," Blythe said to Cordova.

Tom watched for a few moments before asking, "There's no sound?"

"No." Cordova turned a dial and the video jumped forward, several seconds at a time. Heather's image made jerky gestures, and she uncrossed and re-crossed her legs. Declan remained virtually motionless.

"Hang on," Tom said. "Can we just watch for a few seconds?"

Blythe nodded at Cordova who slowed the video back to normal speed.

Tom leaned closer. Hard to see Heather's face from the angle, but he watched her body language. Her dangling foot tapped the air. She ran her hand over her face, smoothed back her hair. "Looks nervous."

Blythe spoke to Cordova. "Okay. Let's go forward." Cordova twisted the dial. When Heather Moss rose from her chair, the corporal slowed the speed again.

Heather moved across the cell and sat on the cot beside Declan.

"Do they normally do that?" Tom looked from Cordova to Aaronson.

"The therapists are not supposed to have any physical contact with the inmates, no," Aaronson said. "It's unusual she would sit beside him, but it didn't indicate anything to the deputy on duty at the time."

They continued to watch as Heather and Declan talked in close proximity. About a minute passed. Then Heather made a move and Blythe pointed at the screen. "There. See? Freeze that. Okay, go back a little bit — good. Now play that at quarter speed."

Cordova went through the commands and Tom watched as Heather appeared to reach behind Declan, just for a second. Then she stood up and crossed back to her chair.

Tom could feel Blythe watching him and he turned his head toward her. She raised her eyebrows.

The video continued. Heather Moss left the room. Declan sat for a moment, unmoving, then stood. It was impossible to say for sure, but it looked like his hand swept the bed, picking up a small item, like an envelope. He concealed it from the camera until, a few seconds later, the same hand went to his mouth.

"Okay, forward again . . ." Blythe said. Declan paced the cell at high speeds, going in circles, like a broken toy. When there was an aberration in his movement, Cordova slowed down. Then the corporal turned her head from the screen.

Tom didn't have that luxury. He watched as Declan bent over, holding his stomach. The inmate dropped to his knees, in obvious pain. Deputy Rizzo appeared in the shot, got close to Declan, but the inmate held up his hand. Then he projectile-vomited. Rizzo disappeared from the cell.

"Deputy Rizzo left to get the jail doctor at that moment," Aaronson said. Tom thought the captain's voice sounded far away.

On screen, Declan shuddered and shook. He got unsteadily to his feet, his pants soiled. Then he dropped again and went into convulsions, sprays of blood coming from his mouth.

"And there he's seizing, biting his tongue," Blythe said. "Okay. That's enough."

Cordova returned her attention to the console and pressed a button, causing the screen to go dark.

Tom backed away from the monitor and stared off, thinking.

"I mean, we got her." Blythe said. "There's no getting around that video. She comes in, she's not searched, she goes into the suicide watch area, meets Declan. Sits beside him, we can see her pass him something, she leaves, looks like he shakes open a small envelope, pops something in his mouth. A few minutes later, he's vomiting, biting off his tongue."

"Okay," Blythe said to Aaronson. "Can we bring your people in now?"

Aaronson let out a breath and stood. "Alright. Give me a minute."

He left and Blythe rolled her chair closer to Tom. They looked at each other, communicating the horror of what they'd seen.

* * *

The control room was big enough to contain all the deputies and corrections officers who'd been rounded up, but without enough chairs, so that half of them were sitting, half standing.

A muscular deputy with a bald head was seated, bouncing his knee — Rizzo. A corrections officer, her hair pulled back in a tight braid, gazed through a large reinforced pane of glass overlooking the common area. A few inmates were out there, watching television or playing cards.

"Good morning," Blythe said. "Thank you all for coming. I know it's a massive effort to keep this place running, we promise not to detain you long. And we appreciate the captain's quick response to rally you together so we could talk."

Blythe glanced at Aaronson, who crossed his arms.

She resumed, "So, some of you we're going to speak to individually, but for now we wanted to brief you as a group. As you may know, Howard Michael Declan was recently arrested for disorderly conduct, disturbing the peace, and assaulting an officer. That all landed him here. His initial mental health screen was high, and he was placed in the on-watch area where he awaited further evaluation and arraignment."

She turned towards a bank of monitors, showing camera views all over the jail, including the security checkpoint.

"At 8:51 this morning, Heather Moss, a therapist from County Mental Health, came to evaluate Declan for continued suicide risk. She entered the east wing through the main doors and approached security."

Blythe stooped over the controls and said something to Cordova, who rotated the dial. On the main screen, an image jerked to life, and Tom watched as an overhead camera captured Heather Moss as she stepped up to the table beside the metal detectors. She had a green bag over her shoulder which she set down as a female C.O. approached her with a smile. They had a short conversation as the C.O. scanned the ID badge pinned to Heather's chest.

Tom watched along with the others as a deputy, the same one who'd escorted Tom through security over an hour before, led Heather to a door off to the side of the metal detector, keyed it for entry, and they stepped through. Heather's bag was left behind; she carried only a notepad with her, probably a pen.

Tom asked, "You let clinicians in — therapists — with writing utensils?"

"Not to booking," Aaronson said. "There are pens attached to the tables in there. But therapists — they gotta have something to write with."

By this point, Tom thought, she must've had the small envelope in her pocket, or maybe tucked between the pages of her notepad.

Cordova pushed a button and new image displayed on the main screen. Heather walked down a corridor to another door, on her way to the east wing.

Blythe said, "You can see that she's entered the jail and passed into the on-watch area without any sort of search. Just like that, she's on her way."

Cordova grabbed the dial again. Heather Moss froze in motion on the screen.

Blythe faced the group: "We believe Mrs. Moss had something on her person which was then used to kill Howard Declan."

The first to speak up was the female C.O. with the braid. Her nametag read Howser. She'd been the one on screen, chatting with Heather Moss, scanning her ID: "Mrs. Moss has been coming in to see inmates for over a year. We just streamlined it. I mean . . ." Howser looked around as if to find support among the other guards. All Tom saw were hangdog expressions.

Blythe held up a hand. "We understand the reasons why you'd let in someone like Moss without the full range of security checks. Why we're here is because that convenience was exploited, and ostensibly resulted in someone's death. I've spoken with the medical examiner, and we're close to determining that Declan died from—"

"Who is he?" It was another corrections officer, McNeill, with a blond buzz cut and a dusting of freckles. "He someone important? Murder witness or something?"

"Let's just hold those questions for now, okay? Declan likely died from potassium cyanide, probably a dose of over three hundred milligrams, wrapped in a fast-dissolving shell. Brain death occurs within minutes, and the heart stops beating shortly after."

"That's true?" McNeill glanced around the room. "I thought that was from movies or something. Spy fiction."

"If you want, you can look up its uses in the military and yes, espionage organizations. Or read about the Tamil Tigers in Sri Lanka's civil war, who wore potassium cyanide necklaces they could eat in case they were captured by the Sri Lankan Army."

McNeill's mouth snapped shut.

Blythe continued, "For our investigation, we'll consider its availability online, for one thing, via the deep web. It's probably obtainable on the street, too, if you know where to look."

Howser spoke. "It causes people to throw up like that? That's awful . . ."

Tom gave Rizzo another look. The deputy was pale, his eyes searching the floor, probably reliving the moment he watched Declan drop to the floor. Which one of them was working for Palumbo? McNeill? Rizzo? Anybody? Or had letting in a mental health counselor just become routine, like Howser said?

"Symptoms of the poisoning can vary to a degree," Blythe continued. "But typically within a few minutes, the person loses consciousness, suffers convulsions. Death is caused by cerebral hypoxia. Potassium cyanide basically starves your blood of oxygen until you die."

Tom looked at Heather, suspended in mid-stride on the video, imagining the tiny death-capsule she was carrying. He thought of her reaching around Declan, placing the tiny envelope behind him. Where had she gotten such a lethal chemical?

"Back to the leak," Blythe said. "Could anyone, besides Heather Moss and the people in this room, know that therapists sometimes get a pass on security? Maybe someone who's spent time in lock-up? Do any inmates ever have a view on the security area?"

Howser shook her head. "No. Not at all. They are taken in and out of jail on the other side of the building. They never see the security entrance. But, Moss could have said something about it to a colleague, even a friend . . ."

"She's not supposed to speak about anything that happens at the jail," Aaronson said.

Tom did the calculations in his mind — maybe inmates weren't privy to the comings and goings of the security area, and matters were kept confidential from outsiders, but about ten staffers knew the situation, along with one in-house clinician who worked directly for the jail, and potentially others from County Mental Health. Then there were lawyers who came in to see their clients — and who knew how many of those. To figure out anyone who'd either bypassed security or knew about people bypassing security was a tall order.

He stepped closer to the control desk and looked over all the monitors, the computers processing all of the information they displayed. Sweeping his hand across the dials and buttons, he asked, "How does this work? This CCTV, this is all digital, yeah? Hard-wired or wireless?"

"Both," said Cordova. "The basic system is wired. But the analog is converted to digital by this machine here. So we can take what we call the clean feed and broadcast it wirelessly."

"Broadcast it to where?"

"Both the captain and the sheriff can access the clean feed remotely."

Tom glanced at Aaronson, who looked away.

Cordova said, "Hackers?"

"I don't know." But as Tom turned back to the controls, he was thinking it. Someone — anyone — with the capabilities of hacking the clean feed broadcast to the higher-ups could monitor it from afar. Perhaps even wait until they found the right candidate. Someone like Heather Moss, let into the complex without much ado.

Someone with something to lose, like her precious daughters, who would have no choice but to cooperate.

CHAPTER SIX

A dilemma: incarcerating Heather Moss at Everglades County Jail meant bringing her back to the scene of the crime. But criminal suspects didn't go to state or federal prison before sentencing. That left neighboring counties such as Lee or Charlotte, but Turnbull decided against it, opting to put her in segregated housing within the Everglades jail, and bringing in fresh C.O.s who hadn't been on duty yet that day.

Tom set out his tape recorder and clicked it on. The jail had dressed Heather Moss in inmate fatigues so she now looked eerily similar to Howard Declan. Her wrists were shackled in front of her, but she wore a placid expression, her eyes shining.

Sitting beside Tom, Blythe noted the date, time, the persons present in the room for the benefit of the recording.

Heather Moss glanced at the recorder. "I've called my lawyer. He should be here any minute."

Blythe scowled. "Okay — though that strikes me as a little odd. You've said you have nothing to hide, you've been cooperating from the start."

Heather smiled politely. "Agent Blythe, I've been a clinical therapist for almost ten years. I understand a little about the system. Please don't take it personally, I know you have a job to do. I'm just protecting myself and my girls the best I know how."

Blythe gave Tom a long look. The door opened and a man came in wearing a rumpled brown suit. He set his briefcase on the table and shook the agents' hands. "Robert Ernst. I'm Mrs. Moss's attorney." He glanced at the tape recorder on the table, then sat down beside Heather. "How are you doing? Are you okay? Are they treating you alright?"

Another look from Blythe, who rolled her eyes.

"Okay," she said. "So, can we continue?"

Ernst settled in. "The charge against my client is fleeing the scene of a crime?"

"That's the current charge filed. Now we go to the prosecutor, and based on our recommendation, we can add to that charge."

Ernst stared back at Blythe. "Such as?"

"We'll let you know once charges are prepared and issue a warrant."

Ernst shook his head. "You can't keep her in here for fleeing the scene. She's never been arrested; has no criminal record. She's a single mother of two young girls and an upstanding member of the community. I'll request she's released on her own recognizance."

Tom watched Heather carefully as Ernst spoke. Her eyes were downcast. It was hard to get a read on what she might be thinking. Finally, she looked up, right at him.

"How are my girls?"

"I've just checked and they're perfectly okay. They're playing. I told them to make sure Olivia has art supplies."

Tom was happy to see his smile reflected back in Heather's face.

Blythe cleared her throat. "Okay, Mrs. Moss. If your attorney will permit it, we'd like to get into the events of this morning. Let's talk about what happened."

Heather glanced at Ernst, who nodded and snapped open his briefcase. He was in his forties, balding, with a mole on his upper cheek.

"I was on my way to work," Heather said, "running late. I got a phone call."

"I'm sure you've checked my client's phone," Ernst interrupted.

"We have," Blythe answered. "Our forensic team found that a call was received this morning at 7:58, lasted for seven minutes."

"They said that they were watching my girls," Heather said. "They described what each of them was wearing, what they were doing. They said they would hurt them if I didn't do exactly what they said."

Tom saw Heather's lower lip begin to tremble. The therapist was fighting to keep composure, but her blue eyes were welling up.

"You're saying 'they'," Blythe commented. "Did you speak to more than one person?"

"No. I don't know."

"You don't know?" Blythe cut Tom a sidelong look. "Was it like a party line?"

"It was some kind of computer voice. It said 'we' several times. 'We're watching. We will hurt them.'"

Tom interrupted. "Focusing on the voice — what do you mean, 'like a computer?' You mean like the, ah, the group Anonymous? That sort of thing?"

"Yes. I've seen someone at the clinic — not my own client, but another therapist's — with an assistive device that provided speech output. They were in a wheelchair, like Stephen Hawking. But this voice was, I don't know, *better* sounding, more human. I imagine they have different versions or something?" She stared off, shook her head. "I really don't know."

"Okay. So no way to guess an age or gender?" Tom asked. "Or an accent?"

"No. Not at all. I can tell you he or she talked a lot. He told me Florida was a nice place to live. He told me his people were sitting outside of my daughter's school. He described to me what Olivia was wearing."

Heather was repeating herself, growing upset again. A tear escaped her left eye and tracked down her cheek.

Ernst rose from the table and went to the door, alerted the guard with a knock. "Can I get some tissues in here?" The guard outside nodded and radioed the request. Ernst closed the door and sat back down.

Tom spoke to Heather. "Like Agent Blythe said, we have your phone. We've got the number and we'll do everything we can to track this person down and get to the bottom of it."

Ernst faced her. "Why don't you tell them about the vehicle you saw."

She nodded. "The caller said he could see me. I looked around and thought I maybe saw a black SUV."

"Like a Chevy Tahoe?"

"I don't know. It could be. It was big, four doors. I only saw it, you know, in my mirrors."

"Anything remarkable about the vehicle?"

"Tinted windows, I think."

"Any chance you caught the license plate?"

"No. Sorry." She glanced at Tom's bandaged hand. "Thank you for what you did this morning."

He felt his cheeks warming. "Anyone would have done the same thing."

"The girls — they were so scared . . ." Heather became emotional again, turning her face away, as if embarrassed.

The door opened and the guard set a box of tissues on the table. Heather looked at it blankly for a moment, then plucked one out. She wiped her eyes and blew her nose. She made as if to put the wadded tissue in her pocket. Then she laughed. "I have no — no pockets to . . ."

"It's okay," Tom said. "Just set it aside."

After tidying up her tear-streaked face, her eyes acquired the blank look of fear. "Am I going to be charged with murder?"

"No," Ernst answered. "There's no way they can charge you with murder. This was not your fault, and that's clear to them, right?" The lawyer looked between Tom and Blythe.

Blythe answered. "Right now there's no felony complaint. But there could be. And as a capital offense, it could go before a grand jury."

"We can waive that," Ernst said to Heather.

"Why would we waive a grand jury?"

"Because as both these agents know, grand juries almost always return an indictment. It's a rubber stamp."

"The statewide prosecutor has an obligation to present exculpatory evidence," Blythe said and shifted in her seat. "Your client was the last person with Howard Declan. The video shows she — it looks like she passed him something. I think you, and your client, need to be prepared for the charge. But, again, that would be for the grand jury to decide, or there would be a preliminary hearing."

Heather leaned back, tilted her face toward the ceiling and blew out a long breath. "Murder," she repeated quietly. "Oh my God."

Ernst patted her hand. "No. Never gonna happen. It's okay . . ."

"Mrs. Moss," Tom said quickly. "Please just answer me this — the call that came in on your phone this morning went on for over seven minutes. You say the caller threatened you, threatened your *daughters* in order to convince you to go along. And through all that talking, he could have said something —anything — which could help us. We don't want this to be on you, Heather."

There was a lot going on behind her eyes — tragedy sitting just inside her gaze. "Yeah, he talked. He talked a lot. He said he'd been watching me. He knew how I came into the jail and lately had bypassed security. I tried to argue, I tried to reason with them, but then he said . . ."

"What?"

"He said, 'We're not normal, rational people.'"

The room fell silent, just the low buzzing of the wall clock.

She spoke again. "He also said — he was talking about a truck that was driving near me on the road — he said, it was 'probably full of illegals'. But that's it. That's all I remember. For the next two hours, all I could think about was my girls."

Tears cupped in her eyes again.

Tom said, "We're going to figure this out. Okay?"

Blythe leaned forward, interlacing her fingers on the table. "Mrs. Moss, did you look inside the envelope at any time?"

"You don't have to answer that," Ernst cut in.

Blythe rolled her shoulders. "What did you think was in the envelope? Weren't you curious?"

"The caller made it clear I shouldn't look inside."

She hadn't exactly answered the question, Tom thought, and felt a weight slide over his heart. But maybe she was just trying to protect herself, her daughters all along, like she said, hadn't looked, hadn't wanted to look.

Ernst was getting agitated. "Heather, you don't have to answer any more of this."

"Oh, come on," said Blythe. "You want exculpatory evidence? Let her tell us her story. Let us figure out what happened, and if she's on the level then it can only help her."

The lawyer's eyes flitted back and forth between the agents. "No prosecutor or judge would dream of charging this woman with murder, not when she was so clearly under duress. What you need to be doing right now,

52

Agents Blythe and Lange, in my humble opinion, is going after the person who threatened my client, threatened her daughters. You need to be going after the people who wanted Howard Declan dead."

CHAPTER SEVEN

Howard Declan had a home in North Naples, where narrow streets wound through a residential neighborhood filled with modest homes like Heather Moss's, one-story places with small front lawns. The lowering sun threw long shadows over ground wet from the afternoon rain. A sheriff's deputy parked in front.

Tom pulled up across from the deputy, Blythe riding in the passenger seat beside him, finishing up on a phone call to the communications department of the state bureau.

"Okay," she said into the phone. "That could be helpful." She scribbled something on the pad balanced on her knees.

Tom watched little kids further down the street pushing themselves around on scooters, silhouetted by the setting sun. They reminded him of the photos on Heather Moss's fridge.

"Thanks, Matt," Blythe said into the phone. "And can you pass this on to Cheyenne in Research: we want the full workup on Declan — all the agencies. Let's get his income tax returns, employment history, residences; run him through the department of public safety, corrections, all that. I want to know when his last check-up at the doctor was and the color of his urine. Thank her for me."

Blythe hung up, gazed toward the same playing kids as she spoke to Tom. "So this technology — this electronic device providing speech output — there's a few different versions on the market. A lot of it is used by special schools, places for the blind, mute, autistic, etcetera. There's something called an AAC, which is . . ." she read from her notes, "an 'augmented or alternative communication device.' That's usually a computer program which synthesizes speech from text." Blythe shook her head, sighed. "Weird story, if you asked me — someone is driving around with a computer in their car, telling Moss what to do with this . . . voice?"

"Are there mobile versions?" Tom asked. "Seems like these days you could get a phone app or something."

"I don't know."

"Let's ask him — Matt. Can you call him back?"

Blythe gave Tom a sidelong look, opened her mouth, closed it. She dialed Matt again, asked him, listened. Then said, "Uh-huh. Huh. Okay, thanks," and hung up. "Matt said there's something called 'Fusion', which is a portable device for people who can't speak."

"Okay, yeah — a speech synthesizer. You type in one end, a voice comes out the other."

"I still don't know how someone would use it as they drove, though, not at the same time . . ."

"Maybe it's just to mask the voice."

When Blythe didn't respond, he continued: "We should look at the companies who sell it anyway. Plus we'll keep an ear to the street for any black market purchases of potassium cyanide. Maybe we can come around to a couple of C.I.s, see if anything shakes out of the bag."

Finished, he pressed back in the seat and stared out at Declan's house. Declan's lawn was dominated by a short, squat palm tree that resembled a pineapple. "And we're going to talk with some of the jail staff individually?"

"Correct. I've lined up McNeill — can't wait to get in a room alone with him — Cordova, Howser, Clements, and Rizzo."

Tom thought of the muscular guard with the Mr. Clean haircut. "Rizzo is the one who watched Howard Declan go into convulsions, vomit, and chew off his tongue."

"That's right. Cordova was working the CCTV. Howser, as you know, was one of the two who let Heather Moss in. The other is named Pendleton."

"What about the floater? She was the deputy who brought me in, brought Heather in, too."

"That's Clements. She had a family thing, is coming back in this afternoon. I'll be talking to her, too."

"And we'll talk to the other clinicians from County Mental Health."

"That's the plan. You ready? Any more questions or requests?"

Tom frowned at her, then the two agents got out. They crossed the street and greeted the deputy, signed their names on his clipboard. The deputy led them to Declan's front door, letting them in with a key.

Tom stepped into the gloomy house. The air was hot and breathless, redolent of must and neglect. There was an air conditioning unit sitting in one of the windows with a red light flashing on the console. All the other windows were closed.

Blythe moved off down a hallway and Tom stepped into the kitchen. A fridge with no pictures, just a magnet advertising an auto salvage yard, a couple of unwashed dishes in the sink. In general, though, the place was much neater than Heather Moss's house. This was the home of a single man, no kids.

Tom moved through the house, noticing a stack of *The Week* magazines in the living room, bookshelves against one wall containing several computer manuals. A closed laptop sat on a desk in the corner.

There was a fair amount of unwashed laundry in the bedroom closet. The roll of toilet paper in the bathroom was almost gone. A single toothbrush on the sink.

The house featured a small, screened-in back porch and Tom spied a chest on the ground, unlocked. With his latex gloves on, he lifted the lid and peered inside to find stacks of papers and photos, a couple of photo albums. He squatted down and pushed the materials around, halting when he found a picture of Howard Declan with his arm around a woman. She had a wild head of red hair streaked with gray. That and the lines in her skin put her at about fifty, fifty-five years old. Tom dug a bit deeper through the photos and found more pictures of the woman. They looked like a couple, riding bikes, taking trips, lounging at the beach. Declan was on the tall side, skinny, with a beakish nose.

Tom pulled out one of the photo albums. The very first page showed a much younger Declan and a younger red-head getting hitched. She wore a white bridal gown, he was in a black tuxedo. They cut the cake. He fed her a piece, and some got on her nose. They were laughing.

Tom set the album aside, got on his knees and kept digging. There was a fly-fishing brochure for upstate New York, a pamphlet for camping in the Smoky Mountains, and a random newspaper article covering a classic car rally that had come to town several years before. He picked up a set of keys sitting on the bottom.

"What've you got?"

Blythe startled him. He turned and saw her standing in the doorway leading back into the house.

"Photos, mementos, random stuff. Keys." He gestured to the pile of photos he'd set aside which featured the red-head. "And Declan was married."

Blythe held up her own find, a couple of documents. She rattled them softly. "Divorced."

Tom got to his feet and she handed him the paperwork, saying, "Top drawer in the living room desk."

Tom looked it over. "Name was Barbara." He passed the divorce certificate back to Blythe. "Who's been established as Declan's next of kin?"

"So far, no one. He was an only child with no kids of his own. His parents are both deceased. The ME's office is currently searching for any cousins, which is way down the list in the order of precedence."

"What about her?"

"Legally, she has no rights as a claimant. And we don't need her to identify the body; he was already IDed the moment he was processed into county jail. So, she's nobody."

"She's someone we should talk to."

"Agreed." Blythe sauntered past him out onto the screened-in porch. "Jeez, it's nice out here. Stuffy in there, like a crypt."

"Guy's been living alone for a while."

Blythe sat down on the wicker love seat in the center of the room. She seemed to gaze out into the twilit back yard, as if soaking in the eventide.

"We gonna get the medical on this guy, find out he had all sorts of mental problems?" Tom asked.

"I don't know."

"Maybe 'Barbara' knows whether he ever worked for Palumbo, or ever witnessed anything."

"You think Heather Moss is innocent, huh?"

Tom was struck by the question. "Innocent? You don't believe someone called her up this morning?"

"What if *she's* working for Palumbo?"

"We haven't found any evidence of that. And someone just tried to kill her."

"Well, Declan is definitely connected."

"What did Declan supposedly see or know exactly?"

Her eyebrows went up. "You don't know?"

"I mean, like I said this morning, I know he was questioned by Everglades County a month ago as part of their ongoing investigation into Palumbo. But I don't know what he did for Palumbo, or how exactly he was connected."

Now her forehead wrinkled and she smirked. "I know you've been keeping up on Palumbo, Tom. Turnbull knows, too. Nobody's faulting you for doing a little work outside of normal business hours, okay? That's why we called you in early, wanted you on this."

"Okay . . ."

"Palumbo isn't like these commercial fishermen families running dope; he thinks he's a celebrity. But they've got means that he doesn't. They've got families, boats; they make deals a mile off shore where no one can watch. Palumbo's been trying to capture a piece of that. Get them working for him. So apparently he had a sit-down with Edgar Vasquez."

"Vasquez? The same Vasquez that had the car accident a couple months ago?"

"The very same." Blythe's eyelids drooped to half-mast. "Come on, Tom. Stop being cute."

He held up his hands. "I won't deny I've been keeping my own tabs on Palumbo. But we're talking about mostly old stuff. Anyway, I've been up to here in Nick's affairs for the past six months — liquidating his house, his realty business, settling everything has taken the bulk of my time, you know, when I'm not babysitting the governor or doing therapy."

She looked away, into the pine trees. "Fair enough. Well, the consensus is that Vasquez wasn't going to go for Palumbo's offer. They met a few times, didn't quite come to agreeable terms, let's say, then Vasquez just happens to have a terrible car wreck; car just happens to go plowing into a tractor-trailer, killing him and his wife."

"I definitely didn't know about that. You serious? What are we talking — cut brakes? Brake fluid? That shit doesn't happen."

"County CID found evidence of some kind of tampering. But it all went into the sand trap of vice narcotics, top secret, you know the drill. All I heard was that it was death by vehicle sabotage. Yeah, it happens."

"Okay . . . and Declan was an auto mechanic. So that's the connection — he wasn't a witness to something; he supposedly had a hand in this vehicle sabotage."

"Right."

Tom thought of what he'd seen of Declan's place so far — nothing that necessarily screamed "auto mechanic", except maybe for the newspaper article on the classic car rally. Maybe the magnet on the fridge. "Has Declan been under surveillance?"

"That I don't know."

"Maybe he was getting set to roll on Palumbo, admit he was involved? Then he has some sort of mental breakdown? Tries to commit suicide by cop?"

"I think he might've been scared of something, yeah." She pulled out of her relaxed position, leaned forward, elbows on her knees. "And maybe it was eating him, this fear that Palumbo's crew was going to come around and snuff him out because he was going to talk. But like I'm telling you, this is all protected by court order. Same as the last time we dealt with the Palumbo investigation." She gave him a long look through the gloom.

"Declan gets arrested, goes to jail, where Palumbo gets to him anyway," Tom said.

"By sending in Heather Moss as a vector for his suicide."

"By *forcing* her."

He waited for her to object, something about how he tended to get this way . . . that he was too soft, or was led by his man-parts instead of his brain. There was no doubt he found Heather Moss alluring, but that wasn't why he thought she was innocent of murder. She'd been protecting her children, plain and simple.

He didn't have kids, and his parents were long gone — well before Nick had punched out — but he imagined that, in healthy families, parents were willing to lay their life down for their kids, to do whatever it took to protect them. Heather Moss had done just that.

"Okay," he said, "So Declan is going to flip for the state, maybe confess to rigging the brakes on the car Vasquez was driving, or whatever, but he goes crazy first. Why not just commit suicide then?"

"Maybe he's a coward. Needs someone else to do it. Tried to get the cops to take him down when he went parading around in front of his house *al fresco,* then made a move on a service weapon."

"He readily took that pill," Tom said, remembering the video. "But at that point, he's safely tucked away in jail. If he's a coward, why not follow through and sing for the state, go into witness relocation? He'd disappear."

She cut him a hard look. "Maybe because Palumbo has people everywhere, even in county lock-up — people who specialize in 'the disappeared'. Maybe Declan was terrified of a fate worse than death. This was a small mercy shown by Palumbo, a literal 'get out of jail free' card."

Tom stared off into the shifting shadows outside Declan's back porch.

Blythe suddenly clapped her hands, the sound loud in the quiet space, and stood up. "Let's get home, get an early start tomorrow. Lots to go through."

She breezed past him, wafting a musky perfume in her wake.

He followed her into the main part of the house and glanced at the laptop. "I think we need to take this stuff into evidence. At least get the computer sequestered."

"Tomorrow," Blythe said, nearing the front door.

Tom stopped in the center of the living room. "You trust leaving Declan's stuff here overnight? That lone deputy out front isn't going to stop someone who really wants to get in here to destroy anything Declan might've been harboring, incriminating information on Palumbo, maybe — proof of something, who knows."

Blythe stopped in front of the door and turned around. She'd seemed subtly adversarial since their meeting with Heather Moss. And Tom knew the senior agent had her rebellious side — if she felt encumbered by procedure, sometimes she just went around it. Heather's lawyer had pissed her off.

Then again, she'd learned how playing fast and loose could backfire on her as it had during their last case.

"Alright," she said, taking out her phone. "You're right. Let's see if we can get this packed up tonight. Where do we want to start?"

Tom grabbed the keys he'd set on the floor. "Maybe with these, see what they fit."

CHAPTER EIGHT

Tom opened his door just before midnight. The place was pitch black. He snapped on a light and headed into the kitchen. Setting his bag on the table, he leaned into the fridge for a cool drink. There were two Heinekens left over from the previous night, spent with Katie Mills. He popped the bottle cap off one of them and flicked it in the sink where it clattered around and came to a rest. Leaning against the countertop, he took a long swig and checked his phone, swished through photos he'd taken throughout the day: Declan's dismal, neglected house, Heather's cheerier, more lived-in space with toys strewn about.

Then he checked his texts, hoping maybe he'd gotten a message from Katie, already suspecting he hadn't.

He moved to the table and sat down, took another gulp of the beer. The cool, effervescent liquid felt good on his throat. His body ached and he should have been tired but he felt like sleep was still a ways off. He thought for a moment and then punched in a number on his phone.

"Tom?" Jack Vance sounded happy to hear from him.

"Hey, Jack. I'm only calling so late because I'm lonely and I have no friends."

Vance laughed. "Well, you know I'm up. I'm afraid to sleep. Too old — don't know if I'll wake up."

"How's the cooking coming along?"

"Eh, I'm over it."

"*What*? You were one gazpacho away from master chef. What happened?"

"I'm into stamps now."

Tom was silent.

"I'm kidding," Vance said. "Listen, no, you know what it is, I been putting a lot of effort into the business. My snowbird watch thing. But, honestly, the stuff you gotta know on computers today just to compete — I do Facebook, okay? But a website? Now I gotta pay someone to build me a website. Who did Nick use?"

"Nick did it himself, actually."

"Oh, see, there you go. You know, I think I'll just get some low-grade security job. Sit in the booth, some nice little gated community like yours."

Tom took a swig of the beer. "Hey, I'll ask."

"How's the new place?"

"The new place is good. I didn't have much to move in."

"Traveling light. That's the best way."

Tom already felt better. Vance was retired Air Force, and had been his neighbor in Naples. He'd helped Tom out of a couple jams. It was true; Vance was his only real friend now that Nick was gone.

"How's Katie?"

Tom flinched, but it was what he'd expected, and, if he was honest with himself, partly why he was calling. He and Katie had gone out to dinner with Vance a couple times, favoring a burger joint near Collier Boulevard. Katie and the older man had gotten along so well Tom sometimes felt like a third wheel. In a good way.

"Katie's great," Tom said. "She, ah, she's busy with work, and ah, things are good . . ."

"Uh-huh. So you haven't popped the question, is what you're saying."

Tom let loose an unexpected laugh. "No, no, I haven't. Not quite. We, ah, you know, we've been taking it slow."

"Tommy. You're talking to a man who spent thirty-eight years married to a woman, God rest Margaret's soul. And you know I never much had the patience to beat around the bush . . ."

Tom took another swallow of liquid courage. "Okay. So, Katie left this morning and I don't think she's coming back."

He waited for Vance's quick-witted response, but the ex-military man was quiet. Finally, Vance said, "Yeah, well, there is that. You took quite a knock, Tommy. And you haven't had it so easy. The kind of stuff that's happened to you, that can make it hard to let someone—"

"None of us have had it easy. Katie's had loss, too. And I'm on a case right now . . ." He drifted, remembering the damage he saw in Heather Moss's eyes. Thinking of her family photo on the fridge in her house. The unimaginable tragedy it had to be to lose your life partner, the father of your little girls. ". . . It's already shaping up to be pretty big."

Vance said, "You're back in action, huh?"

"Yeah, back with IFS. Fully-reinstated as of today. No more working Governor Protection."

"How was that?"

"It was alright. Lots of standing around playing secret service." Tom rose and put the empty beer bottle in the sink. He headed out of the kitchen toward the living room. "They wanted to keep me on with the department, but keep me at arm's length — you know? See if I had a permanent bug in my system."

"Well I'm glad things seem to be working out." Vance said.

"Yeah — listen, thanks for talking and — I just wanted to ask you — I know you're a private guy, and I respect that, and you're retired . . ."

"Spit it out, Tommy."

"What do you know about the Palumbo family? You know Palumbo owns the dog track, that he makes his money off poker, but that County VNB has a long history with him for other reasons. They went through a lot of targets before they got to Palumbo distributing dope."

Vance sighed. "I bet they did. Listen, here's what I'll say, and not just about Palumbo, but what I see as the big picture: Mexico is the source of everything now. Okay, they're growing pot and poppy and they've got meth labs. Southwest Florida is getting real popular for drug-running because we don't have a lot of assets down here; Everglades County has a tiny little marine patrol, the Coast Guard is way up in Tampa. So it's wide open for a guy like Palumbo to make moves. That's what I know."

"You think he's—"

"I think Palumbo is probably right in the middle of all this, and Palumbo is bold, but he's also smart. But this is coming out of what I know from your case, when you were down here. And, yeah, I talk to some of the guys; I read between the lines in the newspapers. Mostly, I'm old and I don't know shit."

"There's a guy," Tom said, "might've been getting set to flip on Palumbo for something. Turns up dead while he's on suicide watch at the jail. And somebody helped him do it."

Vance was silent a moment. "And you're thinking Palumbo."

"You think that's something he would do? Go after a guy like that? Sitting in jail?"

"I wouldn't put it past him. But there would have to be something really, really substantial this person knew for this level of action."

"Maybe doing a little work on someone's car, making it not work so good — that's enough to get him in a relationship with VNB, or even the feds?"

"Hmm. Maybe vice narcotics, not sure about the feds."

"You ever heard of anything like that actually going down?"

"Vehicle sabotage? Yeah. Time to time. But if you want my honest opinion . . ."

"I do."

"I'm not sure I see it. I'm not saying it didn't happen, just, there'd be something else going on for someone like Palumbo to go full-on like you describe. Because I didn't see this thing about the jail on the news, but the shooting; that's on all the networks — I've seen your face every half hour. Media been hounding you?"

"I took a couple calls, referred them to the Coms Office, who've been instructed not to say shit. The press conference is going to be a lot of nothing, too. But you're saying—"

"I'm not saying anything," said Vance. "It sounds like *you* are. You're thinking about putting Palumbo into this thing at the jail, and you were at this drive-by, so I'm guessing it all goes together."

They were quiet a moment, Tom rotating the empty beer bottle around on the table.

"Alright, Tommy. Listen, keep your head down. And if you see Katie again, you tell her old Jack said hi, okay?"

"You got it. Thanks, Jack."

* * *

With the second beer, he sat down on the couch facing the wall, then stared up at what was plastered all over it.

Blythe was right — he'd been moonlighting all along.

It had taken a couple of weeks, but he'd covered nearly the whole wall in photos, news clippings and his own handwritten notes, forming an intricate web, connected by strands of yarn.

His eyes roved over the many headshots of Palumbo's family and crew. He was so familiar with the family tree he'd created on Palumbo he could map it out with his eyes closed.

Katie hadn't quite approved. "This violates a few regulations," she'd said. But after he explained how there was no direct line of sight on the room so no one outside could see the wall unless they were thirty feet high in the trees behind his townhouse using binoculars, he realized she'd been more concerned about his state of mind than his extra-jurisdictional police work.

She didn't care about the regulations. She cared that it was about Nick, thinking that Tom had become obsessed.

Had he?

Mario Palumbo sat in the center of the web, near the top. The picture was a black-and-white press photo taken using a telephoto lens and showed Palumbo getting into a GMC Yukon. The shot had been used in an exposé on the track in Bonita Springs, and the crumbling enterprise that was dog racing.

On either side of Palumbo, linked by a length of green yarn, were Palumbo's number one and number two guys; Ben Franco and Rodney Lamotta. Franco was bald and beady-eyed, Lamotta looked like some pro wrestler after his career ended and the make-up came off. Each of their photos branched into a filigree of strands pointing to more photos, some actually printed pictures, some newspaper clippings that were yellowing with age. Beside almost every image was a sheet of paper bearing the name, date of birth, suspected aliases.

In the lower right corner was Nick. Nick's sheet of paper also came with a date of death.

Finally, running along top of the collage was a timeline, linking notable events — including Nick's death — in a chain. Several strands of yarn threaded from the timeline down to certain photos. Almost every strand eventually led back to Mario Palumbo, the sort of Godfather of it all.

Howard Declan wasn't up there.

Tom stared at Palumbo's picture, thinking, *I hope it is you behind this, you son of a bitch.*

CHAPTER NINE

THURSDAY

The statewide attorney's office felt like an ice box. Tom and Blythe sat down at a large desk and the secretary who led them in closed the door behind her as she left. Tom glanced at his watch: two minutes before nine a.m. Bob Mandi walked in, a prosecutor with a face so round and scrubbed it looked almost childlike.

Mandi took his seat at the desk and set out a file, glanced up at the agents. "Good Morning." After scanning a few documents, he leaned back in his chair and crossed his arms. "So where are we?"

"Well, let's just come right to it," Blythe said, crossing her legs. She was wearing a skirt today and Tom noticed a small bruise near her knee. "Heather Moss has virtually no record. She's a mental health counselor with Everglades County. Recently widowed, has two daughters. Moss claims she received a call on her cellular yesterday morning instructing her to bring a small package already in her possession to Declan. The caller threatened the lives of her daughters and was very compelling that they could carry out those threats."

"How so?"

"They described the girls in detail. Where they were, what they were wearing."

"So we're talking about multiple persons, working in concert."

"That's what we believe at this point," Blythe said.

"And this package. Some kind of lethal pill? And this led directly to . . ." Mandi flipped a page in the file and squinted at what was written. "Cerebral hypoxia?"

"Following a violent seizure, yes." Blythe shifted and re-crossed her legs the other way. "That's the preliminary finding. The full autopsy is expected to conclude later today."

Mandi was still looking down. "Does she lock her car?"

"I'm sorry?"

He glanced up, and his eyes flitted between Blythe and Tom. "Is Heather Moss in the habit of locking her car? Did you ask her?"

"We haven't yet."

He folded his hands on the desk. "Because the poison was already in her car, you said."

"In her bag," Tom answered, edging forward in his chair.

"And where was her bag?"

"Probably in the house."

"'Probably.' How about her house? Does she lock it up at night?"

"The package," Tom said, "a manila envelope, the kind you might put keys in, was very small. Could have been dropped into her bag at any point."

Mandi studied Tom a moment, then his eyes flitted to Blythe. "And you're looking into that — what is it called?"

"Could be something called Syntox," Blythe said, "a controversial suicide pill. Or it could be homemade.

People used to keep potassium cyanide hidden inside false teeth."

"Why would anyone want to do that?"

"It was called the 'L-pill' in World War II, developed by British and American secret services."

"Is that a fact?"

"It is."

"So someone, at some time, could have dropped the pill in her bag, homemade or otherwise. Maybe she doesn't clean her bag out that often, or pay too much attention to what's in it?"

Blythe shrugged.

"And of course the manila envelope is being tested for prints."

Blythe nodded. "Her car has been impounded, the clothes she was wearing are at the lab — we're doing everything we can."

"Everything you can to show that she is the victim here, it seems." His cherubic face seemed to darken. "What have you got on the *other* victim, Howard Declan?"

"We're still mining for details," Blythe said quickly. "But right now we think it's likely he worked for Mario Palumbo in some capacity, and that he may have been involved in the death of Edgar Vasquez."

Mandi sifted through some papers and pulled up a sheet, squinted at it, took out his half-framed reading glasses and put them on. "So, Everglades CID on this — they did the crime scene investigation on the Vasquez accident, and there's no conclusion of brake tampering or something like that. In fact, there's really nothing conclusive here at all." He slapped the paper down on the desk.

"Well, you know why that is, sir. Palumbo has been a County vice narcotics case for two years. Because Vasquez was part of another trafficking group, and he was purportedly meeting with Palumbo, all this falls under

VNB purview. And certain information gets protected by court order."

"Yes, I know that."

"Vice narcotics have been focused on the trafficking, trying to get to Palumbo by working their way up. But it was CID that handled the Vasquez crime scene, as you say, and it basically went nowhere. That could mean they didn't find tampering, but it could also mean they did, and vice narcotics has been working off that information."

Mandi reddened, as if his blood pressure was rising. "Have you considered Heather Moss might be making this up? That she wanted Declan dead for her own reasons?"

Tom spoke, beating Blythe to it. "Of course we've considered it. But there's nothing so far that shows any motivation. Nothing in her history that shows any intersection between Moss and Declan. She'd never met him before yesterday morning."

"Maybe not *Declan*, per se," Mandi said, "but someone like him. An inmate. A person with psychological problems . . . Maybe Moss is sick of dealing with people and their problems and wanted to just do something. Has she been psychologically evaluated? From what I'm seeing here, the only thing she has to corroborate her story is a cell phone call that lasted seven minutes. And we have no idea what was said."

"With all due respect, sir, I think that's stretching," Tom said.

"Oh, you do, huh?" Mandi glared at him. "Look, I'm poking at this, seeing what gives. We've got a dead man, we've got a woman who's gone in to see him, gives him a pill, he dies. You know and I know the autopsy will confirm that. What we can't confirm is what was said to Moss on the phone. What happened with the caller's number?"

"Nothing," Blythe said. "Out of service. Probably a burner phone, thrown away or destroyed after use."

Mandi picked up a crumb on the desk, tossed it in the wastebasket. "What's your recommendation, Special Agents Blythe and Lange?"

"Hold the murder charge," Tom said. "She might be an unwitting participant here, but she's not a cold-blooded killer. Let us work."

Mandi bit his thumbnail and looked off at a wall of books in the office. "We can't know what was said. We can't know that anyone was watching her daughters. So far you haven't produced any witnesses at the school or day care who saw someone or something suspicious."

"No," Blythe responded.

"And you've floated this idea that Mario Palumbo used her to go after Declan because of something Declan did in relation to Edgar Vasquez, but we don't have any proof of that, if there *is* proof, and even if there is it will take some time and some legal maneuvering to get at."

"County CID investigated before they ran into the vice narcotics firewall," Blythe said. "Declan was questioned in relation to Vasquez. He had his own auto shop for years. In his statement, he admits to frequenting the dog track as a customer."

"But he denies anything incriminating. Never worked for Palumbo, he said."

"Maybe because he was terrified."

Mandi seemed to think about it all, his eyes roving over the files in front of him. "Okay, well, if she's loosed, what's to stop *her* from being terrified? And running?"

"She turned herself in," Tom said.

"Maybe she thought she'd be safe in jail. And maybe she is."

"Not necessarily," Blythe said. "There's eight hundred inmates in Everglades County Jail. Palumbo's got an estimated three hundred in his employ — and those are just the legit people on his payroll. Someone could get to her."

"So, what happens when she gets out?" Mandi shifted in his chair, making it squeak. "She gets shot at again?"

Blythe waved a hand in the air. "Either way, the *fact* that she was shot at supports the theory this is related to organized crime. It makes no sense that she goes after Declan for some other reason, then just happens to be targeted for murder on the same day."

It took Mandi another moment. "Alright. Look, truth be told, I'm inclined to agree with you. But please, tell me, what else is going on with Palumbo as a lead? What have we got? I can't put Heather Moss out on the street when she's on video passing Declan the pill that kills him. Not without someone else to put in the hot seat; it's insane. And where can we go from here? Your Carrie Anne Gallo case last year intersected with County VNB's open investigation on Palumbo's drug network, but once that investigation was closed, it was the end of collaboration."

"We need to begin anew," Blythe said. "Let's bring in Sergeant Coburn, County vice narcotics. See what we can find out on Declan, and what Coby's surveillance shows on any of Palumbo's men yesterday morning."

Mandi ran fingers over his mouth and sighed. "This leaves me in a tough spot."

"What about the feds, sir?" Tom asked.

Mandi's eyes seemed to flash. "No." The word boomed in his spacious office.

"No?"

He shook his head. "No. We're not . . . This . . ." He glanced away again, then said in a quieter voice, "The FBI's hands are tied here. I've already spoken with them. Anything to do with this runs counter to their interests right now."

"Counter to their interests?" Tom checked on Blythe but she wasn't returning eye contact.

"Yes," Mandi said. "Counter. You don't have a shred of evidence this links to Palumbo, and there are sensitive operations ongoing all over the place."

Tom held the man's eye, but didn't argue.

Mandi softened. "Look, I admit it looks like she was used, then they tried to get rid of her. But, we need that shooter. Or we need that caller. In the meantime, we can treat this as her being a witness to gang violence. Okay? That's how it plays. But *someone* is going to have to answer for the death of Howard Declan, and the feds aren't going to touch it with a ten-foot pole. You're on your own there. We've already held her for one day. The arraignment is this afternoon, press conference to follow. You need to find me something. Now."

CHAPTER TEN

Sergeant Danny Coburn pushed half the cheeseburger into his mouth and bit down. The smell of fried grease wafted out the pass-through window of the eatery's kitchen. A kid, all of sixteen, leaned into the window with a waiter's pad as the next hungry customers in the queue stepped forward. Coburn nodded towards some shaded picnic tables in the distance. "Let's sit over there."

He led Tom and Blythe out of the cabana. Tom glanced at the beach as they walked, the sparkling Gulf beyond, a few seagulls circling the air. It wasn't yet tourist season, but a few bold swimmers were out in the water — probably northerners. Colorful umbrellas dotted the sand. A couple of kids played Frisbee by the grassy edge. A lone woman in a red sunhat read a book.

Coburn sat down at the picnic table, already finished with the second half of the burger and licking his fingers. He wore a flower-print bathing suit and a white, unbuttoned short-sleeved shirt, revealing his considerably hairy stomach.

"Thanks for meeting with us." Blythe swung a leg over the bench and sat with it between her legs. "Sorry to bother you on your day off."

Tom edged onto the corner of the bench next to Blythe.

Coburn shrugged and gazed off toward the ocean. "No rest for the wicked."

Blythe asked, "You here with Sherry and the kids?"

Coburn nodded and pointed. It was hard to see them clearly through the brushy barrier between the park area and the beach, but Tom glimpsed a woman with a couple of kids leaping around her.

"I didn't know you were married," Tom said. "How many kids?"

"Five." The sergeant glanced at Tom then folded his hands and stared off the other way, into the parking lot. "Was working fifteen, sixteen hours a day for about six months there for a while. This is the first day off I've had in a long time."

Blythe said, "You know why we're here, Coby..."

He shifted his weight a little, and the picnic table squeaked. "It's not going to be easy. I already spoke to my guys, but this information won't get you very far."

"Why not?"

"Well, Palumbo's about the most fun we've had yet. These guys are good at counter-surveillance and getting better all the time. We've got all these guys up on a wire, but we're not getting the information we need from traditional surveillance. So, we go to the StingRay. But as I'm sure you know there's all kinds of pushback using cell tower simulators. Washington State passed legislation that requires a warrant, so did California and Colorado. It's supposed to happen here, too. There's a bill floating around in the state legislature."

"There's grounds for a warrant in this case," Tom said.

Coburn gave him a tight look. "We've been tracking this crew for two years."

"You mean it could be retroactive."

"New laws that say we need a warrant could make our previous surveillance inadmissible in court. It's fucked up."

Blythe swept a hand in the air, as if brushing away Coburn's words. She leaned in and stabbed the table with her finger. "We need to know where Palumbo's people were yesterday morning, between seven and ten a.m., anyone near the jail, or on Tangerine Drive in Bonita Springs, or both. And we need to know if anyone made a call from that 945 number."

"So you've said, and so we face the same problem we faced last year." He held up his hands. "Guys, this information is protected. I can't just pass surveillance on to any other law enforcement outside my unit."

"Coby, Bob Mandi is behind us on this. Anything you give us is just for him, and us."

Coburn looked around as if to catch someone watching, then pulled a tin of chewing tobacco from his pocket, stuck a wad of it under his lip. "Alright. So far, my guys don't see that anyone was near the county jail. Or the clinic. Or on Tangerine Drive. Closest cellular subscriber the StingRay picked up — closest subscriber who is part of *our* gang of suspects, okay — was on the other side of Fort Myers, thirty miles away. But not using 945."

Blythe sat back, presumably to let this information settle in. Then she shook her head. "Might not even matter. They could have called Moss from anywhere."

Coburn scratched his stomach, then spit to one side. "The StingRay collects calls made. You gave me Moss's number, too, so my guys ran it against all calls that were placed from someone in Palumbo's network we've been tracking currently."

"How many people is that?" Tom asked.

"Right now, twenty-two. We've had as many as thirty-five. But they dump their phones, they switch up, they're taking videos, checking out everything. I told you, the technology goes both ways. Every new toy we've got, they find a way to subvert it."

The table shook as Coburn stood up. "Sorry, I don't have anything else to tell you. I've got to get back."

Tom rose, too. "Anyone under your surveillance ever use the 945 number?"

Coburn shrugged. "It's not a real area code. It's a prepaid number. To answer your question, yes, I've seen it here and there."

Blythe looked like she was grappling with a decision. "Coby, we need another favor."

He gazed off toward the beach. "Lauren, come on . . ."

"Unless we know for sure Palumbo can be ruled out, we can't say he's definitely not behind this. All you need to do is back us up with Bob Mandi. Tell him you've seen the 945 number before."

He kept his back to them, looking toward the beach.

Tom stood up and stepped beside him. "Heather Moss has two little girls," Tom said. "She's a single mother — her husband is dead. Right now those girls are with DFS while she sits in County. If we can't show Mandi *something*, just the possibility of Palumbo's network behind this, Moss is going to get hit with a murder charge in a couple hours."

The big man's chest rose and fell with a sigh. Tom knew Coby wanted Palumbo just as badly as anybody else, and was frustrated by his own system. "Fine. I'll call Mandi. You'll have my support."

"Thank you, Coby."

"What about Howard Declan?" Tom asked. "What can you tell us about him?"

Coburn turned back toward them, spit to the side again. "Nothing."

"Nothing?"

"We never had Declan under direct surveillance."

"Okay, but CID came to question him about the Vasquez car accident . . ."

"They did some old-fashioned investigating, Lange. They had witnesses who said Vasquez was at the dog track the night he died. They questioned dozens of people who'd been there. Declan was one of them. That's it."

Blythe stepped in front of him and shook his hand. "Give my best to Sherry and the kids."

Coburn shook her hand and nodded at Tom. Then he strode off toward the beach.

Blythe slowly sat back down.

Tom waited a few seconds before sharing his thoughts. "He's not happy about it. I'm not sure I am either. And he said Declan wasn't under 'direct surveillance'. What's that mean?"

Blythe considered his words before she spoke. "Listen, Tom, as long as we're all sharing secrets here, getting everything out in the open, I gotta bone to pick. I don't want to go down this road with you again. You weren't forthcoming with me yesterday — you'd already heard about Declan's death. You didn't say how."

Tom looked down at the table. Someone had etched their initials into the picnic table and enclosed them in a crude heart. "I was with Katie Mills yesterday morning. She got the call first, that's how I knew what was happening at the county jail. Okay?"

Blythe said nothing for a moment, then, "Okay. Anything else?"

"No."

She turned her head, her eyes shining in the sunlight. "Alright. Let's go back to Mandi with this 945 number thing and see if it sticks."

* * *

The statewide prosecutor had his suit on, about to head into court, his briefcase open, packed with papers.

He was just getting off the phone when they stepped into his office.

"That was Sergeant Coburn," he said. "You two threaten his life?"

"A little," Blythe said.

Mandi shook his head and looked down. "It's thin. It's paper thin. Let this woman go because Mario Palumbo's organization *could* have been using a prepaid with this prefix number? Ultra-thin."

"Plus there was an attempt to *kill* her," Blythe reminded. "You seem to keep forgetting that."

"No, no I'm not forgetting it. I'm thinking about exactly that. You two are coming at me like her legal team. She's a single mother, separated from her daughters — they're probably all safer where they are. What happens if we let her go and someone comes after her again?"

"We're going to protect her," Tom said.

Mandi fixed him with a grave look, then snapped the briefcase closed on his desk. "And you're prepared for that?"

"Yes."

"And Turnbull cleared it?"

Tom pulled a file from his bag. "Application for funding victim and witness protection is right here." He placed the thick form on Mandi's desk and slid it toward him. "Your signature is required on page two, sir."

Mandi continued to clock Tom a moment before lowering his eyes. He snatched the paperwork off the desk and fanned through the pages. "And you've attached the itemization of expenses?"

"Yes, sir."

"And you're aware that the Protection Review Committee may approve or deny, in whole or in part, all reimbursements requested?"

"Yes."

"You realize you're supposed to submit this thirty days prior to the next Violent Crimes and Drug Control meeting — which is next week."

"Yes."

Mandi continued flipping pages. At last, he set the application down and raised a hand. Tom stuck a pen in Mandi's grip. The pen hovered in the air, Mandi's eyes scudded over the text in front of him, then he looked up.

"Forty-eight hours."

"Forty-eight hours?"

"That's the condition. That's how long you have to get me real evidence that Mario Palumbo is behind this. If you can't, I'll rescind my endorsement and VCDC will halt the process before you're even approved."

"And Heather Moss goes without protection? How does that make sense?"

"Then I'll recommend an astronomical bail she can't pay or bond and she can stay right where she is, Lange. Take it or leave it." Without waiting for a response, Mandi scribbled his signature. Tom thought the prosecutor had a flair for the dramatic. He also thought forty-eight hours was a hell of a time crunch and they were gambling with someone's life.

"Your ROC will have to go out of pocket on this for now," Mandi said. "Maybe you, personally, too."

"That's fine."

Mandi handed back the paperwork and Tom slipped it into a large envelope. The envelope was already addressed to the VCDC Coordinator in Tallahassee and stamped with the proper postage. Tom passed the whole thing back to Mandi. "Can you have your secretary place this with the outgoing mail?"

Mandi snatched the envelope out of Tom's grip. "Jesus, when did you find time to put this together?"

"Last night."

"You sleep at all, Agent Lange?"

"I got a good four hours, sir."

CHAPTER ELEVEN

The judge came out of chambers and walked to the bench, her black robe flowing. With Blythe gone to prepare for the press conference, Tom sat alone at the back of the courtroom. After the judge sat down, three inmates were paraded into a holding area and lined up behind the bulletproof glass. Heather Moss peered out into the courtroom, found Tom and offered a broken smile.

Bob Mandi stood and addressed the judge, his voice booming through the room as he read his statement: "Your honor, the People have issued the criminal complaint against the defendant, Heather Moss, for fleeing the scene of a crime."

The judge looked at Heather Moss, who'd been brought to the door of the holding cell, opened by the bailiff. "And how does the defendant plead?"

"Not guilty, your honor." Moss's voice cracked on the words and she cleared her throat.

Robert Ernst addressed the bench. "Your honor, my client was worried for her children. Their lives had been threatened. She had every intention of turning herself in to the proper authorities once she'd verified that they were safe. She's not a flight risk. I request that Mrs. Moss be released on her own recognizance."

The judge faced the statewide prosecutor.

Mandi waved a hand in the air. "Your honor, the People concede the defendant's release."

"Very well." The judge shuffled some papers at the bench before she gazed across the courtroom at Moss again. "Mrs. Moss, I understand the extenuating circumstances of your actions. And as a mother, I recognize and appreciate the emotion involved. But it is the opinion of this court that you should have notified the police immediately. The defendant shall return to county jail for release procedure, and a preliminary hearing is set for one week from today. Dismissed."

The judge then announced the next case as the bailiff ushered Heather deeper into the holding cell. The inner door opened and she stepped out of sight.

* * *

Tom met with Ernst in the large hallway outside the courtroom. The lawyer smiled at him, looking relieved. Tom shook his hand, said, "Surprised you went for the not-guilty plea on a misdemeanor."

"It's still something that would be on her record. She was a mother worried for her children and she had no idea what had happened."

Tom wasn't going to argue. Perhaps what Heather Moss needed was a tenacious lawyer in her corner.

"As soon as she processes out," Ernst said, "Mrs. Moss wants to head directly to the Department of Family Services and collect her children."

Tom nodded. "Of course. But I'm going to stay with her, and I have a detail waiting to accompany us. How is Heather? Is she alright?"

"Well, she's a wreck. She's terrified, and she's never been away from her girls, not for a single night since her husband died."

"You know her personally?"

Ernst nodded. "I'm sort of a family friend. I went to college with Glenn, her husband. But I passed the bar in Florida six years ago, set up shop here."

"Think I've seen you around," Tom said.

"Yeah. I think I've seen you, too. Well — you had the Carrie Gallo case. I read about it. Body turns up in Rookery Bay, no ID, nothing."

"Yeah . . ."

"That looked like a tough one. But you brought it home; I heard the guy got life without parole. Pretty impressive."

Tom glanced away, wanting a change of subject. He asked, "Have you ever represented Mrs. Moss before?"

"No, but, I helped her tend to the affairs after Glenn died."

"He was a store manager for Home Depot?"

Ernst nodded again.

"So what were you guys . . . college friends as undergrads?"

"Glenn was pre-law. He was a good student, too. But he dropped out."

"Oh yeah? Why?"

The lawyer shrugged. "He had a change of heart, I guess. Met Heather, decided he wanted a different kind of life. He said studying law had been more for his parents than anyone else. But, we kept in touch. Had some good times back then."

Tom put on a smile. "I'll bet." Then he let the smile slide off as he looked around at the few other people waiting outside the courtroom, some sitting in the few chairs provided, others leaning against the wall or standing in the hallway, huddled in conversation. He needed to get going, but was curious about Glenn. "Can I ask you — how did he die?"

"Cancer. He had Hodgkin's Disease."

"Ah, that's terrible. Sorry to hear that."

Ernst shook his head. "Healthy guy, too. Athletic, non-smoker. He even did a few of those triathlons. Just one of these really unfortunate cases. Cancer gets anyone, I guess."

"Scary."

"Very scary."

"Yeah. Okay, well . . ." Tom stuck out his hand.

"So, on your Gallo case — you came up against some unsavory people."

"I don't really—"

"What I've heard was that Declan was a potential state witness. What if those same people were involved here? For my client's sake, I really hope that's where this investigation is headed."

"You know I can't discuss that."

Ernst nodded, this time put his hand out.

Tom branded his face with a fresh smile on top of the quick handshake. "Been nice talking to you."

He hurried down the wide staircase to the street below, his footfalls echoing in the cavernous space. He needed to get to the ROC for a meeting with the Internal Affairs Bureau since he'd been involved in the shooting. He'd tried to call Katie for a ride, but she wasn't answering. Had to take a damned cab.

* * *

The meeting with IAB on the officer-involved shooting was thorough but went quickly enough. Tom thanked his state bureau representative for being there and headed for the crime lab, anxious to find out any results on the multiple forensic fronts.

Veronica Morley held up the small manila envelope inside a plastic baggie. "Dusted, lifted, nothing there but the elimination prints provided for Heather Moss."

In another section of the ROC that was a giant, warehouse-sized room, techs in lab coats shot bullets into blocks of gel while wearing yellow eye goggles and ear buds. Tom had to cover his own ears as he searched for John Armstrong, a ballistic specialist.

Armstrong closed the door to his office, muffling some of the thunderous gunfire. He reviewed documents on a clipboard he held and shouted, a hazard of his job. "Okay. So, Moss case. We're still looking at trajectories, but from cartridge casings found at the scene, we've determined .223 caliber rounds discharged from an AR-15. Twenty-eight rounds discharged in total. We're entering all evidence into NIBIN."

"Thank you. And can we look at where those rounds ended up?"

Armstrong went through a stack of pictures showing Heather's house, the vehicles parked in front. Tom looked at bullet holes in his Crown Vic, in the deputy's cruiser. Heather's Honda was unmarred. Several rounds had impacted the front of the house, on the low side.

Armstrong pointed at a picture of the lawn. "We found five rounds in the ground. The house sits on a little rise, so . . ."

"And inside?"

"Just two rounds reached the interior of the house."

Tom recognized the hallway where Sergeant Sanchez had been slumped in shock and bewilderment. There was a dark hole in the back wall. Another picture showed where a round had penetrated the short wall between the kitchen and hallway. And one large diagram showed the entire ordeal: a spray of bullets from the vehicle in the road toward the house, their trajectories indicated with red lines, the sites of their impacts red circles.

"Thank you," Tom said, getting an eyeful. "Let me know what else you come up with."

"Will do," Armstrong yelled.

Tom wandered into the bull pen and found his desk, ears ringing from all the shooting. He twisted in his swivel chair and tapped his pen on the Formica.

Twenty-eight rounds.

He thought of bending his body over Olivia Moss. The bits of mortar dust that specked her hair like snowflakes when the hail of gunfire was over.

Twenty-eight rounds, and only two made it into the house, plus the Honda was untouched; his own vehicle had taken the brunt of the damage.

Weird.

With almost thirty shots fired, none hit the presumed target. That was a good thing, but the lack of accuracy didn't support the idea of a trained killer.

* * *

A state trooper working the desk took the papers from Tom, flipped through them, then handed the packet back. "You've got to fill out the page so Tallahassee sends down the new vehicle." He tapped the page with a finger.

Tom shook his head. "I need something today."

The trooper blinked. "Something happen to your ride?"

"You could say that."

"You want the same thing?"

"I need an upgrade," Tom said. "Something family-sized."

The trooper just stared a moment, then took the form back. "Okay. I'll show you what we've got out back."

He led Tom past a full slate of vehicles, the evening sun spangling off the steel and polished chrome. Crown Victorias, Impalas, and a couple of fast-looking Mustangs. At the end of the row, Tom saw what he wanted.

They headed over and the trooper opened up the Dodge Durango SUV for Tom to have a look.

He glanced at the big monitor between the front seats, considering how conspicuous it would be to anyone who might be hunting for Heather Moss. The MDT was easy to spot. There was also a push bar mounted to the front of the chassis. And if they knew where to look, they'd see the emergency lights installed on the mirrors, and where the windshield met the roof. The license plate gave it away, too — 445DSI — the letters referring to "Domestic Security and Investigations." The vehicle was not exactly anonymous, but it would have to do.

"Do we have any child seats?"

Again the trooper looked baffled. "Uhm, I'll check."

Tom pulled his head out of the interior. "Need one for a six year-old and one for a two year-old."

* * *

Blythe came down the hall at speed, shaking her head. "What a nightmare."

Tom didn't press for details, knew she was talking about the upcoming press conference, events which Blythe generally hated and considered a burden.

They turned into the office of their researcher. Cheyenne Holman's smallish office was crammed with papers, two desktop computers, plus a laptop. She had long brown hair down to the middle of her back and a wide, pleasant smile.

"So I've done the full workup on Howard Michael Declan," she said. "Definitely interesting in the finances department; I went three years back. The first year, he shows quite a bit of taxable gambling income. Mostly, though, it's pretty break-even — he itemizes each year, reporting his losses to offset taxes owed on winnings. But then he starts a downward slope, and never really recovers." She looked up at the agents. "He died pretty deep in debt."

"No inheritors, correct?" Tom asked.

"Correct. And nothing besides the house in North Naples to inherit. He worked at an auto body shop and salvage yard in Cape Coral for close to thirty years. The place was recently sold." She clicked the keys on one of the computers. "Was bought by Gary Reuben Enterprises, Lake County. They're in the junk dealing business; I looked them up on BizQuest."

"So the house will probably go toward his debts?"

"Yes. Probate court has assumed temporary possession of Declan's estate. They'll pay off the outstanding debts."

Tom leaned back and glanced at Blythe, thinking that the "outstanding debts" were very likely losses on dog racing. Mario Palumbo was going to be getting back the money Howard Declan had lost at the track. If Declan wasn't involved in the Vasquez incident, maybe he was killed for his debt?

"How much did he owe?" Tom asked.

"Almost three hundred thousand."

"Yeah, there goes the house," Blythe commented. "And he 'breaks even' all over again."

Tom asked Blythe, "Did you reach Barbara, his ex?"

"She was very sorry to hear about it, but she hasn't been in touch with Declan for years. She wasn't surprised by the intestacy, said Declan never really was a planner, she'd tried to get him to consider drawing up a will, once, and he just sloughed it off."

"No last will and testament," Tom said. "Guy lived fast and dangerous."

"He didn't have anyone to leave anything to, and maybe he knew he was going to wind up with his pockets turned out. Sounds like he had a real problem."

"Criminal record?" Tom asked Cheyenne.

"He was pretty unremarkable in that regard. He had speeding tickets aplenty, even a suspended license for too many points, but aside from liking to drive fast, guy's clean."

The picture on Declan was coming clearer: Not so much an obvious criminal as a guy without much to call his own. No wife, no kids, no assets. Maybe living in fear of Palumbo, certainly living in the red. A guy willing to take a pill that promised to end it all.

CHAPTER TWELVE

While Blythe and Bob Mandi were finally talking to reporters, telling them what they could — which wasn't much — Heather Moss was outside the county jail, standing in the center of a swarm of deputies and state troopers. None of the officers had information on the particulars of Heather's case, or knew that the substantial security was meant to keep her safe from possible retribution from Mario Palumbo and his crew. They only knew she was to be protected. That was all they needed.

Tom pulled up, got out and opened the passenger door for her.

"I feel like some sort of ambassador," she said. "This is really all for me?"

A trooper cruiser idled in front of the Durango, about to lead them to the Department of Family Services on the other side of the complex. Another cruiser rolled into position at the rear. Tom had been foolish to think any of this could be low-profile. Witness protection was not like witness relocation. He returned to the driver's seat as Heather drew the seatbelt across her midriff and clicked in.

The lead car got going, took the service road, which circled round the complex, Tom following close behind. They traveled alongside the high fence with its unending coil of cyclone wire, then made a turn.

Heather let out a trembling breath as the jail receded in the mirrors.

"Probably never thought you'd be on this end of the system," Tom said.

"No." She placed her hands in her lap and kneaded her knuckles. Then she cracked the joints, the popping noises a surprise.

"You alright?"

"I miss my children. I hope they're okay."

"I called last night around midnight. Both girls were sleeping soundly."

She faced him. "Thank you. So, what happens now?"

"What happens now is you're going into witness protection. So far we've done damage control best as we could; we're telling the press that this is highly sensitive, to completely back off — no one even knows you're being released today, okay? So we have to be careful who you talk to."

She covered her mouth, then seemed to compose herself. "What about my job? My house?"

"You'll be in seclusion at first, someone with you and the girls around the clock. We'll work things out with the clinic. Your house should be fine — there'll be someone keeping an eye on it."

"My God. How did these people find me? Who put that thing in my car?"

"We're going to find out."

"Are they the same people who shot at me? Are we going to be safe?"

He glanced at her, tried to be comforting. "That's the plan, to keep you safe."

Heather put her head in her hands and rubbed her face, smoothed back her hair. "Ugh. I need a shower . . . What about school? Poor Olivia."

"Unfortunately, we'll have to keep Olivia out of school and Abigail out of day care for now . . ."

"Where are we going to stay — if we're not going home?"

Tom didn't answer. After a couple seconds, Heather gave him a penetrating look and repeated the question. "Where are we staying?"

"I've booked a hotel."

"A hotel?" She averted her eyes. "Is that normal? I would've expected some government-subsidized housing. Like a safe house, or something?"

Tom got a better grip on the steering wheel. They were arriving at the Department of Family Services. The jail was still visible through the rear window.

"I'll level with you," he said. "Witness protection can be tricky. This is a state-run program we're working with right now, and it takes time. You have to understand, most witness protection and security programs are about protecting criminals who are informing on their bosses or organizations. So, they're already in jail, and this all gets set up while they're just sitting there. But, you're out."

"Because I'm not guilty of anything."

Tom felt her cool gaze, and she turned to look out the window. Her words hung in the air, but he thought they'd sounded unconvinced. No doubt she was still grappling with the role she'd played in Declan's death; questioning her actions, wondering if she might have done something different, which would have led to another, more favorable, outcome. One in which no one died. He knew he would have been. He wasn't much for analyzing himself — the department shrink did it for him — but he was pretty sure he knew how to pile on the guilt and second-guessing.

Heather continued to massage her hands, the knuckles no longer popping.

The lead trooper pulled up in front of the DFS, a single-story gray building. Tom stopped behind him and faced Heather. "At this point, here's how we consider it: you're being treated as an eye witness to a gang killing, or what we call a street crime. The federal government is not intervening here, this is just us. You can leave anytime. But I seriously recommend that you don't."

Since her own clothes had been booked into evidence, Heather had been given a pair of navy blue slacks and a white t-shirt to wear. She had no make-up on, but she was naturally pretty, a kind of Dutch look to her — wavy blonde hair that nested on her shoulders, average height, slender frame.

A deep crease formed between her eyebrows and she leaned back a bit. "I understand all of that, and please understand I am very grateful. Okay? I'm sorry I'm so on edge right now, I just don't know how I'm going to stay in a single room with my girls for — how long? A few weeks? Longer? I mean, even a few days and those girls will be climbing the walls. I probably will be, too."

"There's a pool." He knew it was a weak offering and smiled.

"A pool . . ." She broke into a smile and laughed. She put a hand over her eyes and swiped her fingers across her forehead.

"It's heated," Tom said.

* * *

The girls came running and Heather swept them into her arms. Olivia was rapid-fire talking about her overnight adventure, her younger sister chiming in with the last word in nearly every sentence. "Eat! Bed! Teevee!"

Watching Heather embrace her daughters, and seeing the way the girls adored their mother, Tom felt a tightness in his chest. He caught the gaze of a social worker who offered a soft smile. Tom made his way to her and asked how things had gone.

"Very good. They're extremely polite girls." The social worker looked over Tom's shoulder at the family reunion. "We're pulling for her," she said. "Heather is one of the good ones. Whatever you have to do . . ."

Tom nodded and returned to Heather and her daughters, glancing at the state troopers waiting outside the glass doors.

"Okay, let's get going."

Olivia stared up at him. "Hey, I know you."

"Hey, I know you, too."

Two minutes later they were strapping the girls into their car seats. A trooper from each of the vehicles stood guard, backs to the Durango, as Tom wrestled with the older girl's harness.

"In the middle there," Heather said, pointing to the clasp. "The shoulder belts snap together right there. Then the whole thing goes into the buckle between her legs."

Tom nodded. A bead of sweat rolled down his nose. Olivia was looking out the window, oblivious to his struggle. "Mom, do we have any snacks?"

"No snacks, baby."

Heather was more dexterous when it came to the child seats and already had Abigail snapped in. She kept kissing the girl, smoothing her wispy hair. Tears continued to brim in Heather's eyes, but Tom thought she was a pillar of strength.

"There," Tom said at last. "Good to go."

Heather got up on her tip-toes and leaned over Abigail, stretched across the back seat and grabbed a strap. She yanked on it. "Needs to be a little tighter."

More runnels of sweat coursed down the sides of Tom's face. It wasn't even that hot out. He couldn't imagine having to maneuver these kids in and out of car seats multiple times a day. Torture.

Heather grasped the tension strap and gave it a yank. The whole harness cinched around Olivia to the point Tom thought it would cut off the girl's circulation, but Olivia didn't seem bothered.

One of the troopers came over with two heavy Kevlar blankets.

"These are ballistic blankets," Tom explained. "This is an armored vehicle, but these are fireproof, will resist any fragmentation." He unfolded one and wrapped it around Olivia, who acted like it was the most normal thing in the world. The trooper went around and placed the second blanket over Abigail, fastening it around the child seat with Velcro straps.

Heather looked uneasy. Tom grabbed something else from one of the troopers, held it out to Heather, who blanched at the sight of it. "This is standard-duty body armor. It's pretty comfortable."

As Tom was helping Heather get into the armored vest, Olivia asked, "How about twist, Mommy? Do we have twist?"

"No, honey, no twist."

Dressed in the special armor, Heather gave Abigail one more peck on the nose before closing the door. She got in the front passenger seat and Tom slipped behind the wheel, giving her a look. "Twist?"

"I put a mixture of two kinds of cereal in a plastic bag. We call it 'twist'."

"Gotcha." He kept the vehicle in park a moment. "You'll get used to the vest."

"I don't want to."

Then they were rolling again, this time leaving the whole complex behind — the jail, DFS. Tom kept his eyes moving.

"Where's my bag?" Heather asked.

"It's at the ROC."

"The ROC?"

"Regional Operations Center. It's a mixture of crime lab and administrative offices."

"It's a twist," Olivia said, from the back seat.

"Exactly."

* * *

The troopers kept their lights off. The convoy moved at a good clip, threading through the thick traffic. The sun burst from behind parting clouds and Tom put on his sunglasses.

Abigail squirmed in under the ballistic blanket. Olivia asked: "Are we going home?"

"No, we're not going home." Heather turned to the girls. "We're going to a hotel."

"A hotel? Like a vacation?"

"Yep. Like a vacation."

"But Mom, I don't have my bag packed."

"That's okay, baby. We'll get everything we need."

Heather faced forward again. They turned off 41 onto Immokalee Road, and an odor filled the car. Tom flicked another look at Heather, who was smiling. A real smile, showing the person she was before this supernova of danger and fear had exploded her life.

"We might need some pull-ups," she said. "It's a type of diaper for potty-training. Abby has been doing the big-girl potty, right honey?"

"Ight!"

Heather lowered her voice. "But sometimes we have a little accident."

"Is that what that is?"

She nodded and kept looking him.

"Now?" he asked.

"You got any on you?"

"Can it wait?"

"How far are we going?"

"Just ten more minutes."

"But how soon until we get some supplies?"

"Maybe an hour."

"I'd really like to change her. They put a diaper on her at DFS, but I'd rather she didn't sit in it for that long."

Tom took out his cell phone and called the lead trooper, explained that they needed to make a detour. "We have to, ah, pick up a few personal items for the family."

* * *

They pulled into a shopping center and parked a distance away from the store entrance. Tom had Heather write down everything she needed. By the time she was done with the list, it was a dozen items long.

The trooper gave it a look and said nothing, just glanced in at Tom and his passengers, then trotted off to do the shopping.

"I bet he didn't expect this was going to be part of his day," Heather said.

Other troopers stood around, giving them cover. Tom made small talk with Olivia while they waited and Heather broke the news to the girl that she was going to miss school. Olivia had a lot of questions, and Heather fielded most of them.

Tom admired her. She didn't lie to her daughters outright but was nimble with the truth.

When the trooper returned, Heather requested Tom open the back hatch of the Durango. Among the purchased items was a box of wipes. With the troopers and Tom forming a human shield around the back of the vehicle, Heather changed the two year-old in what had to be record time. She folded up the used diaper, fastened it to itself with the sticky straps, and held it out to him. "Evidence?"

"No, we can let that one go," Tom said. He nodded to the trooper beside him who took it and moved off, looking a bit green.

CHAPTER THIRTEEN

The hotel had been selected for its location — off the beaten path but still relatively close to Naples and Fort Myers — but also for its set up. It was seven stories high, with five potential entrances on the ground floor; the main entrance of the lobby, a door off the kitchen, and a second service door which led to a rear loading dock. The two stairwells were exit-only and an alarm would sound when opened. The kitchen door also had an exit, but no alarm.

A security detail awaited their arrival. One agent was posted at each door. There would be three eight-hour shifts going around the clock. Nine agents just on lower building security, then three shifts upstairs on the top floor, where the room was. Twelve agents every day. A single day was going to cost upwards of three thousand dollars, just in manpower.

Tom recognized the agent guarding the room as Damien Culpepper. After Tom helped Heather and her girls settle in, he stepped out into the hall and shook the man's hand.

Culpepper, a Florida native with a permanent tan, raised his blond eyebrows. "Pretty crazy."

"Yeah . . . they pulled you from Governor Protection, huh?"

"Yeah." Culpepper loaded a stick of gum into his mouth. "Want one?"

"Sure, thanks." Tom unwrapped the piece handed to him.

"So you're back on normal duties, huh?" Culpepper got a crooked smile. "You never said why you were there, but I know you didn't sign up for Governor Protection . . ."

Tom had thought of it as being sidelined, but there was no need to insult what Culpepper did — protecting the governor was important work. "I needed out of investigations," Tom said, "while they ran me through therapy."

Culpepper accepted this with a nod. "Gotcha. Shit, first day back in the field and you've got this mega case and you're pulling all these strings. I guess therapy worked."

Tom gave the hallway a look up and down, chewed his gum and commented no further on it. Two elevators on the east end beside the stairwell, and on the west end the hall made a turn out of sight. "What's the word on all this?"

"You want me to blow smoke up your ass or do you want the unvarnished truth?"

"I'll take unvarnished."

"People think this is crazy." He looked at the room door, marked 702, slightly ajar. Sounds of the TV drifted through the crack — rubbery cartoon voices. Culpepper said, "A few people think a potential murderer is out walking around with protection. The rest just think it's excessive."

"The rest?"

"Well . . ." The agent smirked. "Not me."

"It's excessive to protect a woman whose daughters have been threatened the way they were?"

Culpepper put up his hands and shifted the gum between his cheeks. "Hey, don't shoot the messenger, right? No, I mean, everybody gets that. But there's just a sentiment, is all I'm saying . . ."

"That we should've kept her in jail?"

He shrugged. "Like I said, I'm not complaining. This is better than working GP, less travel, closer to home. But, you know, taxpayers are already floating the bill for the jail, and social services, and now there's this." He raised and dropped his shoulders a second time. "You know how it is."

"Yeah." Tom peered into the room. Heather's shape blurred past. She wanted to call people — her parents, brother, friends — assure everyone she was alright. The shooting at her home had been widely reported. They'd gone over most of the protocols, about what to say and what not to say to the people she spoke with. The phones at the hotel had been checked for security and the one in the room outfitted with a recorder. But officially, she still needed to be briefed by someone from the Violent Crime and Drug Control Council; they were supposed to be arriving presently.

Tom's phone rang in his pocket. He nodded at Culpepper and wandered down the hall as he took the call.

"Hey, Lauren," he said.

"You got a minute to meet me downstairs?"

"For you? I got five."

"That joke is older than I am," she said.

* * *

Blythe had brought them a couple of hot coffees. They sat in her Crown Vic, facing west, watching the sun slide slowly towards a horizon of tall, slender trees. Tom had a file folder with him which he let sit on his lap.

She nodded her head towards the vegetation.

"You know what we're looking at, there?"

Tom sipped his coffee. "Woods?"

"Very good, Agent Lange. Virgin bald cypress, that's correct." She pointed with her cup of coffee. "That's the Corkscrew Swamp Sanctuary." She cut him a look. "But I'm sure you knew that."

He smiled, took another sip.

She said, "Thirteen thousand acres in the heart of the Corkscrew Watershed. Seven hundred acres of the largest remaining virgin bald cypress forest in the world, and home to the largest nesting colony of wood storks in the country. That's a federally endangered species, I might add." She glanced around, pointing out more with her cup. "I guess it's not a bad spot you've picked, is my point. You've got Orangetree two miles down the road there, and then Ave Maria five miles back that way. Ten minutes to the Immokalee Regional Airport, too."

"Don't forget the casino."

Blythe ducked her head to get a look up at the hotel. "And how is our guest doing?"

"She's okay."

"You watch the news?"

"I've seen a little."

"Well, you know we've kept her anonymous. But the media was all over the shooting, they know who she is, they're speculating that the shooting is related to Declan's death because they know she does mental health work for the jail. So, they're looking for her. Is she going to be able to handle all this?"

He shifted in his seat. He felt a sudden urge for a cigarette but tried to ignore it. "I guess that all depends on what 'this' is."

The air changed and the good humor seemed to drain from Agent Blythe.

Tom stared into his coffee a moment, then took a quick swig. He set the cup down in the cup holder in the console and folded his arms. The ideas were dancing in his head, but he waited for Blythe to speak.

"What's going on, Lange? What are you thinking?"

He wasn't sure if he was ready to present his ideas.

She said, "You don't think Palumbo is behind this? Come on. Talk to me. What's going on in your head?"

There was no letting it lie. "Mario Palumbo has a team of lawyers that cost him probably half a million per year, each," Tom said. "He's been charged with five felonies in the past six years, beaten every one of them. Four settled out of court, one trial. Almost never gets his hands dirty. Meanwhile, Coby's been monitoring his cocaine network for two years; got dates, times, and civilian informants coming out his ass, but nothing. Thousands of kilos have been taken off the street and Coby's interdiction team has busted a dozen of Palumbo's drug runners. But nobody takes a deal, nobody flips. The only thing left is for the feds to come in and drop a RICO cluster-bomb. But they aren't making any moves."

She pointed in the air again, leaning in towards Tom, her face darkening a shade. "Declan is *dead*. A civilian was leveraged to commit murder, for Christ's sake. This type of crime is exactly why the RICO act was passed in the first place."

He nodded. "I know."

"The whole thing *stinks* of organized crime; like Mandi said, it's textbook."

"I know."

"Stop saying, 'I know'." Blythe turned away and stared out at the vegetation filling the distance.

Tom took a drink, giving her a moment. "My point is, even *if* Declan had dealings with Palumbo, was he really going to turn? Was he an actual threat to Palumbo? This guy with nothing, in debt, with no proof he ever even *worked* for Palumbo."

"Maybe he was an informant for Coby."

"Maybe. I thought about that. And taking out a C.I., okay, that might be textbook. But like this? Palumbo using a *therapist*? Then going after her? It's pushing it."

"Tom, I get it."

"Alright. So, what did the other clinicians have to say?"

She tapped her fingers against the steering wheel. "I spoke with all four County Mental Health clinicians who visit the jail. Moss is the only on-call clinician, but she also has regular shifts twice a week to do counseling, or evaluations if there are any. Yesterday was her regular shift."

"So it sounds like she's a constant," Tom said.

"What does that mean?"

"Whoever was looking at Heather Moss knew she'd either get called in or she'd be there as per her regular shift."

"Well, the jail does have an in-house clinician, the one who evaluated Declan when he first came in, scored him high enough that Heather Moss had to follow up the next day."

He lifted the file off his lap. "Right — this is the police report on Declan's arrest and his intake information at the jail. The in-house clinician only does the intake, and it's in a different area to where inmates process in. The in-house clinician recommended Declan be put on watch for suicidal ideation. The inmates need to be evaluated every 24 hours to see if they're still a danger to themselves or others, and Heather was on shift for that next check-up."

"I know all this. What's the—"

"Why would Palumbo wait for this guy to be put in jail where he was so hard to reach? Why go to all this trouble to use someone like Heather Moss when Palumbo could have reached out at any time and gotten to Declan? Edgar Vasquez and his wife died almost two months ago in that car wreck. So for all that time, if Declan was the guy to sabotage their car, he's just sitting around his house, and Palumbo waits to kill him once he's in jail?"

"Palumbo was afraid he would crack under pressure in jail. Declan had been keeping quiet, Palumbo was laying off until now."

Tom shook his head. "I don't think so. Someone knew he'd willingly take that pill, kill himself."

"Declan owed money to the track, too."

"Okay, but, we're back to the same question — why wait until he's in jail? *Unless* someone wanted Heather Moss to be the person who handed him that little package."

She stared at him directly. "I don't understand you. If there's anyone who — look, you realize if you get what you're pushing for; if we can't show Palumbo is behind this, we can't protect this woman and her daughters. You just rigged all this up for them, you've got them in wit-pro, and now you're pushing back . . ."

"What I'm saying, Lauren, is that she's definitely in danger, but it might not be from Palumbo. It might be from someone who selected her specifically."

"Why?"

"At this point, I have no idea."

Her exasperation with him seemed to fade. Still, she tapped her nails against the steering wheel again. "Alright. Look. Talk to her. Find out everything you can."

"I plan to."

"Good."

Blythe keyed the ignition and the Crown Vic's powerful V-6 engine roared to life. "I'll call you in the morning. Now get out."

He raised a hand as she turned around in the parking lot and watched her cruise away on Immokalee Road.

CHAPTER FOURTEEN

"I never had him as a client before," Heather said. She was on her knees beside the tub, up to her elbows in soap suds. "I didn't know anything about him until two days ago, towards the end of the day when I learned he'd been picked up and was at the jail."

Tom sat in one of the hotel room chairs, watching Heather through the open bathroom door. "So how do you refer to someone in this situation? Clinically speaking."

Heather flinched as one of the girls made a splash in the water. Then she reached in and must've tickled Abigail, because the girl giggled, the sound bright and contagious. Tom chuckled. Heather rang out a wet washcloth and leaned in again, her words canned by the tiled walls surrounding the tub: "Well, we refer to anyone who we see at the clinic a 'client'. But when we service the jail, the jail is the actual client."

Tom sobered. "So, how would you be referring to Declan, in your documentation, in conversations with your supervisor, etcetera?"

"As 'inmate'."

He scribbled a note on the pad resting on the table beside him. "Because of this type of relationship, how does confidentiality work?"

"Actually, that's the first thing I say when I see an inmate. I tell them that, ordinarily as a mental health counselor, things they say would be kept in confidence. But as county jail has retained my services, I'm obliged to share information with them regarding any risk I assess. Any danger I feel the inmate poses to themselves, or to the jail staff. Hey, hey, take it easy, girls."

The splashing intensified, both Olivia and Abigail giggling now, hidden behind the half-closed opaque doors enclosing the tub. Then the laughter turned to bickering. "Give it back, Abby," Heather said. "Give it back to your sister. Here. Here's yours, right here."

"And that doesn't cause them to just shut down on you?" Tom folded his arms and leaned back in the chair.

Heather wiped her brow with the upper part of her arm. She was still dressed in the navy blue slacks and white t-shirt. The t-shirt was wet and clinging to her skin in places. Tom could see part of her bra showing through.

She gave him a look and he felt a pang of guilt like he'd been caught in a licentious thought, but her mind was elsewhere. "Actually, it tends to help build rapport. You know, in a lot of these situations, people feel like they have no one they can trust. Up is down, their lives are a mess. And I give it to them straight."

Tom absorbed this. "But wasn't Declan already on a watch when you arrived?"

She nodded. "The regular jail clinician placed him on watch, based on the circumstances of his arrest and how he presented when he arrived."

"I've seen that report," Tom said. "It says he seemed depressed, and he wouldn't — or couldn't — explain the circumstances of his arrest. The clinician writes that Declan seemed utterly resigned. She thought Declan might try to hurt himself. But I want to know what *you* thought; your report."

Heather got to her feet and moved away from the tub, lowered her voice. "Can we do this, ah — the girls . . ."

Tom put up his hand. "Right. Sorry. Sure, we can pick this up a little later."

But she lingered in the doorway a moment, looking at him. "Listen," she whispered, "I left. I went to get my girls and get as far away as I could. Then I was arrested. I never made a report."

"No, I know." He said, matching her volume. "But you did talk to him. You did evaluate him."

"I guess you could call it that. But the girls were on my mind the entire time. I wasn't really in the frame of mind to, you know . . . I was . . ." Heather looked back at the girls, then to Tom again. "You're trying to catch me out. You're not going to find anything."

"I'm . . ." he started, but she'd busted him.

She moved back to the tub, settled onto her knees. "Are the clothes coming? These girls are turning into prunes."

"Yeah. Should be any minute."

Terrified was likely the word she'd been about to say, he thought. *I was terrified.*

There was a knock at the door.

"That could be them now." Tom rose from the chair and started to the entrance. He stepped over to the door, not crossing in front of it. Resting his palm on the grip of his sidearm, he peered into the keyhole.

Two agents were in the hallway. Culpepper, and a woman Tom didn't recognize. They were smiling and talking, Culpepper facing the door. He raised a hand and knocked again by rapping the door with his knuckles once, pausing, then three times, pausing, then twice.

Tom slid unlocked the bolt, slid the chain away, opened up.

"Here you go, boss," Culpepper handed over a black duffel bag and two shopping bags. Behind Tom in the bathroom, the girls continued to chatter and splash. Culpepper looked past Tom. "Everything good in here?"

"Everything's good. Thank you."

Culpepper gave a brief nod, then backed out, closing the door as he went. Tom re-bolted and chained it. Then he set the bags on the nearest double bed and went through them.

"Is it the clothes?" Heather's voice carried from the bathroom.

"Yes." He set aside two sets of tiny pajamas. Then some things intended for Heather — undergarments, yoga pants, a couple t-shirts — all of which she'd requested from her personal belongings. The crime lab had had to check and sign off on the items, and it took time and personnel. Tom had thought familiar things would be nice for Heather and the girls. But any more clothes or personal effects would be purchased new. It was easier and less costly in the long run.

He set out some hair brushes and toiletries, plus two small pillows and two stuffed animals. Held up the stuffed frog and gave it a look, then set it beside the teddy bear. There were three books — *A Fly Buzzed By, The Echoing Well,* and an adult paperback, *A Man Called Ove.* The first book was for little children. *The Echoing Well* was Young Adult.

He tipped the duffel bag over and shook it. Ran his hand along the lining, and through the two end pockets. Nothing.

Tom heard the water sucking down the bathtub drain, put the clothes back into the bag and brought it to the bathroom door, handed it in discreetly, keeping his head turned.

"Thank you."

"There's more diapers out here, too. Everything."

He returned to the bed and sat on the edge, fished around in the shopping bags. Abigail waddled out of the bathroom, wrapped up from her neck to her ankles in a white hotel towel. She took a few steps into the room, then looked up at him.

"Hi," Tom said.

Abigail did an about-face and waddled straight back, tripped on the towel and went sprawling, started crying, which quickly escalated into full-on wailing. Tom moved to pick her up, but Heather beat him to it. She smiled at him and sat down with Abigail on the closed toilet, soothed and shushed her. "You're alright. You're okay."

Olivia stood up in the tub, and Tom withdrew again. He sat on the bed and waited for Heather to dress the girls. Olivia came out first, wearing pajamas covered in abstract art patterns. She hopped up on the chair and gave Tom's notepad a look. He rose and quickly grabbed it up.

"Are those your police notes?"

"That's right."

Olivia blinked up at him. "Did you know my daddy?"

He shook his head. "No, I'm sorry. I didn't."

"He died."

"I know."

"He had cancer."

"I'm very sorry." Tom headed for the door, called to Heather, "I'll check in with you a little later then, okay?"

"What about food?" she asked, out of sight. "You said room service is okay?"

"Yes. We're supervising any meals that are requested . . ." He trailed off, realizing Olivia was watching him closely. "Sure, room service is good. I hear they have good ice cream."

"Ice cream!" Olivia shouted, and leaped from the chair.

"Green-green!" Abigail chimed in from the bathroom.

"Thanks for that . . ."

"I think they have twist flavor, too." He grinned at Olivia and opened the door with both girls shouting, "Twist! Twist!"

* * *

In his hotel bathroom, Tom rolled his head on his shoulders, feeling the kinks in his neck. It was going on nine p.m., and he figured Heather would be putting the girls to bed by now. Their rooms were adjacent and he'd heard Abigail crying a bit at one point.

It hadn't been his intent to say anything really inappropriate in front of the girls — not that he was sure exactly where that line would be drawn. But Heather was right, he'd been fishing, curious how she'd react with her daughters around. Not sure exactly what he thought she'd reveal, just maybe something; he'd know it if he saw it.

But he hadn't seen it, he didn't think. Just that she was smart. And a gifted multitasker.

He changed the bandage on his hand, ran a toothbrush over his teeth and splashed some water on his face. Blotted his face with a towel and gazed at his reflection in the mirror: the small scar beneath his eye seemed to stand out. According to Nick, the scar was from the night Tom had tried to stop his father from hitting his mother. Tom didn't remember the incident, but he could recall other nights.

He tossed the towel aside and shut off the bathroom light. Pulled out his laptop at the desk by the window. After logging into the secure state bureau database he brought up the search engine, typed in a name.

Glenn Moss had been born in Poughkeepsie, New York in 1975. He'd gone to college at Hofstra University where he'd been pre-law and a lacrosse player. He'd switched majors to business, graduated and gone to work for Home Depot as an assistant manager, quickly ascended to manager. He seemed to be living an ordinary and upstanding life when he'd met Heather. The two had gotten married, and Olivia had arrived six months later. The family lived in Nyack, an artsy community on the Hudson River, a half-hour north of New York City.

Tom found hospital records, a funeral service itinerary, and an obituary in the Rockland Journal News, Nyack's paper:

Loving father. Devoted Husband. Survived by his wife, Heather, and their two children, Olivia and Abigail, as well as a brother, Charles Arthur Moss TSgt, USAF…

It went on, Tom read it, then composed a quick email to Cheyenne Holman, asking her to do a little more digging on Heather, her late husband Glenn, and his brother, an Air Force technical sergeant.

The knock on the hotel room door gave Tom a start.

One knock, three knocks, two knocks.

He closed down the laptop and moved to the door, unsnapped his thong holster and peered through the walleye. Damien Culpepper was standing in the hallway with Heather Moss.

Tom opened up. "Everything okay?"

"Yeah. Girls are asleep." She spoke in a whisper even though she was well outside the room. "I thought you wanted to talk a little bit more."

"I do — I just figured I'd come to you."

Heather shook her head. "Abby would wake up. Trust me, I'm not thrilled to be away from them, even if it's only next door. But to tell you the truth I know I'm not going to sleep anytime soon and it's either this or I lay there in the dark with my thoughts."

"Come on in."

Heather moved past him, wafting a scent of hotel shampoo and soap. Tom glanced at Culpepper who gave a nod and said, "I'll be right outside their door. Won't move an inch."

"Thank you." Tom closed the door gently and moved into the room.

He gestured to the cushioned chair in the corner. "Have a seat." Heather settled in and he sat back at the desk. "These rooms aren't bad, huh?" He glanced around.

"Yeah. They're nice."

"And you're hanging in there so far?"

She shrugged, leaned back and drummed the sides of the chair with her hands. "I have no idea."

"When you woke up this morning . . ."

"Right. It was just any other day. I mean, I know this is going to sound strange, but it was actually a little bit tough of a morning to begin with. Nothing like this . . . *Nothing* like this. Just that the girls were giving me some trouble, I was running late. Almost like there was something in the air . . . I dunno." She shook her head, asked, "You got something to drink?"

"I can get just about anything you want. Right here in the room there's some bottled water, but I can—"

"No." She seemed to think better of it. "Water's fine. Thank you."

Tom went to the mini-fridge and pulled out one for her, one for him. She took a long drink, wiped her mouth with the back of her hand and looked off.

Suddenly she was shaking. She dropped her head between her legs, her entire body trembling. "Oh God," she moaned. "I'm so sorry . . ."

Tom moved beside her and placed a tentative hand on her shoulder. Her skin radiated hot, the back of her neck shiny and damp. She tried to speak through the spasms wracking her body. It was hard to understand everything she was saying, but he caught the gist of it: despite feeling she'd done what she had to do to keep her daughters safe, she'd caused someone's death, and felt deep remorse. It seemed to crush her.

"Does he . . ." she stammered, "Does he have family? Oh God . . ."

"Not that we know of," Tom said. "Just an ex-wife. He seems like a loner."

She raised her head. Her face was flushed, her eyes shining. She wiped away the tears with her hand and Tom grabbed her some tissues, handed them to her. He went back to the desk chair, giving her some space.

She got under control, met his gaze. "You asked what I thought of Declan."

"I did."

"Well, I think I know what you're really asking. Did he say something to me that was some kind of sensitive information? And the answer is, no. He didn't. I can tell you what he did talk about, though. His wife. How he regretted that they'd never had children. He regretted the divorce."

Tom unfolded his arms, acutely aware of his body language all of the sudden. He tried to sit casually and draped his arm on the chair. "But did you . . . what did you think of him? If none of the things that happened this morning happened — if you'd never gotten the phone call on your way to work, what would you have thought of him?"

"A sad man. A lonely person; one who was having a psychotic break."

"Would you have recommended another 24-hour watch?"

"Yes."

"And how did you determine that?"

Her look lingered a moment. "He said, 'I don't deserve to live.'"

A silence developed in the room, and Heather drank the rest of her water. The woman who'd showed up at his room door five minutes ago had been lively, almost vivacious, but now she looked peaked. Tom felt guilt swelling up, but he knew the questions were necessary.

"This guy," he said, "walking around in his front yard naked, a neighbor calls the police. They show up, try talking to him, move in on him, and he goes for one of their guns. Boom, he gets arrested, they take him in. Then,

116

he's in jail, and this . . . thing happens. He takes this lethal pill. But I'm also wondering, you know — you said psychotic break. Was this guy really out there? Was he hearing voices? I mean . . ."

She shook her head, her eyes wet and unfocused. "I don't know. I don't think he was schizophrenic or had de-realization, nothing organic like that. He wasn't on any meds, had no history of mental health disorders. But I really wasn't able to . . . That's all I can say."

"I understand. And he never mentioned anything about a man named Mario Palumbo?"

"No."

"How about Edgar Vasquez?"

"Vasquez? No."

"But did he seem paranoid at all, worried people were after him?"

She daubed at her eyes with a wadded tissue. "He seemed afraid of something. Of judgment. I'm not sure if from the law, something in his head, or something else."

"And he never explained why he was naked, walking around in front of his house?"

"Mr. Lange . . . Agent Lange, Howard Declan experienced an episode of acute, primary psychosis. He hadn't been sleeping, maybe for weeks, and was probably disassociated. But I only had forty-five minutes with him, and like I said, I had a lot going on. And this is an initial assessment, part of an ongoing process; I have no concrete answer for why he did what he did."

She rose, a bit unsteadily, and brushed a strand of hair from her face. Tom started to get out of the chair, but she put out her hand. "I do think Howard Declan had some kind of secret. Okay? I won't presume to know what, but something was eating away at him." Her gaze had sharpened to become direct. "Some clients have organic, degenerative conditions; a physical problem with their brain. But Declan had no history of that. If pushed, I'd say he was like the rest of us — even if we're sane, we all have the potential to be consumed by regret, by guilt, to the point it pushes us to extremes."

Tom's gears were turning, thinking about money Declan owed, if that was the extent of his burden. Then his mind hopped tracks. "Heather," he said quietly, "I want to share something with you. I want to be straight with you."

"Oh? You trying to build a rapport with me now?" The corner of her mouth curled into a slight smile.

"Maybe. But I want you to really consider this. Okay?"

"Okay."

"I don't know how long this protection is going to last. We need to prove that it's someone specific who targeted Declan, who used you, and that's been challenging. I just want to prepare you that we may come to the end of this very shortly."

She took this in, then nodded. "Well, we'll cross that bridge when we come to it."

Tom had one more question. "How about you?"

"How about me what?"

"Can you think of anyone who would want to do something like this to you?"

Her eyes widened with surprise. "You mean, put me through all this? Set me up as some kind of murderer? No, Agent Lange. Thank God I can answer that one. No one."

* * *

Lange saw Heather Moss back to her room, and Culpepper let her in with a magnetic key. Heather said goodnight and closed the door.

"Hey," Tom said to Culpepper, "You still smoke?"

"Yeah, the gum is just to get me through. But don't tell anybody. Nothing more on the outs these days than being a smoker."

"Give me one to keep me quiet."

"You're the boss, boss."

Culpepper pulled out a pack of Camels and shook one out. "Need a light?"

"Yeah. Thanks. I'll be back."

* * *

He stood in the parking lot, looking off into the dark pine and cypress trees of the Corkscrew Swamp. The faintly metallic smell of the marsh wetlands hung in the air. He flicked the lighter and fed the flame to the Camel between his lips and the aroma of burning tobacco took over.

Before his parents died, he'd had woods to play in. But since there hadn't been a lot of families taking in foster kids where he grew up, he and Nick had gotten bounced around between a few homes in the city. Some of the families were strict, others let kids roam, and Tom got to know the streets.

Lots of different types on the street, but they had something in common — they'd either learned how to survive or were learning.

Heather Moss was interesting because he couldn't quite peg her. She was smart; when Blythe asked if she'd been curious what was in the envelope, Heather had stuck to the facts — she'd been instructed not to look. Didn't say whether she'd obeyed that instruction or not. Either she knew the system or had that survival instinct. Maybe both.

He'd asked her if she could think of anyone setting her up, and this time her response was more direct — no — but it snagged him: he wasn't sure if she hadn't been able to think of anyone, or if there was someone she didn't want to think of.

Or maybe couldn't.

His phone vibrated, and Tom saw Blythe's incoming number. The time was almost eleven.

"Hey, what's up?" Tom asked.

"There's been another murder."

He just stood there a moment. "Well, it's an unfortunately common occurrence."

She wasn't into the humor. "Everglades City. I need you at the field office first thing tomorrow. We're going to have a look at the crime scene video."

"Is there a connection between Howard Declan and this person?"

"You could say that."

CHAPTER FIFTEEN

FRIDAY

"So this happened four days ago," Blythe said. She sat at her desk and booted up her computer. "A day before Howard Declan was arrested."

Tom set his bag down and looked around the single-room Naples field office. Since his reassignment to Governor Protection, he'd only stopped in once to pick up a few personal belongings. No other agent had been posted in his absence — Blythe had been working alone. There was coffee in the pot and Tom poured himself a cup.

"That's old," she said without turning around. She opened a file on the computer and brought up a video.

Tom sipped anyway. Bitter and cold, just right. He moved beside her. "Okay, let's have a look."

"So this is Everglades City. Everglades City is very small, one way in, one way out. It's a tight fishing community, everyone tends to know one another." She pressed the Play button. A large, rundown boat was moored to a rickety-looking dock along a swampy inlet.

The camera operator, likely a tech from the county's crime scene bureau, panned for a 180-degree view. To the right was an overwater bungalow, looking about ready to fall in. "Sheriff's Department took the call and recorded this video," Blythe said. "But they called in the state bureau because—"

"The Everglades are also under our jurisdiction. Got it."

"Well, technically, this is Big Cypress Preserve. It was supposed to be part of the Everglades National Park, but it hadn't been purchased from the private owners yet. So it's its own thing. But yes, that's why the state bureau was initially notified. An agent came in from Miami. Rhodes."

The shot panned left, passing by the boat, and revealed nothing but more swamp stretching away in the other direction, bristling with mangrove. The low clouds formed a dark and dismal sky.

Tom felt his nerves start to crawl. "So why are we looking at it now?"

"Just watch."

The tech walked towards the boat. There were voices, then a sheriff's deputy came into view, followed by someone in a suit. Blythe pointed. "There's Rhodes."

The deputy led Rhodes along the dock, the tech operating the camera trailing them. The deputy and Rhodes stepped aboard. It looked like a fishing schooner — glimpses of a dirty net piled on the deck, fishing poles scattered about, an overturned bucket leaking some kind of bait.

The team moved through the pilothouse and the shot swept over the rudimentary controls: steering wheel, throttle, toggles to ignite and trim the inboard engine. Then the image framed a narrow set of stairs. The deputy started down, then Rhodes; the camera followed.

A cramped living quarters was in disarray. Clothes strewn about, dishes piled in the tiny kitchen, a few books on the floor.

The shot swung toward the bed.

"Oh boy . . ." Tom sucked in a breath. "There he is."

The dead man's eyes were wide open, staring up at the ceiling. One of his eyes had turned dark red. There was a crusty ring around his mouth.

". . . appears to be some kind of overdose." The deputy on camera was speaking to Rhodes. "You have the vomit here around the mouth, and there's signs that the decedent soiled himself. Could be postmortem though." The deputy's hand, sheathed in a blue plastic glove, pushed aside a blanket partially covering the body to reveal the bespoke excretions.

"Ah, God . . ." Tom said. "Just like Declan?"

Blythe leaned back in her chair. "The director of the Miami ROC called Turnbull this morning. The medical examiner said this was likely poison, something that attacked the central nervous system."

Tom rubbed a hand over his mouth. Two men, potentially killed in the same way. "The chemical is the same? Potassium cyanide?"

"They're still doing confirmatory testing. Both district medical examiners are working on it, and the lab in Miami."

The tour had continued while they discussed, the video wandering the living quarters. The deputy pointed out a laptop sitting on a small, built-in desk. Hard to be sure, but looked like a new MacBook Pro.

"So this can't be Declan's killer in a murder-suicide because this guy's death predates Declan's."

"Correct. He died two days before Declan."

"Who is he?"

"Well, depends on who you talk to, some say he's a genius. His name is Brian Hamer, though he's used different identities in the past. He's thirty-two now, he forged his first ID when he was seventeen. And he made himself a few hundred grand in tax fraud by the time he was twenty-one."

"A modern pirate," Tom commented. "A hacker type."

Blythe paused the video and pulled up Brian Hamer's file on the computer. Tom scanned a list of names as she continued.

"All these aliases belong to dead people. Hamer was filing tax returns under the names of deceased persons and the IRS wasn't cross-checking. When he ran out of those, he targeted living persons, mostly unemployed. He did this for a few years and made a small fortune before he was eventually caught by the IRS and FBI."

"He went to prison?" Tom saw the dates on Hamer's rap sheet.

Blythe nodded. "For just a couple years."

"That's a slap on the wrist. How'd he beat it?"

"Like I said, smart kid. The feds used a StingRay to finally catch him, and that was the key. Hamer mounted his own defense, basically highlighted the whole violation-of-privacy issue raised by StingRays and cell tower simulators in general. The FBI backed down and recommended time served."

Something tugged at the back of Tom's thoughts. Something Coby had said. "They probably just wanted him to go away. Not shine too much light on the StingRay controversy."

"Yeah." Blythe returned her attention to the screen, then backed up the footage about a minute. They were looking at Brian Hamer as he stared up at the low, angled ceiling above his bed, eyes open, body probably still warm, bacteria swarming in his guts.

"Who called this in?" Tom asked.

She pulled out a notepad from her breast pocket. "Hamer's girlfriend, Iowa Schnell. Showed up with coffee and bagels and found him."

"Iowa?"

"She thought he'd overdosed."

"Schnell?"

"You can't make this stuff up."

"What kind of a user was he?"

Blythe shrugged and put away the pad, then looked up at him. "Why don't you ask her?"

"You want me to go interview her? What about Rhodes? You said this was four days ago."

"Sure, Rhodes talked to her, they searched her place for drugs, weapons, talked to a few neighbors, not much, and they sort of wrote it off as an OD, maybe a suicide. But now that we're considering these two cases possibly linked, it's top-drawer again, and maybe Iowa can answer a few more questions for us."

They both watched the screen as the cops in Everglades City finished the tour and headed off the boat. The video went dark.

Tom moved to the sink and dumped out the rest of the bad coffee, ran the tap and drank water out of the mug. When he turned around, Blythe was watching him from her desk chair.

"Do you have a problem going down there?"

"I wanted to get to Declan's today. Have another look at his place. Drop by the evidence room and give his laptop a look. I mean, the clock is running on this thing with witness protection."

"I'm aware."

"And I wanted to check the school where Olivia went, and Abigail's day care. Even if it wasn't Palumbo, someone was watching those girls."

His mind drifted a moment, imagining Olivia as she sat in her classroom, Abigail stacking building blocks at day care. A shadowy figure lurking outside of each place. And the thing with Coby — what was it? He'd said Declan was never under 'direct surveillance'.

Blythe pushed back from her desk but remained seated in the wheelie chair. She was dressed in a dark gray suit and white shirt. She always looked incredibly put-together. Tom wondered if even a hurricane could ruffle her appearance.

"You getting attached?" Blythe asked.

"Attached?"

She just gazed across the room at him a moment. "You swimming your laps in the morning? Getting plenty of rest? Or are you running around at night, staying up 'til all hours writing applications for witness protection?"

His skin seemed to tighten. "So — we should've charged Heather Moss with murder?"

Blythe stood and slowly crossed the space toward him, her eyes cunning. "I'm just asking. Are you taking care of yourself? Or are you doing just what you did on the Gallo case?"

"What did I do on the Gallo case?"

She clucked her tongue as if he should know. "Running on emotions, losing objectivity."

"Lauren, come on, what the hell . . ." He felt trapped. She had such a way about her. He stayed pinned against the sink like he couldn't escape her.

"You went through a lot of shit with the Gallo case," she said, "no doubt. Not only your brother, but what happened with McDermott."

"I'm fine — Jesus. Everybody keeps looking at me like I'm about to light on fire or something."

But her comments brought back bad memories. During the investigation into the murder of Carrie Anne Gallo, he'd threatened a guy named Josh McDermott, a woman-beater. McDermott had broken into Tom's condo and tried to kill him for it. The County crime scene bureau eventually collected enough evidence to help put McDermott away, but by then Tom had decided to leave Naples. It was no longer, for him, the "happiest city in the US". He'd taken some of the money from liquidating Nick's estate, bought the place in Bonita Springs.

"I had six months with the state psychiatrist, twice a week," Tom said.

"And you spent six months working Governor Protection, which puts you in a sort of mindset. Those are long hours, and your job is to be paranoid. I'm just checking in with you, Tom, making sure you're good to go."

"I am." He eased aside as she took more coffee from the cabinets, stuck a filter in the machine and scooped in grinds for a fresh pot. The aroma soon filled the small room.

"And I know you've had a lot on your plate with your brother's stuff. So, don't take offense, but has that all been settled? Because we're awfully close here, with these two things. We've got Declan in debt for gambling, and your brother had his debts, too."

Tom drew a deep breath, let it out, and with it, the tension. Blythe was right — like Howard Declan, Nick had owed money to Palumbo. But not for dogs; for poker. Nick had gone to work for Palumbo to work out the debt. "Yeah, there are similarities," he said. "But unlike Declan, Nick had made a will. I got a lawyer, we dealt with the probate court, settled it. I haven't inherited any debt."

Not legally, anyway, he thought.

"Good," Blythe said. "So, head down to Everglades City, talk to Rhodes, interview Hamer's girlfriend. Okay? I'll keep an eye on Heather Moss and keep looking at Declan — Matt's working on his laptop, his phone, and Cheyenne's still checking into the work history. We've got to see if there's something that connects these two beyond the suicide pill."

She spread her hands across the counter top and lowered her head. "You're a good agent, Tom. You've got good instincts, and you're thorough."

"You mean obsessed. That's what you wanted to say."

"If there's one thing you've taught me, it pays to be thorough."

Both of them knew that the Carrie Anne Gallo case had been compromised, in part, by Blythe's impulsivity.

"That's nice of you to say." He was taken aback that she'd admit it.

She stuck her own finger in the air. "Just one. Just one thing you've taught me. Don't go fondling yourself over it."

He started to gather his things, pulling his suit coat from the back of his desk chair.

"Listen," she said, "have another look at the school and day care if you want, before you go down."

"Good. I will."

She squared her shoulders with him. "Oh and here's a heads-up — Agent Rhodes thinks he's a cowboy. Like, a cowboy-cowboy. So, beware."

Tom didn't press for elaboration. He pushed out the door into the bright sunshine.

CHAPTER SIXTEEN

He headed south out of Fort Myers, stopped in Bonita Springs, took Old 41 through the downtown area. Crossed the Imperial River and passed Riverside Park with its giant water fountain, ancient Banyan trees and the Liles Hotel Historic Plaza, a two-story building with blue awnings over four-paned windows. A sign near the seashell-shaped Music and Events stage declared a blues music festival was coming next week.

Turning down Dean Street, Lange found Olivia's school was in morning recess. The bright laughter and burble of children's voices was audible the moment he stepped out of the Durango. First he walked a wide circle around the building, a cheerier place than the ones he remembered growing up in New York, then wandered into the front office where the woman with the high pile of gray hair recognized him from the day before.

"Hello, officer. Is everything alright? Is Olivia alright?"

He smiled and glanced at the faces of the other administrators, knowing they'd surely seen the news on the shooting at Heather's house.

"Olivia's doing great. I was hoping I could get some basic information from you?"

"Of course."

The others in the office tried to resume normal business while Tom asked his few questions, but he sensed them eavesdropping. He gave the bank of camera monitors at the back of the office another look, then wandered back out to the street, stood looking at the school. He pictured someone, perhaps sitting in a dark SUV, maybe a Chevy Tahoe, watching.

The building was two stories, housing grades K-5. Olivia was in second grade. According to the paperwork he'd gotten from the front desk, her classroom faced south, on the top floor, overlooking the playground. The playground was built to resemble some kind of fairy tale. Children darted in and out of a couple tiny wooden houses, balanced on connecting bridges, climbed over sculptures of animals — a giant Grizzly bear with pegs bore three little ones who dangled like ornaments.

On the far side was a parking lot, a few cars parked, palm trees rustling in the balmy breeze. He walked there, stopped and turned back. Spied the top of a man's head in the room. The man moved closer to the window — likely a teacher, dressed in a tweed vest, eating an apple and talking on a cellular — but he was still only visible from the waist up. There was no way someone could see any little children seated at their desks, not from this angle.

Continuing around the building yielded no better viewing opportunities. He doubted a person could know what Olivia Moss was doing, or wearing, if she was in that classroom, by watching from outside the school.

Interesting.

* * *

Gillian Hough was pleasant, relaxed, with dark hair tied back in a ponytail, dressed in jeans and a t-shirt. She smiled and let Tom into her home. There were four little children in a playroom. They hushed and stared as Tom stepped in.

"Hello," he said.

Only one was brave enough to return the greeting, a little boy with a runny nose. "Hi."

Tom squatted down beside the boy. "What's your name?"

"Mario."

Tom smiled at the other children, then turned back to the bold boy. "Mario, did you know you have the same first name as a famous race car driver? Mario Andretti?"

Mario made a big nod — Tom was afraid the kid was going to give himself whiplash. "Uh-huh. But Mommy says that's just a co-insense."

"A coincidence?"

Another huge nod, and then Mario swiped his forearm across his nose.

Tom stood back up and faced Gillian, who hovered close.

"You mind if I have a quick look around?"

"Of course not."

"And, this room — this is where the children spend most of the day?"

"Yes. Or in the kitchen for snack time and lunch. And we go outside at least once, unless it's too hot."

"Did you go outside two mornings ago?"

She nodded. "I think so. For about a half an hour."

Tom took stock of the surroundings: a low set of shelves, teeming with children's books, a dollhouse the same height as the children. Bins filled with toys, a tiny table and chairs with kiddie cutlery. In the corner was an adult-sized desk and wheelie chair. A laptop was open on the desk, facing the room.

Gillian must've seen him looking at it. "I sometimes play a movie at rest time. Some of the bigger kids don't sleep, but they lay quietly and watch."

"Does it stay open like that all day?"

"Uhm, yeah, I guess it does. I'm usually on email before the first kids arrive. It goes into sleep mode."

Tom nodded and moved off. Gillian needed to stay and supervise the kids, so after thanking her again he showed himself out and wandered the side yard where the children played.

It was a good set-up, with homemade swings, a clubhouse, a sandbox. The area was residential, homes on either side and off the back. A single-story home, Gillian's place lent itself to spying, with unobstructed views of the playroom if someone was in the side yard. From the street, though, the same problem presented itself — hard, if not impossible to watch a little girl like Abigail as she went through her morning routine from there.

CHAPTER SEVENTEEN

It was seventy miles to Carnestown, just a couple miles north of Everglades City, and he made it there in under an hour, the Durango's gas tank running on fumes by the time he pulled into the Sheriff's Station. The small brick building sat back from a field of parched grass, dwarfed by a massive communications tower scraping the dusty blue sky. Just beyond the weather-beaten sign for the station was one for Big Cypress National Preserve, over a thousand square miles of mangroves, alligators, and venomous snakes.

Two men were sitting in chairs beneath the awning framing the front of the station. They watched as Tom hopped out of the Durango and hurried over. One was in a brown uniform, the other in a cowboy hat and leather boots.

"You Rhodes?"

The man tipped back the hat with his finger knuckle and looked up at Tom through reflective Aviator sunglasses. He wore blue jeans and a rumpled short-sleeved button-down shirt.

"I might be."

"Is she here?"

"She left."

"She left?" Tom looked around at the wall of green vegetation on one side, the gas station at the intersection of 41 and 29, and thought he saw a female figure walking.

"Relax, amigo. She just wanted to go get herself a sandwich. We've been waiting on you awhile."

Tom squinted in the distance to determine if the figure was coming or going. It looked like she was headed in their direction.

"This is Sergeant Mackey." Rhodes said. "He was the first to respond to the 911 call."

Tom remembered him from the video and leaned in for a quick handshake. "Nice to meet you."

Rhodes was balancing on the back two legs of his chair but leaned forward so all four touched down. He stood slowly and drew closer, close enough that Tom could smell traces of tobacco on his breath. The agent looked like he hadn't shaved in a few days. He stared off at Iowa Schnell, making her way back to the station along the road shoulder, taking her time. "This one's a real hoot. I don't know how much more you're going to get out of her than I did, but I'd like to see it."

Tom glanced behind them at Mackey, who was suppressing a smile.

"Me neither," Tom said. "But will you do me a favor? Will you bring her to me when she gets here?"

"Sure."

He turned and strode in through the glass doors into the cooler climate inside the precinct.

The officer at the front desk gave Tom a look. "Help you, sir?"

"Bathroom?"

"Right there."

He'd needed to void his bladder since leaving Bonita Springs. Probably half the reason he'd driven so fast.

After he finished his business and washed up, Tom walked around inside the small station. There was one corridor feeding three rooms. One door was ajar, revealing a set of lockers, one led to the single holding cell. The only other door had to be the interrogation room.

It was drab, one scratched-up table, two chairs, and no windows. A camera hung in the upper corner. He sat down and composed himself, setting out his notepad and pen and audio recorder. When Rhodes walked in with Iowa Schnell a minute later, Tom pursed his lips and remained seated.

Another thing he'd learned growing up: the guys in charge were always sitting down, quiet, waiting for you.

She gave him a wary look as she took her chair across the table. Her hair was frazzled with the humidity — either that or purposely teased to look unkempt. Peroxide blonde, the darker roots showing, the curls reminded Tom of later Meg Ryan years. She had fuller lips than Ryan, though. Eyes light brown instead of blue. Skin deeply tanned. She wore a white tank top over a black sports bra and a ripped pair of blue jean shorts. She set a plastic bag in front of her.

"I gotta be at work in an hour," she said. "Lunch shift starts at noon."

"I appreciate your patience. You work at the diner on 41?"

"Yup."

Rhodes closed the door. He folded his arms and leaned against the wall. He still had his cowboy hat on but the shades dangled from his shirt pocket. His eyes were light blue, so much so that the pupils looked like floating flints of coal. His gaze flitted back and forth between Tom and Iowa Schnell.

"First," Tom began, "let me say I'm very sorry about what happened to your boyfriend, Brian."

"Did you know him?" She pulled a sandwich from the bag and started to unwrap it. Tom thought he smelled pastrami.

"No. But, my condolences," he said.

"Thanks, that's nice." She picked up the food — a feat, considering how long her peach-colored fingernails were — and took a big chomp out of it. She chewed a moment, picked up a napkin with equally impressive dexterity, and wiped her mouth. Her many bracelets clacked together. "Sorry," she said around a mouthful. "I'm so hungry."

"I know you've already gone over all of this—"

"First with the deputies, then with Agent Rhodes. Uh-huh."

"Right. I'm not asking you to rehash everything. That's on tape and I can watch it anyway. Just a few questions and then I'll let you get on your way to work."

"Yup." She tilted her head and took another swift bite.

Tom glanced at his notes. "You told the Sherriff's Department that you met Brian Hamer two months ago, correct?"

She dipped her head in a nod, chewing, then, partly covering her mouth with her hand, looked between the two agents. "How does it work again? There's just so many of you guys. You got agents and troopers and deputies . . ."

"I know. It's complicated. Agent Rhodes and I are with the state bureau."

"That's like FBI?"

"Well — the FBI is federal. But think of us like a mini-FBI, just for the state of Florida."

"Okay. 'Mini-FBI'. I like it." Her eyes flashed, and Tom thought she was flirting.

He shot Rhodes a look but the agent's expression was inscrutable, his pale blue eyes fixed on Iowa Schnell as she destroyed the pastrami sandwich. She paused, tore the cap

136

from a bottle of Snapple Iced Tea, and took a long gulp. Set the bottle on the table and burped. Then she giggled. "Excuse me."

"Not a problem. Now, Miss Schnell—"

"Call me Iowa. I hate the name Schnell. Almost changed it a few times. But then I kept it, on account of the property."

"The property — you mean the trailer on - Chokoloskee Island?"

"No. I bought that. I mean my daddy's place on the river. You know, where the boat was."

She picked up the sandwich again.

"Iowa, can you just pause for a few minutes? Focus on me, if you can, and we'll get through this more quickly. You met Brian two months ago. Where, here?"

"No, on Marco Island." She turned to Rhodes. "You didn't say he was going to be this uptight."

Rhodes said nothing. Iowa pouted and looked over the wreckage of her lunch.

"So you met on Marco Island. Was it exactly two months ago?"

She blinked at him. Then glanced up at the ceiling, as if in thought. "Uhm, eight . . . maybe eight or nine weeks. Better?"

"What were you doing there, on Marco Island?"

"A party."

"You were at a party."

"Mhhmm."

"And he was at the party?"

"That's right, sir." She pulled apart a bag of potato chips and stuck one in her mouth, staring defiantly at him as she chewed.

"Okay. So you meet, and then what?"

"I thought you said . . ." She sighed and rolled her eyes. "Fine. Here it *all is again*. I met Brian, he had a boat, we went on it, we did a little — you know. We partied, we messed around. He was nice."

"Whose party was it?"

"Oh, just some resort. Jenny knew about it. It was on the beach, well, the beach at this swanky resort. They own it, or, I don't know. They were having some anniversary or something."

"And it was open to the public?"

"Hey, I don't ask. Jenny knew someone who knew someone."

Tom thought maybe Jenny looked like Iowa Schnell. It was usually no problem for two women like that to cross the velvet rope.

"I was there for just a couple hours; outside most of the time. I met Brian and he said he had a boat, so we went out on it, stayed out all night. The next morning he asked me if I wanted a ride home. I was like, 'okay.' And then he drove the boat back here. We partied some more until I had to go back to work. When I got *back* from work, he was still around. So I was like, 'Wow, this guy is something.'"

"You mean you liked him? Or what? Thought he was strange?"

She shrugged and poked at her sandwich. "You never know with men."

Tom cleared his throat and shuffled through his papers to the 911 transcript. "When you called emergency services, you thought he'd overdosed. Was Brian a heavy user?"

She glanced at Rhodes as if thinking about whether she had to answer. "Listen, now — I'm not the suspect. I was at work, okay?"

"We know, Iowa," Tom said. "These are just questions; you're helping us understand what Brian was like. Was he a heavy user?"

"Define heavy . . ."

"Weekly. Daily. Did he use cocaine? Pills? Anything else? You said you 'partied'."

Another look at Rhodes, then, to Tom, "I just meant we had some drinks. I don't know if he did anything else, but when I found him like that, he looked like someone who'd overdosed. I mean, didn't he? What happened to him?"

"Still trying to figure that out. Did Brian use his computer a lot?"

"Sure. I guess."

"Do you know what he did for work?"

"Not really. He was into nerdy stuff. That was the part of him I was like, meh. I mean, he fished a little, but he talked about this boring stuff sometimes."

"Could you be more specific?"

She rolled her eyes to the ceiling. "Oh, I don't know. Nerdy computer things."

"Iowa, if you can remember anything at all, it would be very helpful. Details matter."

She sighed. "RF detectors? He was on the phone once, saying — I don't know, maybe frequency . . . something."

"Frequency finders?"

"Maybe."

Tom scribbled some notes. "Did he ever say anything about wireless detection?"

"I don't know."

"What about artificial voice synthesizers?"

"What? Look, I really need to get going."

Tom waited.

"No, I don't know. That was his business. Now can I —"

"Almost done. If you could just go back to when you met him, he had this boat, you guys drove it down here — was he staying on the boat?"

"Look, after we met, I don't know, a couple days later, because Jenny was on shift . . . yeah. So the next day, I asked him if he wanted to come over to my place and stay."

"On Chokoloskee."

"Right. On the island."

"And then what? A few weeks go by . . ."

"Yeah." She shrugged. "You know, we partied, we fucked, we went out on his boat a few times. And when he didn't come home for two days, I went out to the boat and found him like that." She took another chip from the bag and ate it, Tom thought, in a way meant to convey mourning.

"And the spot where he parked the boat — you said your family owns that? The property there?"

"Right. My daddy."

"And where's your daddy?"

Rhodes spoke up for the first time. "Hardee Correctional."

Tom returned his attention to Iowa. "And your mother? Any other siblings around here?"

She shook her head, but didn't elaborate.

"Whose idea was it for him to park his boat there — yours, or his?"

She blinked, and Tom thought she was genuinely fuzzy on the details. Partying, indeed.

"I think it was . . . mine. Yeah. I told him, er, he said we ought to go for a ride, and then I told him about my dad's place down here. Yeah. That was it."

Tom clicked off his pen and folded his arms. He leaned back a little. "Iowa, did Brian ever say anything about someone who might want to hurt him?"

"No."

"How about friends who came to visit him?"

"Not that I know of. Hey, I work six, sometimes seven shifts a week at that shithole. I get done work, sometimes me and Jenny, we go up to Naples, or Marco, I would just go home to Brian. He was sweet." She studied the contents of her gas station purchase some more.

"And he never said anything. About his life, his past, who his friends were, nothing."

"Jesus," she said. She glanced at the impassive Rhodes again, standing there like the Marlboro Man with one boot heel pressed against the wall. "No. Okay? He talked about no one. You're making me feel stupid. Alright?"

Tom uncrossed his arms, held up his hands. "I'm sorry, I don't mean to."

"Well, you do, alright? Making it seem like I was with someone for almost two months and didn't know anything about them. Some people are just *private*, okay? You guys always think people are hiding something from you, maybe they just want their privacy, okay? Don't want you looking in every second, seeing everything they do." She grabbed up her items and stuffed them in the bag. Flakes of lettuce remained behind on the table. Then she stood and glared at Rhodes. "Can I go now?"

Rhodes cut Tom a look.

Tom nodded.

Rhodes barely moved, just extending his arm to push open the door.

Iowa Schnell gave Tom one last glance over her shoulder as she left, her bright hair bobbing, bracelets clanking, remnants of food still on the table. She didn't strike him as a 'private' sort of person, if that was what she'd meant.

CHAPTER EIGHTEEN

The cost per gallon at the local gas station was cheaper than anywhere in Naples or Bonita Springs. Tom stood with the spigot in the gas tank looking into the intersection of 41 and 29.

He pulled out his phone and used one hand to thumb through his contacts. Blythe's voice mail picked up, he listened to it and left a message.

"Blythe — hey, so I'm down here in Big Cypress country. Just talked to Schnell . . . She's an interesting character." The trigger on the spigot popped and Tom returned it to the holster. He switched the phone between his ears and looked up at the communications tower jutting from the Sheriff's Station next door. "Listen, I think Hamer was into something with computers, maybe even counter-surveillance. Makes sense with his history. I'm even thinking — well, maybe we should just talk. Call me back."

He hung up and headed into the gas station convenience store. He'd already swiped his card at the pump but he wanted a pack of smokes.

He looked through the glass wall as the clerk rang up his purchase. Route 41 led back home, 29 stretched on toward Everglades City. One way in, one way out. As he exited the convenience store he saw Agent Rhodes pull into the gas station. Rhodes drove a white Impala with mud splattered on the sides, around the wheel wells and doors.

Tom approached as Rhodes slowed to a stop and rolled down his window. "We doing this or what? It's not every day such a fine upstanding young man as you invites me to lunch."

Tom turned back to the Durango. Called over his shoulder, "I'll follow you."

* * *

The truck-stop diner was only half-full, though it was smack in the middle of the lunch hour. Tom and Rhodes had their pick of a couple tables and chose a booth by the window. Rhodes slid across the seat until he was up against the plate glass overlooking the highway. He lifted his hat, ran a hand through his silvery hair, set the hat back on his head.

Iowa Schnell showed up, preoccupied with the waitress pad she was scribbling in. She snapped her gum and looked up at the agents. "You two again?" She looked the same except she'd tied a grease-stained apron around her waist.

"I'll take a black coffee," Rhodes said.

"Just water," Tom said.

She gave them each a look, snapped her gum again and walked off.

Rhodes watched her go. "There's a lot of beef in that steak."

Tom felt himself grimace. "Please. You could be her father."

"I could be a lot of people's father." Rhodes perched the hat back on his head. "Anyway, she's not my type. Now, Blythe, on the other hand, Blythe's more my speed. For one thing, we're both Southern."

"I thought Southerners didn't consider Florida part of the South."

"The panhandle is. It's more Texas than Florida."

"Is that where you get your accent from?"

"Accent?" Rhodes pulled a face. "What accent?"

"Blythe doesn't have a Southern accent."

"She probably had it driven out of her in the military."

"I don't think that's how it works . . ."

Rhodes shrugged. He settled in, put his leg up on the seat and tipped his hat down like he was going to take a nap.

Iowa returned with their drinks. Tom thought the water looked a little brown. He hadn't even glanced at the menu yet. But Rhodes held up two fingers. "*Dos especiales, por favor.*"

Iowa turned on her heel, writing without looking at her pad, and her swaying hips carried her back through the diner toward the kitchen. The bell rang as an order came up.

"She's not telling us everything," Tom said in a low voice.

"No shit."

"What do you know about counter-surveillance?"

Rhodes dropped his leg down and sat up. He leaned against the table, his blue eyes locking on Tom. "Like what?"

"Frequency finders, bug detectors, wireless camera detectors."

"What do I know? I know it's getting harder every day to put surveillance up on the bad guys and get anything out of it. Plus, down here, you got this family of stone crab fishermen, and they go out onto the water and make their deals, very hard to keep on top of it."

"It's the Vasquez family down here."

"That's right. I mean, this is your county. I'm sure VNB has a moving truck's worth of files on Vasquez. I mean, as a manner of speaking. Most of it's all digital."

"So why are you here?"

"Aside from my charm? I guess I'm here because Everglades City is equidistant to Fort Myers and Miami and I was available."

"How's Miami these days?"

"Gone crazy. Columbia stopped taking down their poppy fields and marine interdiction has just about died. So, yeah, we've taken a greater interest in this little area."

Tom thought about Jack Vance saying drug traffickers were proliferating in southwest Florida. And Coby mentioning counter-surveillance acuity among Palumbo's crew.

"I did a little research and a lot of this counter-surveillance stuff is available online," Tom said. "Companies like Red House Security, Gotcha Tech, there's a few others."

"One thing that's out there," Rhodes said, "called a Brat, this thing scrambles a cell phone location. So you're tracking a guy, you head to Tampa, he's over in Nogales."

Tom nodded. "So, this Brian Hamer was a smart guy. IQ probably somewhere around 160. Managed to defraud the government out of hundreds of thousands of dollars. He evaded the authorities for years. I'm thinking he excelled at counter-surveillance. Not to mention he pretty much lawyered himself out of the whole fraud thing."

"Well, sure. But he wasn't alone. In the lawyering."

"No?"

Rhodes sipped his coffee. "No. He had help. Some ACLU lawyer took an interest in the Fourth Amendment aspect, helped him to file the Motion to Suppress that was enough for the feds to back down. The feds didn't want it to become a huge deal. For one thing, these are methods you don't want the bad guys knowing about. For another, yeah, it's a constitutional gray area. But the courts hadn't caught on yet."

He'd thought the same thing about the FBI letting Hamer off the hook — the feds hadn't wanted use of

StingRays to become more public information than it already was. And they were going ahead where there was no judicial precedent.

"Hamer started to become something of a civil rights crusader after that," Rhodes said. "Kept his real name, though, and I think stayed working above board."

"Yeah, but he was doing something to make a buck. What if he was contracting out services to do a little hacking and spying? Maybe for Palumbo."

Rhodes shrugged. "Yeah, I'm sure. Once a thief, you know? He'd stayed up in Michigan for the rest of his probation, then wound up down here . . . So, right, I see where you're going — Hamer hacked the county jail, had a look at who was coming and going freely through security."

"Yeah. Like that." Tom looked around the diner at the various patrons eating and chatting. Mostly men. Iowa Schnell was hip-swinging her way among the tables, grinning, jawing her gum and revealing eyefuls of thighs and cleavage as she leaned over to pour coffees.

Rhodes sniffed, sat back, put his arm up on the seatback.

Tom asked, "Who was the ACLU lawyer?"

"Uhm, I forget. Indian guy. Ayaan-something. I can look it up for you."

Tom was lost in thought when Iowa slid the two steaming plates in front of the agents. She offered a manufactured smile and asked, "Anything else?"

He looked over the pile of steak, eggs, hash browns and white toast saturated with butter. Enough to stop a heart after the third bite. What had Blythe been saying about taking care of himself? At this rate he'd be looking like Rhodes in five years. He said to Iowa, "Is your friend Jenny here?"

"No. She's off today."

"I'd like to have a look at your place on the island. If it's alright with you."

"Fine." She couldn't get away fast enough. Rhodes gave Tom a glance, waggled his eyebrows, tucked into the food.

CHAPTER NINETEEN

There was Everglades City, which was small, population around four hundred, everything bushy and green but dry, souvenir shops all over, modest homes, and then there was Chokoloskee Island, accessible by taking a long causeway across the bay called Smallwood Drive. The island was quaint, just as dry, like a pancake of floured dough, with many fishing and island-touring charters along its edges. There was one trailer park and it looked out on the ocean. Rhodes pulled in ahead. Tom got out, white dust boiling in the air, the scents of fish and salt water, and walked with Rhodes to a trailer modified to look like a small house.

The agent waved a hand like a *maître d'*. "Here you go." He opened the door, said, "After you," and Tom stepped inside.

Iowa Schnell wasn't much of a housekeeper, her place as messy as Hamer's boat. Rhodes stayed by the door as Tom poked around, moving first into the small bedroom — walled in fake wood panels, the double bed just a mattress and box spring, unmade. The bathroom smelled sweet and sticky with hairspray. Only the kitchen was kept, not a dish in the sink or stain on the counter.

"I had a K-9 unit here," Rhodes said from the doorway. "Found nothing. If there were any drugs, Miss Iowa got rid of them before we were ever here. We took a few of Hamer's personal effects into evidence. Nothing earth-shattering."

Tom checked the cabinets below the sink. "Where's the trash?"

"Say what?"

"Trash. Refuse. The British say 'rubbish'."

Rhodes turned his head to look outside. "The bins all line up over at the road there. I don't think there's any way of determining whose crap is whose though. That's what we call it in Texas. 'Crap.'"

Tom scanned everything one more time then nudged past Rhodes. Back outside, he circled the trailer, which sat on several stacks of concrete blocks for a foundation. He headed for the row of trash bins but detoured toward a pile of junk.

Rhodes caught up as Tom browsed some ragged pieces of corrugated metal, a busted microwave, a battered DVD player. Tom moved on to a stack of cardboard and sifted through it. Postal boxes that had been broken down, some bearing the Amazon smile logo.

"That's the recycling," Rhodes said.

"Why'd you move from Texas to Florida?"

"It's a long story. It begins with a woman, ends with me broke and looking for a job."

"You weren't always dying to be a state cop?"

"My daddy had a ranch outside of Houston. That was my future. I still go back, much as I can."

Tom grabbed the corner of a shiny collapsed box and slipped it from the stack. He rotated it around in the air as Rhodes came closer. "Fusion?" The agent scratched his head.

Tom felt a little rush. "This is a synthetic voice generator. People who can't speak use it." He looked into Rhodes' eyes. "Very possible that the person who called

Heather Moss was using something like this. See here? It comes with phone adapters. You plug it in, then type what you want to say."

Rhodes blinked. "But Hamer was dead by the time Heather Moss got that phone call."

"Right. But I'm thinking he detected the wireless signal from the jail cameras going to the sheriff, hacked in, found out about Heather Moss's easy access. This is a guy who knows his tech. Someone hired him to get all this stuff, to do this. Then they killed him and got Heather Moss to finish the job on Declan. We need to look at Hamer's laptop history."

"Already on it. Where to next, Columbo?"

"Please don't call me that. Well, okay. If you must."

* * *

Ten minutes later Lange was stepping aboard the fifty-foot schooner where Brian Hamer had died. The deck looked like it had on the video: neglected, as if no one who'd boarded in the past few months was doing any real fishing or chartering, just keeping up appearances to that effect. The bait was bits of dead fish, desiccated in the sun, smelling something awful.

"We ran the hull identification and vessel registration numbers," Rhodes said. "The boat was registered seven weeks ago at the local tax collector's office in Marco Island. Proof of ownership came from a place called Aquatropics — they sell new and used boats. Mostly fishing boats. This one was used. Way used."

Tom squeezed down the narrow stairs beneath the pilothouse into the living quarters below. Everything about it was claustrophobic — low ceilings, small porthole windows. Smelled bad in there, too. Like death.

The bed where Hamer was found had been stripped to the mattress, but his fluids had soaked through and stained the blue-striped fabric. Everything had been photographed and documented; still, Tom wore plastic gloves as he moved around the cramped space.

In the tiny bathroom — Rhodes called it a "bulkhead" — Tom opened the medicine cabinet and peered inside. There was a near-empty bottle of *Pepto Bismol,* an aid for stomach troubles. Some Aspirin, a heavily-used toothbrush, a couple of Q-Tips.

"The techs didn't take this stuff to the ROC?"

Rhodes stuck his head in the doorway. "They got the sheets, mud on the carpeting, blood on the walls, dusted it, the whole nine yards."

"Yeah well, they missed the trash at Iowa's trailer, and look what we found. Let's bag this stuff. You got any bags?"

Rhodes just gave Tom a look.

"Come on," Tom said. "You got anything we could put these toiletries in?"

Rhodes slipped out of the doorway and Tom heard him climb the stairs and leave the boat, mumbling as he went.

Tom stepped out of the bulkhead and continued to rummage around in the main quarters, pulling out the drawers of a small dresser bolted to the wall. He poked around at some underwear and socks, then found a couple of blank postcards, both from Marco Island. A beaded necklace, a bottle of cologne, a hair brush, a belt, some swim trunks faded from years of use.

There were dirty dishes in the sink nearby. A pot with dried-up noodle remnants congealed inside. Two cabinets above the sink — dishes and a wooden box inside. He pulled out the wooden box, shook it gently, heard the cutlery clattering inside. He put it back and closed the cabinets, saw more drawers beneath the blood-stained bed.

Tom got down on his knees and pulled the drawers out. Each one was empty. But the way the bed was built, he thought there was more hollow space in the drawer housing. He set each drawer aside and clicked on his pen light, bent and looked around in the space.

He heard Rhodes clomping back down the stairs behind him.

"There," Rhodes said. He'd brought a small evidence bag with him. "I'm pretty proud of myself, I have to admit, keeping these in my — what have you got?"

"Nothing."

Tom got back to his feet. They bagged up the items and Rhodes left. Tom looked around the small space one last time, trying to see it with fresh eyes, thinking about Mario Palumbo going through all this trouble to get Howard Declan — and then also thinking about a serial killer who targeted men.

But that was a long shot, at best. What else linked the men besides the ostensible poisoning? His vibrating phone interrupted his train of thought. Blythe.

"Hey," Tom said, "where have you been?"

"I've been to Declan's and then I was with Matt, going through his laptop. Tom, we got something."

Her voice held a tremor he didn't like.

"What?"

"Declan's computer drive looked like someone tried to wipe it. But Matt found a way to retrieve the data . . . turns out it's loaded with child pornography. Mostly pictures, a couple videos."

Tom felt heavy. He leaned against the small counter. "No shit — Declan? Was he making the stuff? Or just consuming?"

"No evidence on this machine he was making anything, probably consuming only. Anyway, I got your message. And I'm thinking you might be on to something with Hamer's involvement, with hacking and counter-surveillance. Maybe someone finds out about Declan, what he's doing, and then goes after him by hiring Hamer? Hamer then hacks the jail CCTV, finds out about Heather Moss getting it easy going through security, uses her to give Declan the suicide pill. Then they retire Hamer's services."

Tom's gaze landed on the stained mattress as he absorbed Blythe's theory.

Rhodes thumped down the stairs, on his own phone call.

"Hang on a sec, Blythe." Tom nodded at Rhodes.

"I'm on with the computer tech from Miami ROC," Rhodes said. "Hamer's hard drive has been totally wiped. Tech thinks there was probably a program used which is kind of like a self-destruct. She tried to salvage it, but it's not looking good."

With Rhodes crammed in the small space alongside Tom, two conversations ongoing, the walls started to close in. Tom squeezed past Rhodes, up the stairs and out into the fresh air.

"Did you hear what Rhodes said?"

"I heard."

"Alright," Tom said. "Sounds like someone tried to wipe Declan's hard drive the same way, but it didn't work?"

"I don't know," Blythe said.

"I'm on my way back. See you in a bit."

"Drive safe."

Tom pulled his pack of smokes from the Durango and lit up. Rhodes ambled over.

"Can I get one of those?"

With both of them puffing, Tom gazed at the boat bobbing in the water. Beyond it was a bend in the river, several smaller creeks branching into the mangrove. The boat was in need of a paint job, bulky, not the kind of watercraft typical of Everglades City, airboat tours and fishing charters. Brian Hamer's boat was moored on property owned by Ned Schnell, Iowa's incarcerated father. There was an old airboat sitting above the ground on railroad ties a few yards away with *Jungle Ned* in faded letters.

Tom inhaled the smoke, tried to calm his nerves.

"Blythe said Declan's laptop had child pornography on it."

"Ah, Jesus."

"So what have we got? Someone who goes after an extortionist and a pedophile?"

"Well, that, or you're looking at it the wrong way. Could be Hamer is behind the whole thing, he found out about Declan, decided to kill him, and *he's* the one who hired out someone to threaten Heather, carry the whole thing out."

Tom shook his head. "I don't think so. He offs himself before he gets the satisfaction of seeing Declan dead? No, I think there's someone we don't know about yet, pulling the strings."

"Huh." Rhodes mashed his used-up smoke in the dirt with a boot heel, doffed his cowboy hat and smoothed back his silver hair. "Let's go." Rhodes started towards his vehicle. "I got some calls to make, a shit ton of paperwork."

Tom kept smoking, staring at the boat. "Hamer's laptop was wiped, but Declan's still had all the incriminating data . . ."

"Yeah? Well, see there you go. Because Hamer was saying, 'Look at this guy.'"

"They tried to wipe it."

"Maybe, or could have just deleted the browsing history, moved things into the trash, make it look that way, easy for cops to find. 'Look at this guy,' they're saying, 'he deserves to die.' Shit, I don't know, maybe he did. Or maybe this thing is just what it looks like: it's Mario Palumbo using this guy Declan to fuck up Edgar Vasquez's car, killing him. Then Palumbo takes Declan out. Either way, this Declan guy sounds like a sick son of a bitch."

Tom was staring at the overwater bungalow, he'd go through that next. "Well, maybe he deserved to be arrested and tried, but no one has the right to dispense their own justice like that."

Rhodes' eyes seemed to grow a shade darker. "Yeah, okay. You wait until you've been doing this job a few more years."

"What? Then I'll learn to disregard the law, you're saying?"

"Oh for Christ's sake . . ."

Rhodes marched back to the vehicle, boots crunching the grit. Tom heard the door slam. He didn't move. He just took another drag, then dropped the smoldering butt to the ground, started toward the bungalow.

"We went through all that!" Rhodes called.

Tom kept going. Heard Rhodes bang out of the vehicle again, cursing. "That place is about ready to collapse, Lange. Nothing in there. Try walking around, you're liable to fall through the floorboards, and the alligators will fucking eat you."

CHAPTER TWENTY

Rhodes had been right, not much in the bungalow but some discarded lumber, a few old buoys, sun-faded and peeling. A hole in the floor. Tom looked down and swore he saw an alligator just beneath the murky surface, like Rhodes said, waiting for him to drop though.

He took the Durango and headed north, grateful to see the miles of mangrove receding in the rear-view mirror, found his thoughts wandering to Katie. In the rush of the past couple days, he hadn't been able to focus on the fact that she'd split up with him.

Two weeks ago they'd been having dinner at Buffalo Chips, a spot close to his condo. Charming place, if you liked dimly lit and coated in grease, the walls crowded with funky decorations like license plates and snake skins. Most of the dinner had passed without talking, then Katie had brought up a past relationship. She'd seen a guy for a few months who'd worked in the DA's office.

"First I thought, you know, it was just cops that suffered from emotional unavailability. But it's not. It's just some people."

"Emotional unavailability?"

She'd given him a look like he knew exactly what she was talking about — maybe he had.

Halfway to Naples, his phone vibrated. His first hope was that it was Katie.

You're very persistent, Agent Lange.

Tom slammed on the brakes and pulled the Durango off onto the shoulder. The raised dirt was billowing around the car as he typed a return message.

Who is this?

A few seconds elapsed and the phone vibrated with a new text from the same 945 number.

I know all about you.

Tom stared off into the thick wall of vegetation alongside the road. His heart hammered, his hands shook with adrenaline. *I know all about you.* What did that mean? He didn't like it. At the same time, this could be a major break.

He punched out a response: *What do you want?*

He waited again, trying to remain calm, breathing deep through his nose. There was no reply. Instead, his phone chirped and read, *Message failed to send.*

Shit.

Somewhere, he imagined, there was a room. Filled with monitors, phones, frequency finders and wireless detectors. A type of high-tech doomsday bunker. Someone was sitting there, at the controls, but Tom couldn't see his face.

* * *

Tom found Agent Culpepper in the hallway, standing guard outside Heather's hotel room. He'd had the drive to think and ease himself down, but his adrenaline level was still high.

I know all about you.

Could be a bluff, could be nothing, or maybe it only referred to him, personally. But it might mean Heather and the girls, their whereabouts.

"Evening," Culpepper said.

Tom kept his voice down. "Everybody okay?"

Culpepper sensed something was off. "They're the same as they were when you called a half hour ago — what's going on?"

"How did they do today?"

"Good." The agent seemed to let it go, then referred to a spiral notebook he was holding. "Two trips to the pool, and that's about it. Lots of cartoons, sounded like a fight between the girls at one point, little one crying for a good fifteen minutes straight. Amazing. I don't know how people do it."

"I'll be in my room." Tom started toward the door, eager to have a shower, grab a moment, when he heard Heather come out of her room.

"I thought I heard voices," she whispered. "Can we talk?"

"Of course. Come on in."

He used the key card and held the door for Heather. "How was your day?"

Heather stopped in the center of the room and turned. Tom watched her as he set down his bag on the bed. He could already see it on her face before she spoke.

"I'm sorry — this is crazy. I don't know how much more of it I can handle. We're cooped up in here; it's only been two days." She sat down in the chair and ran shaky fingers through her hair. "I know this is for our own good, but it's just — it's not sustainable. Isn't there a house or something? Somewhere with a backyard?"

Tom sat on the bed and rubbed his knees a moment. "I know this is not ideal for you, for two young girls. But it looks like things are changing on our end anyway."

"What do you mean?"

"I mean this, all this, is conditional, like I said before. And I'm afraid it's not looking like we're able to meet those conditions."

She cocked an eyebrow. "You can't prove that this guy Palumbo was behind what happened to me."

"We're working as hard as we can. But you're right. I can't prove it."

"Have there been any other — I don't know — breaks in the case?"

He thought about telling her about the 945 call but decided against it.

"I've been going over this all day," Heather said, "running through a list of old clients in my head. Even back to New York. Someone who might have been pissed off. Lost their kids or their jobs, or went to jail because of me. And I mean, I think I'm a good therapist. But that stuff happens. I had a client once say they wanted to kill me. And I reported it, right away, to the police." She gave him a long look, the desperation swimming in her eyes, then she blinked. "I'm rambling, sorry. I haven't really had another adult to talk to all day and I'm crawling out of my skin."

"It's okay. I know this is hard." But he was glad to hear it — maybe her earlier reluctance to name anyone came from her professional obligations to confidentiality.

He rose and took a bottle of water from the fridge. He offered her one but she declined. After a swallow, he said, "There's been another murder. I've just come from the death scene."

She frowned. "At the jail?"

"Somewhere else."

"But you think it's connected?"

"It looks like it. Same type of death. And the victim might have owned a Fusion — that's a device to manufacture a voice. You ever heard of Brian Hamer?"

She shook her head. "I haven't. Who is he?"

"He had a fairly high-profile case about ten years ago. It took a lot to find him and bring him in. He was offered legal counsel, *pro bono*. An ACLU lawyer, but there were possibly others he reached out to while he was building his case. And he got out."

She just stared back, then it was her turn to stand. She paced the room. "This is . . . I don't know what this is. So this guy was after *me*? Why? I don't understand."

"Well, we don't know *who* the target is for sure. You and Declan are connected by what happened. But one of you is the constant, the other is the variable. Meaning, maybe someone wanted to get rid of Declan and used whatever means they could."

"I thought you said that was doubtful because they waited until he was in jail?"

"Well, doubtful that Palumbo waited until he was in jail. But it could have been someone else."

"Someone after Declan. Nothing to do with me."

"I wish I could say for sure. For now, it's open to question."

She slowly sat down on the bed again, her expression haunted.

"Going through these old clients in your head," he said, "that's a good idea. Think about anyone who would want to upset your life."

She nodded, and stared off into the room.

"Maybe you could write the names down?" he asked. "If someone threatened you, that releases you from confidentiality, doesn't it? Who was the man you reported?"

"It was a woman. Forty-eight years old, living with her aged mother. They had rats in their home. She told me about them and I notified the local Sheriff's Department. There were rats everywhere. They removed the both of them and put the mother in a home. The next time I saw her, she blamed me. Said she wanted to see me die. And I reported it. They came and they got her and they took her away, too."

"Is that why you came down to Florida?"

Heather wrinkled her forehead. "That was a long time ago. Glenn was still alive. No, I came down to Florida for other reasons."

"Can you tell me something about those reasons?"

Heather stood and walked to the window. She pushed aside the curtain and looked down the ten stories to the swamp stretching into the distance. She sighed. "Glenn and I were very happy. He was everything to us. It was just the three of us; me and him and Olivia — she'd just been born when we found out about his condition."

She let the curtains close, turned and stared into the corner a moment.

"It's . . . you know. It's just like they say, but it's a totally different thing to live it. Have you ever lost someone?"

"I have."

She studied his face, then nodded. "So you know. But then, to be diagnosed with something like that — and we had hope; they tell you that if you catch Hodgkin's early, you can beat it, and we caught it early. So we just, you know, kept living life. I got pregnant again. And then — Glenn was fighting for his life while his second child was coming into the world."

"I'm sorry."

"He saw Abigail born, and then he died. She was three weeks old. One day he was holding his baby in his arms, the next day the hospital was calling me and saying he was gone."

She sat down on the bed again. "You know, I've been so angry. I didn't know what to do for a long time, I just went through the motions. Those poor girls . . ." She looked at the wall, as if envisioning her daughters sleeping on the other side of it. Then she shrugged. "I just decided we needed to make a change."

She drew a deep breath and let it slowly out. He resisted the impulse to comfort her, pick her up out of the chair and put his arms around her.

"I couldn't take it anymore. Everyone at work. My parents. Our friends. The look on their faces. It was just too much."

"I understand," Tom said, thinking about leaving Naples. "And how did you pick Florida?"

Her gaze traveled to the carpeted floor and her brows drew together in another pensive expression. "Partly it was just impulse — get as far away as possible. And Glenn's friend, Robert, was down here."

"Your lawyer."

"Yeah."

"That's why? Are you very close?"

"No, that's not why. He's not why. He suggested it, and it was so radical it just seemed . . . I was lost. I'd stayed with my parents for a while, but I had to make a change, and while the girls were still young. I didn't want to wait and transition them after they had friends and everything. Olivia started school here. You don't know how . . . well, you might. You might know what it does to you, how you can't focus. I knew I wasn't going to last in New York. That if I stayed there, I'd lose it completely."

Heather got back to her feet. "I'm not sure if that helps you at all. And I'm sure you have things to do." She crossed to the door and Tom followed, reeling from her abrupt change in mood.

He unlocked the door and she stepped over the threshold.

"Your insights were right about Howard Declan," he said suddenly. "You thought he had a secret. He did."

Her eyes lit up. "What secret?"

"He was doing some very bad things. That's all I can say right now."

"And that's why you're thinking it's possible he was the target after all?"

Tom nodded.

After she thought for a moment, Heather said, "Unfortunately, that doesn't make it any better. Whether he was into something bad or not."

He nodded. "No, I guess it doesn't."

She started away then stopped again. "This is the craziest thing I've ever been involved in. And I've always been able to land on my feet. I don't mean to say I'm some kind of great person. But I've been able to deal with a lot." She searched his eyes. "You're going to figure this out, right? I'm going to be able to rebuild my life? Again?"

"That's what I'm trying to do."

Her look lingered. Then she lowered her eyes and walked away. Culpepper escorted her the few feet to her door and she disappeared into the entryway without looking back.

* * *

"The VCDC reviewed the request for protection," Turnbull said on the hotel room phone. "They're turning us down."

"We still have a few hours." Tom sat wrapped in a towel, his hair wet from the shower.

"Lange, Bob Mandi hasn't rescinded his endorsement, they've just rejected it, flat out. They'll reimburse up to this point. But there's no compelling evidence that this is Mario Palumbo."

"We found child pornography on Declan's laptop. Someone could have been after him."

"Right, but who? The connection to Brian Hamer is there, but if he's the assailant, he's dead. And if he's not, we're miles from knowing, let alone being able to prove, who is. In the meantime, we can keep an eye on Heather, but no wit-pro."

Tom stood, feeling angry, clenching his towel closed. "Someone threatened her *children*. And whoever it is, is still out there. Blythe told you about the text I got tonight?"

"She did. And you've turned in your phone, and we'll work on it. But, listen, Lange, the witness protection program is funded for a hundred grand. Supplies are running low and reimbursement is a state legislature thing. The money is just not there. I'm sorry."

"What about the security detail? I've got a dozen agents here."

"I've just pulled them out. Except for the position on the top floor, outside of the witness's room."

He meant Culpepper. Tom felt like he was running out of moves. He didn't want to be insubordinate, but he really worried for Heather and her daughters and it made him grasping, desperate. Without witness protection they were vulnerable. Either to Palumbo or to this new player in the game. "What am I supposed to do with them? Send them home?"

"I'm doing everything I can. Between our agents and Everglades County, we can keep someone posted for weeks. For as long as it takes . . ."

Tom was shaking his head. "They're not going back there." He recalled the dark SUV rolling slowly past Heather's house on the sun-drenched street. The tip of the rifle sticking out of the window. The bullets raking the house and car.

"What about friends in the area? Any family?"

Tom sighed and sat back on the bed. "She has parents in upstate New York, a brother in Nevada, but she hasn't even spoken to them about this yet. She seems pretty isolated."

"There's got to be someone."

Tom wanted a cigarette. He pulled on his pants as Turnbull spoke. "Listen, you like Culpepper? You know him from Governor Protection, yeah? You two worked together?"

Tom slipped a t-shirt over his head and put the phone back to his ear. "Sure. Yeah, I like him."

"Then Culpepper stays with you. And the room is already paid for another couple days."

"Thank you, sir."

"Hang in there, Lange. We'll figure this one out."

Tom hung up. Sat staring at his bag in the closet, then pulled it out. He dressed, strapped into his shoulder holster, checked his Glock, slipped it in.

Then he made another phone call.

CHAPTER TWENTY-ONE

He slipped out of the room and nodded to Culpepper, who leaned against the wall, checking his phone. Tom waved a pack of cigarettes so the agent could see it, then pressed the button for the elevator.

Outside, the night sky was mostly clear, several bright stars flickering. A few ragged clouds slid across the dark sky, slipping over the moon.

You're very persistent, Agent Lange.

Tom circled the hotel perimeter, keeping watch on all the cars, anticipating movement inside any one of them.

Halfway around to the front entrance, he passed alongside the swamp. The cypress tree line was about fifty yards away from the parking lot curb.

He froze, hearing something crackling through the undergrowth.

I know all about you.

More crackling sounds and something trampled the brush, then a splash as it encountered water. His heart knocked against the breastplate of his Kevlar vest and he tried to steady his breathing. The swamp fell silent, but for the chorus of insects and small reptiles chirruping in the dark.

A vehicle approached, a throaty engine gurgling in the damp night. Tom broke out of his trance and resumed moving toward the front of the hotel, jogging now, keeping close to the building. He slowed as he neared the corner, saw a Chevy Camaro turn into the parking lot.

The Camaro found a spot near the entrance, and Sergeant Danny Coburn got out.

Tom released a pent-up breath and stepped into the open.

Coburn was dressed in civvies, jeans, and a t-shirt advertising University of Florida — *Go Gators!* He saw Tom, made a nod, then ducked back into the car for something before he strode over, his boots making crisp sounds on the asphalt.

"Evening, Lange."

"Thanks for coming."

Coburn frowned. "You in trouble, huh? Word is your wit protection has fallen through."

"Word travels fast." Tom hadn't said anything to Coburn about it on the phone, just asked him to meet.

Coburn glanced up at the lit windows of the hotel. "She's got a couple of young ones, you said?"

"Two little girls."

Coburn hooked his thumbs through the pockets of his jeans. Tom glanced at the black holster clipped to his belt, the pistol grip protruding. Tom remembered seeing Coburn's own family at the beach, a couple of girls among them.

"So, what's up?" Coburn asked.

"I wanted to ask you about something you said, yesterday, about Declan."

"Okay . . ."

"You said that you never had him under direct surveillance."

Coburn cut Tom a look, then gazed off toward the dark wall of pine and cypress. "You're a smart kid. Bit cocky, but that'll change. I liked you on that Gallo case and I told you there was a place for you with vice narcotics, but it looks like you found your way back to where you wanted to be."

"I don't know if where I am right now is where I want to be. I feel like there's a lot of moving parts, and I'm not sure what connects and what doesn't."

Coburn nodded. "You'll have that. Sounds about right. You know, this shit is like a war. And in war, you might make some mistakes. But you're looking out for your buddies. You gotta draw the line somewhere. And you gotta ask yourself how much good you're doing. And if the answer is, at the end of the day, you think you're making the world safer, then . . ." He shrugged. "Then you gotta do what you gotta do to stay in the game."

Tom felt something cold stirring in his gut. He recalled Rhodes saying, too, that opinions changed with experience. He pulled out a cigarette, lit up and watched Coburn through the rising smoke. "What are you talking about, Coby?"

Coburn pulled a tin of chewing tobacco from his pocket, took a pinch between his thumb and forefinger and tucked it behind his lower lip.

Tom watched as Coburn stuffed the tin in his back pocket. "Hard candies not doing the trick anymore?"

"Yeah, I can see you've quit smoking."

Tom held up his hands in innocence. "Hey, I'm commiserating, not judging."

"So, look. We've had Palumbo on a wiretap for two years. Longest case of my life, I'm working sixteen-hour days. But he's always changing it up. Different guys coming and going. And we know he's talking to Vasquez, because we've got eyes on Vasquez, too."

"You think this thing, all this, could be Vasquez's people? Getting back at Palumbo?"

"Timing is off for that. Listen to what I'm saying — we're watching, we're working our C.I.s, but these guys are throwing surveillance, and then we find out that Palumbo and Vasquez are meeting. So, we come in with the StingRay, just before Edgar Vasquez dies. We said fuck it; we've got to have a look at this whole thing."

"But you can't use that information," Tom said. "You can't get a warrant for bulk-data collection. Is that what you're talking about?"

"We do what it takes to get the work done, get the bad guys put away. The politicians, the law-makers, they struggle to keep up. Everybody wants to uphold the Constitution. I want to. So no, we don't use the StingRay information directly."

"My understanding," Tom said, "is that because a StingRay casts a wide net when it mimics a cell tower, it picks up every phone in range. And that's the violation of third-party privacy, the Fourth Amendment issue. The laws aren't in lock-step with the tech, but things eventually change, get caught up, right? We have to be patient."

Coburn's eyebrows went up and he spat to the side. "You're not giving me advice, are you, Lange?"

"I'm just telling you what I understand."

Coburn looked away. "You know, I came here to . . . aww, fuck it." He started walking back to his Camaro.

Tom caught up, tossing his cigarette. "Ah, man, hang on . . ."

The big vice cop turned on his heel and drove a finger into Tom's chest. "When you see the shit I've seen, the shit half these cops out here have seen, and the fucking bad guys who slip through the cracks, you might change your tune."

Tom glanced at the finger. "Easy, Coby."

Coburn just glared, then his expression broke up into a big smile, and he laughed. "You're a fucking piece of work. I heard about you, you know. Blythe said you're ashamed of your own past; you think you're white trash or something and you get all revved up trying to prove you're not. You're ready to fucking go toe-to-toe with the world, right? A warrior for justice. You hide behind your bullshit, Lange, but you're the same as anyone else."

Tom bristled with adrenaline but kept cool. "Why don't you just talk to me straight. You agreed to meet me; you know something."

The smile evaporated and Coburn gritted his teeth. He outweighed Tom by fifty pounds. Tom's heart hammered against his ribs. "Fine. You wanna know? CID came in and did their interviews with witnesses after Vasquez was last seen at the restaurant at the dog track. And we talk to CID, and we share what information we can, we try to work together. Everybody knows he was meeting with Palumbo, that Palumbo wanted the action Vasquez had going on. We got pictures of them, we put Vasquez up on surveillance for a while, but he slipped it. Then we used the StingRay. Declan was there."

Tom absorbed it. "Okay. Declan was at the track, gambling or something, and the StingRay got his phone data. Is that right? Then, what, that's how you learned he was working for Palumbo?"

Coburn stared off a moment, not responding.

"Did you find evidence that Declan was involved with the sabotage of Vasquez's vehicle, but couldn't act on it?"

Finally, Coburn answered. "No. What we got from his phone was something else." Coburn spat to the side, said, "This guy had child pornography in his emails."

"Okay. Well, we found that, too. So — what did you do?"

Coburn stared back, silent. Some of the anger faded from his eyes and he leaned back a bit, watching Tom closely.

Tom had to ask: "Did you act on this information somehow?"

Coburn turned his head to the side and spat another brown stream. He fished the tobacco out of his mouth and threw it away, wiped his mouth with the back of his hand and turned toward the Camaro. "Forget it, Lange." Coburn opened the car door, sank into the driver's seat.

"Coby . . ."

The big man cranked the engine, the Camaro roared to life. He spoke out the open window. "*I* didn't act on it, Lange; someone else got a hold of it."

"Got a hold of it? How?" But Tom thought he already knew.

Coburn dropped the shifter into drive and faced forward. "We were hacked, Lange. This whole thing started with us."

Tom grabbed the door, leaned in. "You mean, you've got all this private information on people — and someone came in and swiped it?"

"Get your hand off the car."

"When? When did this happen?"

"About six weeks ago. Now let go."

Tom pointed at the hotel behind him. "What about that woman? And her little girls? You've got a family, Coby, that's why you're here. Whoever took Declan's information from you, the evidence of what was in his phone, his emails, they used it. I don't know how, but— Were you able to trace the hack?"

Coburn slammed his hands on the steering wheel. "You think I haven't done everything I can? It's a whole new world out there. We gain a little ground, we get something new that can help us, then the courts are working against us, the public gets outraged — meanwhile these fucking guys out here on the street get to use that technology all day long. And they're getting better. They're better at it than we are because we have all the rules, and they have none."

"Okay . . ." Tom's pulse was racing but he tried to calm down, calm Coburn down. "I understand. You tried. But someone got access to all this information. And now they're using it. They're using it and there's a woman and her daughters caught in the middle."

Coburn turned back to Tom, and there was genuine concern in his eyes. "What happened to her, or those little girls, has *nothing* to do with me." He looked out the windshield again. "I shouldn't have fuckin' come . . ."

"No, you should have. I'm glad you did."

"That's all I can say. Let go of the car, I have to go."

"We've got to bring this to Blythe, to Turnbull . . ."

"No."

"No?" Tom felt the anger flaring. "You've unwittingly given up court-protected surveillance on civilians. Did Palumbo's people hack you? Or Vasquez's? I need something on him, Coby, or she's out on the street with her girls!"

Coburn slammed the shifter back into park and opened the door so fast Tom stumbled back. Then the big vice cop grabbed Tom by the shirt and threw him against the side of the Camaro. Tom had to suppress every instinct to fight back.

Coburn breathed heavily, the lingering odor of his tobacco blasting up Tom's nostrils. He slowly released his grip, and Tom slid down the side of the Camaro, his weight returning to the ground.

"We don't know," Coburn said at last. "They didn't leave any fucking trace. But I can tell you I don't think it was Palumbo — we didn't have anything incriminating Declan in that way. He just looks like some guy who went to the track a lot, gambled, was sick in the head, that's it."

"Then who? Vasquez?"

"Maybe."

"Coby, what about someone inside? One of us? Someone who found out about Declan and wanted to go where the law couldn't?"

Coburn was still upset. He'd turned bright red in the face. He coughed a few times like he was having trouble breathing, then shoved Tom aside and opened the door to the Camaro again.

"Coby — you alright?"

This time Tom didn't try to stop him. He couldn't have, anyway. The vehicle leapt away a second later, tires squawking.

Tom watched it race out of the parking lot, then turn onto the highway and speed away. The big engine faded into the night and the sounds of insects in the neighboring swamp gradually filled the void.

Then, ripping through the silence — the unmistakable screech of tires, followed by a metal-shredding crash.

CHAPTER TWENTY-TWO

The blood sang in Tom's ears. He sprinted across the lawn between the parking lot and the highway. It was late and the road was quiet, the streetlights throwing crisscrossing cones of light over the asphalt.

In the distance, the traffic light turned red. On the other side of the intersection, the Camaro was off the road. There was a second car beside it, the front crumpled, hood smoking.

Tom's lungs burned and he panted for breath. Almost there. Someone was trying to get out of the second vehicle, a white compact car. They were shoving their weight against the door, the metal groaning until they got it open and staggered out into the street. A young woman with blood running from her scalp. She blinked and looked around at the accident.

There was no movement in the Camaro.

Tom reached the woman and took gentle hold of her. "Are you alright?"

She seemed disoriented. But she blinked and stared at the Camaro. "They just swerved right into me . . ."

"Sit down, okay. Over here."

Tom walked her to the other side of the road. Some cars were coming through now, drivers ogling the scene, slowing. Tom waved them through and sat the woman down in the grass, well away from the asphalt. "Just stay right here, okay? Ambulance is on the way. What's your name?"

"Terri."

"Terri. You feel okay? Feel sick to your stomach?"

She shook her head. "My head hurts. The air bag deployed." She raised her arm and showed him a red mark. "My hand, too. I think I hit it. I don't know. They just swerved. Right into me."

"Terri, I need your phone. Do you have a phone?"

She dug it out and handed it over. He dialed 911, gave his shield number, the location, describing the scene in bursts: "Officer involved. Send paramedics. Contact Special Agent Blythe."

He handed it back to her.

"Thanks. Okay. Just sit tight."

He ran back toward the Camaro, picking his way through more slowing vehicles.

He stopped in the middle of the highway when he saw one of them was a black SUV. The chrome on the rear hatch spelled Tahoe.

"Hey!" Tom pulled his gun. "Hey — *fuck*   stop! Florida State Police!" He jogged toward the vehicle, aiming the gun down.

The SUV jerked forward and raced away, lurching to pass other vehicles in its way. Tom ran faster, caught sight of two numbers and a letter: 18-E. It hooked around a bend, squealing the tires, slipped out of sight.

Tom slowed, stopped, put the Glock in its holster. He returned to the Camaro, found Coburn inside. Coburn looked dead. But not from the accident.

"Oh, Jesus."

He yanked open the door and Danny Coburn flopped halfway out of the car. There was vomit on the steering wheel, and some on his shirt. A thin tendril of blood threaded from his nose. His arms slipped off his chest and his hand landed in the grass.

There was a round shape in Coburn's breast pocket. His tin of chewing tobacco.

* * *

The female motorist was loaded into the back of an ambulance. There were cops everywhere — local PD out of Orangetree, plus highway patrol and few from County.

"Agent Lange?"

A state trooper was asking Tom questions, but he'd already told them everything he knew. He looked off at the hotel rising out of the night, a quarter mile away. He hadn't seen the Tahoe again, but he wanted to get back to Heather Moss right away.

"Like I said, tell the ME he needs to look for poison. Potassium cyanide, or something similar. I gotta go."

"Aren't you going to—?"

Tom glanced at the Camaro one more time. The troopers first on scene had cordoned off the area as per Tom's request. Coburn still hung halfway out of the vehicle, crime scene tape flapping in the breeze around him. Then Tom ran.

They'd been very careful to make sure all food coming into Heather's hotel room was safe. No ordering take-out, nothing from outside the hotel, only food prepared in the kitchen downstairs, overseen by an agent. But now the agents were gone. Heather could order a midnight snack. Or the killer could try to get to her in another way.

Because they seemed to be picking off everyone surrounding the case, anyone who knew or might've known who they were. And Heather Moss, whether she was aware or not, could be one of those people. She'd certainly been in close proximity to Declan. Tom believed in Heather, but she might not have told him every detail about her interaction with Declan, what he might have told her. The killer could still be after her.

He reached the hotel, winded again. Instead of going through the main entrance he circled around to the rear loading dock and hurried up the ramp, shoved his way through a cluster of empty laundry bins. The door was locked. He used the key he'd been given by the hotel manager and slipped inside.

At this late hour, the kitchen was semi-dark and quiet, redolent of spoiled food and grease. One man in a greasy apron was mopping an area near tall chrome refrigerators. He glanced at Tom, who had his badge ready. "Anyone order something for room 702?"

The cook moved toward a huge, cast iron range dominating the room. A couple of yellow tickets hung over the line, rattling in the air sucked up a massive exhaust fan. "No, nothing for 702."

Tom pushed through another door and into a service hallway. From there he stepped into the stairwell.

The door banged shut behind him, the sound reverberating. He started up. Stopped on the second floor when a door above him opened and closed.

Footsteps scratched over the concrete stairs.

Tom stayed pressed against the wall, breathing shallow, hearing his heart beat in his ears.

Another door slammed. No more footsteps. He continued on up.

Just before the fourth floor, he skidded to a stop when the door opened again. A man in a bathrobe held a bucket. The man went white as a sheet and stared down at Tom, half a flight below him, and at the gun in Tom's grip.

"Ice machine is out, uh, on my floor."

"Sorry."

The hotel guest moved down the stairs, grimacing as he passed Tom, spared one last nervous look before opening the third-floor door.

Tom continued up. Reached the top floor and rounded the corner, found Culpepper still surfing the internet on his phone, oblivious to the chaos outside.

CHAPTER TWENTY-THREE

"We're going?" Culpepper's eyes got wide.

"We're going," Tom said.

He started into his room, and Culpepper caught up to him. "Hey — everybody got pulled this evening except me. We lost the wit-pro?"

Culpepper looked Tom up and down, worry hardening his boyish features. "You're bleeding, Lange. And you look like you just ran a marathon. What the hell is happening?"

Tom noticed his pants were dirty, bits of mud and grass clung to his shoes. The bandage on his hand was flapping loose. "What's happening is we were denied funding. And with the security detail gone, someone could move in on us."

"Who? Something happen out there?" Culpepper started away, as if to the windows at the end of the hallway.

"Damien, the hotel isn't safe. People know we're here."

"You gonna call the ROC? Speak to Turnbull?"

"Already did; he's working on it. But his hands are tied. He's got the assistant commissioner to deal with."

"I don't get it. She's clearly in danger."

"Exactly. And that's all that matters."

Culpepper seemed to weigh all of this as his eyes wandered the hallway. Then he nodded. "Alright. Let's get them out of here."

Tom clamped a hand on Culpepper's shoulder. "Let me borrow your phone."

He slipped into his room and stripped out of his clothes, threw the filthy bandage in the trash, dressed in clean clothes, packed up his computer and a hold-all of files. Before leaving, he moved aside the curtain and looked out at the emergency lights blazing in the distance. He couldn't believe Coburn was dead.

He keyed in Blythe's number.

"Lauren?"

"Tom? Whose phone is this?"

"I'm getting Heather and the girls out. It's Culpepper's phone. He's the only guy I got left."

"Now? You're taking them now?"

"Yes, now. I saw it, Lauren — black Tahoe, smoked out windows. Same as yesterday."

She was silent. Tom could hear radio chatter in the background.

"Are you at the scene?" he asked.

"Yes."

"I got a partial on the plate — 18-E. Can you relay it to Machado, Pierce, get them on DMV? And meet me downstairs in ten minutes."

He hung up, left the room and set his bags down in the corridor. Culpepper opened up Heather's room with the key card. He expected to find her sleeping, but as he moved into the space he saw her silhouette in front of the window. The girls were sharing one of the two double beds; two small unmoving lumps.

She turned as Tom neared and went to him, quickly.

180

"What's going on? Everything alright?"

"There was an accident. We gotta go."

"Why? We're not safe?"

He'd come into the room with all sorts of plans about what he would say to her, how he would motivate but not alarm her. As he looked into her eyes, shining in the semidarkness, those plans vanished.

"No," he said. "We're not safe."

* * *

Culpepper led the way to the elevators. Tom held Olivia, her head draped over his shoulder. She was asleep but stirring. Heather was beside him, Abigail passed out in her arms, the girl wearing footie pajamas.

"We left all the bags," Heather said. "Our things . . ."

"We'll get them later."

They waited in silence as the elevator rose to the top floor and the doors opened.

"Let's take the stairs instead," Tom said.

No one argued as they stepped into the stairwell and started down. The girls were becoming more awake with all the movement.

"Mommy?" Olivia was bleary-eyed with sleep.

"It's okay, honey. Just a little adventure. Hang on tight to Agent Lange."

They rounded the flights down. Nearing the ground floor, Heather said, "I don't understand. How could they just take away the security?"

"We're going to resubmit," Tom said. "We'll contact the U.S. Marshall Service. But, it's going to take a little while."

As they poured out of the stairwell into the lobby, Olivia arched her head back to look at Tom. Then she looked around for Heather. "It's night time."

"Yeah."

"You look sweaty."

"Guess I'm out of shape."

Tom moved them toward a section of couches and chairs near the front. The hotel security guard was watching, as was the lone clerk at the wide front desk. Tom set Olivia in one of the chairs, spoke briefly to the security guard, and told Culpepper to sit tight with the girls.

Then he pushed through the front door and stepped out into the humid night.

He scanned the parking lot for any potential threats. Over a hundred cars, impossible to discern a black SUV parked among them. He reached the Durango, the alarm chirped as he pressed the fob. He piloted the vehicle to the entrance, pulling right up to the doors with barely any room to spare.

Culpepper saw him through the glass, got Heather moving. Heather still carried Abigail, who was awake now, too, and looking at everything with depthless eyes. Seeing Heather's face released an unexpected memory — Tom and Nick as little boys, and their mother putting them into the back of the family Jeep in the middle of the night.

The rear door opened and Tom snapped back to attention. He hopped out of the Durango, kept his eyes moving. Heather put Abigail in her car seat, while Tom helped Olivia into hers.

"Where are we going?" Olivia asked.

"I don't know, honey."

A vehicle approached. Tom tensed, then recognized Blythe's Crown Vic.

He finished snapping Olivia in. Culpepper had moved to the front of the Durango, but now he approached Blythe's car as it slowed. His hand rested on the grip of his weapon.

"It's okay," Tom said to Culpepper. "She's with us."

He turned back to Heather.

"Where do you want me?" Their eyes connected across the back seat.

"In between them. Get under those blankets, okay?"

"Okay." Heather grunted and squeezed into the Durango's back seat. "Well, let's see if Mommy's butt can fit in here . . ."

Despite the tension, the late hour, Tom felt his heart lift at her humor.

With the three of them secured in the Durango, he closed the door and headed toward Blythe, who'd parked in front and gotten out.

She looked ashen in the hotel lobby light, concern wrinkling her forehead. "What's going on, Tom? What the hell happened? Why was Coburn here?"

Tom moved them out of Culpepper's earshot. The agent seemed to understand and repositioned himself beside the Durango, guarding the family inside.

"Coby came to talk to me, Lauren. I called him."

"About what?"

"To discuss Declan. Coby's unit was hacked. Data on Palumbo's crew, and data on Declan was stolen electronically."

"Declan? He said Declan was never under surveillance."

"Not directly, he said. But they had bulk data, collected from everyone in range of the StingRay used to watch Palumbo and Vasquez; to watch the track. And that info was used against Declan. My guess is someone executed him because the normal channels wouldn't have worked."

"What? Who?"

"I still don't think Palumbo would be this elaborate. As for Vasquez it doesn't make a lot of sense. Coby thought the timing was off. So, maybe other cops."

"Other *cops*?"

"I said maybe, I don't know. Or, some sort of para-law enforcement. Someone who wanted to take Declan down for the child pornography, but couldn't go about it through the courts, the prosecutors, because of the privacy issue."

She raised her eyebrows at him. "Those are serious fucking allegations, Tom."

"I know they are. But this is coming from Coby. He was obviously blowing the whistle. What did the ME say?"

"Well, he only just got there a few minutes before I did . . ."

Tom waited. He knew Blythe had already assessed the scene on the highway and would have her suspicions. Lauren Blythe was not a time-waster. "He said it looked like Coburn had suffered some kind of attack. Like a stroke or a heart attack, lost control and collided with the other driver."

"He was killed the same way as Declan and Hamer. He was given potassium cyanide."

"How?"

"I think his tobacco. We need to get his tin checked."

Her frown deepened. "Come on . . . This is . . ." She put her hands on her hips, swept the night with her gaze, said, "God *dammit*."

"It sounds like someone is picking off people who are close to this thing, or a part of it. Brian Hamer probably performed the hack. Heather Moss was the instrument they used to kill Declan, and Coby suspected it has to do with this theft of their surveillance information."

"All this for a small-town pedophile? Now who's suggesting something overly elaborate?"

"Well, Coby was working with CID, everybody hoping to make the case that Declan was involved with the Edgar Vasquez car accident. Maybe someone was pressuring Declan to talk, threatening to expose him unless he turned state's on Palumbo."

"See?" Her eyes were sharp. "So we're back to Palumbo again. Palumbo kills Declan so he won't talk."

Tom shook his head. "But Coby didn't say anything about evidence that Declan was really involved."

"Doesn't mean he wasn't. Declan was seen at the dog track all the time. His trade was auto mechanics." She bit down on the words. "*Fuck*, Tom. This thing is a fucking merry-go-round."

"Nobody slashes brake lines, and you know it. Even if Declan messed with Vasquez's car computer or something . . ." Tom trailed off, new ideas forming, then jumped back on track: "Either way, yeah, if we're back to Palumbo, we're back to it still not adding up that Palumbo would wait until Declan was in jail." Tom glanced into the Durango, at the expectant faces of Heather and the two girls. "Lauren, I gotta get them out of here."

"You're sure you saw the same vehicle."

"Same as the drive-by. Dark SUV. Did anything come back yet on the tags?"

"Not yet, but, Tom . . ." She stuck out her chin, spread her hands. "What? You're not going to tell me where you're going? Tom, this isn't . . ."

He knew what she wanted to say, that he was doing an end-run around procedure. Not too long ago the shoe had been on the other foot. But he had no choice; at this point, it all had to be quiet, off the air, because who knew how deep this thing went.

He avoided her glare and opened the door to the Durango. "I'll call you when I get there."

Culpepper sensed imminent departure and circled round to the passenger side, got in. As soon as the door closed, Tom hit the gas.

CHAPTER TWENTY-FOUR

"Here it is," Tom said. "Home sweet home."

He'd watched their backs every mile between the hotel and here and was as sure as he could be that they hadn't been followed. They'd entered the gated community where he lived, the security guard giving them quite the look. Otherwise, middle of the night, not a soul around.

"This is where you live?" Olivia asked.

"Yes ma'am."

"Which one? All the houses look the same."

"Livy . . ." Heather said.

"Yeah, they do," Tom said, pulling into his short driveway. And it was a good thing, too. Plus, he'd been in Bonita Springs so briefly he hadn't even updated his address in the state bureau's registry yet. The only people who knew he lived here besides Blythe were Katie Mills and Jack Vance.

"They all look the same," Olivia repeated. "Gnome sayin'?"

Tom shared a glance with Culpepper. The agent formed a crooked grin as Olivia spelled out: "G-n-o-m-e. The 'G' is silent. Gnome sayin'?"

He hit the button, the garage door opened and he rolled in, killed the engine, pressed the button again and the garage closed up.

Safe.

"Alright girls," Heather said. She started unstrapping their harnesses. "Ready?"

Abigail was fully awake. "Eddy!"

Tom got out, circled round to Olivia and helped her out. She had rings of fatigue beneath the bright pools of her eyes. Tom thought she looked a lot like her mother. "You a spelling bee champ or what?"

"No. I got third place in the spelling bee."

"Well that's alright," Tom said.

Culpepper helped Abigail and Heather out the other side, then they made their way into the condo. Heather took the girls upstairs to get them settled back into bed.

Tom went into the kitchen with Culpepper, got them a glass of water each. They listened to upstairs commotion — the patter of little feet down the hallway, the running of tap water, flushing of the toilet. The soft murmur of Heather's voice and occasional chirp from Abigail.

"Nice place," Culpepper said.

"I thought it was more than I needed."

"Well you never know when you're going to have refugees staying over." He drank the last of his water with a gulp. "Where do you want me, boss?"

Tom collected the glasses and brought them to the sink. "You know I started up with the department six months *after* you, right?"

"You mentioned while we were on GP. But you're still the boss anyway."

"Thanks for this, Damien."

He could still feel the adrenaline, like an electric current through his body. And something else, more than a mere sense of duty to Heather's girls, an ache to keep them safe.

Standing in the doorway, Culpepper winked. They'd kept the kitchen lights off, but the agent was faintly backlit by the lone illuminated lamp in the living room.

"No prob," Culpepper said. "I still have three hours on my shift. You want me right out in front of the door?"

"That would be great; keep out of sight if you can."

"I'll check in with you at six."

Culpepper was quiet as he stepped out of the condo.

* * *

Tom heard soft footfalls coming down the carpeted stairs. Heather walked into the living room, rolling the sleeves of her sweatshirt. Then she stopped and gave the wall a long look.

"This is interesting." She used a voice Tom thought was practiced in the art of keeping the girls asleep, somewhere in between normal volume and a whisper. She was gazing at his collage of photos and news clippings.

"Let's go in here."

He led her into the kitchen and offered her a seat at the table. Then he leaned against the sink counter. "Everybody okay?"

"Took a little bit to get Abigail settled again. We had to go through the whole nightly ritual all over again — brushing her teeth, having a glass of water, sitting on the potty. I found a new toothbrush still in the packaging, hope that's okay."

"Anything you need. You hungry? Want a drink?"

"I can get it."

She rose from the table. He stepped aside as she picked up one of the glasses out of the sink and ran the tap into it.

"Agent Culpepper and I just used those."

She took a big drink of water and smacked her lips. "Please. I pick boogers out of little girl noses with my pinky finger." She finished the water, set the empty glass back in the sink. Then she returned to the table and sat down. "So. Agent Lange. What is going on?"

"You can call me Tom, if you want."

"Okay, Tom. How bad is it?"

"Until I know for sure, I'm being overly cautious."

"Isn't this unusual, though? Taking civilians involved in a case into your home?"

"It is. But, given the circumstances, it seemed like the right call."

"I'm not questioning your judgment, just wondering if you'll get in trouble for something like this."

"Probably. But I think we're in uncharted territory."

"I didn't know there was any of that left."

"Uncharted territory?"

She nodded, keeping a straight face despite their banter. "Yeah."

They both lapsed into silence, and Tom pictured Coburn, flopped out of his Camaro, the stars glinting in the sky above.

When he focused on Heather again, he found her staring at the gun tucked against his ribs.

"Where do you keep your weapons?"

"This one stays with me." He lifted his arm so she could get a look at the lightweight Glock.

She blinked, asked, "Is that a good gun?"

"It's got a short frame, a heavier trigger pull than the other Glocks. Made by an Austrian manufacturer, they're reliable, good in the heat . . ." He trailed off, sensing that she was no gun enthusiast. Neither was he, especially, it was just part of the job. "I have one other. I keep it downstairs in the garage, secured by a cable inside a locked cabinet. Nothing anyone can get their hands on except me."

She looked at him, slowly nodded, and he thought she was finally showing some real fatigue.

"Let's try to get some rest, alright? We can talk more in the morning, and I'll explain what I can."

She nodded again, tried to stifle a yawn with her fist, then stood up from the table. He led her into the living room and waited at the bottom of the stairs. When he turned back, she was looking at his wall again.

Her eyes seemed to trace the web of yarn connecting events, people, and headlines. She pointed to the picture in the center. "That's Palumbo?"

He neared her, hoping she'd continue on upstairs. But she squared her shoulders with the wall, took a step toward it. "Yeah that's him."

"But you don't think he's got anything to do with this anymore."

"I really don't know."

He zeroed in on an aerial shot of the dog track, showing the grandstands smattered with a few patrons, the tiny shapes of dogs cutting lines through the muddy track. A newspaper article taped beside it focused on the dwindling returns dog racing brought the track owners, and the use of high-stakes power to keep the money coming in.

Then another article, this one on a shooting in Tampa, linked to drug traffickers. A third, from the *Tampa Bay Herald*, linking the chain of drug distribution to the track. Tom had highlighted several portions which referenced the involvement of the Everglades County vice and narcotics bureau. There was an inset picture of Sergeant Danny Coburn.

Tom was staring at it, thinking about Coburn's now fatherless kids, when Heather spoke.

"Didn't we pass the track on the way here? It's, like a mile away. Coincidence?"

Tom didn't know how to answer. He'd looked at several places after making the decision to leave Naples, and chose his new home for multiple factors. But there was no denying that close proximity to Palumbo's dog track was one of them.

Heather asked, "You always take your work home with you like this?"

"This was my first assignment."

"So you wanted to hit it out of the park."

"A woman was found dead in Rookery Bay. Carrie Anne Gallo?"

Heather sat down on the couch facing the wall. She seemed wide-awake again, the fatigue gone. "I remember that. I read about her. It was after I'd been down here a few months. That was you, huh? Who was she? Or can't you say?"

He eased onto the couch beside her. "She'd been a prostitute and was stripping at a club in Tampa. Palumbo owned the club."

"Oh, okay," Heather said, the lamplight catching her eyes. "I see."

"My case intersected with a pre-existing County VNB investigation on Palumbo, which is ongoing."

"Right, right . . . So you state guys, you handle that stuff, huh? A murder case, a body in the water? I always thought you went after white collar crimes, police corruption, things like that."

"That's part of it. There's also domestic security, Governor Protection — what I was doing until just recently. But criminal investigations — IFS — that's a big part. A lot of what we do is help with multi-jurisdictional cases."

"Like me. I work in Everglades County, live in Lee County. That it?"

Tom felt a heat creeping up his neck, the way she was looking at him.

"What else?" she asked.

He blinked. "What else? What else do we do?"

She tilted her head toward the wall. "About this. You said it was a vice narcotics case. So have you been assisting them? Or opening your own case? You just told me you were on Governor Protection . . ."

"We really should get some sleep." But he didn't move, and neither did she.

"Where's your family?"

Tom clucked his tongue and ran a hand over the back of his neck. He kneaded the flesh there, looking down.

"Wow," Heather said. "That's a telling response." She turned back to the collage. "I'm remembering more of this now. Reading about it . . ." She rose from the couch and moved toward the wall, toward one of the clippings. "Nick Lange?"

Nick's mention twisted Tom's gut.

She read from the clipping, her lips moving, just whispers. She covered her mouth with her hand. "Oh . . ."

She slowly returned to the couch, sat down. After a silence, she asked, "Is that your brother?"

"Yeah."

"His death had something to do with the case, I take it? With Palumbo?"

She was blunt, and he was feeling more and more uncomfortable. But it wasn't her fault. He'd brought her here, he was the one with his work splattered all over the wall in his living room. She deserved an explanation.

"Nick got into debt with Palumbo and allegedly went to work for him to pay it down. When vice narcotics closed in on Nick, he ran."

She absorbed this and leaned against the couch cushion on her side. "That's got to be tough. Palumbo still out there, business as usual, investigation ongoing . . . so, can I ask you?"

"Go ahead."

"Nick owed money to these people, and he passed — how does that work? Is debt inheritable like that?"

"It's complicated, but, the short answer is, no. Not in this case. Not legally."

She blew some hair out of her face, sighed, and said, "I don't mean any offense, but this has 'conflict of interest' all over it."

"I know it does."

"Yet here we are."

"Here we are."

She looked into his eyes. "Were you and Nick close?"

"I guess so." He watched as she pushed off her shoes, brought her bare feet up onto the couch.

"Is this okay?"

"Of course."

"So, you and Nick . . ."

He let out a breath, feeling some of the day's tension ebbing. "We grew up as foster kids. From when I was eight, to eighteen."

"Where? Around here?"

"No. Westchester County in New York. In New Rochelle, and later in Yonkers."

She nodded. "I wasn't far from there. In Nyack. But you probably know that."

"I do."

"What was foster care like?"

"It was okay. We got separated at one point."

"That had to be tough."

He took a breath, let it out slow. "I didn't like being without Nick. But then we came back together — I was turning fourteen — and we lived with the Johnsons."

She raised her eyebrows, inviting him to share more.

"Marvin Johnson. He was a pastor. And his wife Monique. They had two kids of their own who'd already grown and gone off to college. Which was a big deal. Then when Nick was old enough to leave, he ended up hanging around the area. He got an apartment, waited the two years for me to be eighteen."

"Then you moved down here together?"

"We messed around up there for a couple years, then we came down. Nick got into real estate, I went to school. Then I started up doing this."

Heather brushed a strand of hair away and smiled softly. Her level of comfort was disarming. He was used to court-appointed psychiatrists and stuffy offices, being obligated to talk about himself. He'd never shared these things with anyone outside of that. Not even with Katie.

"How often do you think about him?"

"Every day." Tom stared down at his cut hand, which seemed to be healing. "You know what's funny is, Nick's real estate website is still up. I drafted an email to the host server to ask them to take it down, but then I ended up not sending it. Even his Facebook page is still there . . ." Tom looked up at her. "What about you? You must think of your husband every day, too."

"I do. And I see him in the faces of the girls. It's unbelievable how hard it is, how it never goes away. People say it leaves a hole in your life, but for me it's like a wall. Your thoughts turn there, and there's this wall, preventing you from seeing that person, from talking to them, from touching them. Like they're not dead, but away somewhere, and you don't know where, and can't get to them."

He didn't respond and Heather closed her eyes. "I don't know what you do with that. Two years, and I still don't know. I guess you get used to having that wall there."

She suddenly blinked and sat up. Tom tensed and leaned toward her. "What is it?"

Heather looked toward the stairs. "I thought I heard Abby." She swung her legs off the couch and slipped on her shoes, cocked her head. "Maybe not. But, I better head up."

He stood as she got to her feet and moved through the living room. She glanced over as she began ascending the stairs. "Good night, Tom. Thanks for talking."

"Good night."

She paused with her hand on the banister. "What's next?"

"What's next is I've got a new lead. Tomorrow I'll talk with my supervisor and director, and we're going to figure this thing out. 'Gnome sayin'?'"

She smiled as she drifted up the stairs and out of sight.

CHAPTER TWENTY-FIVE

SATURDAY

Culpepper had left at dawn, after keeping out of sight in the shadows and lush vegetation crowding the door; Tom stood in front of the townhouse, dressed in sweatpants, t-shirt, sandals. Just another guy out for a morning smoke in case anyone was watching. Like the woman walking her little Yorkie as the sun came up. Tom raised his hand in a wave. She seemed to hurry her pace and the dog yipped.

Blythe's Crown Vic came up the street and pulled into his driveway.

"When did you start that up again?" She scowled at the cigarette as she got out.

"I'll quit soon."

She handed him a new phone. "There's your replacement."

"Thank you."

"Matt said that—"

He placed a hand on her wrist. "Hang on. Not here."

Her eyes closed in a long blink. "Jesus, Lange . . ."

Between townhouses was a walkway bisecting swathes of mid-size shrubs, Formosa lavender Azaleas. Tom gestured to a short, wrought-iron bench as a gecko darted across their path. Blythe gave him another look that said *you're crazy* and sat down.

Tom mashed out his cigarette on the ground and tossed it in a nearby can, took a seat beside Blythe.

"So," she said, "Matt had a look at your phone, tried to trace the call, no luck — there's no phone in service with that number. Also, the number that sent you the text last night is different from the one in Heather's phone from the morning of Declan's murder."

"But they're both 945."

"We're watching all the towers, if any phone pings from a 945, we're having a look. It's thousands of phones."

"How is Turnbull handling this?"

"Handling what? That you've absconded with a witness in a murder case and her two daughters? Won't say where they are? He's about an inch away from hauling you in, Tom, reassigning you. Again."

Tom nodded at the door into his place. "They're inside."

Her eyes widened. "You brought them *home*?"

"No one knows, and that's the point. This is gated, twenty-four hour security—"

"You mean the retired rent-a-cop who stared at my tits when he let me in?"

"There's a camera that took a shot of your license plate for one thing."

Her mouth dropped open. "You're not using these people as *bait* Tom?"

"Of course not."

"What about the agent with you? Culpepper?"

"I trust him. He'll be back a little later. He's getting their things; he'll be careful no one follows him."

Blythe stared off at the shrubbery, but Tom knew she wasn't thinking about the *Arboricola* landscaping. He pointed at the small case she was holding. "What've you got?"

She sighed and unzipped it, pulled out two dossiers, handed them over. "Pierce did the legwork on this. He started with a hundred and forty-two Chevy Tahoes in Lee County with plates beginning 18-E. One hundred forty-two registrants, twenty-six with some sort of record, just two felons, Daryl Trenton and Todd Whitcomb."

Tom looked at pictures of Whitcomb first — a mug shot, plus two candid photos, one of Whitcomb on a boat, and another of him and a young woman. According to his record, Todd Whitcomb was a rapist. The young woman pictured was one of several who'd filed charges against him. He owned a 2014 Chevy Tahoe.

"He's a registered sex offender," Blythe said. "He's also a financial manager living on Sanibel Island."

Tom moved on to the next guy, Daryl Trenton. Trenton's file included a mug shot, and one still shot pulled from a video camera. The image showed a man in a baseball cap and dark sunglasses in the midst of a hold-up.

"And that's a convenience store in Immokalee. Trenton is doing five years for armed robbery."

Tom flipped to the last page and saw Trenton's driver's license and vehicle registration. He was the proud owner of a 2009 Chevy Tahoe, jet-black. But he wasn't driving it anywhere, not from behind bars.

"He could be loaning it out," Tom said. "Anyone could be driving that Tahoe with Trenton in jail."

"Correct. Or maybe it's just sitting in a yard somewhere with a blown gasket."

"What about stolen vehicles?"

"I thought you'd ask. Only one report of a stolen Chevy Tahoe for Lee County. It belonged to this man, Larry Boyle, a school teacher in North Naples."

Tom looked at the stolen vehicle report, taken by the Lee County Sheriff's Department. "This was filed in early December. All this stuff keeps coming back to two months ago, or thereabouts."

He sensed her mounting frustration and she crossed her arms. "Either one of them strike you as working for Palumbo? Or maybe Vasquez? Come across one of them in your extracurricular activities? I see you've set up your new place a stone's throw from the dog track."

"I've never seen them before. Whitcomb doesn't fit in. Maybe Trenton? But doubtful. Palumbo's guys don't go around robbing convenience stores. But that doesn't mean Trenton isn't involved with what's happening."

She tapped the paperwork with a short fingernail. "You think either one of these guys is smart enough to pull off what happened with Heather Moss? One's a rapist, the other's a thug robbing a convenience store. They're hacking county jail security, procuring potassium cyanide, rolling around with AR-15s?"

"We won't know until we look. Maybe Whitcomb — you've got to have some brains to manipulate money. But I don't think it matters — Brian Hamer was the one used for his technical skills. I found the Fusion packaging at Iowa Schnell's trailer park. Don't you see how it's going? Hamer provided the technical know-how, then he was murdered. Coburn's unit was hacked, supplying the info on Declan who is then murdered, too. One of these guys just does the short work. Some kind of muscle, maybe."

"How exactly did Coburn have information on Declan? He was wiretapping him? So he was a suspect."

"No. Like I said last night, Declan wasn't on their list, they weren't surveilling him."

"Last night was crazy. Refresh my memory."

"There was a hack into the data on Palumbo, including the bulk collection. You know how a StingRay works by mimicking a cell phone tower, right, it turns your phone into a tracking device without having to go through the phone company. But the StingRay is imprecise; it's like a trawler net and collects information from all the phones in range — it can tell you strength of signal, unique identifying numbers on the hardware, even the calls being made at the time, the data being used, the internet being surfed."

"But they didn't find evidence Declan was working with Palumbo. They found the pornography. And *then* they were hacked."

"Exactly."

She shifted a little, turning toward him as she followed the line of thought. "Maybe Palumbo has gotten tech-savvy, or uses Hamer, and hacks Coby's unit. And he finds out that Declan is a pedophile. Even Palumbo has his standards. So then he kills Declan."

"And we're back to Palumbo waiting until he goes to jail, which seems unnecessarily complicated. Like you said last night, this whole thing has just got us going round and round, chasing our tails, and maybe that's part of the point."

"Part of what point?"

"I'm still working that out. But, look, Coby sounded like he didn't think it was Palumbo, either. I think he was about to tell me who he thought it was — but then he left. The drug was already having an effect on him. What is the autopsy showing?"

"It's currently inconclusive," Blythe said. "But two labs are working on it. Declan's pill was a gelatin ampule. Hamer drank some; they haven't shown how yet. Same poison, three different mediums. Coburn's chew was laced with KCN — potassium chloride. How the hell did it get into his chewing tobacco?"

"Same way that envelope got into Heather Moss's purse. Someone had to get close to him. So until we know who's ultimately pulling these strings, I'm keeping Heather and her daughters safe."

Another gecko ran out onto the walkway, stopped, jittered a moment and then darted back beneath the shrubs. The sun was starting to shine down between the buildings. Blythe's mouth formed a thin line, her eyes hard and cunning. "I'd like to speak to Mrs. Moss now, if you don't mind." She stood up, smoothing out her pants, brushing off her backside.

"Absolutely. And then, let's pick up Whitcomb and talk to Trenton in jail, check the stolen vehicle. Somebody fired on Heather's house from a Tahoe. And then it was out last night on the street where Coby died. We need that vehicle."

"I know we do. But it's all the more reason, Lange, why this still looks like Palumbo or Vasquez; even if some of these elements seem to militate against it, these are mob-style executions and drive-by shootings. We just need evidence that Declan was working for Palumbo. We find that, and we're solid." Blythe's eyebrows went up. "What now?"

"Well, it was a drive-by shooting, yeah — where no one was hit. Twenty-eight shots were fired, not a single injury. Doesn't sound like a pro to me, Lauren. Sounds like a thug with bad aim."

* * *

The two girls were sitting around Tom's kitchen table. Olivia's blonde hair was a wild nest of spun gold, her eyes bleary from sleep. Abigail's darker hair stuck out in clumps and there was a princess sticker caught on the sleeve of her pajamas.

Heather was going through the cabinets. "Okay, girls, a can of tuna, or these year-old pretzels? Your choice."

"I haven't been here a year . . ." Tom said from the doorway. He grabbed the bag of pretzels and gave it a look. "Okay . . . brought these from my other place. Busted. Good morning, everybody. How did you sleep?"

"Seep!" Abigail patted the table and swung her legs in the chair.

Heather slowly closed the cabinet door, taking a look at Blythe.

Blythe nudged past Tom and walked into the kitchen. "Mrs. Moss, how are you doing?"

They shared a quick handshake. "Nice to see you again, Agent Blythe." Heather moved to the table and sat down.

Blythe smiled at the girls. "Hello."

The girls just stared back.

"Olivia," said Heather. "Say hello to Agent Blythe."

"Hello."

"I just thought I'd check in with you, see how you're holding up," Blythe said.

Tom thought Blythe sounded peculiar but was coming to understand that his supervisor wasn't always natural with people. A lot of the time he wasn't sure he was, either.

The door opened and Culpepper stepped in, his arms loaded with grocery bags, a duffel hanging from his shoulder. He dropped the duffel in the living room, walked into the kitchen and halted when he saw everyone. "Whoa. It's a party. Hello."

Or, Tom thought, some kind of strange, dysfunctional family. "Agent Culpepper, this is Agent Blythe."

Culpepper set the groceries down by the sink, then shook with Blythe. Tom nodded toward groceries. "More tuna and pretzels."

Heather stood, smirking, and went through the bags, pulling out boxes of cereal, oatmeal, eggs. Culpepper headed for the door. "You know where to find me." He tipped a nod at Blythe before leaving.

"Well," said Blythe. "I know this probably isn't what you expected when you agreed to witness protection. If there's any—"

"This is fine," Heather interrupted. "We're very grateful to Agent Lange. To both of you."

He'd never seen Blythe quite so flustered. There were times he'd wondered if she even had a touch of Asperger's — she could be brusque and distant — but he'd never seen her at a real loss for words. She smiled at the two girls again, then pursed her lips, glanced at Heather, and backed out of the kitchen.

Tom followed her into the living room and found her standing in front of his wall. He was getting used to the reaction: "You got to be kidding me, Lange."

"I'm going to take it down. With them here, I just haven't gotten to it."

"Let's go. Right now. We're talking to Turnbull."

She walked out the door without looking back. Tom jogged upstairs, changed into his suit, slipped into his shoulder holster, jotted down a note. When he came back down, Heather was leaning in the kitchen doorway, wearing an expectant expression.

"Agent Culpepper will be here all day," he said and handed her the note. "If you need anything, I wrote down my new number. Okay?"

She nodded. He held the gaze of her arresting eyes. Then he hurried outside.

CHAPTER TWENTY-SIX

"We can't tell him," Tom said. Blythe drove her Crown Vic and he rode shotgun. "I don't know how deep this goes."

"Tom, I think you're losing it. You've got a witness locked away *at your own house* and you don't want to tell our regional director."

"I'm going to draw up the paperwork and submit it to the U.S. Marshalls. Until then, I want her location undisclosed."

"You want her . . ." Blythe was too pissed off to finish her sentence. A dark vein protruded on her temple. "Jesus. Jesus, Tom. Alright, listen. You're probably not going to like what I say next. I *know* you're not going to like it."

"What?"

"A reminder that we're both mandated reporters for any child endangerment."

Tom felt the hairs on the back of his neck. "You wouldn't — Lauren, you can't. She's a single parent. Heather is all those girls know—"

"And those girls are potentially at risk."

"How? How are they at risk? Between me and Culpepper, we're watching them around the clock. It's a gated community. No one knows where they are. Lauren, no—"

"Tom, they were shot at! Whether or not they're at imminent risk is for a judge to decide. That judge okayed the girls released back to their mother *per witness protection*. But wit-pro is out and the DFS needs to do their investigation."

"Stop it, Lauren, come on . . ."

"And you called Coby out to the hotel — look what happened to him. Look at his kids. People can get hurt, Tom, clearly. Around you, they can get hurt."

He punched the roof of the car. He hadn't expected to do it, he just suddenly lashed out.

Blythe jumped. She gouged him with her eyes.

"That's it, Tom. Let that violence out. God, I feel like we were just here. You're part of the risk, Tom! What is it? You like her? She ask you about your brother, make you feel all warm and fuzzy inside?"

"Aw *fuck*, Lauren."

She turned into the ROC a bit fast, the tires giving off a squawk. When she hit the brakes for the parking spot, Tom lurched forward. He'd never been so angry with her. Even if Coby had been a friend, even if she was hurting — she made him feel small. He already felt bad enough.

"You've got to give me time, Lauren. Get the paperwork together, contact the Marshall's service . . ."

"And when are you going to pull together that paperwork? Before or after we're shaking down two ex-cons who happen to drive Tahoes? Before or after we figure out who's been sending messages to your *own phone,* or before you tear down sensitive information on an organized crime figure from your fucking wall? Tom, I feel like your mother. And I don't like feeling that way. It was a mistake to bring you back in. You're not ready."

Blythe threw open the driver's side door, stepped out then leaned back in. "You may never be ready."

He stared at her. "We have no idea how long this investigation could take. If a judge finds for imminent risk, those girls could get placed in homes. They could be separated." He gritted his teeth. "You're cold, Lauren."

Images jumbled through his mind, memories of him and Nick as kids. Nick crying, people in suits standing around. Tom being pulled away from his brother.

She slammed the door in his face. He got out, feeling heavy and buzzed. For early February, the day was blazing hot, waves of heat coming off the tarmac. It suddenly seemed like hell.

Blythe swiped her ID card and pushed in through the main doors. Tom slipped in after her, followed her path down the corridor to Turnbull's office. When she reached his door she gave it a hard rap of her knuckles, but didn't wait for an invitation.

They barged into the room with Turnbull on the phone. The director glared at them, instantly getting the picture. "I'll call you back." He hung up, and stood. "What is going on?"

Neither of them spoke. Tom just stood, simmering, feeling the anger emanate from Blythe.

"Lange? You want to tell me where our witness is for the Declan case?"

"I told you I'd work something out, sir. I did."

His eyebrows climbed onto his forehead, and Turnbull leaned across the desk, as if to better hear. "And?"

"And I don't think it's safe to say right now, sir. I'm sorry."

Turnbull just blinked. His eyes flitted to Blythe for a moment, then fixed on Tom again. "You're not going to tell *me* where the witness is?"

"I have reason to believe that County VNB could be compromised. And that the infection could also be here at the state bureau. I don't know for sure, but I'm being cautious."

Turnbull glanced at Blythe once more, and then stood fully upright and crossed his arms. "This is about last night. What was Sergeant Coburn doing at the hotel in Orangetree?"

"Confessing," Tom said.

"Confessing?"

"Yes, sir. That sensitive information on open cases — including civilians — has been stolen and someone is acting on—"

"Stop," Turnbull said. He came around the large desk, darted past the agents and closed his door, drew the blinds. Then he loomed behind them, like a drill sergeant. "Sit down, both of you. For God's sake."

Tom moved into one of the two chairs facing the desk. Finally, Blythe did too.

Turnbull resettled in his chair. "Coby's unit has leaks?"

"Someone got information on Howard Declan, and who knows how many other people, inside Palumbo's organization and outside. They came in through the computer system — VNB have been upgrading to digital file-keeping for years now."

The director absorbed this. "So, what do you want to do?"

Blythe sighed demonstrably, clearly irritated Turnbull was willing to entertain any of Tom's ideas. Tom ignored her and ticked off the plan on his fingers.

"I think we have to put aside Palumbo and Vasquez for good. Start looking closer to home. Someone had to get close to Coby to poison him, someone he knew, maybe trusted."

"Who are you talking about?"

"Maybe ex-cops."

Blythe swore under her breath. Tom pressed on: "We start with Everglades County, maybe anyone who's gotten entangled with IAB, resigned, or even retired. Plus we ought to take a look at the jail staff — and not just the ones on shift during Declan's death — even prosecutors and defense attorneys."

"That's a hundred people," Blythe muttered.

Tom ignored her. "The idea is, it could be someone who's grown frustrated by the system. Seeing people slip through the cracks, getting off with a slap on the wrist, or missed altogether. Someone who thinks they're righteous, doing the work that the law is too slow, or too complex, to handle."

"It's ludicrous to assume this is someone in law enforcement, or some random civilian," Blythe said. "This is someone hitting back at Coby's unit. Wasn't this all about counter-surveillance? Palumbo hires someone to hack Coby's unit, weaken it, create all this chaos. Coby has been after Palumbo for two *years*. This is Mario Palumbo's move against him. You've got nothing but wild paranoia to support your ideas."

"I've got a vehicle that Heather saw the morning Declan died, that later showed up at her house and opened fire, but only two rounds penetrated the house. You're right, I've been studying Palumbo on my own. This is too out there, too sloppy for him. And I've got Coby telling me that the VNB had nothing on Howard Declan, just that he was some guy who showed up to gamble on greyhounds. Then Coby died, and it was someone close enough to poison him."

She avoided his gaze and spoke directly to Turnbull. "I think Agent Lange has become a danger, Director Turnbull. He's making unilateral decisions, and this is something personal for him, to do with his brother. It was a mistake to bring him back in; it was too soon, there are too many conflicts. And he's emotionally unstable."

"Emotionally unstable?"

She jammed a look at him. "Was that you who slammed a fist in my car just now?"

Turnbull's gaze dropped to Tom's hand. Fresh blood seeped from one of his reopened glass cuts.

"That's enough," Turnbull said. "Both of you." He let out a sigh and leaned onto his elbows. Then he bent further forward, threading his fingers into his thick red hair. Tom had never seen the director lose composure. He suddenly felt guilty, like this was all his fault. Like Blythe was right, and he was way out of bounds, running on emotions.

Turnbull spoke slowly, raising his face to them again. "We're the FDLE. And part of our charter is to investigate law enforcement corruption." When he looked at Blythe, there was sympathy in his eyes. "I know Coby was a friend. I know this is hard. But we've got to consider the possibility that leaked — or hacked — information is being acted on by a civilian or in some back-channel way. Blythe, you've been all through the interviews with the deputies there, and the other County clinicians?"

She nodded. She still wouldn't look at him, but Tom thought she'd mellowed some. "I have. While it's still in the realm of possibility that someone working for the county passed on the details about Heather Moss slipping through security, I tend to abide by the theory that the CCTV was hacked, and security spied on. For one thing, as we're seeing, it's easier to get around firewalls and break codes than to deal with people. And to confirm that, if you think about it, anyone who was involved or knows about it is winding up dead. But none of the staff or outside clinicians have been threatened that we know of."

"Agent Blythe and I are in agreement here," Tom said when Turnbull looked at him. "I went to the school and the day care. No real clean lines of sight at either place. But the school has cameras, the day care had a laptop with a camera. I don't think someone was there personally, but I think the girls were being watched all the same. I'm only acting in the interest of Heather Moss."

"You're not her lawyer," Blythe muttered. "And you had her pegged as innocent from the first moment you laid eyes on her."

"Again, not true. Heather Moss is like anyone else — she's protecting her family. And she protects her clients. I'm actually not sure she's been completely forthcoming with me about who she thinks might have targeted her."

"Targeted her? Does she think she's been *targeted*? How aggrandizing."

"My words, not hers."

Turnbull leveled a hand in the air to silence them. "Listen, this is someone with some high-tech capabilities. And we're thinking Brian Hamer was responsible for finding the lapse in county jail security, and perhaps now this hack of Coby's unit. When did Coby say this happened?"

"Two months ago," Tom answered.

"Okay. So let's say Hamer gets into Coby's files two months ago. And he's spying on the jail. But then he dies. So who's texting you now?" He read from a sheet of paper on his desk. "Who's saying, *You're very persistent, Agent Lange?*" Turnbull looked at each of them. "Give me a guess. Give me *something*."

"We've got nobody," Blythe answered.

"I don't know who's making the calls," Tom admitted. He felt like he needed air.

"God," Turnbull said. He leaned back and his chair squeaked. "Then it sounds like these two felons, Whitcomb and Trenton, are our next move. And searching for the stolen Tahoe. Otherwise, this list of former mental health clients, disgruntled ex-cops and persons in criminal justice is a mile long."

Tom stood. He glanced around the room, not really seeing anything, unsure of whether to leave or not. But he suddenly needed to get out. The intense urge was on him to escape, like he was trapped.

"Lange?" Turnbull cocked his head.

Tom thought about Heather's girls getting taken away from their mother.

"Lange? You with us?"

"I just need a minute. I'll be right back."

He opened the door and headed down the corridor before Blythe or Turnbull could object.

* * *

Outside, Tom put his hands on his knees and bent forward. He drew in a few deep breaths through his nose, feeling the heat beat down on his skin.

He thought about Iowa Schnell, upset about cops digging into private lives. Coburn saying how time wore a cop down, made him or her see things differently.

His foster father, Marvin Johnson, quoting scripture — how every way of man was justified in his own mind.

The ends justified the means, especially when you believed fully enough in the results. Was this really some ex-cop or para-law enforcement going after Declan for pedophilia? Acting in the dark because the police couldn't do anything legally with third-party information? Or was he projecting his own angst, reliving the Gallo case when Blythe had sought to put away a suspect on shaky evidence?

Was Blythe right about him? Had he been getting too riled up? Too attached? All this time, he'd been preaching about adherence to the law while playing by his own rules . . .

A hypocrite.

Things would get better, starting now. Tom stood upright, turned his face to the sun and closed his eyes. He needed to apologize to Blythe. This was his own fault for keeping her at a distance. He kept everyone at a distance — been doing it for years. As a result, Katie didn't feel close to him. All he wanted was not to be alone anymore yet he pushed everyone away.

He could start to make amends. They were going to get to the bottom of this whole thing.

As he started to feel calmer, better, Tom felt his phone vibrate in his pocket. He thought maybe it was Heather, and pulled it out.

It was a text, and the number started with the digits 945.

How do you live with your secrets?
Do they keep you up at night?

He glanced around the parking lot, feeling panicked again. A few agents were coming and going through the side door. A plane was flying low, likely headed for the Fort Myers airport.

His thumbs dabbed at the screen and he sent a return message.

How did you get this number?

The small red words finally appeared beneath his attempted text:

Message failed to send.

* * *

He strode back down the corridor toward Turnbull's office, a darkness stirring in the back of his mind.

Secrets? What secrets?

He slowed his pace. The heat was creeping up his neck again. He needed to assume the worst. Otherwise he could lose everything.

He slipped the phone into his pocket. Couldn't show them. Not right now. If the secret was what he thought it might be, the only thing it could be, maybe never. He grabbed the doorknob and found Turnbull's office locked.

Blythe opened up and stepped aside to let Tom through. He stopped in front of Turnbull's desk. He knew they'd just been carrying on without him, but the air felt charged.

"Everything okay?" Turnbull took a sip from a mug bearing the FDLE shield logo.

"I'm fine. I'm sorry."

Turnbull relieved Tom of having to explain, waving a hand in the air. "It's alright. You've been under a lot of stress. This is a lot for an agent to carry around."

Blythe was on her feet. She barely looked at Tom when Turnbull continued, "So, a couple of things: We're going to talk to the judge so we can have a look at Coby's files. If we can get through the protective order we can see what was going on with Coby these past few weeks. In the meantime, I just called Lee County, and they'll meet you at Todd Whitcomb's house on Sanibel Island. We've got the PC with this guy's record, his registered Tahoe, we can have a look. Okay?"

Turnbull stood up behind his desk and gave them each a heavy look. "I want this all done by the book. Lange, you're one pen stroke away from being back in Governor Protection and back in therapy. Blythe — you two better kiss and make up."

CHAPTER TWENTY-SEVEN

They sped across the Sanibel Causeway; sparkling, turquoise water spread out on either side the curving strip of land. People were parked off the road, gathered at picnic tables along the narrow shore, fishermen casting their lines. Pelicans circled above, their dark shapes like pterodactyls.

Blythe drove, exuding an icy cool. Tom thought his phone vibrated and surreptitiously gave it a look. She noticed.

"Everything good?" There was an edge to her tone.

He put the phone away, just a phantom sensation. "Look, Lauren, I'm sorry."

"Sorry?"

He searched for the right words. "I know we have this . . . thing between us."

"What are you talking about?"

"Come on. Why you making this so hard?"

"Maybe because I don't know what you're talking about. The only thing we have between us is how cocky you are, how you think you can do whatever you want when you want to."

"I'm not cocky—"

"Oh please. You could stand to do some time in a human resources workshop, let's put it that way. I do what I have to do, but I'm a professional, and I keep it that way."

He wanted them to be past it, but it seemed like there was more to come out: "Lauren, you froze me out during the Gallo case. How long did you know about Nick's involvement with Palumbo? Maybe you could have come and told me but you had it in for Raymond Bosco and nothing was going to stand in your way. Not even your own partner."

She gave him a look that could cut steel, then jerked her eyes back to the road. They were almost to the island. "So that's it, Tom. That's it. You been saving that up, waiting for just the right moment to blame me for your brother? I couldn't say anything to you. That's what professionals do. I keep my distance, so what? At least I'm not sleeping with any cops."

It was a cheap shot, and Tom felt his muscles turn to gristle. He tipped his head back and let out a boiling breath. "Goddammit, Lauren . . . Goddammit."

It was like she'd lost all respect for him. He never realized how much he needed approval until Blythe. Busting his ass in college to double major in criminology and sociology, graduating *cum laude*, getting top marks on his Officer Certification, working for the Investigations and Forensic Science arm of the FDLE — was it all just because he'd never feel good enough?

You're very persistent, Agent Lange.

How do you live with your secrets?

The anger was on him like an animal. "You still planning to report to DFS about Heather Moss's daughters?"

"I'm going to do what is required of me by law. Try to remember when you used to feel the same way."

They arrived at Todd Whitcomb's mid-island townhome. It had views of the ocean, a decent-sized lawn, trimmed to perfection. A Lee County cruiser was sitting in the driveway next to a white luxury car. Two retirement age women rolled past on bicycles, giving the police concerned looks.

Blythe parked on the narrow street and got out. Tom followed into the hot day, gripped by the sense that this was all some sort of manipulation, someone pulling their strings. The Chevy Tahoe thing was bait, and he'd taken it. He just didn't understand. Bait for what?

"Afternoon," said the Lee County deputy. He stood beside the cruiser. Another deputy got out the other side.

"Yeah, we know all about this guy," the first said, leading them up the steep steps to the front door. "He's a real prize. Slept with two girls a couple years ago, one fifteen, the other sixteen. Then flies off to New York the next day to make millions from other rich people's money. These masters-of-the-universe types think they're above the law." The deputy knocked on the door.

Tom and Lauren crowded together on the small porch, barely enough room for them and the deputy. The other officer stood on the front lawn, keeping a watchful eye. The first pressed the button and the doorbell rang.

Whitcomb hadn't responded to their initial phone call, and now he failed to come to the door. Tom left the porch and circled the house. No grass growing, the yard was made of sand. He found a back door and tried the knob. Locked. He gently rattled the door in its frame and looked for trip wires. Nothing, and no deadbolt. It was easy to use a credit card, slide it over the lock plate and pop the door open.

"Hello?" He cautiously stepped into a laundry room: white towels neatly folded on metal shelving above the washer and dryer, the air perfumed by detergent. "Florida Department of Law Enforcement. Todd Whitcomb? You here?"

He passed through the laundry room and into the main area. "Hello?" The townhome was well-appointed but didn't look lived-in. According to their information, Whitcomb considered it his full-time residence, and there were no other properties he owned.

Tom saw the shadows of Blythe and the Lee County deputy behind the curtain hanging over the front door. He unlocked it and opened up.

Blythe stepped past him without meeting his gaze and moved deeper into the house, the officer trailing behind her. He spoke to Tom. "So this guy is a suspect in that jail-poison murder?"

Tom swung open the refrigerator door as Blythe climbed to the second floor. The fridge was empty except for a bottle of San Pellegrino and some condiments in the door. "He's one of two Chevy Tahoe owners from this county with a felony record."

"Oh," said the deputy.

Everything was tidy and clean in the dining area and living room. A remote control sat on the coffee table, placed at an angle. Tom leaned into the bathroom, listening to Blythe's footsteps upstairs. The roll of toilet paper was folded into a point. A housekeeper had been here recently. Either that or Whitcomb had OCD.

Tom found the door to the adjoining garage. Empty. He pulled out his phone and first dialed Fort Myers airport. Afterward, he made two more calls, finally discovering that there was a 2014 Chevy Tahoe parked in the lot for airplane travelers. Whitcomb had taken a flight out of the area six days prior.

Great.

He was about to go up to tell Blythe when he noticed another smaller building between the townhouse and the beach. The sky beyond was bright blue, the Gulf breezes keeping the clouds pushed back over the mainland. He walked to the outbuilding, probably used to store a boat, beach items, but the door was locked and he cupped his hands against a pane of glass.

Not a boathouse after all. The place looked remodeled.

The deputy had wandered out behind Tom. Tom turned to face him, jerked a thumb over his shoulder. "Deadbolt on this one."

The deputy shrugged. "I mean, you guys have the PC, right? Like you said this guy owns a vehicle seen at a couple of crimes . . ."

Tom spun back around, got his balance, and kicked. The door rattled but didn't open. He kicked again, letting all the frustration of the past few days come blasting out his shoe heel, and the door gave way.

He looked over the damage, doing a quick calculation of the cost. A couple of hundred bucks was a small price to pay if this was a domestic terrorist's center of operations. The place was dark, thick curtains enclosing the windows against the sun on the beach side. He found a light switch on the wall and snapped it on.

"Holy shit."

Expensive-looking computer equipment dominated a long desk including an iMac computer with two huge screens. Two walls bore inlaid shelves stocked with Blu-ray movies and unmarked DVDs. A digital video camera sat on a tripod in the center of the room. The camera was aimed at a Queen-sized bed, neatly made up with satin sheets. In the far corner was a short bar, and on top a couple half-full bottles of liquor. With his gloves still on, Tom slid a random DVD case from the shelves and read the cover. "Marlena" had been handwritten in marker. There was no date.

He moved to the computer and gave the mouse a shake. The system booted up and the home screen asked for a password. Tom looked around, found a flat screen TV with a Blu-ray player hooked up and turned it on, slipped in the DVD, then stood back to watch.

An image showed a bed — the one in this room. The lighting was much subtler, the camera placement about the same.

He heard the sounds of kissing from the computer speakers. Then a woman stepped back into the video on screen, followed by a man. She looked of age. They continued to make out, then he pulled the silk teddy she was wearing up over her head. Her breasts bobbed into place, and she shook her hair. The man groped and kissed her, started sucking on her chest.

Tom recognized him. Todd Whitcomb.

"Well, okay," the deputy said. "A little homemade porn?"

Whitcomb gave the woman a push and she bounced onto the bed. She was smiling as he stripped naked, kicking off his shoes. Then he climbed onto the bed after her.

"What the hell is this?" Blythe darkened the doorway, then stepped into the room.

On the screen, Whitcomb pulled down Marlena's underwear, kissed her leg, and moved on top of her.

"What . . .?" Blythe moved closer.

Whitcomb and Marlena had sex. Tom realized he was holding his breath, wincing, wary of the moment it became violent and Whitcomb started to hurt her.

He never did. Two and a half minutes into the recording, Blythe said, "Shut it off."

"But he could—"

"I said kill it."

Tom hit the pause button on the player. Whitcomb and Marlena froze on screen, mid-coitus, her hair thrown back as she rode on top of him. His face was just visible around her body, his eyes wide open, staring up at her.

Blythe browsed the items on the long desk. "What is all this?"

Tom dragged his eyes from the screen and went through the equipment on the desk with her. There was a device for copying DVDs, something called a "mixer", and another box labeled "Xtended Graphix".

"He's got some kind of home video studio," Tom said.

Blythe quickly browsed the library of movies and DVDs.

"I checked with the local airports," Tom continued. "Whitcomb's been gone almost a week."

She gave the deputy a look, then turned to Tom. "Then what are we doing in here?"

Tom felt a sinking sensation. "Nothing. Let's go. He can bill me for the door."

* * *

They separated after Todd Whitcomb's house, deciding they'd cover more ground each on their own. But Tom knew the real reason Blythe was headed off to the jail to speak to Daryl Trenton on her own — they couldn't stand to be around each other anymore. He made the long drive south to Marco Island wondering if they would ever be on the same page together.

Marco was more heavily developed than Sanibel, full of business plazas, marinas and golf courses. Jack Vance sometimes spoke of Florida from years past. He'd made yearly trips down with his then-living wife long before his retirement. Back then, he'd told Tom, southwest Florida was still wild. There was little left that was wild about Marco Island; the inland waterways were man-made, the southern tip was stocked with resort hotels.

Brian Hamer met Iowa Schnell at a party near Tigertail Beach; Tom got the exact address from Agent Rhodes. The Silver Shell Hotel and Resort was right on the water, with white sand beaches and Palapa bars with bamboo roofs. It was still early, not quite two in the afternoon, but the bars were crowded. Tom entered the restaurant, Starfish Grill, the scent of smoked salmon in the air, dining room filled with chatter and the clash of cutlery as patrons tucked into their meals. A hostess gave him a bright smile.

"Hello sir, one for lunch?"

"I'm actually looking for the manager."

The smile faltered. "Oh — is everything alright?"

"Everything is fine." He showed her his badge. "I just have a few questions."

"Right this way, sir."

The hostess led him to the bar toward the back of the dining room. An attractive older woman was drinking a glass of red wine, talking with some guests. She looked over at their arrival.

"Mrs. Shannon? This policeman would like to have a word with you."

"Thank you, Kayla." Mrs. Shannon was Blythe's age, dressed in a black skirt and black V-neck, subtle eye shadow and glittering earrings. "Can I help you?"

"Tom Lange, Department of Law Enforcement."

Shannon smiled demurely at the guests beside her. "Excuse me," she said to them, and they huddled together, turning their backs. She gave Tom a studied look. "FDLE? I spoke with one of you a couple days ago."

"I know; just a follow up. Sorry about the intrusion. Is there a private place we can talk?"

He wasn't sure if she was going to cooperate. Shannon took a drink from her goblet of wine and then stepped down from the bar stool. "Follow me, please."

She led him back through the kitchen. The chef tossed a piece of fish into a hot pan, sending up billows of steam. A busser with a huge tray of dirty dishes nearly ran into them. Two servers, dressed in black, stood in line awaiting their food and gave Tom a look. Shannon pushed through another door, they went down a short corridor and she keyed into her private office.

"Please, have a seat."

The room was small, completely cluttered with a mixture of kitchen items and paperwork. They sat facing across her desk. "Okay. What can I do for you?"

He opened the file he was carrying, placed a picture of Brian Hamer on her desk. She glanced at it for half a second, sighed. "Like I told the other detective, I don't know who that is."

He laid a picture of Iowa Schnell beside the one of Hamer. Another cursory look from Shannon. "No, not her either."

"You're sure."

"Mr—"

"Agent Lange."

"Agent Lange, this was — what? A little over two months ago? We had a party to celebrate our tenth anniversary here, so December 1st. There were three hundred people invited, plus all the guests. The other agent went through our guest list, and neither of these two people was registered."

Tom set out another picture. She continued to gaze at him for a moment, then had a look.

"He's a financial manager. Name is Todd Whitcomb. May I see your guest list again?"

She looked dismayed. "I don't have the guest list here for the hotel. This is the manager's office for the restaurant. You'll have to go into the lobby and ask for Mr. Burton. Or, just get it from your other agent. He has it."

"I will. But, you don't recognize him?"

"No, I'm sorry, I don't."

Tom had one final picture. Shannon stared down at the photo of Edgar Vasquez, the recognition showing on her face. "Yes, I know who that is."

"Was he here the night of your party?"

Her eyes snapped up. "No. He'd just been in his accident by then."

"So, you know him from before."

"Mr. Vasquez and his wife Carmella have been guests at the hotel a few times, yes."

Tom put the pictures away and stood up. "Thank you for your time."

CHAPTER TWENTY-EIGHT

Heather's face fell when she saw him. "Oh man. Tough day at the office?"

He tried to smile but probably failed.

She pointed to the kitchen. "I made some dinner. Culpepper said you called him, thought you'd be home around now. I fed him already. It's not much, just some pasta."

The mention of food brought him out of it a little bit. He set down his bag and pulled out a chair at the kitchen table. "Where are the girls?"

"Upstairs. They're in the bedroom, watching a movie. Hope that's okay."

"Of course." He took a seat, watching as she plated some spaghetti. He didn't have the heart to tell her about Blythe and DFS coming to evaluate Heather and the girls, to take them away. Not just yet. He needed a minute first.

"How much sauce?" Heather asked. "Dripped or drowned?"

"Drowned."

She ladled sauce from a pot on the stove, expertly swirling it over the pasta. He smelled the onions and peppers, saw the steam rising as she set the dish down in front of him. Then she ducked into the fridge and placed some shredded parmesan on the table, opened the cabinet and took down the pepper grinder.

"You know more about my kitchen than I do," he said.

Finally, she set out cutlery, then joined him with her own dish. "You keep yourself busy when you're pent-up."

He took a bite, savoring the flavors just long enough to get the damned food in his empty stomach. After he'd eaten enough to appease the monster inside, he dabbed his mouth with a napkin and looked across the table at her. "Are you doing okay?"

She raised her eyebrows and shrugged, twirling pasta into a spoon. "I gotta say, it's actually been nice having more time with the girls. You know, you think of single parenting and you imagine someone just up to their eyeballs in kids all the time." She took a bite, chewed, looking lost in thought. After she swallowed she said, "And it's like that, but it's also a lot of time apart. I work all week. It's good I get out at four, but it's still long days for the girls."

The anxiety curdled the food in his stomach. But he wanted to put off the inevitable a moment longer. "What does Olivia do? School doesn't go until four, does it?"

"Ha. No. She goes to an after-school program. It's right there in the same building, like a built-in day care. But I drop them off in the morning before eight and pick them up after four. So it's still about a nine hour day for each of them. That's a lot for two little girls."

Tom's ears pricked, hearing the remorse in her voice at the end. He gazed at her as she set down her fork and spoon and looked out the kitchen window. She seemed to gather herself back together and resumed eating.

"That sounds tough," he said.

"I don't know. Yeah, it is. But they seem okay. They're such good girls. I think I give them a good life."

"I know you do. They're wonderful."

She didn't look at him. He watched her blush, and then her eyes came up, flustering him with their directness. "You were telling me you had, ah, a good experience with the Johnsons. When you were older."

He was coming to think that focusing on other people was part of how Heather coped. He said, "I did, yeah. They were good people. But, Heather, I need to talk to you about something."

She stared at him. "DFS is coming back. I know."

Tom wasn't sure what to say. He'd expected this to be upsetting, but she already knew or suspected.

"I work with DFS all the time," she said. "I understand how this works. I figured when Agent Blythe was here she was going to notify them."

"I'm sorry — I shouldn't even have told her you were here . . ."

Heather raised an eyebrow. "She's your supervisor. And she's only doing what she has to do."

"You're taking this pretty well."

"I'm devastated. But now I have to be really careful, anger only makes all of this grip you tighter. And I spoke to the girls this morning, told them they might have to stay with some other people for a little while."

"How did they take it?"

Heather looked off toward the living room. "They'll be okay."

He didn't know what to say, or if there was anything he could say.

"What about when you were little?" There she was, focusing on him again. "You and Nick, you're about the same age apart as the girls. What was life like for two little Lange boys?"

He smiled through the deep ache rooted inside him. Normally he would provide some pat answer and get out of it. But the least he could do was oblige her with the distracting conversation.

"We had our good times. We had one place we lived, there were woods in the back, and we had a clubhouse. Like, the real deal. Nick even painted a sign, called us 'The Protectors'."

"The protectors?"

"Our job was to protect the woods."

"A couple of budding environmentalists."

He shrugged. "It was somewhere we could get away. You know what I mean? Sacred."

"Sure. You were protecting it from the world."

He looked down at his empty plate. "No one really bothered us."

"Well, then you did a good job."

"Except our father, once. Came out after us, found the clubhouse. And it was kind of over after that. We didn't really . . . you know, we didn't really like it anymore after that."

When he looked up, she was regarding him in a certain way. It didn't make him uncomfortable, but persuaded. He gently set down his fork and spoon, wiped his mouth again, and then stared into her blue eyes. "Our father . . . was violent with our mother. And he beat Nick. He hit me, too, but I never got it as bad."

"Tom. I'm sorry."

He fought the impulse to leave the table. "It happens, I guess."

"Have you talked about it? You said you were seeing someone through your job."

"I didn't talk with him about it. But, I had a shrink when I was a kid. Court-appointed. I think I told you that. We talked about it; he called it an ACE or something."

"Adverse Childhood Experience."

"Yeah, right. One of those. Everyone has those, right? I'm going to get a drink, you want something?" He rose, dropped his dish in the sink and opened the fridge.

"Well, everyone had some bad experiences in childhood, sure. But, certain things, experiencing abuse, witnessing abuse . . . that can have a real long-term effect."

The fridge blasted his face with cool air. "Orange juice? Milk?" He retreated and started going through the lower cabinets. "I think I have some wine around here . . ." He suddenly felt foolish. "Probably not the best time, for that, though."

"It's two cabinets over," she said.

He glanced back at her and she winked. He found the Cabernet and pulled it out, then sifted through the drawer above for the bottle opener. "You sure?"

"Yeah, I can have a glass of wine. Life goes on. I'm not going to down the whole bottle."

He drove the sharp tip of the opener into the wine cork and screwed it down. He had his back to Heather as he spoke. "Our father would have these gregarious, nice-guy spells. Every once in a while he'd take us on a trip. Took my mother to a hotel for the weekend, the only time. I thought maybe he was trying to make it all up to her."

The air made a popping sound as he extracted the cork. "There was a fire at the hotel. A few people died, including my parents." He set the items aside and opened the upper cabinets, found two wine glasses, set them aside.

When the emotion bubbled up, he wasn't expecting it. He spread his hands across the counter, and, feeling dizzy, lowered his head.

Gradually he turned around. Heather was watching him, not with pity, not in judgment; just listening.

There was thumping upstairs, the sound of feet traversing the bedroom. Then pounding down the stairway at the back of the condo. "Mommy?"

Heather got up from the table and intersected Olivia in the living room. Tom heard their voices.

"Abigail pulled my hair," Olivia said.

"She did?"

More pounding upstairs. Going the other direction, like little Abby was running away.

Tom poured a glass of the wine. He listened as Heather moved off with Olivia, headed back up. He was lost in thought about childhood and parenting when his phone vibrated in his bag by the kitchen door. He pulled it out and saw the new text.

How you doing, Tom?

Tom ducked back into the kitchen and was quick to reply.

Tell me who you are.

This time the text went through. He waited, feeling his heart beat a strong rhythm. Then new words appeared.

What would you do to protect your secret?

It was another 945 number. He knew the last digits were different without even having to compare them this time. Who was it? Daryl Trenton was in prison. Todd Whitcomb was a thousand miles away.

He wrote back again. *I'm going to find you.*

Once more he waited. The phone vibrated with the new message.

Check your email.

Tom set down the phone and grabbed his bag. He opened up his laptop on the table, logged into the state bureau's system and entered his email password.

His skin crawled as he scanned the two dozen recent messages. Everything he saw came from someone within the FDLE. Nothing drew his attention — they all seemed non-threatening. He didn't know exactly what he was looking for and needed to go through each one. But he checked his personal email first.

His Gmail account open, Tom pulled his hands back from the laptop as if it had become radioactive. The most recent message, from Citizen-Justice@ymx.com read: *Tom's a Liar.*

He double-tapped the mouse pad and opened the mail.

Tom stared at a picture of his own face, but years younger. Just barely a teenager. A bruise marked one cheek, and his eye was threaded with shattered capillaries. A mug shot.

The heat worked its way up the back of his neck, around his ears as he leaned in to read the text beside the photo. On top was the insignia for Yonkers Police Department. Below that, his name, date of birth, physical characteristics, then the list of charges.

His phone buzzed again. Not a text this time, but an incoming call. The same 945 number.

"Who is this?"

"Pretty heavy stuff, Tommy," the voice was synthesized, flat of affect, just as Heather Moss had described. "Drug possession, destruction of property, assault, resisting arrest — quite a sheet. You were a bad boy."

Tom's mouth was dry, his eyes riveted to the screen. "Those records were sealed."

There was a pause, then: "Tom, anyone today who thinks something is sealed is naïve. People hack the IRS. Elections are influenced. Companies are toppled. Nothing is safe, Tom."

Tom stared at his thirteen year-old self, remembering that day. Many of the events leading up to it were a blur, but nothing was as crisp and clear as being arrested and processed. Below the frame of the mug shot, his knuckles had been scraped bloody.

"Focus, Tommy. Lying on your application for the state bureau is a major offense. Maybe even prison. And you will never, ever, be a cop again."

Tom struggled to find the words. He was still gripped by his memories. After their parents had died in the fire, he and Nick had gone into the foster care system. But it wasn't easy keeping two pre-teen boys together. Tom had fallen in with the wrong crowd. By thirteen, alone, angry at himself for not protecting his mother, he'd wanted to watch the world burn.

Maybe just like his father.

"It is amazing how things work out," the caller said in that toneless electronic lilt. "You are even better than I had hoped." But, Tom realized, the caller wasn't *talking* at all. Rather, he was sitting somewhere typing the words.

"Better for what? For your fucking games?" He was aware his voice was rising. He thought he heard Heather coming back downstairs but couldn't be sure. "You think you're going to threaten me with this?"

Another brief pause. "I know it threatens you. It will undo everything you have worked for. It will completely ruin your life."

Tom strained to hear sounds from the other room. Someone was definitely coming. Heather was being quiet, though, maybe not wanting to disturb him, maybe listening.

He spoke in a harsh whisper. "How did you get that information? And how did you get my new number? Did you hack into the state bureau, too?"

"I get what I want when I want it. Everyone has a secret. Even Mrs. Moss has a secret."

He glanced up at the sound of her name, caught a glimpse of her in the kitchen doorway, then she retreated.

"I am not the bad guy," the caller said. "I am the liberator. Howard Declan was a pedophile. Brian Hamer an extortionist. Your friend Coburn invaded people's privacy."

Tom kept watch on the vacant doorway. "And what about Heather Moss?"

"She is a liar," the caller said. "Just like you, Tom. Only, your real vice is violence."

Tom stood up from the table. As he moved toward the kitchen window he said, "Why Howard Declan? Did you just pick him out of a hat?"

"Everyone serves their purpose, Tom. They walk around, thinking it is fate, or thinking it is God. But, it is not God. It is me they are serving. Just remember what I know about you. When the time comes, you will do exactly what I say. Everyone always does."

"You're trying to justify your pathology. You use people for your amusement, then throw them away, a garden variety psycho, nothing special."

Tom pulled the phone from his ear and looked at the screen. The connection had ended.

CHAPTER TWENTY-NINE

He needed a minute. He couldn't talk to Heather right now. Culpepper was outside and Tom lit up a smoke, hands shaking.

The agent looked worried. "The hell happened in there?"

"Sergeant Coburn said someone hacked his unit, got information on Howard Declan. I believed it, but the guy just confirmed it."

"You *talked* to him?"

Tom nodded. "And he sent me emails."

"What about the call? You said this 945 number was a repeat, different from the others."

"Communications department thinks that these phones are essentially reprogrammed to have a different number. It's the digital equivalent of grinding off serial numbers. Maybe this one repeated, but I doubt we'll ever see it again. This is well thought-out. This guy has been setting this up for a while."

He stared off, thinking about Edgar Vasquez, disappearing two months ago. That event seemed to set the whole thing in motion. The timeline wasn't exactly clear: either just before or after the Everglades County drug-runner went missing, Brian Hamer had shown up on Marco Island — presumably lured to the area by the promise of work — to hack the county jail. But if he'd gotten a bit of an earlier start, he could've been the one to hack Vasquez's brand-new car computer, too, cause the brakes to fail, something. Hamer was, apparently, a genius.

And Vasquez was a rival of Palumbo, so Palumbo had tried to cut a deal. VNB watched the whole thing. Vasquez refused the deal, died. County CID investigated the crash, but it wound up buried under layers of protected surveillance and court orders.

Circumstantial or not, it did all seem to point to Palumbo. The son of a bitch who'd ruined Nick's life was involved in this thing. Blythe had to be right — nothing else made any sense. This was Palumbo bringing the house down around everyone's ears. Now he was reaching out — or someone from inside his organization was — and messing with Tom, too.

But no one had asked Tom for money yet if Nick's debt was involved . . .

Culpepper was staring. "Lange? So the phones are a dead end, alright — what are you thinking? You're talking emails—"

"I'm not expecting much there either."

"You're gonna speak to Matt Forsythe though."

"Yeah, I'll talk to him . . ."

Who are you? One of Palumbo's crew I never learned about? An outside hire?

What do you want from me?

"I'll give you that he seems to have covered his ass pretty good so far," Culpepper said. "I bet he's using proxy servers, rerouting his emails all over the place, running them through some public space to become anonymous." He stuck a smoke in his mouth, and with it wagging between his lips, added, "I was a computer science minor."

Tom suddenly grabbed the cigarette and threw it aside. He mashed out his own half-finished smoke, too.

Culpepper balked at first: "What are you doing?" Then he put it together. "Ah, Jesus. You got to be kidding me. Poison? You think so? God, this is crazy."

A moment later a car pulled up on the street in front. Tom jogged out of the breezeway in time to see the doors opening, DFS workers getting out. The bearded man had a long ponytail and a suit that hung too big, the woman was round-faced and large through the hips with a slight waddle to her walk.

"Agent Lange? We're with the Department of Family Services . . ."

"Yes, I know who you are."

"Then you know we're here to speak to Heather Moss and her children?"

Tom stepped back and extended an arm, led them into the breezeway. Past Culpepper, whose face summed up his own feelings — not only was Heather about to be separated from her daughters, but another location was blown. If DFS knew they were at Tom's house, anyone might.

When he opened the door on the townhouse, Heather was standing in the living room, getting the girls dressed. The sight of their bags — Abigail's backpack with the ducks on it, Olivia's tote with her art supplies sticking out — broke his heart.

The DFS workers introduced themselves, and the woman, Leslie Parker, said, "Mrs. Moss, I'll just come right to the point: we have reason to believe your children are at imminent risk of psychological harm."

Heather finished putting Abigail's little shoes on and stood calmly. Abigail took cover behind one of her legs. Olivia stood solemnly beside her. "I understand," Heather said. "And what reason do you have to believe they're at risk?"

"Well, we talked with Olivia and Abigail during their time with us. Both girls said that they'd been scared by the recent events in their lives, Olivia said she was upset that she might be . . . that something bad might happen to her."

Tom looked at the six year-old, remembered meeting her for the first time, sitting in her mother's car, happily coloring a picture. Minutes later he'd been shielding her from gunfire.

Parker said, "Mrs. Moss, you know how this works. The judge's ruling was contingent on witness protection. Since you're not officially under the care of the state, the judge wants to reconsider the safety of the children."

"You're just doing your job," Heather said, anguish beneath the surface.

"Yes, ma'am," Parker said. "While we conduct our investigation, the girls will be very well taken care of."

"When will we go in front of the judge?"

"With luck, you can see a judge as soon as tomorrow, or maybe the next day."

Two nights without her daughters. Tom was sick at the thought, and they weren't even his kids.

The man with the ponytail squatted down near Abigail. "Hi. Do you remember me? My name is David. And you're Abigail, right?"

Abby clung to her mother's leg. David slowly held out his hand. He turned it over in the air. "You see this? I have a little caterpillar, right here."

Abigail stayed rigid, but Olivia had a peek. "That's not a caterpillar. That's a tattoo."

David smiled. "It's a tattoo *of* a caterpillar. Gnome sayin'?"

Olivia moved closer for another look. She reached out and took David's hand. The man was incredibly gentle, letting her get a real close look at it as Olivia spelled out, "G-n-o-m-e. The G is silent."

He laughed. "That's right. Good memory, Olivia."

By this time Abigail had edged away from her mother's leg, just a little, to try and see the caterpillar. Tom glanced up at Heather. She was smiling at it all, but her chin quivered, her eyes shone with emotion.

It took another five minutes of David easing into Abigail's confidence before they were ready to go. Heather helped Olivia into her sneakers. She hugged them both several times. Tom and Heather followed the DFS workers to the car. David carried Abigail, who was now chatting with him in her broken speech. Olivia held her mother's hand. They embraced again at the curb, then the agents were strapping the girls into child seats.

He knew it was right. He knew it was the system working for the benefit of the children.

It made him feel sick.

The car turned around in the street and drove off.

Tom didn't move or look at Heather.

A garage door rolled open at one of the townhouses in the block across a small, man-made pond. A nice, white sedan pulled out into the street, the headlights popped on and it drove off. The sounds of a TV — evening news — drifted from an open window. Eight months of the year, windows were closed, central air regulating the inside temperatures, but in early February, the nights could get cool.

Heather left the lawn and walked back to the condo. He followed her. Culpepper was standing by in the breezeway, looking like he'd witnessed a tragedy. Tom wanted to talk to Heather, but once inside she moved upstairs and he heard the door close. A minute passed, and she was coming downstairs with her bag.

"I'm going home."

"Heather. I don't think that's a good idea."

She stopped in the living room, the two of them standing in front of the collage wall.

"I understand that, Tom. But I want to go home. I want to be in my house. I can't stay here. Can someone drive me?"

He searched for an argument, but nothing would convince her. And he had no grounds to force the issue. "At least let Culpepper keep an eye on things. He'll sit outside."

"Okay."

"I'll drive you."

* * *

The house on Tangerine Drive still looked like a crime scene. Forensics had finished processing the evidence, but it wasn't in their job description to make repairs. Gunshot windows looked like broken teeth, caution tape crisscrossed the front door. Even the palm trees on the front lawn seemed to bend with remorse.

A mist hung suspended as they stepped out of the Durango, diffusing the streetlights into soft orbs. Fresh orchids scented the humid air. Tom walked Heather to the front door. He felt like they'd been on some long, crazy date, and now it was over.

He slashed the crime scene sticker spanning the door seam and Heather used her key.

"You're going to be alright," he said. "We'll get the girls back. Are you going to call your lawyer?"

"I will, first thing in the morning."

She walked into the gloom, through the living room, leaving him behind in the doorway. In the kitchen, she turned on the overhead light and looked around at the mess and the dishes. Wordlessly flipped on the faucet, let the water run, then shut it off. She started picking toys up from the floor.

After a moment she seemed to remember he was still there and offered a broken smile. "Can I get you anything? You want to come in?"

"No. I'm sure you'd like some time to settle in." He jerked a thumb over his shoulder. "But I'm just going to wait in the car until Culpepper arrives."

"That guy has been working some crazy hours."

"I know. I'm going to get him some relief. And remember, I'm just a text or phone call away."

"Okay." She resumed tidying up.

"Heather, who would do this?"

She held a doll in her hand, stripped of dolly clothing, a smudge of paint on its plastic head. "I told you what I thought. I've considered old clients, new clients. And I came up empty." She looked at him. "You thought this was the man on your wall. I hope you find out, Tom."

Then she turned away, set the doll on the counter and ran the tap water again for the dirty dishes.

Tom left.

CHAPTER THIRTY

Tom watched the shadowy palms shake in the gusting wind and listened to the distant turbulence of thunder as he peered out from the Durango, waiting for Culpepper.

Thunder rumbled again and the first fat drops of rain smacked into the asphalt.

Without turning on his wipers, he watched Heather's home, gone rubbery through the deluge. The houses and vegetation along the street became amorphous shapes.

When Culpepper arrived, Tom traded a few brief words with the agent, promised him shift relief, then drove off.

* * *

He pulled into parking lot at the dog track and found a free space, stared through the windshield at the large, dark building. From his angle the grandstands and racetrack were blocked, but he could see the green awning covering the poker room entrance.

His phone burped, and he answered the incoming call from the ROC.

"Ms. Holman," Tom said to the researcher. "Working late?"

"Well I just love my tiny little office so much I can't bear to leave. Listen; wanted to just follow up with you — I sent you an email, don't know if you saw it yet, I know how busy you are."

"I'm finding things to do with my time."

"It's in reference to Charles Moss, the late Glenn Moss's brother. You asked me to find what I could on him, so, here it is — Charles Moss is older than Glenn by two years. Before the Air Force, he worked as a manager for a couple different department stores. Sort of like Glenn, working for Home Depot — but looking at Charles's tax returns, I'd say Home Depot is much more lucrative than the places Charles worked. Anyway, no criminal record, good health, joined the Air Force and took about seven years to get promoted to technical sergeant, and . . . that's really it."

"Were you able to get an address for him? A number?"

"He's in Stamford, Connecticut. Unmarried, though, no kids, and he's currently on active duty. The trail sort of went dark — I guess the next step is to contact him through the Air Force, but I thought I'd call you first."

"Thank you, Cheyenne. That's good for now." He put the phone away.

The rain pounding the area began to let up. Poker at the track ran late into the night. The doors beneath the awning were propped open and he could see people inside.

He undid a couple of buttons on his white dress shirt, took a breath and got out of the car, traversed the wet asphalt and went inside.

Three men sat belly-up to the bar, a half dozen more at the small round tables spread through the room. The air smelled like stale beer and cologne. The carpet terrifically gaudy, meant to resemble confetti spilled across the floor. Lounge music played from the speakers above the bar. Tom thought he recognized Tony Bennett's singing.

The bartender was a skinny older man with dark smudges under his eyes.

"Help you?"

"How about a Jack and Coke."

Tom glanced around as the bartender fixed the drink. Just about everyone was giving him the eye. Older men, fifties and sixties. One man had jowls that hung below his jawline. They wore suits and floral-print shirts.

"Five-fifty, pal."

Tom fished the money out of his wallet. He smiled and said, "I'm looking for a poker game. Not sure how this works."

The bartender took the money and examined Tom with dark eyes. "Tonight is five hundred dollar High Hand, every half hour. Ends at midnight."

The clock on the wall above the racks of liquor read five minutes to ten. "Great." Tom nodded toward the doors at the back of the bar. "So I just go in through there? Who do I pay?"

The bartender, still holding Tom's cash, blinked down at him. "You gotta qualify first. Full house or better. Then it's two-dollar jackpot rake on all pots over ten dollars."

He was speaking English, but Tom had no idea what the man was saying. Nick used to talk a bit about poker, and Tom had generally tuned-out.

The bartender tilted his head, still trying to get a read on Tom. "You want no-limit, you gotta come in on Fridays." He turned away with the money and rang up the purchase on the old-fashioned register between the liquor racks, looking at Tom in the mirror as he made change.

He set the change on the bar, gave Tom one more look-over: wet hair, unbuttoned shirt, jeans. "You go through those doors, up the stairs. Good luck, buddy."

Tom pocketed the money. Could feel the eyes burning holes in his back as he picked up the drink and left. The heavy double doors closed behind him, smothering out

Tony Bennett, but there was music playing from speakers in the stairwell — smooth jazz.

On the next floor, a wide hallway fed several rooms. Murmuring voices drifted out, the clack of poker chips, someone either coughed or farted. At the back of the hallway was a door with a sign that led to the grandstands, but it said "Closed".

He moved past the rooms, giving them sidelong looks, sipping his drink as he went.

What are you doing here, Tom?

At the end of the hallway he pushed against the crash bar, the door gave. The blue-gray nighttime lighting filled a large space with deep shadows. A wall of glass overlooked the dog track below, the dirt oval lit up by two towers, the drizzle glittering. He thought of Declan. Tall, gangly body, hungry eyes fixed on the track.

Tom moved past the concessions stand, toward the back of the long, rectangular room, to the booths where racing bets were placed.

To the right of the booths, a corridor. His footsteps echoed past closed doors for administration, maintenance, security. The air smelled antiseptic but musty.

"Hey, what are you doing?"

A broad-chested man in a dark suit was standing back at the mouth of the corridor by the betting booths. His slicked hair shone in the lights.

"Poker rooms?"

The man took a few steps, then stopped. He pointed. "Back that way."

Tom sipped his drink to keep up appearances and started walking back. "Sorry," he said as he neared. "Got a little lost I guess."

The man glared at him. "Got lost? What're you doing out here?"

Tom held up his injured hand in peace. "Alright, alright. Sorry. Just wanted to look around. This place is really something, you know?"

In proximity, Tom recognized Rodney Lamotta. His picture had hung on Tom's wall for months, just to the right of Palumbo.

Lamotta scrutinized him and put out an arm to keep him from walking past.

"Let me see some ID, guy."

Tom stopped walking. Took a slow breath. He pulled his badge and showed it to Lamotta. "Okay? Can't a fella get a late game of cards?"

"Yeah, right. I saw you come in, smart guy. Pidgy told me you don't know cards from your ass . . ." He glanced up, eyes a bit wider, like he recognized Tom's last name.

"The fuck are you doing here?"

"Where's Palumbo? He around?"

"The fuck do you want?"

"What do you think?" Tom stepped close. He was on the tall side, but Lamotta was taller. Heavier. Tom stared up into his face.

Lamotta kept clocking him, cold in the eyes, mouth twitching a little bit, then he said, "Hold on." He stepped away, looking aside at Tom, but punching at his phone. A moment later he was mumbling into it, still watching Tom, then said, "Yeah, alright." He slipped the phone into the pocket of his double-breasted suit coat.

"Let's take a drive."

"He's not here?"

"No. He ain't here. You coming or what? You wouldn't be sneaking around back here if you had a warrant, so either let's go or you can fuck off."

Five minutes later, Tom was riding in the back of an SUV — a blacked-out GMC Yukon, two guys flanking him, Lamotta driving, watching him in the rear-view mirror, unspeaking. Tom kept up with where they were, he'd driven the route enough times, like they were going to Nick's old house, in Naples. But where it would've been one turn for Nick's, Lamotta took another direction, and they were cruising along Gulf Shore Drive, where millionaires kept their gigantic homes, most of them occupied only a couple of weeks of the year.

Palumbo's was like so many of the others: big gate out in front, looking like some Mediterranean castle, perimeter lights trained up on the house, blanching the yellow walls white. Tom spotted at least two guards on the upper levels, hidden behind the palm trees, one of them stepped out onto a balcony as the Yukon rolled up the driveway.

Place was worth twenty-million, at least. Probably ten thousand square feet, would be glorious views of the Gulf on the other side — he could hear the waves slopping against the shore as the men got out and walked him inside.

They were greeted at the door by a guy wearing all black, bald-headed, half-frame glasses perched on his nose. He gave Tom a big smile and Tom saw the fabric of the guy's suit stretch over the gun he carried in his own shoulder holster. They'd already patted Tom down, looking for wires, weapons, found his Glock, and he told them there was no way he was letting them take it.

"I'm Franco," the bald man said. "You must be Tom. Come on in."

"He's carrying."

"I know he's carrying, Rodney. What's your choice, officer?"

"It's a Glock Gen4."

"Gen 4? You asked me they didn't make any improvements on the Gen 3. Did you know, Gaston Glock had no experience with gun design when he started out? Knew polymers, though. But like any Glock model, the sights are poor. And it's a tough trigger pull, don't you think?"

Franco led him into the house, the men, including Lamotta, trailing. Pretty understated for a big ego like Palumbo, Tom thought, ignoring Franco's rambling. Marble floor in the main room, coffered ceiling, some maple millwork detail. Franco opened the door to a room with a big limestone fireplace, and a desk, just as big, sitting by a window overlooking the dark Gulf water.

"It's the kind of gun that's all show, but doesn't deliver. But that's just me."

"Uh-huh." Tom couldn't help but notice the rack of wine against the other wall, the Crestron home theater system. If Nick had seen this place, he would've gotten weak in the knees. Tom never cared about this kind of shit.

"Is Mr. Palumbo coming?"

Franco sat behind the desk, framing himself in the window overlooking the water, and motioned to the men flanking Tom. One of them pulled out a chair, and Tom sat down. Lamotta took the chair beside it.

"So," Franco said, "Rodney tells me you were at the track. Looking for a poker game."

"My brother Nick's dead," Tom said. His heart was in his throat, but he figured it would be better not to draw this out. "And my understanding is, he died owing Palumbo some money. From poker losses. I've been handling Nick's estate — you probably know that — but this is a matter that's off the books."

Franco glanced at Lamotta, then folded his hands, tilted his head at Tom like it was the most interesting thing he'd ever heard. "And you're looking to settle up? That's very respectable of you."

"I'm here to find out if Mario Palumbo, if any of you, had something to do with recent crimes. The murders of Brian Hamer, Howard Michael Declan, Danny Coburn."

Franco grinned so wide the folds in his cheeks pushed his glasses up a bit. He looked from man to man, and Tom heard one of the goons behind him give a little titter. Then Franco looked at Tom, a puzzled expression overcoming his weirdly bare features, asked, "And you think I would just tell you, one way or the other?"

"If it has something to do with me, with Nick, any of it, then yes. I'm willing to settle Nick's outstanding debts. I don't need to be blackmailed; I'm here, I'd like to work it out."

"Blackmailed?" Franco laughed again, then stuck a finger in his eye, worked it around, examined what was there, flicked it, and looked over the men surrounding Tom another time. "When you patted him down, you checked this man for a wire, right?"

Lamotta said, "Yeah, we checked him."

"You check him for balls, too? Find a nice big set? Because this is an interesting tactic for the FDLE. Just walk right in, boom!" He slapped his hands down on the big desk. If it was meant to make Tom flinch, it didn't work. "Boom," Franco said again, "just walk right in and ask point blank."

Tom said nothing, just looked at the bald man, waited.

Franco seemed to lose interest, or cease to be amused. "No, Agent Lange. That's the answer to all your questions: No. Mr. Palumbo runs a respectable business, everything on the level. Some people, like your brother, or Howard Declan, they might have a problem, but that's their own problem, that's not on Mr. Palumbo. There are ways to get support — I hear gamblers' anonymous has a high success rate."

"What's the debt right now?" Tom asked.

Franco glanced at Lamotta, who answered. "It's right around sixty grand."

"And that's with the vig running for the past year?"

Franco got a quizzical look. "The vig? No, that would be illegal, Agent Lange, you'd be talking about a loan shark, extreme high interest rates, extralegal activity. This is all above board. Our interest rates are all in accordance with the criminal usury statutes. Really, this is just a matter of time — our bank will soon make its claim against your brother's estate and this will all get sorted in probate court."

"But you were letting Nick pay off the debt by other means," Tom said, the nerves really starting to throttle him. He could feel the men close behind him, Lamotta's staring eyes, but he stayed fixed on Franco.

"I don't know anything about that," Franco said. "All I know is that you've gone out of your way to come here and talk about repaying your brother's debt, but we don't work that way. Again, that would be illegal." Franco stood up, the palms blowing around out the window as fresh rain swept through. "Now, we've shown you every courtesy, gone out of our way to talk to you, respectfully, but the rest of this will be handled in probate court." He turned away.

"You mentioned Declan had a problem. Was gambling all you meant?"

Franco sort of froze, then slowly turned his head back to Tom. "Well, I would say his other problem is that he's dead. Otherwise, Agent Lange, I don't know, nor do I give a fuck."

One of the men grabbed Tom's shoulder. The touch jacked his pulse but he got up out of the chair, looked Franco in the eye, said, "Thank you."

The men led him out of the room, Franco staying behind in front of that big window, the storm starting to whip again. They moved outside, Tom drenched in seconds, hustled to the car, and they threw him in the back, rather roughly, he thought.

Driving away, Tom said to Lamotta, "I never asked about Edgar Vasquez."

"Guy, I'm tellin' you . . ."

"You're telling me what? You gonna sit there and deny that Palumbo was romancing Vasquez, but Vasquez gave him the cold shoulder, and oops, his car goes speeding up, slams into a semi, kills him and his wife?"

Lamotta just stared in the mirror. Tom didn't speak again until they were back at the track, fifteen minutes later.

"Come on, Lamotta. I know you, you got almost twenty years in this shit, and what's with this guy? Franco's been here, what? Two years? And he's Palumbo's number two guy all of a sudden, living in his house, acting like he runs southwest Florida. If you want to talk, Rodney, now's your chance."

Lamotta's forehead wrinkled. "Get the fuck outta the car."

One of the men opened the door from the back seat, left, yanked Tom out. As soon as he had solid footing, Tom grabbed the guy, whipped his arm around behind his back and shoved him against the car. Pulled his gun out a split second later, jammed it in the guy's ribs. Lamotta and the other guy banged out of the car, came running around, but Lamotta stopped the other henchman from doing anything. "Whoa, whoa," Lamotta said. "Hey, Lange, what the fuck."

The man Tom had pinned grit his teeth and moaned as Tom applied upward pressure on the arm, edging it to the breaking point. Tom leaned toward his ear: "What's your name?"

"Fuck you."

"Yeah? Fuck me?" Tom stared at Lamotta, who was keeping his distance. The other guy had his gun out, pointed down. The rain blurred everything out, warm and soaking. Tom let go of the guy, took a couple big steps back. The guy turned around, rubbing his wrist. He grinned at Tom, a humorless expression that deepened the lines around his eyes. "You're fucking pathetic. That's what you got, tough guy?"

Tom took off his shoulder holster. Let it drop. Pulled out his badge, held it up for the men to see, tossed it aside.

"Come on," he said to the guy he'd antagonized. "Come on, motherfucker. Any of you. Fucking come on. I'm not a cop. Right now I'm nothing."

Tom heard footsteps. He quickly moved toward the main concourse just in time to see two more men come running out from under the green awning. They slowed when they saw what was going on.

Five to one, Tom thought.

Those odds were just fine.

* * *

He drove too fast, blood still running from his cut eye, but that jumbled mix of anger and frustration that had been building the past two days — the volume had been turned down. At least for now.

Fuck it. He didn't care that Palumbo's men might have killed him. To feel that way was scary, dangerous, but true. Ben Franco had acted coy, but Tom doubted Palumbo's number two guy actually knew anything about what happened to Declan. Or, maybe he did; maybe that bald creep was making moves to impress Palumbo, or even to supersede him. If so, Tom thought he'd stirred things up enough so that if anyone in Franco's cohort was texting and emailing him, the communication would start to reflect what had happened, one way or the other.

Make them think you're crazy, unpredictable. It was one thing Jack Vance had taught him when they'd spent time together, discussing the job. Do right by your co-workers, be straight, but the bad guys shouldn't know whether you were coming or going.

Sane or insane.

CHAPTER THIRTY-ONE

SUNDAY

He was staring up at the ceiling through a blurred, puffy eye, alone in his bed, sorting through his various aches and pains. He looked over to the side Katie had slept on, as much as three or four times a week for the past few months. No one there.

His phone rang. Tom checked the time, not yet seven a.m.

"Director Turnbull. Good morning."

"Lange, we caught a major break. I've been working with County VNB, Coby's unit. The death investigation has allowed a few things to open up."

Tom sat up, bright bolts of pain in his head and neck. "And?"

"Turns out Coby has been working with a C.I., a guy named André Rapp. Normally that would be protected information, but these are special circumstances. Rapp was busted a few years ago for possession of a controlled substance with intent to distribute. He's tied to the Palumbo family. He did two years at Hardee and Coby turned him into a C.I. Reporting on other members of the Palumbo family, what they were doing in there, all that. He gets out and Coby keeps working him. But a week ago he stole a car."

"A Chevy Tahoe."

"2010 model, took it from a Costco shopping center. Coby found out, went to check up on Rapp at his apartment in Immokalee."

Tom got dressed as he listened. Jeans, plain black t-shirt, shoulder holster.

"So Coby knew. About the Tahoe — he linked it to Heather Moss and our investigation."

"It seems so."

"Tried to handle it himself by talking to Rapp?"

"You're going to get him," Turnbull said. "Blythe will meet you with a team at the ROC in a half an hour."

"I'll be there in twenty minutes."

* * *

Tom manipulated the Kevlar vest, trying to make it more comfortable as the SWAT vehicle barreled down the highway. Blythe sat in the back seat with him, her body rocking with the movement of the vehicle, her lips a thin line. She was wearing her own bulletproof vest.

There were five other SWAT members in the huge vehicle, something that looked like it belonged in the military; half tank, half van. The driver turned off the highway onto a residential street, regained speed. Tom looked behind them — a second SWAT vehicle followed.

He checked his weapon for the third time, making sure the magazine and chamber were clear of debris.

"Relax," Blythe said without looking. Then: "You going to tell me what happened to you?"

"No."

She tilted her head back and stared up at the ceiling. "Un-fucking-believable."

A voice up front said: "Here we go."

Tom blew out some air and closed his eyes a moment. He felt the vehicle slow. When he looked, he could see the apartment building; white stucco with rusty water stains beneath a downspout on the corner. Four stories, an exterior stairway that zagged back and forth up one side.

The vehicle jerked to a halt. The doors all opened at once, the team spilled out into the late morning. Blythe squeezed past Tom and he stepped out last.

SWAT was fast, already moving up the stairs like Special Forces on a raid. Blythe ascended the stairs after them, and Tom followed. He noticed a child, too young for school, standing with his scooter over by the dirty pool opposite the parking lot. The little boy was staring at the men and women in black clothes streaming up to the third floor, now gliding along the balcony, everything quiet, just the whisper of clothing and subtle clacking of body armor.

Tom hustled to the floor, came around the corner just as two SWAT used a battering ram on apartment 3-F. The door burst open and they poured inside.

"André Rapp! Florida State Police! We have a warrant!"

Tom braced himself and stepped through the door, yanked off his sunglasses. More shouts and commotion. A black streak as a SWAT member moved between doorways, checking rooms, the tip of his Colt M4 Carbine leading the way. The apartment was unkempt: a derelict couch faced an enormous flat screen, the TV canted at an angle, a crummy particle-board table sagging beneath it. Hot, stolid air, like Declan's place, smelling of burnt eggs.

"Here! Here!"

Tom darted around Blythe and entered the room where the SWAT member had gone. André Rapp was on his bed, just a mattress and a box spring. He crossed his arms across his face as the SWAT team surrounded him, weapons trained.

Blythe nudged past Tom, holding out the warrant. "André Thomas Rapp?"

The guy looked pale for a Floridian, like he'd been holed up in this apartment for too long. His ginger hair was long and frizzy, tied back in a loose ponytail. When he spoke, Tom saw a missing tooth on the lower deck.

"Jesus, guys! Jesus! How many of you are—? Jesus!"

"Are you André Rapp?" Blythe stopped right at the foot of the bed.

"Yes! Yes. Christ. I didn't do nothing. What are you doing in my house?" He stayed supine, holding up his hands. "You guys scared the shit out of me."

"Mr. Rapp, we have a warrant for your arrest."

"For what? Jesus! For what? I told you, I didn't do nothing. I'm clean."

"We're going to need you to come with us," Blythe said.

Tom looked around the gloomy bedroom. No windows; the only light came from a fish tank in the corner. Clothes littered the stained carpet. A chintzy desk and a cheap chair occupied one corner, a few papers scattered about.

"Get him up, please."

Two SWAT members did as she asked and hauled André Rapp out of bed. He raised his arms over his head. He was wearing a tank top and an ugly pink pair of shorts, no shoes, and stunk like he hadn't washed his ass in a few days. They walked him out of the room, Blythe reading him his rights.

"Let me get my sandals!" Rapp whined. "Jesus!"

Tom hunted in the mess and found a pair of battered sandals, kicked them over to Rapp. The man stared at Tom's cuts and bruises, and Tom stared back. Rapp stuck his feet into the sandals and the SWAT jerked him away.

Tom lingered in the room. No computer in here, nothing remotely techy or sophisticated. He pulled open a couple dresser drawers. "Got a weapon here . . ."

He quickly snapped on a pair of latex gloves and pulled out the handgun. Looked like a Beretta 9mm. Tom brought it into the living room. They were just about to drag Rapp out the front door.

"This yours?"

"Hey! Hey, yeah, that's mine. It's totally legal, man."

"You're a felon with a handgun license?"

"Ah, man. I got the papers for it."

"Let's go," Blythe said. "Move."

Rapp was hauled outside.

Tom moved through the rest of the apartment and found Rapp's phone charging in the kitchen. The screen was cracked and there was some gummy substance on the corner. He set down the gun, picked up the phone and swished through the log.

Nothing. No texts on Rapp's phone like the ones Tom had received. He left the phone, put the gun back in the drawer and headed out.

The day seemed brighter after the semidarkness of Rapp's apartment. Tom descended the stairs as SWAT loaded Rapp into one of the vehicles and slammed the door.

Blythe was standing on the asphalt, looking at the cars parked in the lot. The slots were numbered, the white paint faded. Tom caught up to her and walked along the slate of cars until they came to an empty spot that corresponded to Rapp's apartment.

No stolen Tahoe.

He started to say something but she stalked back to the waiting SWAT vehicles. "Let's go talk to him," she said over her shoulder.

* * *

"This is bullshit," Rapp said in the interrogation room. "What about my human rights, man?" He sniffed and wiped his nose with the back of one hand, shackled to the other in front of him. "I mean, coming into someone's home like that? What if you gave someone a heart attack? How is that even allowed in our society?"

"You go to a judge," Blythe said. "The judge signs off on a warrant."

"I mean, Christ. It's just not right." He gaped at Tom. "Happened to you? I hope that was from the last guy you steamrolled."

"You should've thought of that before you stole a car," Tom said. He stood by the wall though Blythe had taken her seat across from Rapp.

"I didn't steal no car," Rapp sniveled. "Prove it. Where is it?"

"Doesn't matter where it is. We know you stole it."

"And we know you're working for Mario Palumbo," Blythe said.

"Who?" Rapp's head whipped back and forth, looking at the agents.

"Come on," Blythe pressed. "Let's not do this. We know you sold meth for Palumbo for years before you got sent up. We know that you turned into a C.I. once you were at Hardee. You reported to Sergeant Danny Coburn."

"I don't know who that is, man. I don't know nothing about any of what you're talking about."

"You're in deep shit," Blythe said. "Grand theft auto, violation of your parole, and that's just to begin with. You're going to go away for a long time. Maybe the rest of your life. Unless you cooperate. How many phones you got?"

Rapp looked wounded. Even a hardened criminal was vulnerable to the sting of Blythe. He averted his eyes and seemed to shrink a few inches.

"How many . . . what? Phones I got? One. What the fuck is that supposed to mean?" He shook his head and pooched out his lower lip in self-pity. "This system is *bullshit*, man."

Rapp continued to pout and stare at the table. Tom thought the man was lucky if he had an IQ of a hundred. If he'd managed to rehabilitate his right to own a gun it was doubtful he'd done that on his own, let alone be manipulating cell phones.

"Once again for the recording," Blythe said. "Where were you on the morning of the 23rd, at eleven a.m.?"

"I told you, I was out looking for work. I stopped and saw Bobby Olcheck at the garage in Immokalee. He'll consolidate that."

"You mean corroborate."

"That's what I said."

"You were nowhere near the county jail, or Bonita Springs . . . ?"

"Look," Rapp said, trying to get fierce. "I wasn't anywhere near the jail, or Bonita Springs, and I wasn't anywhere near Orangetree two nights ago. That's a fact."

Blythe tilted her head. "You want to get real, André? You want to just stop this shit and get real with me for a minute? You're not fooling anyone. I told you we know you were a civilian informant. So, what happened? Why'd you boost a Chevy Tahoe, why are you running around in it, showing up at all these crime scenes? Why are you shooting at a woman and her kids in Bonita Springs?"

Tom saw something change in Rapp. It was subtle, like a psychological mask removed. He leaned toward Blythe, his jaw twitching.

"You think I'm afraid of you? Why don't *you* get real for a second, cop. You think I give a shit about going back inside? At least in there I have some chance at protection."

"From whom?"

Rapp glanced at Tom, and rolled his eyes like Blythe was stupid.

"From Mario Palumbo?" Blythe asked. "Because right now, it looks like he put you up to this. Right? So I wouldn't be so sure of how protected you'd be inside. People in jail are dying. So, time to help us, André. Help us put this guy away and stay alive. What did he do? He threatened you? Told you to go after Heather Moss? To poison Sergeant Coburn? We know Coburn met with you two nights ago, just before he died. His movements are tracked, André. He was at your place. When he turned his back, you laced his can of tobacco with potassium cyanide. We're going through your apartment, your trash, we'll find the dropper, or whatever you used. Because he's dead, André. So add to your charges murder one. Killing a cop."

Blythe turned on her heel, her face red. "I'm fucking done with this guy."

For once, Tom thought, the emotions had gotten to Blythe, too. Coburn was a friend. She couldn't help it. He did nothing to stop her, and when the door slammed behind her he faced André Rapp.

"You ever heard of Howard Declan?"

"Who?"

"How about Heather Moss? Know who she is?"

Rapp stared back, his mouth hanging slightly open. Something was working through his mind.

"You know the name, at least. That's the woman you shot at, André. And her two little girls. You're lucky you didn't hit them." Tom reached out and clicked off the recorder. "Or I'd jump across this table and beat you half to death."

Rapp's lower lip trembled, but Tom didn't think it was because of the threat. "He told me not to kill anyone."

"Who? Who told you?"

"He did. The guy who called me. He had a fake voice."

Tom's heart skipped a beat. "Like a voice synthesizer?"

"He told me I wasn't going to kill anyone. Just to make it look good."

Tom considered switching the recorder back on, hesitated. "He said 'make it look good'? The person who called you, put you up to this? Who was it? Ben Franco?"

"Franco? Never heard of him. He never gave a real name, we never met face to face, just those calls. But Palumbo *knew* I was snitching, man. They were gonna come at me. My sister. My ex. My son. Unless I did exactly what they said."

"You're sure it was Palumbo's crew? You know that for a fact? Not someone else?"

"Who else would it be?" Rapp sniffed back some snot and looked down.

"Have you ever heard of Citizen Justice?" Tom stared, hunting for any trace of guile.

The felon blinked. "Citizen Justice?"

"An email address. Citizen-Justice at ymx dot com. Yes? No?"

"Nah, man. I told you, just calls. That's it. Okay, sometimes texts. And all from different numbers."

Tom took in a deep breath, deciding. He turned on the recorder. "You get phone calls and texts. Texts telling you what to do?"

"Yeah. Just check my phone. 945 numbers."

"We will. These calls and texts instructed you to do all this? To shoot at Heather Moss, but not to kill her?"

Rapp lowered his eyes and nodded.

"Speak up, please."

"Yeah. I was supposed to shoot the place up. Try not to hit anyone. Make it look good."

"And Sergeant Coburn."

"Ah, man. You guys, bustin' into my house like that. This is unconstitutional, man. This is system is bullshit."

"So you've said. On the other hand, if you're telling the truth about your gun, you were granted the right to legal ownership after a felony conviction. So, the system isn't all that bad, is it?"

Rapp looked up, back into his woeful act. "This shit violates my human rights. The people of this country won't stand for this. A reckoning is coming, cop. I want a lawyer. I want my lawyer here."

"You got a lawyer? Who's your lawyer? Same person who got you your gun license back?"

Rapp sulked. "What do you care?"

"What's your lawyer's name?"

"I don't know."

"You don't know your lawyer's name?"

His eyes rolled around, bloodshot, the fight drained from him. "That was two years ago or some shit. His name's fuckin Ernie somethin'. Or Eddie."

"Ernie? Eddie? You're fucking with me, André. You're blowing it. This is your shot, André. Your only shot."

"Yeah, Eddie, man, fuck. Or no, that wasn't it. Ernie, maybe, like I said. I don't remember."

"Ernst? Robert Ernst?"

"I'm not admitting nothing. My gun is legal. Listen, you motherfucker — I did what I did to stay alive. I don't care what that bitch says, I *do* have rights, you know. Or don't you cops understand that there are real people in the world, people with—"

Tom closed the door on André Rapp.

CHAPTER THIRTY-TWO

MONDAY

He could access court records online using PACER, which was Public Access to Court Electronic Records, but he didn't trust his laptop and headed to the county courthouse.

Tom took the hallway to the office of the court clerk, his footfalls echoing in the cavernous space. He entered the office and presented his badge to the clerk, then requested to see any court dockets with André Rapp as a defendant or plaintiff.

"Hard copies, please."

Waiting for the clerk to find the information, he drummed his fingers on the counter, glanced up at the camera mounted in the corner.

Wondered who was watching.

She came back with a large file. Tom moved to a room adjacent to the office, which featured a long jury table, several chairs, bookshelves filled with legal reference material and a copy machine in the corner. The court dockets summarized the federal, civil, criminal, and bankruptcy cases on a given date, available to the public. Rapp's file included daily digests during his criminal case for the drug possession. The case was from seven years ago. His lawyer was a man named Alfred Hale. Rapp had pled out and taken his five year bit.

Huh. So much for that.

* * *

Daniel Coburn's memorial service was held without a body; it was on ice at the morgue, one piece in an ongoing investigation. An empty casket adorned the altar, and a picture of the sergeant in his uniform propped on an easel, surrounded by flowers.

Coburn's wife was dressed in black, even wearing a veil. The widow's five children stood soberly beside her, primped and slicked, everyone in their darkest clothes. Their ages ranged from four to seventeen. A girl with an angled blonde hair cut was the eldest, and she carried the youngest on her hip, bouncing the toddler throughout the service, like she was afraid to stop.

Blythe whispered to Tom, but the priest's elocution overwhelmed her voice.

"I said," she repeated, "Sherry really pushed for the expedited memorial service. She's a cop's wife, alright."

It was the first thing Blythe had said to Tom since they'd parted ways after interviewing André Rapp. Not communicating was no way to run an investigation, so they'd been emailing and texting in lieu of actual talk. Pretty much like the rest of the world.

They'd met outside the church and taken their seats together, the air between them retained a brittle tension. She was wearing her hair down but tucked behind her ears; it didn't quite reach her shoulders. She wore a black skirt and suit jacket, a white blouse.

She was right — Coburn hadn't been dead a full two days and there was already a memorial service. A funeral, but minus a corpse. Sherry Coburn probably understood how investigations could drag out and saw no sense in prolonging the grieving process.

He continued to sneak glances at Sherry until he felt eyes on him. Tom turned around and saw Katie Mills a few rows back. She caught his gaze, then looked away.

The church was filled to capacity. The priest's words resonated. Behind his sunglasses Tom's eyes wandered to the stained glass, it took him back to his teenage years with Pastor Johnson. He recognized most of the depictions — the Birth of Jesus, the Ascension of Mary, even some of the more obscure, such as Christ's Charge of Peter. Pastor Johnson had been fond of calling stained glass the poor man's bible, pointing out times when many in a parish were illiterate. "God has a way of getting His message to anyone," the pastor would say.

Even though Tom had spent those Sundays in a Protestant church, the Coburn family's Catholic church felt similar. The lingering smells of incense, the creaking wood of the pews. The effect was calming. His time with the Johnsons had marked a new beginning in his life.

Now the darkness that preceded it was haunting him.

How do you live with your secrets?

When the service ended, he searched for Katie in the crowd. He stayed back as she spoke with Sherry Coburn, and watched as the two of them shared a tearful embrace. Katie bent toward one of the children, a boy with large dimples. She smiled at him through the tears brimming in her eyes, then she moved toward the entrance.

Tom wanted to catch up with her, but he waited with Blythe to pass his condolences on to the widow. He watched Katie stop and talk to some other County cops by the font containing holy water. The font was a young angel holding a basin.

When it was his turn, Tom took Sherry's hand and looked her in the eyes. "I am so sorry for your loss, Mrs. Coburn."

He started to move on, but she held onto him. "You're Agent Lange."

"Yes, ma'am."

She was as tall as Tom, round-faced. Her bright eyes were red from crying behind her veil, but still captivated him. Her grip was strong. "Coby liked you."

"I liked him too."

She moved subtly closer, and her smile vanished. "Don't let this go," she said in a low voice. "I know you picked someone up, I know who he works for. You've got to finish what Coby started. You need to end this, Tom."

She released his hand and stepped back, then immediately turned to Blythe, next in line. Tom eased away, his head heavy with the contradictions. Coburn's work was one of secrecy, but even his wife seemed sure that Palumbo was behind his death.

Unless, though, she'd meant that she knew André Rapp was Coby's C.I. and only that.

The whole thing seemed vulnerable and porous as a sieve. Coburn's surveillance was protected by court order, yet outsiders had access to it thanks to knowing where and how to look for that information. But the more he considered it, the less he thought Shelly's words referred to any of this, exactly. As he drifted toward the exit, he thought her words were an attempt to drown out the complexity, to make things simpler — Coburn was a cop, a good cop, and his death needed to be answered.

He avoided the eyes of other deputies, city cops, state troopers, and prison guards, as he left. It suddenly felt like he was caught in between two worlds — the organized crime of Mario Palumbo, and the tribe of Floridian law enforcement.

Somewhere in the middle of it, pulling strings it seemed, was Citizen Justice. And only Tom knew, only Tom occupied the same ground.

* * *

He managed to catch Katie outside, about a block from the church, getting into her personal vehicle, a compact Honda Fit. She was about to get in but saw him coming and closed the driver's side door.

"Hey," he said, approaching.

"Hey."

She wore the requisite mourning ensemble, black pants and a black button-down shirt. Her brown hair was loose, nesting on her shoulders. Her eyes showed the same fatigue as Sherry's.

"Saw you in there."

"Yeah . . . I can't believe Sherry. That woman is something."

"No kidding." Tom could still feel the cool, dry grip of her hand, her laser eyes seeking his soul. "She's very strong."

"I can't even imagine . . ." Katie sagged against the vehicle. "Left without a husband; five kids. I would be in pieces." She scrutinized his face. "Tom, what did you do?"

"Can we get a cup of coffee?"

Their eyes connected, then she looked at her feet. "Ah, this is a tough time. I *do* want to talk, but right now is . . ."

"It's not about us."

He had her full attention again.

"I mean, I do want to talk about us. Actually, I want to apologize to you. For a lot of things. But right now I need your help. So can we meet? Maybe right around here? Get a table in the back somewhere? It won't take long."

She finally nodded. "Okay. I can give you a half hour. I'm just swamped." He held her door open, she dropped into the seat and looked up. "You must be, too."

There was something in her face that made him wonder if word had gotten out that he'd had Heather Moss stay at his house. He knew Blythe wouldn't talk, or Culpepper, but this was a cop's world, and cops were always watching.

"Yeah, things have been pretty crazy."

* * *

It was hard, sitting across from her, not to reminisce. Katie seemed more like a stranger now than when he'd first met her. He hated to think it was over. If it was, it was his fault.

He'd been far more open with Heather than his own girlfriend. Why? Maybe because with Katie he'd seen a future, and it scared him, so he'd kept a distance.

Funny how that worked.

"Coburn came to see me," he said.

"I know. The night he died."

"He said his unit was hacked."

"He did?"

"We don't know the extent of the damage. Turnbull is scrambling to find any leaks from within the department. The whole thing is obviously being kept under wraps. I'm just telling you because . . . I want you to watch your back."

The waitress appeared, interrupting. They gave their orders, a couple of coffees, a piece of apple pie. Tom thought of Iowa Schnell as he watched the waitress pick her way through the crowded café to put in their order.

Katie was eyeing him. "Tom. What is it? Who hacked Coburn's unit? Palumbo?"

"We don't know."

"Same person as whoever was spying on the jail, though, right?"

"Right. You should protect CID. Talk to your supervisor, make sure your firewalls are all up to date, that sort of thing. Have you gotten any strange messages? Emails or texts?"

"No. I don't know. Not that I know of."

Tom nodded and drummed his fingers, feeling restless. "When is someone going to just fucking take down Palumbo? When are the feds going to make a move? When was Coby? Ever?"

She was silent a moment. "You know how it is, Tom. It takes a lot of time to build a case like that . . ."

"Two years, Katie. Or close to it."

"Sure. Coby's unit put all sorts of people in jail. They get some of them working for them. Others, at least they're off the streets. They make drug seizures. But Palumbo is getting slicker all the time. He's using more boats now, working with other people."

"He was trying to work with the Vasquez family. I think he took out Edgar Vasquez to create a void he could fill, stone crabbers down in Everglades City . . ." Tom shook his head. "It just keeps going on and on. There's no switch to turn it off."

"Maybe this is it. This case. Pinning Declan's death to Palumbo. Proving Palumbo used Declan to get rid of Edgar— Why are you shaking your head?"

"It's not him. It's not Palumbo."

"Why? How can you know?" She pointed at the cut on his face, the bruise around his eye. "Is that where you got this? What — did you just show up, start harassing people?"

"Look at how Declan was killed. Blythe said it: a text book organized crime hit. It's like someone was trying to hand us Palumbo. 'Here's a potential accomplice to a mob murder, and then he gets taken out — *in jail*.'"

Katie's voice was measured. "You think someone in county has been back-channeling? I mean, framing Palumbo when there's already so much real evidence on him?"

"Real evidence? If there's any real evidence, why's he still walking around, breathing the same air as us?"

"Tom, if memory serves, you went to school for criminology. Surely your studies inform you that Palumbo is not the exception to the rule. Organized criminals like him — businessmen — float above the law. You get them

267

on some bullshit charge, they beat it, and it's like bacteria learning to resist the antibodies. He just gets stronger."

"Exactly."

Katie sighed. The waitress arrived with their coffee and pie, blocking her exit.

"Can I get you anything else?" Her gaze traveled between them.

Katie answered, "No, thank you."

When the waitress moved off again, Katie levied a long look at Tom. Her round, pretty face appeared older, he thought he saw a hint of pity in her eyes.

"You think someone inside law enforcement has taken up the mantle, gone where the law can't go, that kind of thing?"

"I think that's more likely than Palumbo making all these moves out of character. People keep saying 'textbook organized crime', but for my money, that's a shot to the back of the head, it's not hacking and spying and poison."

"The world is changing."

"And this guy we rolled up on, André Rapp, he admitted that the person he's working for told him to make it look like a drive-by shooting on Heather Moss, but not to hurt her."

She blinked. She hadn't known that. "So it's some vigilante with a conscience?"

He stared at his coffee, then took a sip of the hot liquid. "Please just tell me if you know anything, Katie."

She stared, then let out a trembling breath. She had yet to touch her own coffee, a tendril of steam rose up from it.

"Okay."

He waited.

"I heard some things. That's all. Just talk."

His heart started to beat a little faster.

"VNB has been frustrated," she said. "For the very reasons you're talking about — Palumbo keeps slipping away. They've made all sorts of busts, interdiction teams picking up drug runners all up and down the coast, but no one flips. No one takes the plea deal. I heard that the feds had gotten involved at one point, there was talk of RICO, but then it just seemed to go away."

"Why?"

She looked defiant. But then she answered. "Because the whole thing is tainted. There was speculation the feds found out about the data breach in Coburn's unit."

"What? They knew? Where's this coming out of?"

"Machado. Her brother is in information tech. There was a big scramble; Machado's brother was working on retooling the whole thing for vice narcotics, adding security, things like that."

"When did this happen?"

"I don't know. Not long ago. All I heard is that there's someone out there messing with this stuff. It's all electronic. Like I said, the world is changing. Staying the same too . . . Listen, I heard one name, and you can't tell anyone that this came from me, Machado, her brother, nobody — do you understand? I heard that—"

"Citizen Justice," he said.

Her face went slack. He heard her swallow. "You already know."

He lifted his phone in the air and rotated it so she could read the screen, but Katie grabbed it. She read the most recent email, then went back through the chain. "Oh my God, Tom. This is it. This is him. You're *emailing* with this guy?"

Tom leaned back and surveyed the café. "I think this guy gets whatever dirt he can find on anyone. Something he can leverage you with. Like Declan, and the child pornography. He's got something on me, too, Katie."

She continued scrolling and looking, and Tom saw it register on her face. Katie sighed heavily and closed her eyes. "That's you?" She shoved the phone back at him and started to leave. "I can't do this, Tom."

"Yeah, that's me. I lied, Katie. On my application for the FDLE. On all the paperwork, every bit of it. That picture is from my arrest when I was fourteen. I'd gotten in a fight with a guy — he was five years older than me — and I nearly killed him. When the cops came, I ran. They caught me, I resisted. They found the drugs I was carrying." He sighed. "I was in possession of crack-cocaine."

She just watched him, stopped in her tracks.

"I would have gone to juvie, but when my case manager found out he notified my psychologist, Dr. Camden. Camden stepped in, talked about what I'd been through. They showed mercy on me, amended the charges, let me off with a strong warning. But I still lied about it all. I've been lying, keeping it a secret, for years."

"Why are you telling me this? In six months you never even—"

"Because *he* knows. Whoever is doing this, whoever killed Declan, Hamer, and now Coby, he knows. He knows that if this comes out, I'm finished with the FDLE."

She stared. "Is he blackmailing you? What's he asking you to do?"

"He hasn't yet."

"You have to tell Blythe. And your director."

"I know."

Silence lingered between them. Tom felt a mix of emotions. He'd been carrying the lie for years. From the moment he'd decided to go into law enforcement right up until one minute ago, knowing that he'd been dishonest, rationalizing that it was all for the greater good. It was exhausting, and he felt unburdened.

But he could have put Katie at further risk. He picked up his phone, which suddenly felt dangerous. Really, just about any device could be weaponized for spying. The phone could be a listening device.

He powered down the phone, staring at it. "And I'm sorry, Katie. I'm sorry I never — I've been afraid to, ah . . . I've been afraid of what you'd think of me. That Nick, with all his problems, Nick was better. He was stronger. Better with people, with everything. I'm just . . . I don't know what I am." The phone off, he pulled the battery.

When he looked up, Katie had tears in her eyes. She wiped her face and sobered as she looked at separated phone and battery. "What are you doing?"

"This guy said something to me. He said everyone does his bidding eventually."

"Well, Tom. You get out in front of it, then. You come clean. Then he can't manipulate you."

"You're right."

He started to get up, stopped. She was watching him closely, worried. "What would he try to get you to do?"

"I don't know." Tom leaned across the table and took her hand. "Thank you, Katie."

"Where are you going now?"

"Heather Moss has court to try and get her kids back this afternoon. I'm headed there. Listen to me. Be careful. I'll check in with you later today."

She looked again at the pieces of phone in his grip. "You gonna send me smoke signals?"

"I'll find you. Talk to you in person. Just like people used to do in the old days."

CHAPTER THIRTY-THREE

Tom met Blythe in front of the county courthouse in a wide angle of shadow. Nearby a lawyer in a white suit was smoking and talking loud into a cell phone; two sheriff deputies were laughing at some joke, one standing in the shadow, the other blanched by the light. They walked up the steps and headed inside. He ventured a question as they went through security.

"How's Rapp holding up?"

"Hasn't stopped talking about his civil rights. Forensics has been all through his apartment, no evidence of potassium cyanide yet. And we still don't have the vehicle. But Mandi is ready to formally charge him on suspicion of murder — he was the last person to see Coburn alive."

"Before I did."

"Right. Before you." Both of them through the security portal, she stopped. "Listen, what I said about you, and Coby . . ."

Tom put up a hand — no apology necessary. "Did Rapp call his lawyer?"

She shook her head, and they resumed walking. "Public defender came in last night and talked with him for fifteen minutes. I don't know that he ever had a real lawyer."

"I went ahead and checked on Rapp's story about his gun license. Turns out, he's telling the truth. I knew about this, never really looked into it — it's called 'relief from the disability of not being able to possess a gun'."

They ascended to the courtroom. Blythe pushed open the door and they slipped into the back. Sitting beside Blythe, who'd effectively sounded the alarm on Heather and her children, was awkward.

Heather had her back to them, standing beside her lawyer. Robert Ernst looked much snappier today, having traded in his rumpled, off-the-rack suit for something fitted. His hair seemed trimmer, even his bald spot shining in the overhead lights of the courtroom was more dignified. Tom listened as Ernst gave the judge an impassioned plea, praising Heather Moss as a mother:

"Your honor, what's happened over the past few days is no fault of my client. Mrs. Moss has provided a loving, stable, and safe environment for her children from the beginning. After the tragic loss of her husband, she relocated to Florida where she's done clinical therapy, providing a valuable service to the community, and helping people every day."

The prosecutor, Ginny Staithe, whom Tom had met during the Gallo case, cut in: "Your honor, this isn't about the virtues of Mrs. Moss's work. But her lawyer does raise an interesting point. After the loss of her husband, Mrs. Moss chose to relocate. But she relocated over a thousand miles away from the friends and family who could help ease the burden of raising two children alone."

"That is out of line," Ernst said, "and irrelevant. People move all the time, for all sorts of reasons. We can't fault someone for their mobility. Our right to ambulate is enshrined in the U.S. Constitution—"

"Alright, alright, Mr. Ernst . . ." The judge raised his hands. "If we can stick to the issue. The issue is the two children, and whether or not they're at risk for psychological or physical harm. Now, when I allowed for the children to be returned to Mrs. Moss after her arrest, it was predicated on her being in witness protection. But she is no longer protected by the state. The court's concern is for the safety of the children."

"Your honor . . ." Ernst sounded gruff. "This is not my client's fault. The state bureau was unable to provide compelling evidence to secure the witness protection."

Tom flinched. It wasn't exactly true. The witness protection had been denied before the time limit proposed by Mandi was up.

Ernst went on. "It's unconscionable to keep children from their mother because of the shortcomings of law enforcement."

"Excuse me, Mr. Ernst. I don't appreciate referendums on the efficacy of police procedure in my courtroom."

"I'm sorry your honor, but—"

Staithe interjected: "And may I remind Mr. Ernst that his client still faces a preliminary hearing for the matter he's referring to — fleeing the scene of a crime. And she's still a major witness in an ongoing investigation — what are Mrs. Moss's children going to do for months of legal proceedings? A trial, if it comes to that?"

"That's completely speculative, and it's not—" Ernst began.

"This is not about penalizing Mrs. Moss," Staithe said quickly. "This is about what's best for her children. Mrs. Moss is involved in a complicated case, one where she's been threatened, her children have been threatened, she's been shot at, and spent time in jail. With due respect to the FDLE, I agree with Mr. Ernst that as they have not been able to exculpate Mrs. Moss with evidence, it puts her in a very difficult position and it leaves her children without an effective parent."

"An effective parent?"

Tom's ears felt hot at the mentions of his failure to find a culprit for the murders. But he was distracted by the way Ernst put his hand around Heather's shoulder. And his mind was running away . . .

"Mrs. Moss has been an exemplary parent," Ernst said. Heather glanced at his hand and he withdrew it. "To have gone through what she has, the loss of a spouse, of her children's *father*, and still be a woman with a career, and an incredible mother. Let's face it, your honor. If there's any referendum, this is about judging Mrs. Moss's ability to be a mother, to provide security for her children. And she's done everything right. After the terrible events at the county jail, the first thing she did, the *very first thing*, was to go get her daughters. Their safety was her number one priority, and it has continued to be. And to their credit, the FDLE sought to further provide protection by taking her to a second undisclosed location after the formal witness protection was denied. And the children were safe. Then DFS pushed to find their location, and *this*, if anything, is what has compromised matters."

Staithe held a hand out toward Ernst. "Your honor, Mr. Ernst has just admitted that the children are in danger."

"I said 'compromised', Ms. Staithe, not 'endangered'."

The judge raised his hands again. As he spoke, Tom watched Ernst lean toward Heather. She seemed to shrink from him a bit. When she turned to look over her shoulder and look at Tom, he felt a jolt.

Tom stood and hurried out of the courtroom, ignoring the looks.

* * *

He got Cheyenne Holman on the landline phone in the clerk's office.

"I've been trying to call you but your cell goes straight to voice mail," she said.

"Did you get something?" Because of the memorial service, he hadn't had time to check other courthouse dockets, like Lee County, and on Sunday the public office had been closed.

"I did," Holman said. "Rapp was a litigant in Lee County in pursuit of rehabilitating his right to possess a gun."

"Was his lawyer Alfred Hale?"

"No, someone else. Legal counsel is listed as Robert J. Ernst. That name mean anything to you?"

"Get me any and all documents including both Rapp and Ernst. Don't email them; have a courier bring hard copies to the Naples field office." Fresh adrenaline twisted through his body. He thanked her and fled the courthouse.

* * *

Blythe met him at the field office, an annex within the courthouse grounds.

When she entered the room, she switched on a light, jumped when she saw Tom waiting for her in the kitchenette, leaning against the counter.

"What are you doing standing here in the dark?"

"I've been thinking."

"Where the hell did you go?"

"What happened at the hearing?"

"The judge went for it. She's getting her kids back. Ernst pulled it out of his ass. I have to admit, he's pretty good . . . What are you holding?"

Blythe set her things down beside her desk. Between her sharp looks and her sharper personality, he had to force the confidence to say what needed to be said.

"I've kept going over it, this idea that whoever is killing these people, they're part of the criminal justice system. Someone who knows cops, criminals, jails — who knows where to look and how to find their secrets.

Someone who's protected by confidentiality. Someone who's everywhere, you know, but nobody you'd really notice."

She crossed her arms and stared across the office. "We have André Rapp still on a 48-hour hold. He stole a Chevy Tahoe. He met with Coburn. He works for Palumbo."

"He said he's been taking orders, jumping through hoops. Text messages threatening his loved ones, telling him what to do . . ."

"From 945 numbers," Blythe said. "We've looked into his phone. And we know from Coby that there are 945 numbers in Palumbo's crew."

"They're generic numbers. Coby had nothing major on anyone using a 945 prepaid. They just pop up here and there, they're burners, don't last long."

"Rapp will talk, all the way up. I know he will. Maybe the others wouldn't, but he's weak."

"Maybe he was led to believe its Palumbo."

She spit out some air and rolled her eyes. "Someone is framing Palumbo? Said the guy who looks like he was in a bar fight? You know I never recommended your suspension on the Gallo case . . ."

"I know. Turnbull did. And you're thinking about it now, I get it."

"You really think someone is framing him? Why? Why would someone do that? Who?"

"At first I thought maybe Vasquez. His people trying to get it out that Palumbo flushed Vasquez down the toilet when he wouldn't agree to terms. Or that Vasquez just lost control of his car, and they're trying to make Palumbo look guilty anyway."

"You said cops, Lange. That's what you said."

"Yeah, or maybe one cop, frustrated by legal limitations. Going after Declan because he was a pedophile, but they couldn't do anything because they'd found out using third-party surveillance." He pushed the

277

papers at her before she could retort. "But now I'm wondering about someone else. Rapp said his lawyer on the gun thing was Eddie or Ernie. He couldn't remember for sure. He was talking about Robert Ernst."

Blythe strode across the office and snatched the papers. She scanned them, the vein in her temple protruding. "Okay. So Ernst was Rapp's lawyer." Her eyes drove at Tom. "It's quite a coincidence."

"Yeah."

She wandered back to her chair and sat down, still looking at the paperwork. "So what does it mean?"

"After I left the courthouse and came here, I called Dale Rhodes."

"And?"

"Rhodes had told me that Brian Hamer, when he was finally busted for the tax fraud, got some help for his defense. Rhodes mentioned a lawyer with the ACLU, but also said he thought Hamer had additional help."

"Robert Ernst . . ."

"Well, there's a problem. Ernst was just a law student at the time. He offered his support, but he's not on record with the courts. Ayaan Anand is, though, the ACLU lawyer. So, I called him."

Blythe waited, leaning forward.

"Anand knew the name. He knows Ernst helped with Brian Hamer's case. He knows the two of them are connected."

She stood. "Well, let's get him on the record."

"That's tricky. Anand was educated here, but is not a citizen. He had a work permit then, but returned to India years ago. We can get a written affidavit from him, preserve it for trial, but on its own, it's circumstantial."

Blythe began pacing. "You really want to heap this all on Heather Moss's lawyer? He just helped her get her kids back. We've got André Rapp, who is going to sing like a bird. This thing is just about to get wrapped up."

"I'm not heaping anything anywhere. I'm just investigating. So, last call I made, just now, was to my friend Jack Vance. He's retired Air Force. Because Heather Moss's brother in-law, Charlie Moss, is on active duty."

"You're thinking Charles Moss might have insight into Ernst?"

"You left the courthouse the other day, after Heather's arraignment, but Ernst and I had a quick talk, and he told me about how he and Glenn had gone to school together, been good friends, and I just want to see if the brother, Charlie, can confirm it. Or, yeah, he might have something to add about Heather, anything in her past that this could be about."

"Sounds like Charles Moss is miles away, disconnected. What's he gonna know?"

Tom shrugged.

She sighed. "Look, you said Coburn made allusions that this wasn't Palumbo. But did he say why he thought that? No. He didn't. Who knows what he meant. Maybe he meant this isn't *like* Palumbo; he's not the hacker type, he's not that sophisticated, etcetera."

Tom sank into his chair. "I feel like we've been here before."

Her eyes flashed. "Do you? Come on, Tom. You've got to let that go. I made mistakes on the Gallo case, so did you. We have to . . . I don't know. We have to forgive each other, I guess."

She sighed, and her body seemed to sag. It occurred to him Blythe had been doing some thinking, too.

"We do," he said. "So, help me with this, Lauren: we don't have physical evidence against Palumbo — no poison, no Tahoe. All we've got is what I saw and heard. Rumor and conjecture, not enough to prosecute."

"You'll talk to Bob Mandi. You'll be deposed, you'll testify. For God's sake, Tom, you're an agent with the FDLE, your word counts . . ."

But did it?

That was the whole point: he'd been checkmated. Because if he pushed for Ernst, he was positive Citizen Justice would release the information on his sordid history. He'd be fired, discredited. He'd be no good at a trial.

On the other hand, why would Citizen Justice do that? Why, if the aim was to make the whole thing look like Palumbo was behind it?

Because you're close. The fact that Citizen Justice was threatening to expose Tom's past could only mean that Tom wasn't following the preferred clue path. He'd gone out of bounds, and this was a way to keep him in line.

Blythe loomed close. "Lange? Hello?"

"Nothing. Just give me a minute."

"If there's any truth to this, that Ernst is involved somehow, then why?"

He pictured the lawyer putting his arm awkwardly and inappropriately around Heather Moss in the courtroom. A gesture that seemed involuntary. And her reaction: pulling away. He thought of the text from the other night: *She's a liar.*

"Let me talk to him. Let me find out what he's after."

"Fine. We'll both go." She started after her things.

"Let me do it, Lauren."

"No way."

"He's already reached out to me. I'm part of this."

She stared at him. "Has there been more contact? Tom? Has there been more contact beyond the texts you received?"

He slowly met her gaze. This was it. Either he went it alone, or he let Blythe in.

CHAPTER THIRTY-FOUR

Tom sat in the Durango, reassembling his cell phone. When it booted back up, he pulled out his business card for Robert Ernst, Attorney at Law. He dialed the number and waited.

"Hello?"

"Mr. Ernst, Agent Tom Lange."

"Agent Lange. Good to hear from you. I just left Heather Moss at DFS. She's about to be reunited with her children."

"That's great, Mr. Ernst. I'm extremely happy to hear that. Do you have a minute to talk?"

"Sure — I'm just headed back to my office. Would you like to meet there? Listen, I just want to say, right off the bat, I'm sorry if anything I said in court was offensive. I really have great respect for what you do, and I know you've done your best on this thing."

Tom thought he detected cool condescension behind the veneer of warm words. But, who knew, maybe it was just lawyer-tone. Maybe it was his own suspicions. "Thank you, Mr. Ernst."

"So, what can I do for you? I have some appointments this afternoon, but I could try to move a few things around. Is it important? Is it about Heather Moss?"

"Indirectly, yes, I think so. Here's what it is: it's recently come to our attention that André Rapp is one of your past clients."

"Rapp, you said? Rapp . . . well, I can check that back at my office."

"He did a bit at Hardee Correctional for methamphetamine distribution. Relatively small time, but connected to Mario Palumbo."

A silence. Then, "Yes, okay — let's see . . . I represented Mr. Rapp on a matter concerning his right to possess a gun. So, is that who you're referring to? How can I help you?"

"Can you tell me, what you're permitted to given confidentiality, how he came to be your client?"

"Well, ah, if I remember . . ."

You remember, thought Tom.

"He contacted me," Ernst said, "after he was out. Said he had a felony record, but needed to protect himself. He was worried about retribution from his former associates. And he hadn't been in any trouble since his release and had undergone drug rehab. Does that help?"

"Mr. Rapp recently stole a black Chevy Tahoe, and a vehicle of the same description was seen outside Heather Moss's house, the morning she was shot at, then later at the scene of Sergeant Coburn's death. The plates are a match."

"Oh my God. You're kidding. I had no idea. I haven't heard from him . . . Is there something more I can do for you?"

"I'm curious about your relationship to him."

"Oh . . . okay, well, like I've laid out, it was strictly professional. I haven't seen or heard from him since we won his case."

"What about your relationship to Heather Moss?"

"How do you mean?"

"Outside of being her counsel."

"Okay. That's a strange segue." There was a sharp bark, and Tom realized Ernst had just laughed. "Well, you know I went to school with her husband. I guess I'd say I'm a family friend. That's it." He paused. "I'm not sure where this is headed, Agent Lange — I really do have some things to tend to this evening. Maybe we could meet tomorrow?"

"Sure. One more question for now. You graduated from law school in New York, but you took your bar in Florida. Why here?"

"Well, because it's Florida, I guess. Because I spent my life shoveling snow before that." Ernst finally sounded agitated. "What do you really want to know, Agent Lange?"

"Did you encourage Heather to move down here after her husband died?"

"'Encourage' her? I would say I suggested it, sure. I was already set up down here, I went back for the funeral. I called her once or twice after that, asked how she was doing. During one conversation, she told me it felt impossible to go on. I suggested a fresh start."

"You suggested Florida."

"Yes."

"Is there any romantic component to your relationship with Heather Moss?"

Silence, except for the sound of the lawyer breathing. "She's the widow of a friend. I tried to help her out as best I could. I don't control her. I suggested a fresh start, I suggested Florida, yes. And then she came down sometime later. Now—"

"My brother was the one who suggested I move down here," Tom said. "I went to school here, then got my job for the state bureau."

"Agent Lange, I'm trying to understand, but I really—"

"Listen, if I had a problem — you know, if I had done something I shouldn't have done in order to get this job, is that something you could help with? Like the way you've helped Heather and her children, or Mr. Rapp?"

Another moment of silence, and this one felt heavy as radon gas. "Are you asking me to represent you, Agent Lange? If so, we can set up an appointment . . ."

Tom stared out into the parking lot, nerves chattering, but feeling okay, too. "I'm just wondering. If I did something as a juvenile, and that came out; if it could cost me my job — is that something you could help with, in a professional capacity?"

When he spoke again, the lawyer's voice was deadpan, flat of affect. "Meet me in Palmona Park in one hour. I'll move some things around. At the Windmill Café. You know where it is?"

"I do. Thanks so much, Mr. Ernst. Can you make it two hours?"

A long silence. "Alright."

"I really appreciate it."

* * *

Palmona Park was a small town of about 1,300 over the Caloosahatchee River, north of Fort Myers. Tom took the exit off 41 and cruised Pine Island Road through a residential area of single-wide trailer homes and palm trees drowsy in the late day heat.

The Windmill was a small café frequented by landscapers and business people who worked in the area. This late in the day, the small plaza where it was located contained only a few cars.

Tom parked the Durango where the parking lot edged against a lush wall of green Mexican heather, dotted with purple blooms. He dug out his phone and placed a call to Culpepper.

"All good here," the agent said. "Heather came back with the little ones just a few minutes ago. Man, even I missed them. Glad they're back together. She's inside putting Abigail down for a late nap. Olivia has the tube on, watching something with pink and purple animals."

"Great. Damien, listen, I'm working on getting you some reinforcement, I promise. We'll let you get outta there for a couple hours."

"Sounds good, boss. But I'm good to go, long as you need me. I just sleep standing up."

"I'm getting you relief. Thanks, Damien."

He started to dial Turnbull to see about another agent to replace Culpepper when there was a knock on the window.

Tom started, looking around. Robert Ernst stood outside the vehicle on the passenger side. Tom rolled it down.

"Hi," said Ernst. He smiled at Tom, the bright sunshine beating down. He pushed his dark sunglasses up onto his scalp and leaned in. "This your ride?"

"It's department-issue."

Ernst looked in the back. "Comes with car seats and everything, huh?" He smiled wider. A different guy than the one on the phone, who'd gotten a bit morose at the end; Ernst seemed renewed, even chipper.

"Hop in," Tom said.

The lawyer popped the door open and slid into the car. Tom tensed, felt a bead of sweat trickle from his armpit.

"So, the Windmill," Tom said. "Why this place?"

"Oh, this is my favorite coffee spot."

"It's a bit out of the way, though."

Ernst shrugged. "Good coffee is good coffee."

Tom rolled up the window and dialed up the AC. He felt his heart softly knocking against the gun holstered to his chest.

Stay calm.

Ernst's eyebrows drew together in a pensive scowl. "So, you're in some trouble, you said on the phone. You want to go in and we can lay it out, see where we're at?"

"Yeah, that would be great. And thanks again for meeting me on such short notice."

Ernst held up his hand. "It's no problem. And, listen, sorry if I was brusque with you on the phone. I get defensive some times. But, hey, I'm a defense attorney, right? Comes with the territory." He flashed a crooked smile and grabbed the door handle.

"It's fine," Tom said. His eyes flicked to the rear-view mirror. The parking lot behind them remained inactive. "But, you're not always a defense attorney, right?"

The lawyer's face darkened, but he kept that airy voice. "What do you mean?"

"I mean when you represented André Rapp. That was civil, not criminal."

Ernst let go of the door. "Well, I don't know how much you know about lawyers, but the vast majority of us have to hustle to stay afloat. Have to diversify. I do it all; criminal, general, domestic."

"That's a full load."

Ernst looked out the windshield. "When you're a lawyer, you have a kind of intimacy with your clients no one else has. It's not dissimilar from what a therapist does, with their own clients. You learn secrets, you know the most personal details." He turned his head and met Tom's gaze again. "Like you, Agent Lange. Seeking my counsel. Now you and I — we'll be connected by that. It's really something, when you think about it."

"And you've helped others in this way," Tom said carefully. "You started early. You helped Brian Hamer when he got into some hot water with the IRS and the FBI."

"Who is that now? I don't think I know that name . . . unless, was that the young man found in Everglades City? A fisherman, or on a fishing boat? I didn't know he was involved with any of that. But it's interesting. I wish I *had* helped in a situation like that . . . Government overreach and the erosion of privacy is something I'm passionate about. With the technology we have today, it's a real mess . . ." He shook his head.

Tom flicked his finger between them. "It's a two-way street, that intimacy. A client needs to know their lawyer, too. I have to do my due diligence, right?"

Ernst threw his head back and laughed. "That's right," he said, nodding. "That's exactly right, Agent Lange. You need to know what you're getting into."

"Brian Hamer. You worked with him. You and Ayaan Anand. This intimacy you're talking about . . ."

Tom's eyes dropped to the man's hands. One of them had disappeared into the dark suit jacket he was wearing.

Tom started after his gun, but Ernst pulled out a small notepad, then a pen, clicked it on. He flicked a look at Tom, then wrote something down, turned it so Tom could read.

I won't tell you what you want to know like this.

His pulse started pounding. "What does that mean? You won't tell me 'what' like this?"

Ernst scowled. "Sorry? I've lost you . . ." and he quickly jotted another phrase:

Lose the wire, we can go somewhere.

Tom wasn't surprised by it, and let out a slow breath. If Ernst was who he was starting to believe, then the lawyer was too smart to walk into a recorded confession. But he'd also know that none of it was directly admissible, since Florida had a two-party consent rule for taped conversations, and there was a lack of predicate — Ernst hadn't identified himself, used a slightly different voice; he could later say someone was impersonating him.

Even so, he was requesting Tom remove the wire before they went any further. And Tom was more anxious to go further than proceed with an already shaky method.

"Blythe," he said, looking away from Ernst, "I'm going off air."

He reached up under his t-shirt, ripped off the microphones, pulled them off his chest and held them palm up toward Ernst. Two little black disks, thin as dimes. "Okay?"

"Where's the transmitter?"

Tom popped open the dashboard compartment, pulled it out, no bigger than a box of matches. He dumped the batteries, threw everything back into the compartment and closed it up.

Ernst smiled demurely. "Now you can follow me. I'm the beige Acura." His voice had dropped back to his more usual pitch. He put a hand on the door again, paused. "Tell your supervisor to stay back — she follows, and it's over. And I'll know if she's following."

CHAPTER THIRTY-FIVE

The sun was slipping toward the Gulf. Tom followed Ernst in the Acura south on 41, back over the river on the Edison Bridge, then back into Fort Myers. He took a left on route 82, past low homes, yards patchy with dirt, then a right turn on Ford Street, into a rundown section of the city. A kid on a bicycle gave him a look as Tom drove past.

The Acura slowed in front of a fence, turned in. Tom waited on the street, checking to see if Blythe was anywhere behind him. She'd texted twice along the drive and he'd texted back, *Am OK, stand by*.

The fence was made from hubcaps, stacked upright and wired together. Two corrugated sheets of metal formed the gate. Ernst undid a padlock, shoved the doors open, glanced at Tom, then drove the Acura in the rest of the way. Tom began following, but Ernst stepped into his path, holding up his hands. With the window down, he could hear Ernst's instruction: "Leave it in the street."

Tom thought for a moment, decided.

Let them think you're crazy.

He pulled the Durango over, killed the engine and got out. Ernst stayed standing in the entryway, and Tom walked through the gate.

An auto salvage yard. Rusted shells of cars, hills of tires, a scraggly pile of lumber, a squat, one-story building, a trailer up on blocks, and a garage.

Who's place? Ernst's? Or someone else's — Howard Declan, the auto mechanic's?

He stopped walking, keeping a little distance from Ernst, watched as the lawyer closed up the gate, this time snapping a padlock closed on the inside. He glanced at Tom, called over, "That's not for you; this just isn't the best neighborhood."

"It's your place? You a lawyer who moonlights as a junk dealer?"

Ernst uttered that short bark laugh, then headed for the garage. "Come on."

They stepped inside, where it was at least ten degrees cooler, and dark. Ernst flipped on the lights.

An empty space, five hundred square feet. Two load-bearing angle-iron pillars in the center. Concrete floor blackened with oil stains. There was a desk in the far corner, dunes of paper piled high. Two large doors with runner tracks that curved up onto the ceiling. Windows blacked out with paint.

The hydraulic arm hissed and the door snapped shut.

Ernst glanced at his watch. He was wearing leather driving gloves. He walked in a ways, stopped beneath the overhead arc sodium lamps, turned back to Tom.

Tom tensed. "So, I'm here. You want to show me something, Robert? You ready to talk?"

The lights shone brightly off the lawyer's scalp and filled his eye sockets with shadow. "One of my clients was an anesthesiologist. Loved to talk. He even knew where people could get powerful sedatives on the street."

Tom felt a rush. Ernst was dying to lay out his whole fucked-up escapade for an appreciative audience. An egotist.

Tom stayed just inside the door. "Okay. So for Declan it was the pill, for Coburn it was his chewing tobacco. What about Hamer?"

"Hamer had a sensitive stomach. Drank a lot of that stuff, Milk of Magnesia. Pepto Bismol."

Tom remembered seeing the bottle in Hamer's medicine cabinet on the boat. The lab had had it for a couple days. It sounded like they were bound to find traces of potassium chloride inside of it.

"Okay, Robert. So Declan, he's a pedophile. Coburn, what did he do?"

"Come on. Information dragnets? Everyday citizens walking around, being spied on? It violates the Constitution; it's fascism, end times. You know better."

"What about Hamer? What was his offense? He seemed pretty anti-government — thought you'd like that."

"Please, Tom. This is beneath you. Hamer was wasting his considerable talents. There's probably nothing worse."

"Fair enough. So. Where do we go from here?"

"Well, the rest of it is up to you, really." Ernst stepped beyond the throw of light, his complexion fading to gray.

"Okay . . . and what does that mean?" There was a catch in Tom's dry throat, and he coughed after the question.

Ernst gave him a bemused smile. "You know what the Russians call it? *Kompromat.* There's a reason I'm an excellent trial lawyer, Tommy, and it's because everyone can be leveraged. You just have to know where to look, *how* to look. If the CIA can do it, I can do it. Really it should be power the people hold. We can spy right back."

Tom shook his head. "If you're talking about my application with the FDLE, I don't think that's going to take you as far as you're thinking. For all you know, I've already told my supervisors." He held up his hands. "I don't know what else I have for you, Robert. You know all my *kompromat*."

Ernst chuckled, walked to the desk on the far side of the room, sat down, glanced at his watch again.

"You waiting for something?"

Ernst just looked up, his eyes shining across the space.

"So, here's what we've got, Tommy. You live at Beachwood, a gated community in Bonita Springs. A fairly recent development — not bad — two pools, tennis courts, a gym, nice set-up. All the houses look alike, but who cares, right? You've got all your amenities. Recently you had a nice woman playing house, there with her two daughters. But she's gone now, because you blew it."

"Heather Moss is under constant watch."

The lawyer affected an understanding scowl, stuck out his lower lip and nodded. "Of course she is. Sure." He slipped a smart phone from his inner pocket, faced it toward Tom.

Tom slowly started across the garage, feeling heavier with each step. The image was small, but he could make out what was there:

Heather's kitchen. Seated at the table were Heather and her two daughters, eating dinner. The camera looking at them had to be above the sink somewhere. Seeing them sit there eating and laughing silently at his table filled Tom with dread. And guilt — he'd obviously gotten cocky, been outplayed by Ernst, missed something vitally important.

"We've been all through that house," Tom said. "This is video from some earlier time."

"I knew you'd go through the house. I didn't put these cameras in until I met with Heather last night to prepare for this morning. I had to improvise, what with your partner throwing Heather under the bus on those kids, but it's all worked out. Better than I could have even planned, I think. You want another view?"

He hit a button and a camera showed the bathroom from a high corner.

"Or how about this one?"

Heather's bedroom. The covers were in a bundle on the bed.

"You can get these little lipstick cameras at Sam's Club and you can watch them from anywhere there's cell service. Pretty cool."

Tom thought of the cameras at Olivia's school. The laptop at Abby's day care. Anywhere there was a lens and an internet connection, Ernst could watch. He gave the impression that he was a group of people, not a single man, because he had eyes all over. But Tom was convinced it was just him; Ernst had taken out other possible conspirators and wasn't working for Palumbo. He was alone and insane, wanting Tom to know just how clever he was.

Ernst waggled his eyebrows and swept the phone through the air like a magician about to perform a trick. "But that's not all, Tommy . . ." He thrust the phone toward Tom again. "Note the man absent from this picture. Damien Lawrence Culpepper. Born November 4th, 1987 in Jacksonville, Florida. Not as much of an up-and-comer as you, Mr. perfect-score-on-his-SOCE, but Damien is a good boy. He listens when he gets a text from your supervisor that he's to take the evening off."

Ernst slipped the phone back into his pocket. "Our little machines tell us what to do, and we do it, no questions asked."

"I just spoke to Culpepper."

"So did I, as you followed me here. Or, I texted. It's the newest thing, I just got it installed — a caller ID faker. No more 945 numbers even necessary."

"He wouldn't just leave without someone there to relieve him."

"Sure he would. He's only human. He's dying for the relief you keep promising but don't deliver. How long have you had him guarding Heather? Three days straight? Come on. She's there, she's alone, and in one phone call — I'll tell her it's urgent — I'll have all three of them come here and meet me."

Tom stared down at Ernst, wanting to wipe that little fucking smile off his face, but confused. "Why? You know all I have to do right now is arrest you."

"Go ahead. You have your gun, you have your badge."

Ernst just sat there. Tom didn't move.

"Why don't you?" The lawyer stood up abruptly, the wheelie chair rolled back and clunked against the wall. "I'll tell you why. Because right now it's just your word against mine. And you are a cop who lied to get into his department, a cop with a record, with documented emotional problems, with conflicts of interest in every direction. I mean, look at your fucking face. Have you looked at your face?"

Tom just breathed, could hear the air whistling through his own nostrils.

Calm. Stay calm.

Ernst pulled a set of keys from his pocket, the same ones he'd used to open the padlocked gate. "Meanwhile, I'm an upstanding lawyer, no criminal record. I got Heather Moss her daughters back after your partner had them taken away. And I'm going to clear her of all charges on the Howard Declan case."

This close, his mask removed, Tom could see the damage in the man's eyes, but also his cunning. He'd been planning this thing for months, maybe years.

"What do you think is going to happen, here?" Tom asked.

They were close together, noses a few inches apart, Tom could smell mint gum on the lawyer's breath and it made him want to vomit.

"You called *me*, Tom."

"You knew I was getting close."

Ernst shrugged, then sauntered away, casually. Tom saw him check his watch again. Then, keeping his back to Tom, said, "Let me have your phone please."

"I don't think so."

"That's the only way this works."

"The way what works? I'm losing patience here . . ."

Ernst turned. "The way we all get what we want."

CHAPTER THIRTY-SIX

The sun was extra-bright after the gloom of the garage and adjoining office. Tom squinted around at the site, at least a half an acre. An engine grew louder as some far off car gained speed, then the sound sank away. No human sounds, no voices. He looked at the second, smaller building within the enclosure. Saw the nose of an intact vehicle poking out behind it, a chrome grille.

"Ah, man," Tom said. Ernst trailed behind as Tom stopped in front of the stolen Tahoe. The tags had been switched but he was sure running the registration would show it belonged to school teacher named Larry Boyle, that it was reported stolen a week earlier.

By André Rapp, Ernst's client.

"Come on," Ernst said. He nodded at the door to the smaller building.

Tom headed toward it. His footsteps crunched across the dirt yard. He'd given Ernst his phone, willing to see where this thing led, thinking Ernst had a point — even if Blythe backed him up, they had no physical evidence to link Ernst to the crimes, and he wasn't about to consent to any confession. He'd been switching phones, rerouting his emails, orchestrating things from a safe distance.

"It's open. Just push it."

Tom faced the door to the smaller building. This one had a window, blinded on the inside. He felt like going through it was a step backwards.

"Tom, go through the door. Stop being a pussy. You know where this is headed, and you want it to go there. Just admit it to yourself, and let's move on."

Tom used his foot to open the door. The first room was a long rectangle with a bank of multi-paned windows overlooking the junkyard. The lights off, dust motes floated in the sunlight streaming in through the dirty, chambered glass. Two long desks faced the windows, file cabinets sat opposite, and a chest of drawers. In the middle of the room was an enormous table, piled with books, technical equipment, clothing. In addition to being a sociopath, Tom pegged the lawyer as a hoarder.

Or, he'd just inherited most of this crap when he'd come into this place. Tom doubted it was a primary location for Ernst, this was a hideaway, something he'd bought to carry on his twisted hidden life.

"So you're Gary Reuben Enterprises? A little shell company you set up to buy this place?"

"First door on the left is the bathroom."

The wooden door was ajar, and he saw a bathtub. One tiny window over the toilet, opaque. The fixtures were old-fashioned — the tub was claw-footed, the sink a small, water-stained basin, the toilet leaning slightly to one side.

Tom continued into the dusty space toward another closed door, a padlock hanging open.

"Step in."

Three computer towers, two large high definition screens, two keyboard decks, a counter with a fleet of go-pro cameras, a pile of coiled cables, a couple microphones.

He noted the sound-baffled walls. This was the control room he'd envisioned all along.

There was a single overhead work light, turned off. The screens were dark except for a screen saver on each — a flock of tumbling umbrellas drifting across the two-dimensional space.

"Sit down, I want you to see something." Ernst gestured to one of the two swivel chairs. Tom sat. The lawyer moved toward one of the screens, tapped the keyboard, waking the system.

"I've set this all up for you. Every step of the way."

"How did you get my information?"

Ernst gave him a sidelong look. "While you cops run around bumping into things, I'm the one who cleans up the mess. I know every judge in my district. Which one likes his coffee black, which one likes his wife to use the dildo on his ass. I know who to call, when to call them, where to apply pressure. And I know the judges from back in New York."

He opened a file on the desktop, highlighted and enlarged several pictures, ones Tom had already seen showing Palumbo and Edgar Vasquez together.

"Here's one of my clients — Edgar Martin Vasquez. I did the divorce from his first wife, and we kept in touch. Like I said, I'm a multifaceted lawyer. He came to me when Palumbo made the overture they start working together. He didn't want to. Say what you want about the drug trade, but it was a family business, and Edgar had a lot of pride, a lot of tradition. He knew when Palumbo offered that he wasn't going to take *No* for an answer. So he put a few things in place."

"Like you."

Ernst shrugged and went on. "Sure, he put me in place because — you could say our interests dovetailed."

"You need me to help the Vasquez family."

"I don't need you; I don't have to do anything I don't want to, unlike most people. Vasquez knew what Palumbo wanted, what he would try if Vasquez refused, and how likely it was Palumbo would get away with a murder. County VNB with their dicks in their hands, FDLE sniffing everyone's ass, helping no one. You of all people understand how short the system falls, right?"

Tom stared at the picture of Edgar Vasquez while Ernst connected to yet another file. Howard Declan replaced Vasquez, his unhappy face filling the screen. "It's all right here: Howard Michael Declan, auto mechanic for thirty years. He did jobs for the Palumbo family. He did one job, his last one, where he sabotaged Edgar's vehicle."

"There's no proof of that."

"Sure there is." Ernst clicked a button and a video began to play. Howard Declan faced the camera. The surroundings looked familiar, like the video had been recorded in the garage:

"My name is Howard Michael Declan. This is my video confession. I've worked for Mario Palumbo for a decade, under the table. I've worked on his cars, on his employee's cars." Declan's face was drawn, his eyes haunted. "Occasionally Mr. Palumbo would ask me to do something I knew wasn't right. But, I did it. Like I did with Edgar Vasquez. It's because of me his vehicle malfunctioned, causing the accident. If anything happens to me, that's why. Because the County police did their investigation, and Palumbo got rid of me."

By the end, Declan had tears rolling down his cheeks. He leaned forward and canceled the record button.

The video ended.

Tom was quiet a moment. "You asked Declan to record that. You found out he was a pedophile and you used that to leverage him. This is a coerced confession; he's as stiff as a board."

"Says who — you? Do we have to go over this again? You're someone who lied on their state police application. So you already confessed to someone. Good for you on the contrition. But let's not forget your documented history of bending the law — wasn't it you who just last year threatened a man who was beating on his girlfriend? You threatened to deport his undocumented workers?"

Another couple flicks of the mouse and Ernst opened new pictures. These of Josh McDermott, now an inmate at Miami-Dade Correctional. One picture was McDermott's headshot. Seeing his face transported Tom back to the attack in his condo, McDermott trying to kill him. But before that, Tom had gone into a bar where McDermott hung out after work as the owner of a landscaping business, threatened to investigate him and his likely undocumented workers, throw suspicion on him for the Carrie Anne Gallo murder. McDermott had been beating up his girlfriend and she was too scared to press charges. Tom had seen red.

Ernst said, "You've got anger management issues, Tom. I've seen it before. Probably comes from your past."

Ernst clucked his tongue and shook his head in mock sympathy. "You've also been ordered to attend therapy — which you never completed, I might add. Not your fault, maybe, but still significant; no clean bill of mental health for you. And let's not forget about the woman and her two daughters, who you took to your home, violating about a dozen statutes, and endangering those children. It's by a slim miracle I was able to get them back into their mother's custody."

Tom felt the weight of it all threatening to crush him. This was how Ernst worked. This was what he did to people, what he had done to Declan. Found out where the wounds were, stuck in his knife, twisted.

"But now," Ernst said with a touch of emotion, "look where you are. Look!" He grew animated, waving his arms, swinging around in the chair. "You're at an auto salvage yard, a place where Declan still had the keys." He lifted the jangling set of keys in the air, and swung them in front of Tom's face like a hypnotist's pendulum. "This is the spare set, but the originals are probably sitting in an evidence room because you never found what they went to, because you never thought to check his old place of business — it was sold to Gary Reuben Enterprises. You're only part right. Gary Reuben doesn't exist. Well, he did at one time, I think he was from Dayton, Ohio. But I had Hamer file some paperwork for Gary Reuben. That was Hamer's specialty — tax fraud — before he became a loser. And, if you look again at Howard Declan's recent correspondence, you'll find emails between him and Mr. Reuben, where Reuben agrees Declan can use the old place to work on his cars, or whatever other crazy projects he's up to."

"What now?"

"What now is for you to do your job, Agent Lange. You've got a taped confession that Howard Declan sabotaged Edgar Vasquez's car, killing him. More importantly, that he did it for Mario Palumbo. All roads lead to Palumbo. And you've got the Tahoe sitting out there, stolen by André Rapp, who was threatened into becoming a lethal delivery boy when Palumbo's hacker, Brian Hamer, discovered he was a C.I. working for Sergeant Coburn."

Tom felt the choke of claustrophobia again. He wanted to get out. But Ernst was still laying it on: "In the Tahoe are Rapp's prints, DNA, and of course, his supply of potassium cyanide, one hypodermic needle and some capsules. Rapp supplied the package to Heather Moss, poisoned Hamer's stomach medicine, and laced Sergeant Coburn's tobacco." The lawyer sniffed, looked over the images he'd collected on screen. "You'll never find traces of me anywhere." He stroked the mouse almost lovingly. "I did it all by remote control."

"That's great," Tom dared. "You ought to be a drone operator."

Ernst blinked. "What?"

Tom waved a hand, stood up.

Ernst sighed and shook his head. "I thought you'd push back a little. So let's have one last look." With a few quick gestures he opened a website.

It had been true when Tom told Heather that he thought of Nick every day, but it had been a few days since Tom had looked at his website. He slowly sat back down.

A picture showed Nick smiling handsomely in his suit. The text spoke to his love of people, his in-depth knowledge of the housing market, his nearly ten years of experience.

Ernst shrank the window down, navigated to a folder on the desktop and opened it up. The folder read "Coby."

The first picture had been taken at the scene of the accident where Nick had flipped his rental car on highway 75, then been hit by a tractor-trailer unable to stop. In the image, Nick was being loaded into the back of an ambulance on a gurney, draped in a white sheet. A press photo.

Ernst scrolled through several more, and Tom watched as the images changed from press photos to surveillance shots. Pictures of Nick's house, Nick getting into his Escalade. Nick outside the dog track, stepping into the poker room with the green awning.

And then, finally, shots of Nick and a bald man.

Ben Franco.

The images were fuzzy, looking through a lace of palm fronds, but it was fairly clear, at least to a cop's eyes, what the men were doing. They were making an exchange, Franco handing off cocaine for Nick to sell.

"These pictures," Ernst said in a quiet voice, "Were taken months before the Carrie Anne Gallo case."

Ernst was now swishing through more surveillance photos, taken from afar. They showed Tom's brother on the ground, fetal position, defensively protecting his head. He was getting kicked and beaten by two thugs as a shadowy figure looked on. Franco? Lamotta? Or even

Palumbo? Hard to say the location, too; it was dark, an oval of light on the tarmac suggesting a nearby streetlight.

The final pictures showed Nick and Tom together. They also bore the mark of surveillance — shallow depth of field, taken from a distance. In one, Nick and Tom, both in sunglasses, having a coffee near the beach, they were smiling.

There was paperwork in the file. Tom felt numb as Ernst navigated through a few PDFs. He didn't need to see much to get the full picture: vice narcotics had known about Nick for some time. They had evidence of Palumbo's men beating him up. But they'd been bound to confidentiality, legally unable to share that surveillance with Agent Tom Lange, even though he was Nick's brother.

Tom understood it all, but felt the charge of anger anyway. Seeing Nick on the ground like that, his aggressor standing near, brought back the worst memories.

"Your department is as fucked up as you are," Ernst said quietly.

"Alright," Tom said.

"This is the truth," Ernst said in that soft voice. "Your brother wasn't important enough to Everglades County to jeopardize building their big case against Palumbo. His death was brushed under the rug, a casualty of the great war between cops and drug lords."

Tom's teeth were on edge. He struggled to keep composure. "Palumbo's good at what he does, he keeps himself insulated. He's got a squad of attorneys working for him."

"See? Fucking lawyers, right?" Ernst came back. "Who would you rather deal with — lawyers who protect someone like Palumbo, who has caused all of this suffering, or someone like me? I get shit done. Where the law is slow and inadequate, I keep things liquid." Ernst's voice was raising now as his oration gained momentum. "*This* is how it has to be. The old ways don't work! You know it, I know it. Palumbo is out there, Ben Franco is out there, day after day, and they're protected by *the law*. You can't tell me that's not a broken system."

Tom couldn't help but stare at the images of Nick. The shots showing him and Franco were the most salient — Franco was well-established as a piece of Palumbo's drug operation. Handing off product to Nick was clear evidence Nick was selling for Palumbo.

"Just take it down."

"Why don't you take *him* down, Tommy? This is your chance. This is *our* chance to do something. The enemy of my enemy is—"

"Fuck," Tom said. He pushed back from the screens and stood up again.

Ernst got up quickly after, his gaze falling to Tom's gun, snug in the shoulder holster.

Tom's head was throbbing, the images of Nick getting beaten stuck in his mind. The grim statistics on Palumbo — the people he'd murdered, directly or indirectly; the countless lives touched by drug addiction, gambling, pain and suffering; just about anyone with rotted teeth or tracks on their arms in the whole of southwest Florida was likely to be a Palumbo victim. The greater good had to count for something. Taking down Palumbo, even like this, must be better than letting him walk away from yet another crime, creating more addicts, more people like Nick.

Ernst was right — Palumbo was in the crosshairs and someone just had to pull the trigger.

Tom took a breath. "What do I do?"

CHAPTER THIRTY-SEVEN

In the main room, Ernst emptied Tom's Glock, stripping the cartridges from the magazine with his thumb. They clattered to the ground. Then the lawyer expertly pulled back the slide, popping the final round from the chamber.

Ernst handed the empty weapon to Tom, grip-out.

Tom slipped it into the leather holster, snapped the thong closed.

The lawyer smiled. A humorless grin, the kind Tom had seen before on the faces of psychopaths awaiting the death penalty. Men missing certain pieces of themselves. Either born remorseless, or built that way by an especially hostile environment.

Beside Ernst were three large boxes, filled with the equipment he'd dismantled in a matter of minutes — hard drive, screens, everything but one camera, which stood on a tripod nearby. "Now, let's get your story straight: You came to meet me at the Windmill to discuss my relationship with Rapp. We talked about my representing him on the gun matter, and in the course of our conversation I mentioned how, on one occasion, Rapp had discussed target shooting at a scrap yard in Fort Myers. It clicked for you, because you knew of an auto salvage yard where Howard Declan was formerly employed. You circled the perimeter, looking in, saw the Tahoe, and that gave you the probable cause you needed to enter; you searched the vehicle."

"I would have called it in immediately."

"Your phone was damaged."

Ernst was handing it over in two pieces — the phone body and the battery. Then he suddenly threw the body against the ground, cracking the screen.

"Fell out of your pocket when you scaled the fence. So you searched the premises for a landline. There's one over there."

Tom looked where Ernst was pointing at the cream-colored rotary-dial phone sitting amid drifts of paperwork and junk. "But before you located the phone, you found this." He patted the camcorder beside him. "You watched what was on it, you found Declan's confession."

Ernst picked up the broken phone, used his foot to sweep away the cartridges littering the dirty floor. "You can pick those up after I leave."

"It won't work."

Holding out the damaged phone, Ernst cocked an eyebrow. "Oh no?"

"It's what cops call an 'orgy of evidence'." Tom took the phone. "Everything here, in one place; too convenient. Plus my supervisor knows I met with you, disengaged the wire."

The lawyer's eyelids fluttered and he looked insulted. "But Agent Lange, I didn't want to be recorded betraying an attorney-client privilege. I told you I had something that might be useful about André Rapp, but asked that it be off the record."

The Tahoe was partly visible through a dirty multi-paned window. Ernst pointed.

"The dash cam is still inside. I even left the Fusion hooked up to a smart phone. It's a 945 number. Tom, I've thought of everything. Even this one last thing, this last thing you have to do to make it airtight."

Tom felt heavy again. "One last thing?"

Ernst looked at the camera. "You're right about one thing — the confession. Palumbo's attorneys will say it looks coerced, and a judge could throw it out. On its own, it's not enough. That's why we need a good old-fashioned paper trail."

"Declan's house is monitored, I told you. I have to sign in. And we booked most everything into evidence already."

"Not this," Ernst said. He nodded to the bag sitting close on the table. "This you missed. It happens. Cops go back for a second look all the time. And cops come and go from the evidence room. You just have a guilty conscience, that's all. But when it's all over, you'll see how it worked out just right."

"You're the boss."

The lawyer narrowed his eyes. "You still having trouble with this? Save yourself from a lifetime of humiliation and dishonor, Tom, and be the hero who finally finds the evidence implicating Mario Palumbo in the death of Edgar Vasquez via Howard Declan. You can charge André Rapp for Declan's murder, the drive-by shooting, and for Hamer and Coburn, all acting on Palumbo's behalf. Rapp will cop to it all; he's dumb as shit. Turn it all over to whomever you want — hell, give it to the feds." His eyes flashed. "Do that and you can get rid of the man who killed your brother."

"How much are they paying you? The Vasquez family."

Ernst picked up a box, grunted with the weight, started to back away. "You let me worry about that." He touched the door behind him, started to pull it open. "Your choice."

"What happens to Heather?"

307

"Her name will be completely cleared. I'll fight the fleeing a crime charge; that's nothing. Help me with these."

Tom grabbed up a box, a feeling of pure unreality washing over him. He was helping a criminal escape with the evidence of his crime.

"It's a sick dream," Tom said. Ernst had the back hatch of the Acura open and Tom set down the box. "It's pure manipulation."

The lawyer shrugged. "Who doesn't manipulate? That's all life is." He went back inside for the final box, Tom following. Box in hand, Ernst swung open the door and left.

Tom popped the gun's magazine and dropped to the ground, frantically scrounging for the ammunition. By the time he located one in the corner, he heard Ernst slam the Acura's hatch closed, fire up the engine. Tom fed the cartridge into the magazine and pushed the magazine back in. He racked the slide, loading the cartridge into the chamber and stepped out.

Ernst had already undone the padlock and swung the first door, was back in the car. He drove through the gate, stopped, pushed the door closed, and as he did, looked through at Tom.

Son of a bitch.

Tom slowly lowered the weapon, holstered it. He listened as Ernst locked the gate from the other side, then got back into the Acura and drove off.

Son of a—

The sun was almost set. Tom walked around the dirt lot, picking his way through the junk, kicking at whatever got in his way, feeling the rage jacking him up, blurring his vision. He got back to the Tahoe. Took out his broken phone and battery from his pockets, reassembled it once more and turned it on.

After a minute, the phone chirped, the operating system was up, and he opened the recording app, searched for the latest file. He'd turned the recorder on just before getting out of the Durango and following Ernst into the scrapyard. He played back the file, listened to static, garbled voices. It wasn't much, not useable in court, but it was something. He heard Ernst saying: *You can get these little lipstick cameras at Sam's Club.*

Heather Moss, and her two girls. Was money Ernst's true motive for all of this? The promise of more work from the surviving Vasquez family members? Was he an anti-government nutcase? Or was this about Heather Moss, too; some kind of twisted, elaborate scheme to possess her?

"Fuck!"

He strode back to the out building and went inside. Eyed the camcorder, found another loose cartridge on the dirty floor. Then he worked his way over to the phone, and plucked the handset from its cradle. Dialed Lauren Blythe.

* * *

Half an hour later, the place was swarming with law enforcement, crime scene technicians crawling in and around the Tahoe. Tom stood beside Blythe in the middle of the scrapyard.

"Sent a car over to Heather Moss," Blythe said. "Everything is good there. So someone texted Culpepper, headed him off, you said?"

"Yeah," Tom said. "I called him to check on Heather and that's when he told me," he lied.

A generator was fired up, lights exploded all around them, turning everything brighter than day. Blake Turnbull walked in through the gate, looking concerned.

"You alright, Lange?" He looked Tom over. "What happened?"

"André Rapp," Tom said, squinting in the harsh light. "Rapp told Robert Ernst that he'd come here in the past, to work on old cars."

"Ernst — that's Moss's attorney?"

Tom gave a nod. "He'd represented Rapp in the past. I found out about it looking through court records."

"But you were recording your meeting with Ernst," Turnbull said, and looked between Tom and Blythe. "Why?"

Blythe just stared at Tom; Tom said to Turnbull, "Because of how he looked to me. Standing in court with Heather. I got some ideas. They didn't pan out, but since Ernst mentioned this place I decided to swing around, try to salvage some of the day."

Turnbull kept looking at the both of them, his lips parted, as if chasing around the right word or thought. "You two have something you're not telling me?"

Blythe beat Tom to it. "We will, sir. As soon as the time is right. At the moment, we have a bit of work ahead of us."

Turnbull seemed to accept this, placed his hands on his hips and looked around. His gaze landed on the Tahoe. "Yeah, I guess so."

They went through the rest of the scene. Tom took Turnbull to where he found Declan's confession. "I'd like you to have another look at Declan's place," Turnbull said. "I want this thing solid when we bring it all to Bob Mandi."

Amazing, Tom thought. Turnbull had just opened the door, figuratively speaking. Now all he had to do was to walk through it and plant the evidence on Declan's connection to Palumbo that Ernst had worked up. And pay a visit to the evidence room, get a hold of Declan's laptop.

Tom felt sick. The bathroom was near and he pushed through the door, dropped to his knees, vomited in the bowl.

CHAPTER THIRTY-EIGHT

The rest of the night was a haze. They'd discussed the prospect of getting Moss and her family back into witness protection. Even if Rapp was off the street, Palumbo was liable to send someone else to silence her. She could corroborate the use of the 945 number, the Fusion voice synthesizer, and she'd seen the Tahoe the morning of Declan's death. She would be a key witness in taking down Palumbo. They had to act fast.

"Might even be witness relocation," Turnbull said. "New identity, new location, the whole nine. We'll see what Mandi thinks, and we'll bring in the Marshals, talk to the FBI, whatever we have to do."

Tom drove slowly down Tangerine Drive, looking out for Ernst's Acura. The lawyer's car wasn't around, but there was a sheriff's deputy sitting in his parked cruiser. Heather Moss's house was dark, probably everybody asleep, and Tom rolled up beside the cruiser, recognized Pierce when the deputy rolled his window down.

"Hey," Tom said. "Everything quiet?"

"Everything's okay," Pierce said. "Lights went off about a half hour ago. Couple hours before that, she was putting the kids to bed."

Tom nodded, looked off at the house, thinking about Ernst's cameras. At some point the lawyer was going to need to take those down. Unless he had a way to explain them away, but Tom didn't think so. Tom said goodbye to Pierce and drove home, keyed into his condo, climbed the stairs feeling like he'd run a marathon. He left the lights off, preferring the gloom as he got the vodka out of the cabinet beneath the sink and poured himself a glass. Sat down in the living room, and stared up at the wall of faces — Palumbo, Franco, Lamotta, Nick. He took a sip of the drink, then another, then finished it. Went back for more.

No one was coming for Heather and her daughters. No one except for Ernst. Even if she went into witness relocation, as her lawyer, he could be privy to her new set-up, follow her. She'd have no one else — she might even let him move in when he asked, and he probably would.

Sick fuck.

Or, that was self-pity talking. She'd seemed leery of Ernst in the courtroom, after all.

Fresh drink in hand, he sat back down on the couch, stared at the wall some more. Told himself that Palumbo deserved it, that even if Ernst was a stone cold serial killer, Palumbo was worse. He'd eluded capture for years, had hundreds of people in his employ, thousands were affected by the drugs he trafficked — it was an evil empire. Sitting right under the noses of a law enforcement system that was powerless to stop him. All this surveillance, civilian informants and busts of offenders further down the chain, cops hoping to work their way up, and they never did, or they got close, made a move, Palumbo beat it. When you had money and high-powered lawyers and you lived in Florida — not much different from Texas, really — you could do that. Tom sat there and looked at the wall and worked himself up into a righteous anger, then got up fast and started tearing at it, clippings and photos fluttering to the ground. He grabbed everything, ripped and crumpled.

When it was over and he was breathing hard, third drink in his hand, an idea started to form. Little bits and pieces coming together, coalescing into something he might be able to work with.

He picked up his replacement phone and called Jack Vance. He'd checked voice mail earlier, had missed several calls from Vance that day, hadn't wanted to speak to him yet, or anyone, but now he did.

Late as it was, old night owl Vance was wide awake.

"Tommy."

"Hey, Jack . . ."

They talked for ten minutes, then Tom made another call, this time to Katie, expecting her voice mail since it was after midnight. But she picked up, and sounded happy to hear from him. "I'm outside," she said.

"What?"

He sat up, set down the empty glass.

"I just pulled up," she told him. "I'm outside your place. Bad time?"

"No — glad you're here."

He'd given Katie the second fob that came with the condo for getting in the automatic gate. He went down to greet her. She walked up the stairs in front of him, opened his door and went in. "Got a new phone already?"

"Yeah. My third in a week."

"You're going through phones and cars like a . . ." She'd reached the living room, and was looking over the wreckage. She clicked on the light. "Doing a little redecorating?"

"You never liked that particular look," Tom said.

She stepped through the pile of papers and photos, then glanced at his empty glass on the coffee table. "Got one for me?"

"Sure." By now he was feeling a little buzzed, a little better. Poured himself one more glass, one for Katie, and they sat on the couch together, facing the bare wall.

"Going to have to put a TV there now or something," she said. "Like normal people." Then she faced him, drawing her leg up onto the couch. "You want to talk?"

Déjà vu.

"About this? Or about us?"

"At Coburn's memorial service you said you wanted to talk about us."

"I do."

She nodded, slowly, gazed into her drink. She held the glass with both hands, took a sip, said, "Do you think it's healthy?"

"What? Us?"

"Yeah. Is what we've had what you'd call a healthy relationship? Two cops, both working long hours, trying to scrape together some kind of relationship that began when someone died." Her eyebrows went up, she took another gulp of the drink, set the glass on the table.

"Healthy as any relationship, I guess."

Now she scowled. "You have limited experience, I take it."

"No," he said. "I know it's not."

"Okay. So. What do you want? Let's say we get back together — well, that presumes we even *were* together . . . What do you see us as, like, where do you see us in a year? In five years? Ten? Do we have a family? Kids? Do you even want children?"

"Sure."

She nodded, like she didn't believe him, and then fell into thinking about everything for a moment. Finally, she said, "Hey — I'm not here to add more complexity to your life. Okay? But I'm wondering, I'm just thinking aloud, you know, if it will ever be any different."

"You asking me if I'm going to resign?"

"It's not that I have a problem with you being a cop . . ."

"I know what you're talking about. I don't know . . . I guess I'm figuring that out."

She nodded again, but her expression betrayed her disappointment, and she stood up, like she was thinking of leaving.

She looked around like she was forgetting something, then reached into her pocket, pulled out the fob to the security gate, held it out to him. "You want this?"

"No. I want you to keep it."

She didn't move. "I'm going to say this — and I hate hearing myself say it — but I think you gotta ask yourself if you actually . . ."

"What?"

"When you came up to me after the service for Coby, and we went to the café — why?" He opened his mouth to reply but she cut him off. "You needed a sounding board? You needed to unburden yourself?"

"I was worried about you."

"And you needed information," she said.

"And you had it."

"Tom . . ." She faded back, away from the couch, glanced at the door. "It's really late. Maybe this — you look exhausted. I just . . ." She was still holding the fob, looking at it.

He stood up. "Just stay. Tonight."

Another glance at the door. "Let me go. Okay?"

"Maybe tomorrow. Come on, you just came all the way here to . . . You don't even have to sleep in the same bed with me. Okay?"

She remained standing there a few more seconds, between him and the door, looked around the room. "How many of those you had to drink?"

He took a cautious step toward her. "Just a couple."

"Why do you want me to stay? You just don't want me to *go*, and that's the whole thing with you. Keep me around, keep me right where you want me . . ."

"I meant what I said today."

"I believe you." She gave him a look that squeezed his heart, made him weak in the knees. "Is that gonna change, though? Or you're going to spend the rest of your life trying to prove something? You gonna spend the rest of your life protecting yourself?"

"I'm working on it. That's gotta be — that's gotta mean something."

She moved to the couch at last, sat back down. Maybe it did.

* * *

Around three in the morning, his eyes popped open. He was on the couch, Katie upstairs in his bed.

He crept down the stairs, entered the garage, snapped on the light. Stood looking at the Durango a moment, then opened the rear doors. He pulled the first car seat out — this one was bigger, Olivia had used it — and set it aside, wrapping all the straps around it. Moved to the other side and unhooked Abigail's, brought it out and set it beside the other.

He stepped in front of the metal cabinet next, dialed the combination lock and popped it open. He kept his set of standard-duty body armor inside, plus a Remington 870 Shotgun, secured by a cable. The key was in another part of the garage and he retrieved it, unlocked the cable, took the gun out with its case, the shells, and loaded it all into the back of the Durango, slipping it beneath a removable panel. The shells were bird shot — 2 ¾" Federal Target Load 12 gauge. Birdshot was powerful but somewhat safer in a residential setting, since it typically wouldn't blast through a plaster wall and come out the other side, injuring or killing some innocent bystander. But it had plenty of stopping power. Just in case he needed it.

CHAPTER THIRTY-NINE

TUESDAY

He stood looking at Katie, asleep in his bed, as he buttoned his shirt. She stirred, opened her eyes. Flashed a smile at him, sat up, blinking, and pushed hair from her face. "This your new stalker routine? With that face . . ."

"I need your help."

"I need coffee."

"It's downstairs," he said, rolling up his sleeves. The temperature was supposed to climb to 90, damn hot for February. He'd been awake since before six, watching the news without really seeing it, but that much he'd registered.

"You sleep at all last night?" She swung her legs out of bed and dropped her head, rolled it around between her shoulders, getting out the kinks.

"A little." Finished with his shirt, he waited and watched as Katie lowered to the floor, started to stretch.

"So what do you need?" she asked. It was hard to get a read on her; last night she'd asked him if he'd just needed a sounding board. He knew what she meant — she wanted to know if he actually saw her, cared about who she was.

He did. But he needed her as a cop, too. It would have to be both, or nothing, this time at least.

"We have to get into the Vasquez case," he said. "I want to see everything on the car, how and why Vasquez went speeding into that truck."

On her back, she raised her right leg, grabbed herself around the quad muscle, and grunted as she pulled. "Not going to happen. Because it was Vasquez and Palumbo, everything is under the purview of vice narcotics, and those are open cases."

"Then we're going to talk to head of CID. Give them a précis of the entire thing, but focus on the murder of Danny Coburn."

She dropped her leg, sat up and gave him a look, seeming to think about it. "Yeah, okay, if we come at it from the angle of Coburn's murder, you might be able to get around some of the privilege." Then she lay back down, raised her other leg. "But that could take days. Weeks."

He watched her a moment longer, wearing her yoga pants and one of his FSU t-shirts, then moved toward her, knelt down and suspended himself above her in a push-up position. She blinked up at him. "Don't."

He eased off her and stood, headed for the door.

She sat up and grabbed his leg before he got away. "Tom."

"Katie, I know what I've done. Do I have to say it?"

"It might help."

She got to her feet beside him, put her hand on his arm. "I've lost people too, you know? Maybe not the same way you did — Nick was really the last person you had. But if you're going to be with someone, if you're going to have a relationship with them, keeping one foot out the door because you're afraid they might leave you . . ."

He crossed the room, on his way out.

"We used to talk about Nick," she said. "That was the whole thing. But then you . . . I don't know. You've got this armor."

She was right behind him.

"All of us, you know, we're — we see it. We know you're hurting. And now this thing with your application. Have you told them? Lauren would support you, I'm sure of it. Turnbull, too. And me. But it's time, Tom, okay? Now's the time."

He stopped in the doorway and looked over his shoulder at her. "Then help me get into the Vasquez case."

* * *

Bob Mandi didn't look surprised to see him.

"Lange. Quite a day you had yesterday." Mandi eyed the file Tom set on the desk, drew a hand across his perfectly scrubbed face and said, "What have we got?"

"Printouts off Declan's laptop. If you remember, there was supposed to be a hard drive wipe, but the wipe didn't work. That's what we're supposed to think."

"Okay . . ."

"Someone left it with plenty of life in it." Tom swept his hand over the file. "These are emails between Declan and a Palumbo subordinate, Ben Franco."

"And what will that give me?"

"It's supposed to support Declan's video confession. That he was employed by Palumbo and Franco to sabotage Edgar Vasquez's car."

Mandi looked at the file like it was his first headache of the day. "Lange, I'm focused on André Rapp. Everything has shifted. We've got the Tahoe, we've got the poison, we've got Rapp. Rapp was made to carry these things out — killing Hamer, Declan, and our own Coburn."

Tom shook his head. "This whole thing hinges on Rapp taking orders through texts and emails. Palumbo has beaten less than this before."

"No one has ever dared to flip on Palumbo," Mandi said. "Rapp's going to sing like a bird. I just got off the phone with his lawyer, and he's going to confess to it all this afternoon."

"His lawyer . . ."

"A PD, name is Jane Willem. Rapp's going to plead guilty across the board, and we're going to use his testimony, execute warrants on Franco and Palumbo as soon as possible."

Tom grabbed the file, held it up the space between them. "What if I told you Palumbo or Franco — neither of them ever had Rapp do anything? Or Declan?"

Mandi sighed. "I'd say you're letting this case get to you."

"Yeah, people tell me that."

"I don't even want to ask where you got those bruises on your face . . ."

"Then don't."

He left.

* * *

Jack Vance was parked outside the Beachwood gate, and Tom stopped the Durango and got out. He found Vance inside the booth chatting with the security guard. The two semi-retirees were laughing like old friends, and Vance turned and gave Tom a big hearty handshake when he stepped into the small room. They said goodbye to the security guard and Vance followed Tom into the community, pulled in behind him in Tom's driveway.

"Nice guy," Vance said about the security guard. "Good gig, too. I think I'm in. Maybe start next week."

"Excellent," Tom said. He always felt mixed emotions around Vance, like he was a friend, but also an authority figure. "Want to come up?"

"Got something cold to drink?"

"Indeed I do."

Inside, Vance looked around, Tom thought he was checking for signs of Katie Mills. There were none — she'd cleaned the place up and left.

Vance settled at the kitchen table as Tom served him up a beer, chose water for himself. After they wet their whistles, Vance smacked his lips and said, "So I had a nice talk with Charlie Moss."

Tom felt a rush. "You were able to track him down?"

"Took a little bit, but yeah, I got him. Tom, he's willing to come in. Give an official statement."

"What's he saying, exactly?"

Vance leaned back, looked out the kitchen window a moment, said, "Ernst told you he was friends with Glenn Moss."

"He did."

Vance nodded. "Charlie says his brother, Glenn, told him once about this guy from school, had kind of an edge to him, paranoid ideas."

"They were friends, though, right? Or weren't they?"

"Yeah. This Glenn seems like he was a real affable guy, got along with everybody; it was just a casual thing, he told Charlie he had a buddy, named Robert Ernst, and Ernst was a little off. So, I did some digging. Called up Hofstra."

"You just called up the school?"

Vance smiled, the many lines in his old face rippling. "You got to know how to talk to people. How to treat them. Hey, I got just enough information so I could do a little more digging, and it turns out this Ernst guy has a past. Comes from quite a bit of money. I talked to some of my old pals in New York and there's a story. Had a real cold childhood, parents estranged but never divorced, some weird situation where they stayed living together, kids growing up in some home like a mausoleum with their parents never speaking. Anyway, Ernst gets kicked out of one school before Hofstra — he was at Cornell."

"What did he do?"

Vance shook his head. "That I couldn't find out. Only that he was expelled. But Charlie — and this guy's a real straight shooter in a crooked town — from what Glenn told Charlie about this guy, Ernst, he's intense. They were friendly a bit at first, Glenn and Ernst, but then Glenn sort of went his own way, dropped out."

"He'd met Heather by then, is the story I got."

Vance took a sip of the beer, nodded his head. "Maybe so. Maybe so. But Ernst stayed in the school, graduated, got his law degree, passed the bar."

"And somewhere in there he was consulting, things like Brian Hamer's Fourth Amendment case."

"Charlie said, you know, coming from Glenn, that Ernst was real anti-government. Had all these conspiracies going about what the government was doing. Deep black budget stuff." Vance lifted his hands. "And he was ambitious as hell, turns out as this libertarian-type lawyer, and he even does some good work, some Clarence Darrow-level civil rights work, but, again, in his mind, there's this ultra-dark, ultra-deep force he's up against, and it's everywhere. Glenn even told Charlie that Ernst once said he admired underground economies — mafias and gangs doing what they wanted, really flexing their liberty."

Vance took another drink, then set the bottle down, a light in his eyes, slight smile on his lips. "You're giving me that look."

Tom was thinking about the secrecy in Vance's own world, that he'd yet to disclose exactly the kind of work he'd done for the Air Force. So he asked, yet again.

"I was a shirt," Vance said at last.

"What's that mean?"

"First shirt. That means I held special duty position, and had the responsibilities of a first sergeant. And so I served as a NCOIC, which is a Noncommissioned Officer in Charge. Satisfied?"

Tom looked into the eyes of his older friend, said, "No," and Vance laughed. But Tom got up from the table, pulled out his phone, his mind swinging to Heather Moss. "Okay, so Charlie knows Ernst has got some ideas about things, maybe he's a bit dangerous . . . Does he try to warn her about this guy? I mean, have they been in communication?"

"Not much. A couple phone calls here and there. I don't think he thought enough about it, and this guy Ernst seemed to be helping her out." Vance grew somber, finished his beer and watched as Tom keyed her number.

Heather answered on the second ring and he did his best to sound casual, upbeat: "Hey, how you doing? How are the girls?"

"They're good, I'm good — how are you?"

"Hanging in there. Did someone from the FBI get in touch?"

"Your supervisor, Blythe, was around this morning, she had an agent with her, she had to be in her twenties. So . . ."

"Good." He flicked a look at Vance, who wore a serious expression. "You're going to get through this, you know?"

"Yeah . . . so you're alright? How are things on your end?"

"Don't worry about me. I'm straight."

"Must feel some relief . . . I mean, from what Blythe told me, it sounds like this could be it for the guy you've been after. What do you call it — the smoking gun." It sounded like she covered the phone a minute, spoke to one of her girls, then the line cleared. "I feel like I'm in one of those movies." She sighed. "And I still have the hearing on Thursday. For the fleeing a crime."

"Your lawyer been in touch recently? What was his name?"

"Robert. Yes. He was here this morning for a minute, and we're going to go over what to expect at the hearing sometime tomorrow. I just . . . I just don't know what to do with myself half the time. My life was so much about routines. I'll be sitting there, doing something with the girls, and it's like I'm a robot that's lost all its programming."

Tom thought he could understand — soon he was apt to be without programming, too. No job — not with the FDLE, anyway. Then again, his work with the bureau had been bumpy to begin with. First case and he got knocked for a loop, sent to do therapy and work Governor Protection, now this — he'd yet to find a rhythm. Unless his rhythm was chaos.

"Well, listen. I'd like to stop by say hello to you and the girls before this all, you know . . . Would that be alright?"

"Of course. Be great to see you, Tom."

"Maybe tomorrow? Only — wait, you said your lawyer would be there, I don't want to interrupt that. What time is he coming?"

Tom felt sure Ernst had by now pulled the cameras, knowing that cops were going to start coming around, preparing Heather for her role in Palumbo's takedown, and her entry into witness relocation. But it was still a gamble to talk to her — Ernst could still be watching some other way, maybe listening. He had to take the risk.

"He said he'd be by at nine, after I've put the girls to bed."

"Alright. Well I'll make my way over before then, okay?"

"Sounds good." She took a breath, let it out, and he could tell she was nervous.

"Hey, I know this is a lot. I mean, that's an understatement. This is your whole life. I just wanted to say, I'm sorry."

"Oh well, Tom, you didn't . . ."

"It's not easy, getting moved around, things beyond your control, you know? I know what you're going through."

She was quiet for a while, and he could hear the chirp of the girls in the background. Then she said in a soft voice, "Thank you."

"See you soon."

He hung up and looked at Vance. The old man gave the air a sniff, said, "So where do we want to pick up Charlie Moss? Tampa? You picking up the tab or is the FBI?"

"I'll pay," said Tom.

Vance got out his phone, preparing to make the call.

"Hey . . ."

Vance looked over.

"After this, maybe we go into business together."

Vance returned his attention to searching his phone for Charlie Moss's number, said, "I haven't even got the security job yet. One day at a time, Tommy boy."

CHAPTER FORTY

WEDNESDAY

When Charlie Moss arrived at the airport, Tom felt like he was smuggling in a celebrity. Not that Moss was ostentatious — he was dressed as a civilian in shorts and a t-shirt, though he had the brush cut and the thousand-yard stare of a military man. Tom met him in the baggage area, but Moss had nothing to claim, so they headed to the Durango.

They were clearing the city, stretching out on highway 75, moving southerly at almost a hundred miles an hour when Moss said, "So how is she?"

"She's good."

Moss ran a hand over his jaw. Tom could see the resemblance to Glenn in the boxy chin, the hooded brow. Charlie Moss looked like he worked out — for a man nearing fifty, he was in good shape. "Heather always was a tough nut," he said.

They didn't speak again until they got off on Imperial Parkway, headed into Bonita Springs, and Tom felt it was time to go over the plan again. The sun was getting low, a garret of clouds on the westerly horizon tinged salmon. "Alright," Tom said. "The feds will have swept the house; Ernst had those cameras installed, but I'm going to just have a check myself. And I'll give you the all-clear once I've prepped Heather."

"She has security, you said?"

"Yes. One federal agent in the house, two outside."

"And they don't know what's going on."

"They've been aware that Everglades vice narcotics bureau was hacked, sensitive information on targets and civilian informants potentially stolen. They've been working with the VNB behind the scenes for weeks. So everything's been on real tight lock down."

"But they're dancing to Robert's tune? They think this Palumbo guy was behind the hack?"

"They do. But there's the other hack that's more important. For us."

"This Vasquez; his car."

"You got it. CID was working with vice narcotics when Vasquez died in the car wreck."

"How can you be sure what they found?"

Tom gave Charlie Moss a quick glance. "I have my sources."

* * *

It was almost full dark when they pulled up to Heather Moss's house. Charlie seemed wistful, quietly staring across the street. "I haven't seen Heather in person since Glenn's funeral," he said. "And I've been so busy . . ."

Tom understood. Charlie felt regret he hadn't been more in touch, and maybe that he hadn't done more to keep Heather protected. "No one could've seen this coming," Tom said, his mind tracing back to the guilt he'd felt the morning Heather was attacked.

"I could have," Charlie said. He seemed to stare at the agent guarding the front door. "Ernst — he's not going to be scared off by all this action? If he's watching?"

"He expects it. He sees feds and he thinks Heather is being treated as a federal witness against Palumbo."

"Got it. That's slick."

Tom said, "Alright. I'm going in. Sit tight."

The FBI agent was already giving him the stink eye as he got out and crossed the street to the unmarked car. The agent rolled down his window. "Help you?"

Tom showed his ID.

Looking at it with half-lidded eyes, the federal agent said, "Who's in the car with you? That the relative?"

"That's him."

The agent looked past Tom at the shape of Charlie, sitting in the Durango. "Well, we're going to have to check him out."

"He's waiting."

The agent spoke into a transmitter on his wrist, and the other fed appeared from the back of the house, walking toward them. The first agent then got out, and his gaze fell to the small zipped case Tom was holding. Tom handed it over and the first agent went through its contents.

"Special Agent Blythe should have briefed you, yeah?"

The first agent said nothing, just handed the case back to Tom, then finally led Tom to the door, showed him in as the second agent approached the Durango.

Heather was on the couch, looked like she'd been dozing with a book. The fed in the house, the young woman Heather had mentioned on the phone, was sitting in a chair in the hallway. Tom flicked a look past her to where a bullet had punched through the dry wall, narrowly missing Sergeant Sanchez. The hole had been covered by a framed picture of Heather and the girls, all smiling. Fitting, Tom thought.

"Hi," Heather said, her eyes still sleepy. "What's going on?"

"Can we sit down?"

"Of course." She gestured to a space on the couch beside her.

Tom said, "In here? In the kitchen?"

Heather showed curiosity, but rose and walked him to the table. Tom scanned for where the camera would have been, just above the sink, maybe hidden in the potted fern that hung there in front of the window. Nothing there now. He pulled out a chair, sat across from her.

"You're kind of weirding me out," Heather said. She seemed a shade paler. "Is everything okay?"

"Fine. Where's your phone?"

"My phone? It's in the — I guess it's over there on the couch, where I was sitting."

"Bear with me." Tom crossed back into the living room, found the phone starting to disappear into the couch cushions. Grabbed it and dislodged the battery, the female agent looking on from her chair in the hallway.

He returned to the kitchen table with the phone and battery, set them down in front of Heather. "Heather, we have some tough stuff to go over, and everything is . . . a bit sensitive right now."

She looked at her dismantled phone with trepidation. "Uhm, okay. But Tom — now you're scaring me."

His own phone buzzed in his pocket. He pulled it out and read the text from Culpepper.

Culpepper had just written: *He's on the move.*

Another text followed immediately: *Just left his place. Headed east. I'm on him.*

Heather looked increasingly alarmed as Tom replied with a quick *OK.*

"Charlie is outside," he told her. "Your brother-in-law. In my car."

"Charlie?" Her eyes widened and she looked over Tom's shoulder, to see out the front windows. Then she started to get up.

"Hang on," Tom said. It was happening quickly. Time had gotten crunched due to Charlie's flight, and Tom hadn't wanted to alert Ernst ahead of time. He was on his way to meet with Heather and prep for the morning hearing, but maybe he was watching the street, too, had seen Tom pull up and enter the house.

"Is something happening with Palumbo?" Heather spoke in a plaintive whisper, her gaze seeking the bedrooms at the other end of the house, where the girls were sleeping. "Is he — Tom, is something happening?"

"What's happening is that your lawyer has been lying to you."

"Robert?" She scowled, but Tom thought he saw a glint of recognition in her eyes. She had to have suspected something. "What do you mean?"

"Tell me everything, okay?"

She leaned back a little. "Robert helped me with the estate. After Glenn died. He's been very supportive . . . I don't understand."

"Robert set all this up. He's the one who put that pill in your bag, he's the one who called you using that voice synthesizer."

She looked shocked, but already growing convinced. "Robert? Doing all of this? That's crazy."

"Well, no. Because so much of this was already in motion. Robert has just come along and tweaked things to his liking."

"Why?"

"Well he's profiting from it. And he's a fucked-up individual. And because he thinks he's in love with you, would be my guess."

Her mouth opened a couple times to respond, color rose from her neck to her face and her eyes searched the room, Tom's face. Finally she lowered her gaze and said, "Ah, God."

"Did you know he had feelings for you?"

Her eyes came back, sharp and wounded. It was all there in her face — shock, disbelief — and yet, guilt. She'd suspected Ernst had feelings, kept it platonic, but perhaps she'd known, on some level, he was expecting her to someday reciprocate. And she hadn't. But she'd never expected this.

She looked toward the street again. "Charlie is out there?"

"Glenn told him things about Robert; Robert's tendency to distort reality. Charlie flew in from Nevada this morning, to help us. To help you."

"Why is he sitting out there in the car?"

"Because I wanted to talk to you first. And because . . ."

Another text from Culpepper. *Just merged onto 75. He's coming to you.*

Tom did the calculation. They had about fifteen minutes before Ernst arrived. He wasn't entirely sure that the lawyer would just pull up out front, be so bold. He was smart, so there had to be contingencies. But he unzipped the case he was carrying and pulled out the two mikes and the transmitter. "I'm going to ask you to wear this. I'm sorry you haven't had more time to absorb all this, that I couldn't tell you sooner. But Robert watches, and he listens. There were cameras in your house not long ago."

She flinched, then looked around. Finally, she stood, and Tom thought he knew what she was thinking. He got up, moved quickly beside her. "They're going to be okay," he said about the girls. "I promise. Okay? There are three federal agents here, plus myself and Charlie. One of my guys — you remember Culpepper — is following Robert. And Agent Blythe and my director, Turnbull, are monitoring everything, standing by with a team."

He sensed her sorting through it all, coming to acceptance, but she was still aiming for the girls' bedroom, about to push past him. "Where is Robert now?"

"On his way here. He's a little early; he might be watching the street, another camera or two somewhere, something."

"He's coming *now*?"

"Which is why you need to put this on." He held out the microphones and transmitter in the palm of his hand. "I doubt he will admit to anything, but we want to get it down anyway."

Heather looked directly into his eyes. In a low voice, said, "You're using me as bait."

"I'm telling you the truth. And by coming here to do that I've alerted Robert, and that's what I expected."

He could see she didn't trust him, and he couldn't blame her.

"I want to talk to Charlie," she said.

"Absolutely. But it will have to be quick. Robert could be just a few minutes away."

* * *

With Ernst in motion, chances were slim he was still watching, or, even if he was, slimmer still he'd be able to make out Charlie Moss's face from a distance on a dark street through a lipstick camera. The agents brought Heather's brother in-law to the door, and he stepped through, and embraced her. They held on to one another for several seconds, Heather saying things with her face buried in Charlie's chest that Tom couldn't pick up. Charlie Moss stroked her hair and glanced at Tom, his eyes sheeting with tears.

Culpepper's text: *On Imperial Parkway. Five minutes out.* Tom ushered the two to the table in the kitchen, where they sat holding hands, talking quietly, and he went about his work.

Back in the Durango, he pulled a two-way radio off a charger in the back, checked in with Blythe.

"We're here," she said. "One street over. You think he's going to show? Or will he scare off?"

Tom waited a minute, watching the dark shapes of men and women moving outside Heather's bedrooms. He felt another twist of guilt — lying to Heather didn't sit very well, but it was for the best. He pressed the button. "I'm hoping he considers the additional manpower is for Heather's safety, like it's all going according to plan. But I don't know. We're just about set."

Blythe came back: "Cutting it close."

"I know."

Tom set the radio down, then quickly squeezed into the body armor he'd brought. If he was right, Ernst still had at least one weapon. He might try and lay waste to anyone and everything if he felt backed into a corner. The agents were sneaking the girls out the back door while Charlie distracted Heather.

He snapped the armor in place, heard Abigail's tiny voice in the distant dark. Tom picked up the radio. "You got them?"

Blythe: "Yeah. We got them."

A text from Culpepper: *Two minutes.*

Tom opened the hidden panel, took out the Remington shotgun, carefully but quickly checked the gun, loaded in the shells, stuffed more in his pockets. He closed the back hatch, jumped into the driver's seat, and drove away in the Durango. He hooked onto the next street, then the next, and knocked over an orange cone holding a spot for him to park. He jogged through the backyard of another property holding the shotgun. A dog started barking, a perimeter light snapped on. He squeezed through a break in the hedging, made his way along another property, then came to Heather's house, squatted in the bougainvillea with a good view on the street. Settled, he stuck the ear bud in, and listened as Heather talked to her brother in-law, Charlie.

". . . but that was in — oh I don't know what year it was. Olivia was just six months old." The transmission came in nice and clean.

Charlie laughed. "Glenn told me she used to do this little monster face. She'd wrinkle up her nose and . . ."

"Yeah, it was like this." Heather stopped talking and Tom heard her take several rapid breaths. He didn't know what they were talking about, but it sounded like reminiscing.

"I'm sorry I missed so much . . ." Charlie said. Then his voice took on a different pitch. "How about Robert — did he ever come around when Glenn was sick? Glenn never said."

"He did, once. Brought flowers to the hospital. It was about two weeks before Glenn . . . you know after that things went pretty quick."

"But did Glenn say anything about him?"

"I don't think he even knew Robert was there."

They fell silent. Charlie said, "Fucking guy." Then, "Excuse my language."

Tom watched the street as they spoke. Culpepper came over the radio. "He turned, guys. He made the turn down Matheson Ave. Be there in thirty seconds."

"Copy," Tom said. "Everybody off." He felt his heart beating harder, studied the street, holding his breath.

The beige Acura rolled into view. Slowed in front of the house, stopped. A moment later, Robert Ernst got out, dressed in jeans and a pink button-down shirt. He ducked back into the vehicle and reemerged with his briefcase. Crossing the street, he pressed his key fob — the Acura chirped and its lights flashed once.

The FBI agent got out of the unmarked car, met Ernst along the front walkway and the two men had a brief exchange. Ernst smiled about something, then nodded, looked around as the agent patted him down. He glanced, just for a moment, toward the spot Tom was hiding. Then he seemed to give the house a long look.

He wasn't going in, Tom thought. Did he see Charlie through the window? He shouldn't have been able to — the kitchen table wasn't in view from the front yard. Something had him spooked, though, Tom could read it in the lawyer's face, his body language — he was stiffening up, losing that cocksure pose.

But then he resumed walking up to the front door, and he went inside.

Tom let go the breath he was holding, listened as Ernst came into the room, closer to the kitchen table, and the microphone. So far so good.

"Robert, this is my brother-in-law, Charlie Moss."

There was some shuffling, like Charlie was getting up from the table. "How do you do."

Ernst said, "It's a pleasure to finally meet you. Heather's told me a lot about you . . . What a surprise."

Charlie: "Well, you know, when I heard about everything Heather was going through."

There was, Tom thought, an awkward silence.

Robert: "How did you hear? Heather didn't call you — did she? She told me you were unreachable."

Charlie: "Saw it on the news, believe it or not."

"National news? Wow, I had no idea."

"Actually I watch Florida news. Yeah. Just — you know. My way of keeping in touch. Listen, I know you two have this hearing to go over tomorrow."

Robert: "No, no. It's alright. We've got a few things, but . . . I don't want to rush you out."

Clear tension in their voices. Ernst was aware something was going on, and Charlie knew it. Heather hadn't said a word. Tom had to make his move, and he had to do it now. If Ernst left the house, he'd go right back to the Acura, grab his weapon. Chances were good he still had the AR-15. The feds were in on what was

335

happening, but had been asked to ignore the vehicle to keep Ernst confident.

Tom crawled into the yard and stood up. From the angle he could just see the back of Charlie's head through the window, half of Ernst's face. Tom ducked down, moved closer to the house, keeping out of sight. They were still talking about whether or not Charlie was going to leave.

Come on, Charlie, Tom thought. *Get to it.*

Charlie did. "Robert, listen. I don't — I mean, I appreciate what you're doing for Heather."

"Well, I'm just doing my job."

Heather spoke up for the first time: "Robert?"

She was nervous. Tom waited.

"I'm going to let you go, Robert."

"What?"

"I'm letting you go as my lawyer. I believe you haven't been honest with me. And I think you've had ideas about what to expect by helping me out. Maybe I . . . if I led you to believe we would ever be more than what we are, I'm sorry."

"Heather . . ."

"There is a conflict of interest here. I'm firing you, Robert, and I'd like you to leave."

Ernst said nothing. The whole room fell silent, and Tom grabbed up the radio. "Move in. He's going to come out. He's going to come out."

Ernst said: "Heather, I don't understand. I don't know what Charlie has told you, but I've only ever had your interests at heart. You think I . . . ? Heather, you're forgetting how we first met. I *introduced* you to Glenn. This is just — what is going on?"

"I remember you introduced me. We met at that dinner, a couple nights before the bike race. I remember that, Robert. And then afterward I saw you a few more times. I remember you came when Glenn was . . . just before he died. And then after that . . . Robert, this is partly on me too. I needed an escape from my life. I accepted your help, and I knew how you felt. But, you're lying about it. And I'm concerned you're lying about more than that. That you've done things. You've done very bad things . . ."

"This is nuts. I can understand you're under pressure here, Heather, a *lot* of pressure, but we have to—"

"She asked you to leave . . . Robert, hey, Robert, what are you doing over there — oh Jesus, put that down, man."

Tom was right at the front door. He pressed the transmitter on the radio: "He's got a gun." Tom could see into the room, the handgun Ernst was pointing, and Tom threw open the door, shouting for Ernst to drop the weapon, to get down, but Ernst spun on him.

He'd had a different weapon stashed in the house and they'd missed it. *Shit.*

Tom had the Remington ready but Heather and Charlie were in close proximity to Ernst. By the time Charlie grabbed Heather and pulled her to the ground, Ernst was running. He crossed into the living room, fired at Tom, twice, both shots missing, and he disappeared into the hallway.

Tom used the radio: "He's coming out the back. He's coming out the back."

"I got him, I got him . . ." Blythe said.

Tom's ears were ringing from the lawyer's two shots, but he heard more gunfire, then shouting. He reached the back door and saw Blythe on the ground, hit. He stopped and checked her, seeing other agents running after Ernst. "I'm alright," she said. She was wearing her armor. "Go."

Tom ran. The other agents had crashed through the bushes hemming the property. Tom followed, hurdling some low shrubs, came out in a neighbor's driveway. There were footfalls out on the street. An agent came over the radio, out of breath: "He's on Dean Street. On Dean Street, headed west."

CHAPTER FORTY-ONE

Chest burning again. Running as fast as he could, Tom was hoping to God that Robert Ernst didn't go into someone's house, try to take a hostage. He shouted into the radio as he booked along: "Anybody see him?"

No response. Tom recognized where he was — Olivia's elementary school was coming up on the right. "Anyone have eyes on? Anyone have—"

Two shots: *Pop pop*. Somewhere up ahead, on the right. A ways beyond the school though; sounded like over on Old 41. Tom threw a glance back, saw a dark shape following him, looked like maybe one of the feds. He reached Old 41 and turned right, saw one of his people sprawled out in the Circle K gas station parking lot. Tom ran to him, saw that it was Culpepper and he was bleeding, dragging himself toward cover, leaving a trail of blood.

"Where is he?"

"He's still on the move." The agent was gasping for breath.

Tom looked up the road — Old 41 was bisected with a median, young palms had recently been planted, propped up with wood framing. Ernst dashed between two of the trees, headed into Riverside Park. Tom waited for the federal agent to catch up, directed her to stay with Culpepper, and took off running again. That was two people down, two people Ernst had fired upon. People Tom thought of as friends. Now Ernst was entering a public space, still armed.

A car came slowly past and Tom ran across the street behind it. As he closed in on the park he saw the people gathering for the first night of a blues music festival. It was on the stage with the roof resembling a massive scallop shell; a semi-circular ridged shape with lighting trusses hung beneath. The band was setting up microphone stands, a musician was testing his drum kit. At least a hundred people were milling about, more wandering in.

Someone screamed. Tom watched the crowd ripple, and people started to run, more shouting and bright screams. He cut through them, yelling for everybody to get down. Then he saw Ernst now on the other side of the crowd, skirting the water fountain, cutting a route toward the large Banyan tree at the far edge of the park. Got on the radio. "He's headed right for the Imperial River."

He ran some more, around the fountain, full sprint across the lawn, saw Ernst drop down onto the docks beside the river.

"He's in the water," someone said over the radio. "He's in the water."

Tom caught sight of another agent up on the bridge spanning the river. The agent stopped, spread his legs, aimed down into the water. It was Blake Turnbull. "Stop! Florida Department of Law Enforcement!"

Tom heard splashing, saw Turnbull get running again. Tom slowed, crept to the edge of the lawn, dropped down in case Ernst was just in the shallow river, waiting for him to show his face. Tom crawled on his elbows and knees to the berm, peeked down at the docks and water. Saw Ernst, and Ernst fired.

The round struck the berm, blasting out flints of concrete. Tom waited, got his gun ready, popped his head up, fired back. Saw his three shots hit the water, and Ernst running away. Tom swung his hips and legs over the berm and dropped onto the dock, ran up to where it ended at the river bank, partly concealing himself behind a rack of rentable kayaks.

"Robert!"

He waited. Couldn't see the lawyer, but heard the sloshing of water.

Ernst's voice floated back: "What?"

"Come on, buddy. There's people all over the place."

Ernst didn't reply, just more slopping of water.

"Fuck," Tom muttered. He looked back, could just see over the edge of the berm into the park, where agents were holding back the foolishly curious, and Turnbull came running up. Tom nodded at him, stripped off his radio, took out his phone, wallet, badge, left them on the dock and slipped into the water.

Warm. Not like the rivers from back home. The few times he'd been able to dabble in nature during those days, the water was cold even in summer. The Imperial was sluggish, the water a kind of steely opaque. The river bent off to the left, and Tom stayed up to his knees along the muddy banks with the Remington, sighting downstream for the crazy fucking lawyer.

Tom made his way around the bend; the train tracks were next, crossing above and he stopped before moving ahead into the short dark tunnel.

"Robert!"

Nothing. No response from the lawyer, no more sounds of him swishing through the water. Tom aimed up at the tracks, down one way, then the other, saw nothing. Then he heard something snap, and someone shouted, followed by a splash.

Saw Ernst on the other side of the tunnel, flailing in the water, holding his gun above his head. It looked like he'd fallen, grabbed a branch and broken it — something floated beside him in the water as he struggled to get back to shore. He turned and looked through the tunnel at Tom, and Tom got moving faster, but the river was getting deep; not shallow beneath the tracks. He went as far as he dared, just above his waist, and strained to keep an eye on the lawyer as Ernst moved back toward the riverbank and out of sight.

There were supposedly manatees in this river.

A few locals said there were gators, too.

Tom grew less comfortable by the second. He didn't want to swim the tunnel.

"Robert? You okay?"

"Fuck you," Ernst called back. "You should have listened."

"Come on, man. Your gun is wet. Listen, I can prove that Vasquez was killed by Ben Franco and his guys. They hacked his car computer, locked up the steering, controlled the acceleration. So that's not on you. Give it up, let's talk."

Tom could just see the edge of the lawyer's arm, leg. The river water cruised through the tunnel, dark shapes moving beneath the surface. Or Tom's mind playing tricks.

Robert's voice: "You won't shoot me?"

"I got enough on my plate, Robert."

There was a long silence, broken by noises behind Tom. He tensed, gave a hunched look behind him, saw a couple of FDLE agents working their way around the river bend toward him, looking even less pleased to be in the water than he was. Tom held a hand up, stopping them, then pointed through the bridge.

The first agent nodded. Then Tom made a gesture suggesting they climb back out of the river, cross the tracks on land so they could flank Ernst. Another nod, the first agent turned back to the second, then they started pushing up through the shrubby riverbank.

Ernst seemed to be staying put. Tom wanted a better view of him. He sighed, waded in deeper, holding the shotgun above the surface. Then he was up to his neck, able to move under the railroad bridge, and as he passed beneath, Robert came into view.

The lawyer had the handgun pointed up under his chin.

"Hey!" Tom tried to move faster, but it was impossible. He'd have to let go of the shotgun, have to swim for it. "Robert, ah, man, come on . . ."

Robert just looked at Tom. "It's not wet," he said, and pulled the trigger.

CHAPTER FORTY-TWO

She was mad at him. Furious. Charlie had to hold her back.

Heather wanted to know why they hadn't just told her what was going on, that they were going to have the girls sneaked out of her own house like that. He tried to explain that he'd wanted everything to feel as normal as possible when Ernst first walked in — "Even if it meant fear in your eyes, fear for your daughters; we just wanted to give you and Charlie the chance to confront him, see what he said."

Tom was still wet, and dried off with one of her bathroom towels as Heather calmed down and was reunited with her girls. The agents had rallied at Heather's house after the river. When Ernst shot himself, Tom had tossed the shotgun to the riverbank, swum for him, knowing it was too late, watching as the lawyer's limp body slipped slowly into the water, listening as the agents in the bushes shouted into their radios and others shouted back.

He'd finally stood there, a stray scream drifting in from the civilians in the park, probably people who'd heard the final gunshot echoing around.

County cops had shown up quick, locked down the scene. Tom walked back, soaked, all the way to Heather's, and eventually, the rest of them had converged there, too, and were mostly standing around outside, smoking, awaiting the cavalry, the questions, and the next moves.

The next moves.

Truth was, Tom hadn't expected Ernst to run. They'd been prepared for it, but the lawyer had been so self-assured and seemingly delusional that there was just as good a chance he'd continue trying to convince Heather and Charlie of what his intentions were; try to worm around the whole thing, continue manipulating them.

And then there was the gun. Probably when clearing out his cameras, Ernst had hidden it in the kitchen, just behind the refrigerator, practically out in the open, where no one had checked. A backup, in case Tom double-crossed him.

Heather was sharp as ever, and she'd seen the doubts in Tom's eyes, and condemned him for it.

She sat with her girls on the couch in her house, and she looked away. As he left, Olivia raised her hand, and Tom waved back.

"I'm sorry," he said to Heather, and stepped outside. It seemed like his life lately was one apology after another. So be it.

* * *

Ben Franco was arrested at Palumbo's Gulf Shore mansion along with half a dozen other Palumbo employees in a massive raid. In his confession, false or otherwise, Rapp had cited Franco as his employer, and vice narcotics had been compelled by the court to turn over the sequestered evidence on the vehicle tampering which led to Edgar Vasquez's death.

An FBI team flooded into the dog track the same day, through the bar, up the stairs, past the poker rooms to the offices near the back of the building. Tom had gone along.

He stood in proximity to Mario Palumbo for the first time; same round face, pock-marked olive complexion as the pictures. Same dark eyes, pursed lips that turned down a bit at the corners in a pout. The feds had reopened their RICO files and were hitting Palumbo with extended criminal penalties for his ongoing criminal organization. He was dressed in a three-piece suit, smelled of cigars and cologne, and he came willingly with the agents, like it was business as usual.

* * *

Blythe clicked her pen on and off, leaning over in her chair, staring at Tom in the Naples field office. Her arm was in a sling; it had been a clean shot, gone straight through. A real miracle this time, not something made to look a certain way.

"So," she said.

"So."

Her eyes lingered on him, then she turned to some papers on her desk. "Talked to Mrs. Shannon, this morning, from the Silver Shell on Marco Island. She came in, looked at photos, and in front of witnesses identified Robert Ernst as someone from her anniversary party. He was there the same night we've put Brian Hamer there. Ernst's computer shows that they'd been talking for months — maybe keeping in touch even for years — but we think that was their first in-person meeting in a long while, kicked this whole thing off. You want coffee? There's some fresh."

"No thanks."

"You off coffee?"

He shrugged. "Think I can be a little high strung. Maybe I don't need it."

She tilted her head, her lip curling into a sly smile. "Smoking?"

"Yeah. Keeps me calm."

"It's poison. They say it's self-destructive."

"One day at a time."

She spun in the chair a half turn, then launched to her feet, adjusted her sling. He watched her move to the kitchenette, asked, "How are you feeling?"

"I'm fine." After she poured a cup, she kept her back to him and said, "We spoke to the judge. In New York. She's still there, in Yonkers."

Tom's ears pricked up. No one had directly discussed the circumstances of his application to the department yet. Blythe slowly turned around, leaned against the counter and took a casual sip. Most casual.

"Blythe? Come on. You're killing me."

She peered at him. "You still want this job?"

"You still want me on this job?"

She set the cup down, looked into a corner for a moment, said, "You know, judges are judges for a reason. They make decisions. This one made a decision to seal your records. She said that given your family situation, what she made of you, she handed out an ACOD. You didn't get in trouble again during the probationary year, so it got dropped."

Tom was on the edge of his seat, now he slowly slumped back, feeling mixed emotions. He'd never looked back from his Yonkers bust, not until he'd been gearing up to be a cop, and then he'd only looked at it with half an eye.

Blythe seemed to pick up on the thought. "We're pretty terrible when it comes to our own lives," she said. "Don't beat yourself up. But regardless of whether the charges were cleared, you still had an obligation to report it when you applied to the department. What this means for you isn't in my hands. If they push you through, though, you've still got about a dozen other issues to deal with if you want to keep working. For one, you've got to finish therapy, and you've got about a month to go through with Internal Affairs."

He slowly got up from the chair, legs rubbery. He crossed to Blythe who watched him come, blushing as he neared. He put his arms around her. She was stiff, but then she softened. He didn't push it though, and quickly let her go.

Her eyes flashed up at him briefly before she stepped away. "And anger management classes, Lange. Starting tomorrow. Non-negotiable."

* * *

Culpepper was asleep in the hospital bed. The machines hooked into him were beeping and hissing. An afternoon storm was grumbling out the windows, palms waving their fronds, the Gulf just visible beyond, a horizon of choppy, gunmetal water.

Tom put a hand on the agent, thanked him but didn't wake him. He sat in the chair in the corner and called Katie.

She didn't answer but he left her a voice message. Then he just sat there.

He jerked awake; been dozing, and his phone was vibrating in his lap. He checked the caller ID and saw Rhodes' number.

"Rhodes," Tom said, "I thought you were a beautiful woman."

"Happens all the time," Rhodes said, then laughed his gravely smoker's laugh. "You get cut loose or what?"

"Not sure yet."

"Hey, so I know it's only been a few days since you cracked this thing, super boy, but how's it going?"

Tom stood, moved away from Culpepper's bed, looked out into the hallway where a couple of nurses were talking quietly. "Well, Palumbo's out on bail. Franco isn't though, so that's something."

"Trial?"

"You know how it goes. Maybe in a year. Palumbo's defense team is piling on the paperwork, filing every motion known to man, trying to get the whole thing thrown out."

"Yeah . . . well, listen; I got a thing. I know you're probably chained to IAB and the legal shenanigans, but I got a boat."

"You got a boat?"

"Yeah. I picked up a boat." Rhodes cackled. "I don't know. I got to get out, you know? See some shit. You want to take a ride? You ought to take some time, man. It's an airboat, like the one from that place . . . *Jungle Ned*. What do you say? Life is short."

"Yeah. Sure."

"Yeah? Alright. Just got to do a little fix-up work on her. I'll call you when she's ready."

Tom canceled the call and went back to the chair, sat down. Stared out as the storm took shape, the sky darkened, the rain fell and slapped against the glass.

A text came in. From Katie this time.

U okay?

He quickly wrote back, feeling light: *Yeah.*

Talk soon, okay?

Okay.

His next call would be to Vance. He deserved to know the whole story, too. If this whole thing with the state bureau ultimately fell apart there was the possibility of them working together . . . But it could wait. Tom put the phone away, let his head fall back.

Rested.

THE END

November 12, 2017
TJB
Etown

Acknowledgments

I'd like to thank Sergeant Andrew Smith, who lives and works in southwest Florida, for his invaluable inspiration and consultation on this book.

My father, James J. Brearton, for his unwavering support of my crazy writing obsession, for facilitating a book set in Florida by living there, and for many of the details that have brought Tom Lange's world to life.

Thanks to my early readers – Bob Sirrine, John Ramirez, and Clare Midgley – for such helpful feedback and constructive criticism. And thanks to all the friends and family in my corner – Dava Clement-Brearton, Jude Brearton, Oak and Ann Clement, Geoff Pierce, David Press, Jennifer Bulkley, Lee Clark Smith, Jennifer Person Beiring, Marie Morgan – you keep me going!

Thank you to Caroline Oakley, my editor for this one, who pushed me to develop and improve critical parts of this story while she pruned the prose. Thanks to Jasper Joffe and everyone at Joffe Books for their continuing enthusiasm and the opportunity to keep sharing these stories with you. And of course my thanks to you, dear reader, for reading, for supporting, for allowing me to keep doing this writing thing.

Without you, and without all of these wonderful people, this book would not be possible.

Thank you for reading this book. If you enjoyed it please leave feedback on Amazon, and if there is anything we missed or you have a question about then please get in touch. The author and publishing team appreciate your feedback and time reading this book.

Our email is office@joffebooks.com

www.joffebooks.com

ALSO BY T.J. BREARTON

HABIT
SURVIVORS
DAYBREAK
BLACK SOUL

DARK WEB
DARK KILLS
GONE

HIGHWATER

DEAD GONE
TRUTH OR DEAD

Made in the USA
Monee, IL
01 January 2020